LIA ANDERSON
DOG PARK MYSTERIES

THE GIRLS

LIA ANDERSON MYSTERIES
by C. A. Newsome

A SHOT IN THE BARK
DROOL BABY
MAXIMUM SECURITY
SNEAK THIEF
MUDDY MOUTH
FUR BOYS
SWAMP MONSTER
THE GIRLS

THE GIRLS

A DOG PARK MYSTERY

LIA ANDERSON DOG PARK MYSTERIES
BOOK 8

C. A. NEWSOME

This is a work of fiction. All of the characters, places and events portrayed in this book are either products of the author's imagination or are used fictitiously. Any resemblance to actual persons or events is coincidental.

THE GIRLS

Two Pup Press
1836 Bruce Avenue
Cincinnati, Ohio 45223

Version 1.02, July 15, 2025

ISBNs
978-1-947085-08-4 (Print)
978-1-947085-07-7 (ebook)

For Marianne

A NOTE TO READERS

For those who find such things useful, a cast of characters is located in the back of this book. There are two versions, the first organized by sphere of activity, while the other is alphabetical.

PROLOGUE
TWO YEARS AGO

ELLEN

Ellen teased the edge of a sizzling goetta patty with her spatula, checking the underside for doneness while potatoes browned on the next burner. The Krups gurgled and hissed on the counter, the aroma of freshly brewed coffee mingling with potatoes and fried onions.

Daniel sat at the kitchen table, lips pursed inside a white, neatly trimmed beard. His 56-year-old frame curled nose-in to her laptop—he refused to get his own—like some Gen Z kid. He looked thirty in the right light. He'd never put on weight (just some edema you never saw because he always wore long pants). His face had that charming boyishness that lasts a lifetime. That face was the reason so many people had trusted him for so long. Or maybe it was the voice. He did most of his business by phone, after all.

Her greyhounds lounged on giant bean bags on the other side of the room. Heads up and expressive ears at attention, the girls reminded her of deer more than dogs, a thought she never shared with the folks at Greyhound Adoption of Greater Cincinnati.

A sonorous voice emitted from Daniel's computer. *"Obstacles are an illusion. Faith is the answer."*

"Ready for coffee?"

Daniel grunted, engrossed in the sermon he watched at least once a week. The message: the bigger the obstacles to the abundance that is your natural birthright, the bigger the rewards when you stand firm and keep sending money to fund a new jet for God's chosen messenger. He'd do better to buy a weekly lottery ticket and be done with it, but lottery tickets don't come with an hour of feel-good gaslighting.

She poured a mug, added a dollop of half-and-half and placed it to his right, in the same spot she'd been placing his coffee for a quarter of a century. Daniel picked it up without looking and took a sip.

"Eggs in five minutes."

Another grunt.

"Are you going into the shop today?"

"I have a delivery to make."

Daniel always did this, procrastinated on big repairs and then spent half a day driving a flute a hundred miles because it was too late to ship it. She gave up talking about it years ago.

Across the room her girls whined, their heads turned toward the front of the house (Connie and Nati were Daniel's girls on paper, but they were really hers. She was the one who loved and fed and took care of them no matter what the people at GAGC thought).

Early for the mail.

A shrilling blast came, like an orchestra in a pitched battle. Her girls ran to the living room, making that rooing noise peculiar to greyhounds. Daniel's nose stayed planted in the laptop.

Ellen gave him a hard look. She turned off the stove, wiped her hands on her apron, and followed the girls.

She'd bought the lovely house across from Parker Woods because it had solid bones and the street was an oasis of peace and gentility. Such a disruption had never happened in her decades here. She stepped between the girls at the large front window, stroking their heads, the soothing noises she made drowned out by the wall of sound.

A dozen young flute players wearing identical yellow tees stood on the grassy slope fronting the preserve, each playing a different song to create the cacophony.

A petite girl with dark, waist-length hair thrust her fist in the air. The noise stopped. She pumped it again. The flautists shouted. Their shouts morphed into a chant, over and over to the beat of a drum:

Where's. My. Flute.

Ellen squinted. Those were the words stacked on their shirts, text-shouting in bold black Helvetica, all caps.

Daniel, what have you done now?

The girl pumped her fist a third time. The chant dropped to a murmur, a susurration. A young man—tall, whip-thin, dark-skinned—stepped out front. He lifted a megaphone and began a defiant rap over the chant.

All I want is to be a musician,
play my flute and make it sound pretty.

> But my pads won't seat and the springs are loose.
> The action is floppy. I sound like a goose.
> They say Flute Doc is the one for you.
> He'll fix you up and make it sound like new.

Ellen didn't have to poke her head out the door to know her neighbors were on their porches, drinking coffee in their robes and watching the show.

"Daniel?"

No answer.

The girls whined. She shushed them with nonsense words and pets and led them back to their kitchen beds. The full company joined in for the chorus, the words audible even in the back of the house.

> You got my flute, flute.
> Where is my flute, flute.
> You stole my flute, flute.
> Give me my flute, flute.
> I want my flute, flute.

Ellen stood in the middle of her kitchen, staring at Daniel. Daniel's nose remained glued to his computer.

"I think it's for you."

> Three weeks come and three weeks go.
> Doc says sorry, I broke my toe.

"It's nothing."

> His supplier closed down. He can't get pads.
> The shop flooded and he can't get in.

"What's this about, Daniel?"

He finally turned to her. Light reflected off the lenses of round, wire-frame glasses, making it impossible to read his expression.

"I already took care of it. She's crazy. Just ignore it."

She. Not the rapper. Had to be the girl with the long hair.

I see a pattern here. I know he's lyin.'
My audition's in two days. Inside I'm dyin.'

It wasn't nothing, and if that girl and her friends were crazy, Daniel made them that way.

I say, give it back and I'll go away.
He says your money's not refundable and anyway
your flute's in a safe, and I lost the combination.

The drum beat built inside Ellen, pressure like rage.

You stole my flute, flute.
Give me my flute, flute.
I want my flute, flute.

I want things, too. "I'm taking the girls for a drive."

"Don't go out there."

Ellen removed her apron.

The doorbell chimed, classic Westminster Cathedral bells. The girls rooed in response.

"Don't answer it."

She grabbed leashes from the basket on the counter. The girls scrambled, racing to the door.

The doorbell chimed again.

"Ellen! I said, don't answer it!"

Ellen hooked leashes to collars and opened the door.

A statuesque blonde stood on the porch, slick in a tailored suit and red lipstick you could spot a mile away. Aubrey Morse, from Channel 7. A young, red-headed hunk aimed a video camera at Ellen. Across the street, the flautists continued chanting to the throbbing drum.

Aubrey Morse shoved a microphone in Ellen's face. "Flutists all over the country are calling Moore Flutes the Bermuda Triangle of repair shops. What can you tell us about the dozens of missing instruments?"

Ellen called back into the house, "Daniel, it's for you." She smiled at Aubrey and her too-bright lipstick and said, "Please excuse us. The girls don't do well with strangers."

Ellen led her girls between the reporter and the cameraman, loaded them in the car and drove away, leaving the front door of the house she loved wide open.

How long would Aubrey stay on the porch, hoping to corner Daniel? How long would Daniel hide in the kitchen, waiting her out? She considered the half-cooked goetta and home fries.

Well, he won't starve.

She checked the clock on her dashboard. *White Castle serves breakfast all day. Maybe Bailey will take a break from work and meet me at Wesleyan.*

1

DAY 1, PART 1

SUNDAY, AUGUST 10, 6:11 AM

CYNTH

THE ROAD WAS DEAD QUIET AS SHE DROVE IN THE PRE-DAWN. Darkened houses sat on the right, with woods rising up the hill across the street. Detective Cynth McFadden rounded a curve. Flashing red and blue lights lit up the gloom, painting the face of the uniform guarding the entrance to Parker Woods. Behind him, crime scene tape blocked the paved walk leading into woods that were dark and ominous in the absence of sun.

She parked, finishing off her coffee and tucking the empty cup in the wastebasket she kept in the passenger footwell. Across from the preserve, houses were lit. Residents in pajamas and robes silently drank coffee on their wide porches, pretending they were only outside to enjoy the last bit of cool before the sun came up. Their dogs gave the game away, staring stiff-bodied and alert at the light show.

Enjoy your Sunday morning entertainment, assholes.

She could have parked on the north side of the preserve, but she wanted to approach the scene from the entrance closest to Ellen Brandt's house. She glanced back up the street. Unlike the neighbors, Brandt was not on her porch. Was she awake? Watching behind her curtains? *I bet she's sleeping in like any rational human being.*

She stepped out into hundred percent humidity that made even the morning chill unpleasant. Which made the lookie Lous on their porches all the more sus, since they all had central air blasting 24/7 this time of year and ought to be inside. The humidity was the reason she'd been up way too early for her run—not that she'd gotten far before the call came.

Have to remember to cancel brunch with Duff and David.

She flexed her shoulder blades inside her jacket, attempting to detach the blouse stuck to her back because she hadn't dried off properly after the shower she didn't have time for.

The humidity will make it a moot point in about thirty seconds.

She glanced down at her slacks, looking for stray crumbs from the egg & sausage sliders she ate on the drive. Too early and the sandwiches sat like lead, but it would be hours before she had another chance. And it beat having her stomach growl while she was with Arseneault.

She was District 5, not Homicide, but Arseneault had asked for her. Peter turned down a spot on his team and a pair of thugs named Hodgkins and Jarvis—AKA Heckle and Jeckle—went over instead. Everyone at District 5 considered their absence a win. That was all she needed to know about Homicide. Until now.

Opportunities are rarely convenient. Her performance here could mark her career. This was her chance to make an impression, step outside the confines of her role at District 5 and the rut she'd found herself in.

Up close, the uniform looked beat. A rookie dispatched to the scene at the end of night shift and stuck here for who knew how long. *Can't be happy about that. Poor guy could use some coffee.* He waved at her, reaching inside the prowler for a clipboard. She stopped to show her badge and sign the log.

"How is it?" she asked.

"Peaceful, except for the body. Could be worse."

It was cooler under the trees, less sticky. A run up the concrete sidewalk through the woods would be a fun change from the high school track across from her apartment. She'd give it a go, suit or no suit, if she had proper shoes. But for some idiotic reason, detectives were expected to dress like office workers, never mind the times her job involved chasing dirtbags. And a request from the head of Homicide required full work drag, whatever time of day or day of the week.

At least it wasn't like the old days. Her great-aunt had to wear a skirt with hose and pumps and carry her gun in her purse. She still told the story about clocking a guy with her purse because she couldn't get to her gun fast enough.

The sidewalk headed up the long, steep grade. As the sidewalk rose, the ground fell away on both sides. She felt like Fred Flintstone walking up the spine of a Brontosaurus. Chopped up trunks of fallen trees scattered across the southern slope like pick up sticks on the layer of rotting leaves.

Folds and gullies riddled the hillside, making Parker Woods unsuited for development. The city made lemons out of lemonade by designating it a preserve. They ran a sidewalk up the hill and hung a sign out front, reaping benefits regarding grants and statistics and virtue signaling.

Not enough light. She kept a headlamp in her trunk. Should have brought it, but Arseneault might think she was weird.

What was anyone doing in the preserve before daybreak? Even now, light barely filtered through the trees well enough to see the walkway. No illumination along the sidewalk. Maybe calling it a preserve was a way to avoid spending money on pedestrian safety.

The ground leveled at the north end of the park, the walk curving as it ran behind the houses on Glen Parker. According to her maps app, the walkway ended at the Hopewell Academy parking lot. A professor had been bludgeoned to death a few years ago. Offsite and never solved. A coincidence?

Maybe not.

Ahead, a sidewalk ran down from Glen Parker, forming a T where the walkways met. The faint pulse of red and blue on the pavement meant another patrol car manning the Glen Parker entrance, and another tired officer on overtime.

Partway up the walk, Captain Arseneault hunkered beside a dark patch of concrete. Two patrol officers searched the area, shoving plants aside with extended tactical batons. A tented evidence marker sat on the concrete, indicating a patch of trampled forget-me-nots.

Good thing the locals are tree huggers. No extraneous trash to confuse things. If there's DNA on a cigarette butt it will be relevant.

Arseneault stood, mournful, hound-dog face staring at a

form on the ground. He was a tall man with a permanent stoop, like Snoopy in a tree doing his vulture act. A Van Dyke beard compensated for a serious receding hairline. He shoved his jacket back and thrust his hands in his pants pockets, something smart cops did at crime scenes to keep from accidentally contaminating evidence.

As she approached, the rusty smell of drying blood fought a pitched battle with Arseneault's recently applied Old Spice and lost. Cynth stopped beside him, looking where he was looking, saying nothing.

Daniel Moore lay, eyes staring, mouth gaping, a fragile husk with the force of his personality gone.

This was why she'd been called. Daniel Moore, flute repairman to the stars who'd destroyed an impeccable, decades-long reputation by stealing a fortune in instruments from dozens of clients. Most of those clients had been hundreds or even thousands of miles away and helpless to do much about it until Moore dipped in the home pond and sparked local outrage.

He'd been the bane of her existence for the months of her investigation, then crickets as Moore's gaslighting and stonewalling caused a slam-dunk case to drag out for close to two years.

A quick confession and a plea bargain would have netted Moore restitution and a few years of probation. Inexplicably, Moore refused to plead. Word was he drove his public defender to drink with his lack of cooperation. Two years, fifty-plus missing flutes, and Moore never told anyone what he did with them. Some turned up in pawn shops. The rest had vanished.

Three months ago the judge figured she'd given Moore enough consideration and scheduled a trial date. Moore reversed course and pled guilty days before trial. Cynth hung her freshly dry-cleaned court suit back in the closet and forgot about him. Sentencing had to have been within the past week or two.

Moore's arms and legs flung at odd angles. Blood trailed from a puncture at the base of his neck, soaking his shirt and the small silver cross he always wore. It seeped onto the concrete, forming a sticky, macabre halo. Absurdly, his beard remained a pristine white.

No visible defensive wounds on his arms. Inanely, the drying blood went well with the adult neutrals of his neatly pressed clothes. *It will be hell getting that out of the concrete.*

She broke the silence. "Who found him?"

Arseneault jerked his chin at milling paw prints smearing the north end of the blood pool. "Neighborhood dog walker named Gail Cook. Pair of Maltese on retractable leashes found our friend before she was close enough to see the body. She's terrified the owners will find out Fluffy and Muffy have acquired a taste for human blood. Other than that, she didn't have much to say."

"Do we need to talk to her?"

"I cut her loose. She stumbled onto Moore hours after it happened. There's nothing she can tell us."

"She say why she was walking dogs in the dark?"

"Owners are out of town and Fluffy and Muffy are incontinent. She was hoping to avoid mopping up a flood in the house."

"Are their names really Fluffy and Muffy?"

"If they aren't, they ought to be."

"Who ID'd him?"

"She did. He's staying with a woman in the neighborhood—" He nodded toward the street. "—on the corner of

Thompson Heights. The poor kid I stuck down on Haight Street was the responding officer. He said everyone at District 5 knew Moore and to call you. Any thoughts?"

"He dressed sharp for a walk in the woods. Hot date? Do guys his age have hot dates?"

"I hope so. He's not much older than me."

Ouch.

Arseneault caught her wince, his face placid. "He didn't usually dress like this?"

"Sweats and old flannel shirts when Davis and I saw him. He might have been dressing down to convince us he wasn't hiding money."

"Was he? Hiding money?"

"A hundred rabid flutists think so, but they're dreaming."

"How exactly did this work?"

"He never said. We pieced together what we know from his victims and people who knew him. Short version is Moore was a lousy businessman who spent big to maintain his brand. His co-hab backstopped his business for years. When she stopped bailing him out, he borrowed money from friends. When he burned those bridges, he pawned client flutes to deal with cash flow issues.

"According to those who knew him, things were always going to turn around next week and he'd redeem the flutes and pay everyone back. Since he was known to take months on repairs, it took owners a while to realize he'd ripped them off. In other cases, he sold consignment flutes and never paid the owners."

"And it got ahead of him to the tune of how much?"

"When I handed the case over to the DA, it was well over a quarter mil. That's instrument value, not retail. He would have gotten much less. There was about 50K more in cases beyond the statute of limitations, that we know of." Cynth nodded at the corpse. "What's your read?"

"Someone knew exactly where to stab him, fast and fatal. They used something round and sharp."

"Like an ice pick? Do people use those anymore?"

"Only in the movies."

"You think Amazon will tell us if they shipped any here recently?"

"Doubtful."

"I'm surprised it didn't happen sooner. Davis swears he had to stop me from strangling Moore at least three times."

Arseneault gave her a sideways look, the corner of his mouth twitching. "Should I treat you like a suspect?"

"If I'd killed him, I would have done it with a satisfyingly heavy blunt object. Or my bare hands."

"An old man like that? How could you live with yourself?"

Department head or no, he rated Cynth's best stink eye. "I'll take a gang banger over his confused grandpa act any day. Watch the videos of our interviews, and imagine yourself stuck in that room for six hours. Anyway, you don't need more suspects than you already have. I'll give you a list. A very long list. Shame about the sidewalk."

"Yeah, no footprints."

Cynth nodded at the eastbound sidewalk. "Hopewell is on the other side of those trees. The school could be involved."

"That crossed my mind. I took this one myself, due to the notoriety of the victim."

Meaning you can't risk pissing off Hopewell after Heckle and Jeckle alienated everyone from the president to the janitor during the Lawrence case. "What's your initial read?"

Arseneault led her to the evidence marker and the assaulted forget-me-nots. "Killer lay in wait here."

"Or a dog took a dump. Moore cried about needing disability. Where's his walker? He tottered in on that thing every time we talked to him. He shouldn't be able to make it here from the street without it." She snorted. "I knew he was faking."

"This is why I need you. You knew him."

"More than I wanted to. I haven't seen him since the case went to the DA. That was more than a year ago."

"What's the disposition of the case? The court website says he had sentencing four days ago, but the record hasn't been entered yet."

"No clue. His ex lives on Haight Street. She should know."

"That close?"

"The ex didn't know. I would have heard the screaming."

"Oh?"

"She had friends tell the prosecutor he was a danger to her. Moore got a no contact order and a juris monitor."

"So his ankle bracelet would alert if he strayed too close to her house. Was he a danger to her?"

Cynth shrugged. "He seemed mild, but you never know with domestics."

"True, that. She might have had reason, if he set himself up within spitting distance. His sentencing would have voided the order."

No bump under Moore's slacks. "Shame he's not still wearing it."

"Having his movements would make things easier."

"Time of death, too.

"Jeffers will have to do that the hard way." He shook his

head. "I keep forgetting. Jeffers won't be back from vacation until Wednesday. We get the new guy."

"Is he any good?"

"I guess we'll find out."

Cynth stared up the walkway to the street. "There are three points of access to this park. Hopewell, Haight, and Glen Parker. Makes sense to ambush him here if you know he lives a block away, but I doubt he let anyone except his lawyer and the jail know where he was staying. Too many haters. How did his killer know?"

"What do you think about the ex?" Arseneault asked.

"Clueless cohab outraged to discover her guy was a crook. Cooperative, but offered nothing that was actually helpful."

"She have reason to be mad at him?"

"She paid all the bills for decades."

"So he was robbing her, too."

"With her cooperation."

"People get madder about being robbed when they agree to it. We need to talk to her. We need to check the place he was staying."

While Arseneault made phone calls, Cynth strolled toward the pulsing lights on Glen Parker. The patrol car sat at an angle across the dogleg where Glen Parker turned north and became Langland. She dodged the crime scene tape, waving at the uniform in the driver's seat.

A tiny playground hugged the side of Langland like an afterthought: a single picnic table, a grill on a post, swings. Perfect hangout for neighborhood druggies except for the honking big, buzz-killer street light.

With the sun full up, she could see the houses. Clapboard. Down market. Some falling into disrepair, but the residents kept things neat. Working class, or retirees on fixed income. Practical people without either the means or the inclination for frills. No bikes or abandoned toys. Older residents, then. No Martha Stewart gardens like Haight Street. Also unlike Haight, nobody was treating their presence as entertainment.

The next block up had to be Thompson Heights. She resisted the urge to check out Moore's house and retraced her steps, heading for the far side of the woods and the back of Hopewell. The sidewalk ended with more crime scene tape and a patrol car guarding an empty parking lot. No flashing lights here. The students were either passed out or too busy nursing hangovers to make use of the practice rooms.

Harsh, McFadden. What musician practices this early in the morning? On a Sunday?

The uniform raised a lazy hand in greeting. She waved back, turning around as she wondered what she expected to find. *A bloody ice pick would be nice.*

She found a morgue tech named Junior photographing Moore's body when she returned. That made the guy in white Tyvek talking to Arseneault the new assistant coroner. She sized him up: short and black; a wiry cyclist build; hair and chinstrap beard about an eighth of an inch long; tribal bracelet tattoo peaking out from his jumpsuit. He had to look up six inches to meet Arseneault's eyes. The heavy, jutting lower lip said he resented every inch.

Arseneault jerked his head to call her over. "This is Dr. Langston. Carter, meet Cynth McFadden from District 5."

He nodded at her, regal and dismissive as he turned back to Arseneault.

Arseneault shifted his attention to Cynth. "The house on

Thompson Heights belongs to a woman named Florence Nygaard. Eighty-one, no record. She come up in your investigation?"

"Never heard of her."

"A uni is sitting on the house until we get a search warrant. I'm headed over to do the death notification. Wanna come?"

"Sure." Cynth nodded at Langston. "Can you check Moore's pockets before we go?"

"Any special reason?"

"If he has his phone, I bet I can get into it."

Arseneault's eyebrows raised.

Langston glowered. "This is irregular."

You've been here less than a week. How would you know?

Arseneault said to Cynth, "Excuse us a minute." He strolled off with Langston, speaking quietly. Cynth imagined the conversation consisted of a conciliatory appeal to Langston's obvious vanity and some masculine cajolery. The pair spoke to Junior. Arseneault returned with a black rectangle in a clear plastic evidence bag.

"You have five minutes before we give it back. You can do anything but take it out of the bag."

The plastic was thin enough for Cynth to operate the phone without removing it. She held it in one hand, pressed the power button, then traced a square around the outer edge of the field of dots on the lock screen. The screen dissolved, replaced by a photo of Moore's dogs covered in app icons.

"Well, well, well," Arseneault said. "You're a woman of talent."

"Moore was lazy. That's the same pattern he used when we took his phone two years ago. Call history or texts?"

"Texts."

Ellen topped the list, with a photo of Brandt on the left.

"Bingo," Cynth said.

"The ex?" Arseneault asked.

"The very estranged ex."

Moore's final message read "OMW." She checked the time. 11:45 PM. Cynth scrolled up to the top of the thread.

FRIDAY, AUGUST 8

Ellen: It's Ellen. I changed providers and they wouldn't let me keep the old number. I'm sorry I said the things I did in court. 3:11 PM

Daniel: I could have gone to prison after what you said. 3:53 PM

Ellen: I know. I'm sorry. I guess I'm still hurt, and I lost it. I can't stop thinking about it. Can we talk? 3:54 PM

Daniel: What is there to talk about? 3:57 PM

Ellen: I miss you. The girls miss you. 3:58 PM

Daniel: You can call. 4:20 PM

Ellen: In person. 4:21 PM

Daniel: You're inviting me over? 5:18 PM

Ellen: I'm not ready for that. Neutral ground. The Lounge. We had good memories there. 5:19 PM

Daniel: When? 6:22 PM

Ellen: Working tonight. Tomorrow. I
have a dinner, so it will be late. 12? I'll
bring the girls. 6:23 PM

Daniel: See you then. 6:45 PM

SATURDAY AUGUST 9

Daniel: OMW 11:45 PM

"They had kids?" Arseneault asked.

"Greyhounds. I'm wondering where this lounge is."

"Excellent question. Maybe a room at Hopewell?"

"Only if he had a death wish. The most expensive flute he stole belonged to a student. A bunch of them protested at his house. They all hated him. Should we talk to Brandt? She may already know we found him."

Arseneault narrowed his eyes. "She doesn't know we accessed the texts. We make a death notification and see how she acts."

"She might not be up yet."

Arseneault looked at his watch. "Or Brandt has been up all night because she stabbed Moore. I want to see if she's twitchy because she hasn't slept. If she's still wearing bloody clothes, I want to catch her in them."

A homey tangle of wildflowers in soft, faded colors fronted Brandt's bungalow. Bailey's design, Lia had said, though it looked like someone played fifty-two card pick up with a bunch of seeds. Maybe it was like hair, where it took a lot of effort to make "just got out of bed" look sexy instead of embarrassing.

She activated the recording app on her phone. Arseneault nodded in approval.

"You think she's playing possum?" Cynth asked as they turned onto Brandt's walkway.

"No telling. She could be on the other side of the door with a gun. We knock, but we don't stand in front of the door."

Cynth wondered when the guys would stop treating her like a candy striper. "You do know I'm SWAT?"

Arseneault gave her an interested look. "Parker said you were primarily a researcher. She didn't say you were Rambo."

Captain Roller was the one who stuck her behind a computer when she made detective. She figured it was a combination of not having confidence in women cops and wanting to stare at her large breasts around the station.

SWAT had been her small revenge on Roller. That and wearing baggy clothes.

Once she qualified for SWAT, he couldn't stand in the way of her taking part in call-outs whenever her schedule allowed. Since she'd been one step up from clerical help, her schedule *always* allowed. And as a woman in law enforcement, it didn't hurt for the guys to know she could kick their balls up over their ears.

Captain Ann Parker took over District 5 and started giving her cases while telling her professional attire was required of all detectives. She also gave Cynth permission to clock anyone who leered at her. She'd said it while an old detective named Sam Robertson was in earshot, which meant everyone in District 5 and beyond heard about it before end of shift, bless his gossipy little heart. Cynth figured that hadn't been an accident.

"Being a researcher makes me available for SWAT."

"I stand corrected."

She unsnapped her gun as Arseneault did the same, a precaution in case they needed to pull weapons. They climbed the steps to the porch and took position on either side of the door. Arseneault punched the doorbell, holding it down for a three count.

Inside, the dogs made weird noises, like they were trying to talk.

"The girls?" Arseneault asked.

"Connie and Nati. Brandt will come to the door just to shut them up."

A muffled "Hush!" as someone padded across the floor. The dogs stopped and the door opened, revealing a tall woman in her fifties, all arms and angles.

Bailey Hughes. What are you doing here?

Groggy-faced, Bailey squinted at them through the screen door, her artificially enhanced red hair messy with sleep and an oversized T-shirt hanging over bare legs. Bailey's dog, a bloodhound named Kita, looked morosely out at them, resembling Arseneault so much Cynth had to stifle a laugh. The greyhounds stood in the center of the room, alert and uncertain.

When Bailey's eyes were fully open they bulged slightly as if she found herself in an alternate dimension and didn't know what to make of it. Considering everything she'd heard about Lia's BFF, it might be true.

Bailey spoke first. "Cynth? What are you doing here?"

"I could ask the same."

"I've been staying with Ellen since Daniel's ankle monitor came off. She's terrified he'll come after her."

Cynth shared a look with Arseneault. "Bailey, this is Captain Arseneault. We need to talk to Ellen. Can we come in?"

Bailey stepped away from the door, grabbing up a pillow and blanket from the couch. The girls, noses level with Cynth's belt, sniffed at them as they passed. Cynth had the absurd vision of the dogs attempting to take their guns. *If cartoon Dobermans can fly fighter jets, the girls can snag my Glock.* She re-snapped her holster, just in case.

Bailey nodded at the couch over the bundled bedclothes in her arms. "Have a seat. I'll get Ellen."

She padded away on bare feet with Kita taking up the rear. The girls sat opposite them, watching in a mildly interested way.

Cynth kept her voice low. "Bailey Hughes is friends with Peter Dourson's girlfriend. This changes things."

"Doesn't it just."

"Wonder why Brandt didn't come out when the dogs were howling."

"Good question."

Brandt emerged from the hall, a petite, older woman wearing a loose tie-dyed top over yoga pants. A wide, stretchy headband restrained gloriously wavy white hair that reminded Cynth of the sexy bed-head look of her garden. Several streaks of soft teal green enhanced the impression. The greyhounds ran to her and she stroked the sleek heads.

"Bailey's getting dressed. She'll be out in a minute." Brandt took an oak rocker. The dogs padded off to a pair of bean bags in the corner. "What did Daniel do?"

Arseneault answered the question with a question. "When was the last time you talked to him?"

"Not through his lawyer?" Brandt rubbed her throat, saying nothing.

Buying time? Searching her memory? As they waited for her to elaborate, the scent of brewing coffee drifted into the room. Bailey entered and silently took a chair. Kita dropped beside her, sighing as her head hit her paws. *You and me both.*

Brandt said, "That was more than a year ago. You remember, Bailey, when he had that court ordered visit."

It had been a cock-up according to the officer assigned to attend. Hinkle was young and brought up to respect his elders and not equipped to deal with Moore's doddering brand of obstruction.

"You haven't spoken since?" Arseneault asked.

Brandt's voice turned brittle. "I saw him in court last week. I spoke to the judge. I did not speak to him. That's it. Whatever he says I did, it didn't happen. I don't even know where to find him. What is this about?"

The dogs went to Brandt, nosing their heads under her hands. Reacting to the tension in her voice? Were they trying to comfort Brandt or seeking reassurance? Trying to distract her from whatever was bothering her? Cynth didn't speak dog, so she could only guess.

Arseneault spoke in a practiced undertaker's voice. "We are very sorry to inform you that Daniel Moore died last night."

Brandt's head jerked back as if she'd been slapped: eyes wide, mouth gaping in an expression much like Daniel's as he lay on the sidewalk. She blinked and looked down as if gathering herself.

"What happened? His health hasn't been good but he

appeared fine Wednesday—if you don't count that stupid walker."

"Someone attacked him in Parker Woods."

Brandt's face read "bewildered." "Across the street? In the *dark*? I didn't hear a gunshot. Did you, Bailey?"

Bailey shook her head.

Brandt continued, "We should have heard it from here. What time was it?"

Arseneault again answered Brandt's question with a question. "Is there any reason he would be in the park at night?"

Brandt bit her lip, started to run a hand through her hair, dislodging the tie-dyed band. She spent a moment putting it right. "I haven't understood why Daniel did anything for years."

Cynth exchanged a look with Arseneault. He nodded. This was the tricky part, where an interview could veer into an interrogation and Miranda territory. The safe bet would be to read Brandt her rights, but doing so was likely to shut her down.

Miranda had two parts: the subject had to be—or believe they were—in police custody and unable to leave, and the questioning had to pertain to the subject's culpability.

In this case they were covered because they were in Brandt's house and she could ask them to leave, but it was better to avoid questions that could get the interview tossed in court. At the same time they didn't want Brandt to realize she was a suspect. That meant walking a tightrope, sharing information and letting Brandt respond without prompting her or asking questions. You couldn't share too much, though. They needed their hold backs.

"Ellen," Cynth said. "We have Daniel's phone. There's a long string of texts from you."

Brandt gave them a how-stupid-are-you look. "No, there isn't."

Arseneault said nothing, putting a skeptical expression on his face and waiting for Brandt to speak.

Brandt snapped, "Whoever texted Daniel, it wasn't me!" Connie and Nati shrieked. The anger vanished from Brandt's face. She leaned over, crooning comfort to the dogs. Once they settled she took a deep breath. "Tell me about it."

"The messages appear to be an attempt at reconciliation. There was an apology for what you said in court."

"I meant every word I said to the judge. You can check my phone. I'll get it for you."

She left, passing by a jumble of tools and leather on the dining room table. Cynth caught Arseneault's eye and jerked her head at the table. Arseneault raised his eyebrows.

Bailey stood, saying, "I'm getting coffee. Would you like some?"

Arseneault declined. Cynth hesitated, then said, "Black for me." White Castle had been ages ago and she needed a jolt. And accepting coffee would lower Brandt's anxiety a notch.

Brandt reentered the room with her phone in hand. "We didn't go anywhere last night. I bought surveillance cameras when Bailey insisted Daniel planned to burn the house down. I have cameras on the front and one on each side. They'll show we never left."

Bailey stiffened as she set a mug in front of Cynth. Cynth bet Bailey had said something like, "Ellen, if you're that worried Daniel will torch the house while you sleep, you'll feel better if you have cameras."

Brandt gave her phone to Arseneault, open to her texts with Moore. He held it so Cynth could see. Nothing since Moore's arrest.

"Do you mind if we see the call history?" Cynth asked.

"Be my guest."

Nothing recent there, either.

"Thank you," Arseneault said, handing back the phone. "What's your number?"

It wasn't the one texting Moore. Arseneault showed Brandt a business card with the number they'd taken from Daniel's phone written on the back. "Do you recognize this number?"

Brandt glanced at the card, passed it to Bailey. "I've never seen it. Bailey?"

Bailey shook her head and gave it back to Arseneault. "What is it?"

Arseneault stuffed it in a pocket. "Not important. Do you know a place called the Lounge?"

"The Lounge?" Ellen asked. "Is that where it happened?"

"You know it then?"

"It's a spot in the woods where we partied when Daniel was at Hopewell. I can't imagine why he'd be there."

Cynth said, "Can either of you think of anyone who wanted to harm Daniel?"

Brandt stared.

Bailey said, "You're kidding, right?"

"Point taken. How about someone who stood out, like they might go through with it?"

Brandt turned to Bailey. "You followed the Facebook group."

"What group?" Arseneault asked.

"A flute group," Bailey said. "Cynth knows about it. A lot of talk about what Daniel deserved, but that's the internet. Most of them didn't even know him. Half of the victims dropped out of the case. Why would they come here to kill him when they weren't willing to show up for a trial?"

"Why do you think they dropped out?" Arseneault asked.

"Bailey, you explain it," Brandt said.

"It's sad. The prosecutor only said they wanted to move on, but you could see how it was. Most of Daniel's victims would have recovered less than two thousand dollars if Daniel ever paid restitution."

"He never will," Brandt said. "If he'd lived, I mean."

Bailey continued, "No restitution for travel costs and loss of income. That would have more than doubled their losses. And I can't blame anyone for not wanting to watch Daniel lie and act like a victim while you know he's never going to admit what he did or tell you what happened to your flute."

Brandt's voice was soft. "I know you didn't mean to, but I wonder if you're the reason they dropped out?"

"What do you mean?"

"You kept telling everyone on Facebook there was no hidden pile of money for restitution."

"I said that for you, so they'd push for prison when the prosecutor sent out his letters to ask what they wanted for sentencing. So you wouldn't have to be afraid of him."

"I know you did. But I think maybe they took it the other way and said, 'what's the point?'"

Arseneault asked, "What happened at the sentencing?"

Brandt huffed and shook her head.

Bailey said, "Since so many people dropped out, he no

longer met the sentencing guidelines for mandatory prison. He got probation and restitution."

Brandt scoffed, "As if he would ever pay a penny."

Bailey said, "The judge piled a lot of conditions on him, but who knows if she would have held him to it?"

"Who came to the sentencing?" Cynth asked.

"A few locals," Bailey said. "Everyone else sent their victim impact statements. Enough of those to fill a two-inch binder."

All of which someone would have to review. "The locals, you have their names?"

"Do you think one of them did it?" Bailey asked.

"We don't think anything yet."

Bailey said, "Dianne"

"Dianne?" Cynth prompted.

"I don't remember last names. Long hair with tiny braids for accents. She came with her friend, Wendy. K Lee, the teacher—"

Cynth said, "I remember her. She bought her flute back from Diamond Pawn and sued Moore to recover her money. Moore ever pay her?"

"Not a cent," Bailey said.

"Have you talked to any of them since the sentencing?"

"There was Dog Day," Bailey said.

"What's Dog Day?" Arseneault said.

"The one day of the year you can walk your dog at Spring Grove Cemetery. They have booths and a 5K, a remembrance ceremony. Ellen runs a booth for Greyhound Adoption of Greater Cincinnati. That's the organization that re-homes retired greyhounds."

Brandt said, "I make dog collars to raise money for charity. I felt so bad about what Daniel put them through. I offered everyone a gift if they came by. They all came."

"They all have dogs?" Arseneault asked.

"No, but I make bracelets and key fobs, too. I just wanted them to have a nice memory. Nobody said anything about Daniel that I remember. It was really busy, so we didn't talk much. Do you want to see my camera feeds?"

Brandt doesn't want to talk about these women. "That may be helpful at some point."

"I can give you my login." She scribbled the information on a scrap of paper and handed it to Arseneault. "Will my fingerprints help? I worked the census years ago. They should still be on file."

"Thank you," Arseneault said. "That's good to know."

"I expect you need me to identify Daniel."

"Not necessary. Detective McFadden's identification was sufficient, and we have his fingerprints."

"Captain, Daniel was my life for thirty years. I need to see him. You understand that, don't you?"

"I'll arrange it." He slapped his thighs and stood to leave.

Cynth nodded her head at the dining room table. "I see you're doing more leatherwork. Can we see?"

Brandt seemed relieved and led them to the table. She held up a wide collar with a Celtic border and "GANDALF" stamped in the leather. Arseneault stroked the leather, admiring the neat holes in the tongue while Brandt explained the process. Cynth listened with half an ear while she scanned the table, inventorying the tools.

Cynth settled into the passenger seat of Arseneault's car. Arseneault said nothing, starting the ignition and conducting a three-point turn. Once headed back to Hamilton Avenue, he said, "What do you think?"

This is a test. Well, she knew her ABCs: Accept nothing. Believe no one. Check everything. It translated into "be skeptical." She hoped being honest didn't flunk her.

"Mixed bag, sir."

Arseneault kept his eyes on the road. "Tell me about that."

"Brandt had motive. I'd say her alibi is soft, but Bailey would never cover for a killer. It would mess with her karma."

"Like that, is she?"

"New Age all the way. An odd duck, but she has a solid moral compass."

"She had to sleep sometime."

"The details need to be explored, but it's a small house. There's a bamboo colony lining a six -foot privacy fence in back."

"A colony?"

"That's what Brandt calls it. I looked it up. It's the official term."

"Huh. Things you learn."

"Point is, you can only get out through the gate and that should trigger her cameras. She wakes up Bailey if she goes out the front door. Camera there, too."

"You don't think she left the house. What's the other side of this?"

"I met Brandt two years ago. I couldn't fault anything she said but she never seemed quite right."

"Explain that."

"I could never see how she lived with Daniel for thirty years and didn't know he was a crook."

"I've interviewed many people who were too decent to imagine what their spouses were up to."

Arseneault was playing devil's advocate with her. She needed to defend herself. "For thirty years?"

"From what you've told me, the people he ripped off for those thirty years just recently figured it out."

"Moore fell into stealing flutes after years of reputable dealing. His early victims were hundreds of miles away and they only knew what he told them. Everyone thought their situation was an anomaly until they started comparing notes online."

"So he wasn't a crook for thirty years."

"No, but he was himself for thirty years, and she lived with him."

"Point taken."

Cynth mentally exhaled. Maybe she wouldn't flunk after all. "Then there's the way she blew up."

"I agree she got excitable for a minute—after we said she'd been texting Moore."

"That's understandable. What bothers me, she turned it off like flipping a switch when her dogs got upset."

"Some people can do that, but I see what you mean."

"That bit about Bailey causing people to drop out of the trial—it felt passive aggressive."

"So, not a nice person. How does that figure in?"

"Not sure it does, but it suggests there's more going on than she wants people to see on the surface."

"Brandt was fine when she showed us her leatherwork."

"The tools fit, but she never impressed me as someone who could calmly demonstrate her murder weapons. If she was that sociopathic, I'd still think she was a sweet, clueless, little—" She remembered Arseneault's age. "—mature woman. She's not ringing my bell. Tickles it a little."

Arseneault nodded, chewing his lip. "You'd expect an undercurrent of smug, greasy excitement. It wasn't there."

"She offered up her cameras. She wouldn't do that if they showed anything."

"I'm more interested in cameras on Thompson Heights."

Cynth forgot her nerves. "You think the person who jumped Moore checked out the residence."

"Bingo. I'd like you to take lead on this."

She stiffened. She was looking for a leg up but this was too much. "I thought I was here to provide background. I don't have the experience. Can I ask why you want me to lead?"

"Moore was yours. More efficient to advise you on the investigation than to get my guys up to speed on a very complicated situation."

She thought about that two-inch binder of victim statements, and a way to test his sincerity. "There're dozens of people to check on and that needs to happen now."

"You can have Hodgkins and Jarvis."

I'd rather eat my own intestines while listening to Nickelback. "Moore's local victims are connected to Hopewell." Where the pair alienated everyone while investigating Lawrence. That had to be a sore point that could wrong-foot the investigation.

"Point taken. What do you suggest?"

"Brent Davis worked with me on the Moore investigation. He hand-held a lot of the victims." A tense alliance due to their complicated history. She didn't want to go there, but anything was better than Heckle and Jeckle. "And there's Peter Dourson. You worked with him before."

TWO YEARS AGO

Cynth sat in Captain Parker's visitor chair with a big, fat target on her ass. Unlike Roller, the new captain was impossible to read. She kept her hands in her lap and out of Parker's line of sight as she clenched and relaxed them. It was a trick she used to keep stress off her face.

She admired Parker, a handsome, no-nonsense woman with mad skills and zero vanity. No matter the event, Parker wore her shoulder-length hair in a simple ponytail and kept her nails trimmed short and unpolished. She qualified for SWAT every year like Cynth did, though she didn't go on call-outs.

Parker reminded her of Vanessa Michael Munroe, ass-kicking heroine of her favorite thriller novels. Like Munroe, Parker's face had firm, simple lines that could pass for male if she needed, or be entirely feminine if the situation called for it. Unlike Munroe, Parker couldn't learn a new language in five minutes and as far as Cynth knew, hadn't killed anyone or blown up any superyachts.

Parker steepled her hands, finger tips tapping their mates. "I reviewed the file. For the record, the DA is an ass. None of this is your fault."

"None of this" was the failure years earlier to treat Moore Flutes as a criminal operation when two women complained Moore was giving them the runaround about their flutes. The DA told Roller—who told her—to refer the women to small claims court instead of pursuing the robust criminal investigation Moore warranted.

With stories on Channel 7 featuring tearful middle-class women, and complaints coming in from all over the country, it wasn't water the DA wanted to carry in an election year. Her damn luck Roller tossed the original complaints at her as a nuisance case to file and forget.

Cynth exhaled, only then realizing she'd been holding her breath. Parker wasn't rolling the shit downhill. She sat back in the visitor's chair, unclenching her hands. "Thank you, sir."

"This is still your case."

Cynth appreciated Parker's confidence in her, but wasn't crazy about picking up this particular ball. "Sir?"

"It has the potential to be much bigger, both in scope and in the public eye. You've spent most of your time here providing backup for other detectives."

Because Roller kept me there.

"I know you like being available for SWAT rollouts, but I think it's time you pushed yourself."

The implication she'd been slacking stung. "I didn't realize I wasn't pulling my weight, sir."

"Take the stick out of your ass. You're a hard worker. Your development fell through the cracks, precisely because you're effective where you are and I had too many fires to put out when Roller retired. You deserve the chance to do more. This is your baby."

Oh, crap. "Thank you for the opportunity, sir."

"Calls are coming in. We need to get on top of this quickly. I'm assigning Davis to help you."

Brent Davis, hot shot pretty boy and total snake. She fell in bed with him years ago, and he'd used her. It didn't matter that he'd been undercover, or that he lied to Internal Affairs so she wouldn't wind up manning a fast food register.

It mattered that he pulled the wool over her eyes with his smooth looks and magnolia voice. She'd bought his story about being a midlevel P & G executive transplanted from Georgia. How could she ever trust him when he could make her believe anything he chose? How could she trust herself when she hadn't seen him for who he was?

The situation had been humiliating and demoralizing and she'd almost left law enforcement over it. Worst of all was him transferring to District 5, his presence reminding her every day she owed her career to him, never mind it was *his* damn op that went pear-shaped.

Only a few trusted friends knew they had history, none of them cops unless you counted IA. Nobody knew the full story except her and Brent. Maybe not even her. Maybe not Brent, either.

"Sir? Is this necessary?"

"Your style is very direct, and it's effective with our usual dirtbags. Daniel Moore isn't a usual dirtbag."

"I can handle him."

"And his victims are high-toned and hysterical. Brent's finesse will come in handy. I'm hoping you'll learn from him. Versatility is a virtue."

Finesse: another word for lying. Resisting would make her look like a whiny bitch, but she still tried. "Sir, Peter Dourson and I have worked well together in the past."

Cynth felt red creeping up her face as Parker examined it.

"Is there something I need to know about Detective Davis?"

Damn Brent, anyway. "No, sir. Not at all."

Parker pushed a binder across the desk to her. "Here's the file and the calls to Channel 7. You're in charge. I trust you'll remind Davis if he forgets."

Cynth had eyes on Arseneault as he turned onto Glen Parker. He stared out the windshield, poking his tongue in his cheek. "I'll talk to Parker and see if Davis is available."

His phone dinged. He pulled over to the side of the road to read the text, then turned the phone so she could see the photo of a bloody spike resembling the tools on Brandt's work table.

"Junior found the murder weapon under Moore's body when they moved it. If Brandt has the strength to shove this through leather, she'd have no problem with an old man's neck."

She'd made the wrong call about Brandt. *Shit, shit, shit.* "Fingerprints?"

"We won't know until they process it at the lab."

Before he could pull back on the road, the phone pinged again. He barked, "Arseneault," then "Damn. It was bound to happen. Thanks for the heads up." He ended the call.

"Channel 7 just showed up. We'll run into them when we round the bend. They don't need to know Moore was staying a block away. Not yet, anyway."

"What do you want to do?"

Arseneault sighed. "Only one way in and out of Thompson Heights, and they're in the way. I suppose I can give them a quick statement, but I can't order them off a public street. No telling how long they'll hang around looking for someone to talk to."

"Is it Aubrey Morse, sir?"

He looked at her oddly. "Why?"

"Give your statement. I have a plan."

Arseneault pulled back on the road. Sure enough, they found the Channel 7 van slewed across the curve where Glen Parker turned into Langland. Bitch-on-wheels Aubrey Morse stood in the road chatting with—more likely harassing—the cop assigned to keep people out of the crime scene.

As Arseneault approached Morse, Cynth veered toward the van where her cousin and parkour buddy Duff busied himself with camera equipment. Cousin Duff was a prime specimen with those rust red dreadlocks down his back and an array of Celtic tattoos celebrating his Scottish heritage.

"Hey, girlfriend," Duff said, straightening to his full 6'4".

"Hey yourself. Sorry about brunch."

"No worries. Aubrey pulled me in, so there is no brunch. At least she called before David started the quiche."

"Knowing David, he made it anyway. He'll tell us later how he ate the whole thing."

"Looks like someone offed your flute guy."

"Can you blame them?"

"We covered the sentencing. I was ready to kill him myself after the bullshit he told the judge. What do you know?"

"You get a bonus for tips?"

Duff laughed. "I wish."

"We spotted the dog walker who found the body heading south on Haight with a harlequin great Dane. You should be able to catch her on Pullan. She won't be hard to spot."

"That's just a few blocks from here."

Aubrey waved him over. He winked at Cynth and grabbed his camera. "Duty calls. Thanks, I owe you."

It took five minutes for Duff to tape a brief statement which likely went, "A man died under suspicious circumstances. We are pursuing all leads." Arseneault wouldn't say much more because what little they knew could compromise the investigation.

Morse handed her mic to Duff. She moved in to say pleasantries to Arseneault and try to wheedle promises of more out of him. Duff caught her attention and whispered in her ear. Morse turned to him, an intent look on her face. She flashed a mechanical smile at Arseneault, said goodbye, then clacked rapidly to the van.

Hah.

By the time Arsenault joined her, Duff had made a U-turn with the van and was heading back to Hamilton and Haight Street.

"Neat trick," Arseneault said. "How did you pull that off?"

"Told the cameraman we spotted the dog walker. He thinks I did him a solid."

"Maybe not the most ethical solution."

"Desperate times, sir."

"That's the truth. I told Morse you'd give her a statement at District 5 for the evening news."

"Sir? This is the thanks I get?"

Florence Nygaard lived in a tired cracker box with faded blue siding, fronted by a cracked concrete walkway, tiny porch, and weedy flower beds. No cameras that Cynth could see. Arseneault waved off the patrol car sitting on the house and punched the bell. Inside, a dog yapped.

What is it with Northside and dogs? It's like a requirement.

They waited several seconds in a pose of solemn respect.

Cynth said, "You think she heard that?"

"If she didn't, she heard the dog. Car's in the drive, so she should be home. Maybe she isn't up yet." Arseneault pressed the bell again. More yapping. "Then again, this might be a two-fer."

"Let's hope not, sir."

Thirty seconds later, the sound of shuffling feet and someone shushing the dog. Not a two-fer, then. The door cracked open, revealing a bloated face, limp, gray hair, and the side of a walker. At her feet, an ancient white fur ball stared up at them with cloudy, alien eyes.

The dog snuffled. The woman said, "Can I help you?"

"Florence Nygaard?"

"Yes?"

"I'm Captain Arseneault from the Cincinnati Police, and this is Detective McFadden."

Blinking and worry on that face now.

"We have some unfortunate news. May we come inside?"

"Oh … well … it's … I'm not ready for company." She turned and called, "Daniel? … Daniel? … I don't know where he is. He should have answered the door. I'm not well."

She backed up with the walker, letting them inside as she made her way to an overstuffed blue recliner next to a nightstand littered with pill bottles, tissues, and a glass jar partially filled with water. The jar explained the delay:

Nygaard had to shove in the teeth she kept near the door because she only wore them when she had company.

From behind, Nygaard was an undifferentiated lump of flesh inside a baggy floral dress. She heaved herself into the chair and the arthritic little dog climbed a miniature set of steps into her lap.

"Close the door, would you? I'm dying. Daniel is supposed to help me, but he's not here. Can you get me a glass of water?"

Arseneault jerked his chin at the kitchen, sending Cynth for the water as he shut the door. Cynth found a plastic tumbler in the dish drainer. As she filled it from the tap, the twin odors of poop and urine wafted up. A lumpy puddle at the back door confirmed what her nose knew.

Nygaard took the tumbler with a shaky hand. "Thank you, dear." The dog circled in her lap and whined. "Can you let Snickerdoodle into the back yard? He's acting like he hasn't been out yet."

Cynth opened the back door, careful not to step into the mess. Snickerdoodle plodded through the puddle on his way out, leaving wet paw prints on the back deck and the ramp down to the yard. He? it? squatted for form, squeezing out a drop or three of urine before hurrying back up the ramp and past Cynth—this time splashing her shoes.

She followed Snickerdoodle into the living room, where he climbed back into Nygaard's lap. She hoped his paws were dry.

When Cynth joined Arseneault on the sofa, he said, "Mrs. Nygaard, when was the last time you saw Daniel Moore?"

"He was here last night when I went to bed. I don't know where he got to. "

"How was he dressed?"

Nygaard gave him an odd look. "Last night? Sweat pants and a flannel shirt. What does that matter?"

"One of your neighbors found Daniel in Parker Woods—"

The face scrunched in confusion. "Found? I don't understand."

Time to rip off the bandage. Cynth looked at Arseneault. He nodded. She said as gently as she could, "He died in the park sometime last night."

"Died? He can't be dead." The gray head shook vigorously. "No. He can't." She looked up at Arseneault, pleading. "I need him. I'm dying."

She meant it literally. Cynth said, "You're terminally ill?"

Nygaard fluttered a hand over the collection of pill bottles crowding the nightstand. "All my organs are in a race to shut down. Daniel moved in to help me. What am I supposed to do?"

"Is there someone we can call?"

The wrinkled face collapsed. "There's nobody I want."

Arseneault sat placidly, not taking the lead. *Another test.* Cynth scanned the room, looking for a clue to anything about Nygaard's life.

Shelves jumbled with dusty knick-knacks lined the walls, interrupted by a decommissioned fireplace. A landscape hung over the mantel, brightly colored and oddly flat, like an adult's idea of how a child would paint.

One end of the mantel held a flag presentation case next to a formal portrait of a marine in dress blues. Too recent to be a husband. A son then, deceased. Not a can of worms she wanted to open. Next to that was a wedding photo, with the bride wearing a 70s Farrah Fawcett feathered cut. A young

Nygaard. She took a discrete peek at Nygaard's hand. She wore a wedding set with a diamond that had to be a carat, surrounded by tiny diamonds. Hubby was deceased, or tucked away in a nursing home. Another can of worms.

Further down, a silver frame held a formal school portrait of a teen-age girl holding a flute. Smaller photos of the same girl at various ages filled in the empty spaces, none of them older than high school.

Cynth nodded at the flute photo. "She's beautiful. Who is she?"

Nygaard blinked at the photos. Tears? Confusion? "That's Natalie. She passed. Daniel was so good to her."

Again with the worms. "I'm so sorry."

"That was years ago. She's at Spring Grove. I ran into Daniel there on her birthday last year. I had no idea he visited her. He was having trouble with Ellen, so I invited him to stay with me. He's been helping me ever since. I don't know what I'll do without him."

"Are you up to answering some questions?"

"I don't understand this. Poor Daniel. How did he die?"

"We're still trying to figure that out. Who knew Daniel was staying with you?"

"I suppose the neighbors, though I don't think he ever introduced himself. He was so ashamed after the lies Ellen told about him. Ellen tossed him out of his own home. She emptied his accounts, and that wrecked his business. Nobody would help him."

"Do you know anyone who would hurt him?"

"Hurt him? Someone did this to him? Someone killed him?"

"That's what we believe."

"Who would hurt him? He was kind to everyone. I don't

know what got into Ellen. Daniel said it started after she hit her head. She wasn't the same anymore."

"Mrs. Nygaard, did you know Daniel was in court Wednesday?"

"Of course he was. He was suing Ellen to get his house back."

Cynth exchanged a look with Arseneault before proceeding. "Ms. Nygaard, Daniel was in court because he stole a quarter million dollars' worth of client flutes. He was sentenced Wednesday."

Nygaard frowned, confused. "That's not right. Ellen stole his house. He told me."

"He pled guilty, Ms. Nygaard."

Nygaard clutched Snickerdoodle and shook her head. "No, that's wrong."

Nygaard was caught in a loop. Keeping her focused would be hard, especially without a friend to hold her hand. Cynth snuck a look at Arseneault. He maintained an attitude of professional compassion that she suspected hid any number of feelings.

Cynth was no good at this, but she'd seen Brent play the nurturer plenty of times. She asked, "Have you eaten today?"

Nygaard turned watery eyes to Cynth. "Daniel gets me something, but I'm not very hungry."

"When was the last time you ate?"

Nygaard waved a hand. "Last night? Soup? I think he made mushroom soup."

"Can I fix you something? Toast? Scrambled eggs? Cereal?" That was most of Cynth's culinary repertoire. If Nygaard wanted an omelet, she was out of luck.

"Daniel makes me an English muffin in the toaster oven.

He spreads a little cream cheese on it. Can you make me some tea? I'm not allowed to drink coffee anymore. Too acid."

"I'll do my best."

She abandoned the field to Arseneault, reminding herself as she rummaged through the cabinets that she was in the kitchen due to rank, not sex. Regardless, she absolutely refused to clean up Snickerdoodle's morning deposit. No doubt Brent would deliver a perfectly toasted muffin, served on a doily with a rose in a bud vase. Brent would also mop and wax the floor while he waited for the toaster oven to ding. It irked.

Cynth was not mopping the floor when the toaster oven dinged. Instead, she had her hands full with boiling water and tea bags. By the time she got to it, the tops of the muffin halves were dark and crunchy. She slathered cream cheese on, hoping to cover up her incompetence. Nygaard might like burnt toast, you never knew. Then again, people got so bent out of shape over food.

She balanced the plate, mug, and silverware, carrying them into the living room. No room on the crowded nightstand. Arseneault spotted the problem and retrieved a rusty TV tray leaning against the fireplace in time for Cynth to dump the food on it instead of the floor.

Nygaard's lips folded in as she looked at the thick coating of cream cheese on her muffin. She scraped most of the offending white stuff off with a knife, looking pointedly at Cynth.

Well, la-di-da. Get your own damn muffin next time. "Do you have family we can call for you?" Cynth asked.

Her face turned mulish. "My son died overseas. They buried him at Arlington years ago. There's no one left."

Cynth stopped herself from wincing and tried again. "A neighbor?"

"I don't want them up in my business. I have a girl I can call if I need anything."

Arseneault's phone pinged. He glanced at the screen. "Mrs. Nygaard, we need to look through Daniel's room. Something there might help us understand what happened. We have a warrant, if you'd like to see it."

Nygaard waved her hand. "I don't know where my glasses are. I doubt I could read it." She nodded at a small hall. "Daniel's bedroom is on the right, after the bathroom. The rest of his things are in the garage."

Cynth remembered piles of junk at Moore's shop and hoped the garage wasn't more of the same. "What kinds of things are in the garage, Mrs. Nygaard?"

"Everything. Ellen locked him out, but that wasn't enough for her. She got Daniel arrested for domestic violence, and he wouldn't hurt a fly. She refused to bail him out, and got a restraining order against him. All made up stuff so she could steal the house. Poor Daniel had to get a court order just to get some clothes. When he went home, they had police there to stand over him. As if he was some kind of criminal!"

Nygaard sniffed. "She'd tossed everything in boxes. Daniel didn't know where to start and they kept rushing him to get out. Then Ellen moved everything to a storage unit at the edge of town and wouldn't let him have access. I had to hire movers to bring those boxes here."

Arseneault asked, "When was the last time he went into the garage?"

"October was warm. It must have been November, to get

his winter coat. He never put it back. His knees. Too much trouble lifting the door."

Unlikely they'd need to go through the boxes.

Daniel's things piled on all available surfaces in his room, smothering the girlish decor underneath: cardboard boxes with the contents scrawled on the sides with marker, courtesy of Ellen and Bailey; plastic crates of files and legal pads undoubtably full of Daniel's endless to-do lists and unreadable notes; clothes, both clean and dirty—and hard to tell which was which.

Daniel slept on a brass bed with a pink duvet and a sweet little bedside lamp. A pink teddy bear sat on the dresser, peeking out from behind a stack of legal pads.

There were more photos of Natalie, casual snapshots with friends. In one she had her arm around a tiny girl with dark, waist-length hair dressed up with a dozen skinny, beaded braids in a sort of fairy look. The fairy girl looked familiar, but Cynth couldn't place her.

Natalie had lived here. How long since she died?

Daniel's walker stood in the corner with a purple cane. Not taken by his killer for a trophy. Daniel had gone a tenth of a mile in the dark without it.

Arseneault handed Cynth a pair of nitrile gloves and seated himself at the tiny desk, claiming that as his territory. Cynth sat on the bed, surveying the top of the nightstand. Lamp, remote for the small flat screen TV on the dresser, water glass, medications, inhaler, and a battered Filofax organizer. Who used *those* anymore?

She set the Filofax beside her on the bed and opened the

nightstand drawer. Hopewell concert programs, class schedules, paperwork, the most recent dated four years earlier. Natalie had died years ago. Nygaard had preserved her room intact. *At least until Moore came along.*

"Well, well," Arseneault said.

Cynth swiveled on the bed to see. "What did you find?"

"Florence Nygaard's legal and financial papers. Moore had power of attorney." He flipped through more papers. "She made him sole beneficiary of her will."

"Of course she did."

Moore's brief bag sat on the floor by the nightstand. Cynth dragged it up on the bed, sorting through the contents. All court stuff: official documents, copies of victim impact statements, legal pads full of Moore's tiny writing. She'd make Brent go through it.

She pulled the side pocket open and peered inside. Pens, antacids, and something small and white she couldn't identify. She slid a gloved hand into the pocket and retrieved a flat plastic square with rounded edges and the word "tile" written on the front.

"Check this out."

Arseneault craned his head around. "What do you have?"

Cynth held her palm out, showing him the bluetooth tracker. "Bet you a dozen donuts there's no Tile app on Moore's phone. Someone was stalking him."

2

DAY 1, PART 2

SUNDAY, AUGUST 10, 8:45 A.M.

LIA

It was a stare down. Lia sat at her favorite dog park picnic table, facing out with her back against the tabletop. She narrowed her eyes at her mutinous Catahoula.

Six-month-old Gypsy stood five feet away with a dirty tennis ball between her paws, staring right back. The pup had bicolored eyes to go with her black on brown merle. Both eyes had started out summer sky blue. One quickly turned brown while the other faded to nearly white. It gave her a deranged appearance that she used to great effect.

Lia tapped her ball chucker against the ground. "Bring it here."

Gypsy picked up the ball, dropped it three inches closer. The pup thrust her muzzle forward. Lia tapped the ground again, this time punctuating each word as she spoke. "Bring." Tap. "It." Tap. "Here." Tap.

49

Gypsy snorted.

Long-time friend Jim McDonald—a retired engineer who reminded her of a cross between Treebeard and Saint Francis of Assisi—was sole witness to this act of rebellion, if you didn't count Chester and Fleece lolling on the table. He extended his walking staff and nudged the ball, rolling it within reach of Lia's chucker. He gave her a bland look.

Lia huffed, "Do I interfere with your parenting?"

"Give her a break. She's just a baby."

"If she wants to chase the ball, she has to bring it back. Enabling her won't teach her anything."

Lia scooped up the ball. Wild with joy, Gypsy bounced in the air like a forty pound Jack Russell terrier and raced down the slope. Lia raised her arm and flung the ball, aiming twenty yards to the right of the spot where Gypsy waited with her tail wagging in canine anticipation. She raced after, stopping short of colliding with the fence as the ball rolled against it. She grabbed the ball, then went on alert, barking with the ball still stuffed in her mouth.

Not alien invaders. Just Steve and Terry pulling into the parking lot with their dogs, Jackson and Penny. The room-mates were of an age with Jim. Lia privately thought of them as Tweedledee and Tweedledum since they were similar in height and build, though Terry had an iron-gray buzz cut and a strong resemblance to Teddy Roosevelt in his portly years and Steve was more balding Pillsbury Doughboy with a well-groomed goatee.

Jim nodded at the tangle of leather on Lia's wrist. "That's pretty."

Lia raised her arm, turning it back and forth, showing off the skinny leather thong that wrapped around her wrist several times. Heart and paw charms hung from the clasp.

The names Gypsy, Chewy, and Honey—who she'd lost to cancer—were stamped in the leather.

"Ellen gave it to me at Dog Day. She made gifts for everyone who came to Daniel's sentencing."

"That was nice of her."

"I think she feels bad they never found all the flutes, even though she had nothing to do with it."

"Criminal, the judge giving him probation after all the people he robbed."

"I guess the judge wanted to give him a chance to make good. That's dumb. The state won't let him operate a business after all the complaints. He told the judge he was applying for disability but would be happy to perform any community service she assigned."

"So he doesn't plan to earn an honest living and has no intention of paying anyone anything."

"The judge didn't buy *that*, at least. She said he had to get a job."

Jim shook his head. "I still can't get over pawning instruments people brought him for repair. What did he think? That they'd forget he had them?"

"Magical thinking. Things would turn around and he'd make everything right. He always was lousy with money. Best we figured, he was robbing Peter to pay Paul to keep up appearances."

"So in his mind he had a noble cause."

Jackson and Penny arrived dragging a bushy six-foot branch. Chewy, having finished his daily perimeter check, supervised noisily.

"Hail, good people," Terry called. And to Jim, "How many tries to get today's Wordle?"

Jim grinned. "Three."

"Bah," Terry said.

Steve laughed. "Took him five to get squid."

Jim elaborated, "Route and snail cover the most used ten letters up front. They gave me S, U, and I in green. Q and D were easy peasy after that."

"Boring words," Terry said. "Adieu has four vowels and flare. I got three letters in the first guess."

Jim snorted. "None in the right place."

Steve picked up the now-abandoned bushy branch and heaved it down the hill. All the dogs except Fleece bolted after it. The border collie lifted her head off her paws and gave Jim a look that said, "kids," then resumed her napping.

Having derailed a pointless argument between Terry and Jim, Steve grinned and said, "I'll stick with Toy Blast."

"Boops and beeps and explosions," Terry said. "A waste of dopamine."

"Bubble wrap," Lia said.

They all stared at her.

Lia continued, "A friend in college was addicted to it. She'd spend hours mindlessly popping the bubbles. Video games are bubble wrap with special effects."

"Not Wordle," Jim and Terry said simultaneously.

Gypsy returned with a tennis ball, this time dropping it close enough for Lia to reach. She extended her chucker. Gypsy snatched the ball away. Lia tapped the ground with the long-handled scoop. Gypsy dropped the ball, then snatched it away again as Lia reached for it.

"She's teasing you," Jim said.

"She has her own special games," Steve said.

"Doesn't she just," Lia said. "A coon hound crowded her at Dog Day and she slipped her collar. Took us ten minutes to corral her. My mistake because I didn't have a ball with me. We finally caught up with her when she stopped to defile a grave. That's the most fun she had all day. I was mortified."

Gypsy gave Lia a wounded expression and relinquished the ball. Lia ruffled the mottled ears. "At least you behaved at the remembrance ceremony."

The X-Files theme sounded from Lia's phone.

Jim said, "Tell Bailey we miss her."

Terry said, "Tell her the blow-up doll keeping her seat warm got mauled by a Rottweiler."

Steve said, "Ask her why she prefers a cemetery full of dead people to hanging with us."

Lia waved them off, turning away to answer the call. "Hey, girlfriend."

"Are you with the others?"

"The usual suspects. Why?"

"Get off by yourself so we can talk."

Odd, and sounded serious. Lia loaded a tennis ball into her chucker and sent it flying for Gypsy before following with Chewy. Several yards from the table, Lia said, "Okay, what's with the secrecy?"

"I'm at Ellen's. Someone killed Daniel last night. Cynth was just here with the head of Homicide. "

"Oh, my god. That's awful."

"Ellen's having a meltdown. I need you."

"What aren't you telling me?"

"More than I can say over the phone. Meet me at Wesleyan. I'll bring White Castle."

Lia sighed, saying goodbye to her quiet day in the studio. "See you in twenty."

"Make it fifteen. I'm desperate."

She returned to the table to grab her leashes.

Jim said, "Leaving us so soon?"

They'll find out soon enough. "The kids and I get to hang out with dead people. Someone killed Daniel Moore last night."

"What happened?" Steve asked.

Terry poked one imperious finger in the air. "A dozen angry flautists stabbed him in the heart."

"After pumping him with a paralytic? I wouldn't be surprised," Steve said.

"Orient Express?," Jim said. "Do musicians read Agatha Christie?"

"Who needs to read when you can watch the remake online?" Steve said.

"The David Suchet version was better," Jim said.

Lia waved goodbye, leaving before the guys asked questions she couldn't answer. Nobody had homicide cases at District 5, not since CPD opened the Homicide unit. Cynth shouldn't be involved.

She considered calling Cynth, but talking to Lia would be item #673 on Cynth's to-do list right now and bothering her would invoke threats of bodily harm. Peter was out in the woods. Doubtful he had cell coverage. He wouldn't know anything, anyway.

The cinderblock echo of two hundred barking dogs drifted through the Volvo's open window as Lia drove through the iron gates that were all that remained of the original fence fronting Wesleyan Cemetery.

Breakfast at the shelter next door, or maybe they were protesting the fact that they were stuck parading up and down Colerain Avenue on their daily walks instead of chasing squirrels across the graves. The scent of baking bread provided an odd counterpoint to the canine serenade, courtesy of a small commercial bakery across the street that specialized in hot dog buns.

Chewy and Gypsy propped up on the windowsill, tails wagging, excited by the invisible dogs, the smell, or perhaps the delightfully decrepit cemetery itself.

Wesleyan was the city's first integrated cemetery. Famous for its role in smuggling twenty-eight escaped slaves through town disguised as a funeral procession, Wesleyan was the historical site the city never wanted. The court forced the city to take over the cemetery around the turn of the millennium after the owner went to prison for misappropriating funds.

There were rumors he'd also resold plots and dumped coffins and remains in the gully behind the property—an urban legend born of the discovery of a bone in the grass. Peter said it was most likely an animal bone.

She and Peter—sans dogs—once hiked the gully looking for discarded gravestones. They found concrete debris and broken pieces of stone that looked like they might be part of a gravestone, but nothing with any text. They found a trash heap with an old bedspring, but no broken coffins. She'd been both relieved and disappointed.

Inside the gate, a large metal sign of the kind found on highways served as a historical marker. Years earlier, a pragmatic soul nailed a small sign to one of the uprights. Crooked vinyl letters said,

PLEASE DON'T WALK DOGS ON GRAVES

At least that's what it said before the letters peeled off. You could still make out the words if you knew they were there.

Officially, dogs weren't allowed. With no enforcement it was a "don't ask, don't tell" situation.

Ancient trees lined the crumbling asphalt drive snaking up the ridge that bisected the cemetery, hiding most of its twenty-seven acres from Colerain Avenue.

Nineteenth century headstones tilted and toppled across the grass as if an earthquake had never been put right. The oldest headstones were made of limestone: tall and thin, with the proportions of a club cracker and just as fragile, the elegant script on the front eroded to illegibility.

The old Volvo reached the top of the ridge, which had been the highest spot for a mile in all directions until cell towers went up. Before the towers, lightning sheared the tops off more than one tree, the damage now hidden by foliage and only detectable by oddly shaped crowns and trunks much too wide for their height.

The back of the ridge sloped gently down. Widely spaced trees soared over the markers, majestic elder statesmen out of a Constable landscape, some with trunks so big it took three people holding hands to encircle them. Short obelisks scattered among the markers.

Fake flowers, half-deflated mylar birthday balloons, garden spinners and pinwheels, toy cars, bows, out of season holiday decorations, and tiny American flags made incongruent splashes of color while providing proof occupants were still remembered.

Seventeen thousand people rested here, though the number of gravestones suggested far fewer. This was the poor person's cemetery. Too many graves were unmarked.

The cemetery ended at a narrow band of woods that hid the Mill Creek gully and, beyond that, an elevated section of I-74.

Runners frequented the looping lanes. Flocks of vultures sunned themselves atop the obelisks in the mornings, stretching their wings and flapping lazily as if they hadn't had their coffee yet. Sometimes coyotes raced across the grounds.

Lia loved it.

A fat, gnarled tree sat in the far corner like something out of a Charles Vess fantasy, marking the edge of four privately owned acres that were mostly ignored except the occasional summer mowing. The lot had likely been bought decades earlier in expectation of selling it to the cemetery, and made worthless when the city took over and shut down burials.

It was a perfect place to run dogs.

Bailey's rusted Toyota truck sat under the Charles Vess tree. Bailey and Kita sprawled on the open tailgate while Ellen's girls wandered languidly through the field. Lia let her dogs loose and hopped up next to Bailey.

Bailey held out a white bag and a paper cup. Chewy and Gypsy stuck close, smelling food.

"This is yours. I already ate."

"That was fast."

"I could only stomach one slider. Nerves will do that to you."

Lia reached into the white bag and pulled out a deep fried hash brown nibbler, which amounted to half a tater tot. She leaned over the edge of the tailgate and offered it to

Gypsy, retrieving another for Chewy before she dug into her sausage and egg slider.

"If Ellen is having a meltdown, shouldn't you be with her?"

"I gave her a Xanax and put her back to bed. She'll be better after she's rested."

"What happened?"

"We don't know." Catching Lia's stink eye, she amended, "Not much, anyway. Someone found Daniel's body in Parker Woods this morning. Cynth said his phone had texts claiming to be from Ellen. It wasn't her. I was with her all night."

The woman who refused to get an alarm system thought nothing of guilting Bailey into being her personal security. Lia was unsure if her uncharitable attitude was due to disliking Ellen or resenting her demands on Bailey's time.

Probably both. "You gave her an alibi. What's the problem?"

"Ellen is convinced the police will arrest her anyway."

Of course she is. "She has cameras. There's no reason to be worried."

"Tell that to Ellen."

"She watches too much TV." Lia fed the last of the hash browns to her dogs and crunched the bag into a ball. "What do you need from me now?"

"Moral support? Ellen is freaking and I'm tapped out."

"Wave Tarot cards at her and tell her everything will be fine."

Bailey laughed. "Unethical but tempting. I tried reading for her years ago. I'd tell her something she didn't want to hear and she'd grab the little white book that comes with every deck and point out how this card and that card could mean different things and demolish the whole thing."

"That's rude."

"A week later, she'd want another reading." Bailey sighed. "Too many people know the truth, but they don't like what they know and they want me to tell them something different. When they hear what they already know from someone who has no knowledge of the situation, it's easier for them to accept."

"But you know everything, so she can dismiss anything the cards tell you as opinion instead of a revelation from the ether."

"Pretty much. If someone spends half an hour telling me all the rotten things their boyfriend does and then the cards say, 'guess what, your boyfriend is rotten,' they aren't impressed."

Lia didn't believe in Tarot, but Bailey had a lot of repeat clients at the website she ran to supplement her gardening. "Haven't your readings for Ellen been reliable over time?"

"The cards know when the querent doesn't respect them and they give me garbage. So I told her reading for people I know gums up my intuition and now she doesn't believe in Tarot."

"Because you won't read for her."

"It's very chicken and egg. Please come."

"I don't know how much help I'll be."

"You have an in with District 5 and you know police stuff."

"No one at District 5 will tell me anything, and I know enough to be stupidly dangerous."

"You know how investigations work. You can tell her not to panic."

"You can tell her not to panic. You've been doing that for two years."

"But she believes you when you say it."

"Could have fooled me," Lia groused. "Fine. I'll drop off the kids and follow you there."

They found Ellen in her Martha Stewart-perfect kitchen, wreathed in the twin aromas of Peruvian coffee and fresh-baked apple crumb cake. She stretched her mouth into a semblance of a smile under hard eyes. Lia blinked and the suspicious expression vanished, replaced by something vague and vulnerable.

"Lia. I didn't realize you were coming."

"You should be resting," Bailey said.

Ellen shoved a hank of wavy, teal-streaked hair out of her face. "I couldn't sleep." She reached into the cupboard, rattling plates.

"Let me do that."

Bailey steered Ellen to the table, where she dropped bonelessly into a chair. Nati and Connie nosed her hands, looking for pets. Kita grumbled and lowered herself onto an area rug, sighing in a way Lia appreciated. *You and me both, girl.*

Lia boosted herself onto a stool at the pass-through counter. She held out a leather-wrapped wrist. "I'm loving my bracelet. Thank you again."

Ellen said nothing.

"I thought Lia could help," Bailey said.

"I don't understand how. Help yourself to crumb cake. I'd get it for you but I'm still shaking." Ellen stroked the girls as she looked out the window, where there was nothing to see except a wall of bamboo. "They think I killed Daniel."

Bailey busied herself with the plates. "You don't know what they think."

"Whatever it is, it isn't good."

"At this point they aren't thinking much of anything," Lia said carefully.

"And how would you know? How do I know you're not here to spy for your boyfriend?" The sharp tone had Nati whining, ears pressed back against her head.

Thank God I dropped the kids off at home.

Bailey cut into the crumb cake. "Peter isn't even in town. He's off in the woods somewhere. I asked her to come because she knows things about investigations."

Ellen squinted at Lia. "What things?"

Thanks a lot, Bailey. Lia racked her brains for basics. "First, Bailey and your cameras prove you didn't leave the house."

"They don't believe her, I know it."

"Even if you didn't have an alibi, they have to place you at the scene of the crime to charge you. If you weren't there, they can't prove you were."

"They planted O.J.'s glove."

Pointless to vouch for Cynth, and not productive to attack a decades-old conspiracy theory. "Did they take anything while they were here?"

"I was out of the room. They did it then."

"You can't plant something after a crime scene is documented. Anything that shows up later can be challenged."

"They can arrest me first."

"Bailey said they found Daniel in the preserve. Do you walk through there?"

"Never. People let aggressive dogs run loose. With all the trees, you don't see them until they're on you. That's why I take the girls to Wesleyan. It's all open. You can see someone a quarter-mile away."

Lia tried again. "That's too bad. If you walked there, it would be difficult to prove anything of yours wasn't left before Daniel was killed. It would be like finding fingerprints in your own house. It would prove nothing."

"I could say I walk there."

Bailey served Ellen a slice of cake and a cup of coffee. "I wouldn't. Some neighbor will tell them you never go there. Your credibility will be gone, right Lia?"

"Don't ever lie. It will come back to bite you. To be conclusive, anything of yours would also need Daniel's blood or DNA, something to tie it to him."

"They can get that. They have the body."

Lia mentally took a deep breath, doing her best to channel Peter's endless patience. "I know you're frightened. But they only want the truth. Why frame you?"

"They always think it's the spouse. You didn't see the way they grilled me this morning."

Bailey set cake and coffee on the counter for Lia, shaking her head imperceptibly. Ellen was exaggerating. Ellen cut her crumb cake into tiny bits with the side of her fork, eating none of it. The girls snuffled the plate but refrained from sneaking bites.

"They have texts saying I wanted to reconcile with Daniel, and they think I lured him out. I haven't texted Daniel since the day they arrested him. I showed them my phone but I could tell they didn't believe me." She dropped her fork, abandoning her demolition project. "They think I killed him."

Lia stole a glance at Kita. Kita twitched her eyebrows, giving Lia a morose bloodhound look. Lia rolled her eyes. Kita whuffed in solidarity.

Bailey squeezed Ellen's shoulder, her large, garden-hardened hand making Ellen look more fragile. "It's going to be okay. They can't prove what you didn't do."

"People get wrongfully convicted all the time."

Lia said, "Peter worked with Captain Arseneault. He's a good man. He won't rush to judgement."

"I'm sure you're right." Ellen pulled a slip of paper out of her pocket and laid it on the table.

"What's this?" Bailey asked.

"That's the number Detective Arseneault showed me. You remember, he asked if we recognized it. I wrote it down."

Bailey handed the paper to Lia, eyebrows raised. It wasn't familiar, but with numbers programmed into phones, who remembered them anymore? Lia shrugged. "You show them your cameras?"

"They weren't interested. They've already made up their minds. You've got to help me."

How the hell am I supposed to do that? "Did they give you the Miranda warning?"

"What does that have to do with anything?"

How to explain? She glanced at Kita, looking for inspiration. Kita rolled on her back and groaned. *Thanks a lot, girlfriend.*

"If they want to ask you anything they can use to establish guilt, they are required to give you the warning first or it can get thrown out. If they didn't Miranda you, they don't suspect you." Not strictly true, but right now Ellen would not be receptive to nuance.

"They asked me where I was and if I texted Daniel."

"Normal interview questions. Early interviews are as much about excluding people as anything. It sounds like you gave them answers that will eliminate you as a suspect."

"Lawyers say never to tell them anything."

Damn shame you didn't call one when Cynth and Arseneault showed up. Then you'd be someone else's problem and I'd be in my studio right now. "Can they trace those texts to you?"

"Of course not!"

"There you go. But if it makes you feel better, call a lawyer."

"Daniel almost bankrupted me when he was alive. I'm not going to let him bankrupt me now that he's dead."

Your funeral. But she didn't say it.

Bailey walked Lia out. Lia stopped on the walkway to key Arseneault's mystery number into her phone before she forgot it. "Ellen is a wee bit excitable."

Bailey grimaced. "I'm not looking forward to the rest of the day. Sure you can't stay?"

"Only if you want a second murder." She looked down the street. A patrol car sat at the entrance to Parker Woods. "Will you be busy later today?"

"I'll hang with Ellen if she wants company. Why?"

"I'm having thoughts. I'll call you later."

WENDY

Wendy hunched over the steering wheel of her ancient Corolla, eyes glued to the road. She hated cramped residential streets, and the road to Hopewell was the worst. You never knew when a dog or a kid on a bike would pop out between parked cars, especially on weekends.

Beside her, Dianne fiddled with one of the tiny braids she constantly wove into her hair. "How was I to know they'd be packed?"

"If we'd left the house when I said, we would have missed the rush."

"Ten minutes won't matter. It's just Hannah the Hun and the other volunteers. Intake doesn't start for five hours."

Wendy navigated the steep drive up to the school. By the time they checked in, it would not be ten minutes, it would be fifteen.

"The purpose of volunteering at flute camp is scoring points." Points a virtual nonentity like Wendy needed. She hoped donating slave labor for the high school camp and flute conference would give her a higher profile. Being late wouldn't impress anyone. "I need to stay in Hannah's good graces."

Wendy steered her car behind the school to the nearly empty parking lot. A police car sat in the back. Bright yellow tape blocked the path into the woods.

"What do you suppose happened?" Wendy asked.

"Don't know, don't care," Dianne said.

Wendy aimed for the cop car. "I'm going to ask."

"I thought you didn't want to be late."

"Can't help that now." She drew abreast of the patrol car and parked.

"Seriously?" Dianne demanded.

"So go on in. I don't care."

Wendy got out. The passenger door slammed as she rounded the hood of her car. The officer looked up as they reached the window. He was older, with a round, paternal face that made her feel comfortable.

"Ladies, what can I do for you?"

"Did something happen here?" Wendy asked.

"You girls go to the school?"

"Yes. We cut through here all the time."

"You want to stop doing that. A man was murdered in the woods last night."

Wendy felt her mouth drop into an "O." She didn't dare look at Dianne. "Who was it?"

"Can't say. I'm just keeping people away from the crime scene."

Beside her, Dianne said, "We really need to go."

"Oh, all right. Thank you, officer."

They hurried toward the school.

Wendy said, "Do you think—"

"Nothing to do with us," Dianne said.

"But we were there. Maybe we should tell someone."

Dianne stopped and turned, eyes narrowed with that stubborn jut of her jaw. She hissed, "No!"

"Did you see anyone?"

"Leave. It. Alone."

"But—"

"Just do like the nice officer said. Steer clear and we'll be fine."

BRENT

The binder landed on Brent's desk, missing his Hogwarts mug. Cynth barked, "Read this."

He swiveled his chair around, tipped it back, folded his arms. "Hello to you, too."

"After you read the file, I need you to review Moore's victim impact statements."

He jerked his chin at the binder. "Seriously?"

Her color up, and the wheat-colored appendage she called a braid frazzled, she narrowed her eyes at him. Today they were the fierce gunmetal gray they turned when she was annoyed.

"You too good to read the file?"

She hated this, hated using him. Perversely, that fact cheered him up. He thought about telling her she was sexy when she was angry—which she truly was (not that she wasn't always sexy, even when she wore polo shirts two sizes too big)—but poking the angry bear under the current circumstance was likely to have less than amusing results.

"I was keeping company with a friend when Parker called me in to assist you. While I don't expect you to express gratitude for me jettisoning a very pleasant Sunday, please do not insult my intelligence. Whatever you've managed to compile so far is too thin to be helpful." And he'd die a thousand deaths before admitting his pleasant Sunday involved driving the grandmother in the apartment next door to mass.

Cynth rolled her eyes so hard Brent expected them to disappear into the back of her head and pop up from the bottom after performing a full rotation. She sneered, "What would *your highness* prefer?"

"A tour of the crime scene would be nice. I understand you need help knocking on doors."

"Whatever. I'm driving."

Parker calling on a Sunday was unusual. That she

assigned him to a murder investigation—one Cynth was leading—it blew his mind.

Whose idea that had been? Not Cynth's. She'd only accepted his help on the original Moore case because she'd rather sauté her own liver and eat it than explain to Parker why she didn't want him on it.

FIVE YEARS AGO

It was a perfect May night. Cynth looked gorgeous, a rose linen sheath setting off her tan and spectacular figure. The wheat-colored hair she normally braided and poked through the back of a CPD ball cap fell in loose waves to her waist. She smiled at him, and his heart sang.

He'd wanted this evening at Boca, wanted to see Cynth in a plush banquette under crystal chandeliers while every man in the place yearned to take his place.

It should have been fun to introduce her to exotic taste combinations while she sneered at plates of food designed for appearance as much—maybe more—as for taste. He'd expected her to say she didn't see the point since it all ended up in your stomach, and what was wrong with a good bratwurst?

She'd never gotten into the spirit of the thing. She'd spent the evening with that vertical crease between her eyebrows, her feather-soft, mourning dove gray eyes gone hard and silver like ball bearings as she sent him the dubious looks he'd expected her to give the food she picked at.

Whatever was bothering her, she wouldn't talk about it

in the restaurant. He'd take her to the riverfront, tease it out of her while they strolled in the moonlight. Then they'd get the evening back on track.

Jerry Morton blew that all to hell.

It was his own fault. You couldn't risk letting a valet have your keys, not when they might be bribed to let someone rifle through your car. He'd parked under Fountain Square instead, opting for the lowest, least-used level of the garage and parking in a slant across two spaces so no one would ding the lovely Mazda MX-5 that was his as long as a P & G exec from Atlanta named Brent Dawson existed.

The first time she'd seen him do this, the tough, vibrant girl of his dreams sneered and said it made him a pretentious asshole. Since that was precisely who he was supposed to be, he'd raised an eyebrow and said, "And your point is?" She'd laughed and continued to date him anyway.

Tonight they'd exited the elevator to find a pair of black SUVs—why were they always black?—spurning a hundred empty spaces to crowd the MX-5 in the vast expanse of concrete.

Jerry freaking Morton from accounting—tall, skinny, and unmistakable in a three-piece suit even fifty yards away—leaned against the hood of the MX-5.

Not here, not now. Mother Mary, not ever around Cynth.

Cynth stiffened, her high heels clattering to a halt on the concrete. He knew what she thought. He had to derail this, now.

"I work with Jerry. It's okay."

"This doesn't feel right."

He winked. "You're a cop. Nothing is supposed to feel right to you."

She searched his eyes. "Why show up in a parking garage? Why not text?"

"He's a strange guy. We make nice for a minute and I get rid of him." He kissed her forehead. "When he sees you in that dress he'll understand."

The dubious look was back in her eyes. He ran his hand up her back, gave her a tiny push. "Jerry can be annoying. Just be chill and let's get this over with."

He mentally took a couple deep breaths and put on his good ole boy face as they approached. "Jerry, my man. What's up?"

Jerry levered off the hood, his eyes taking the scenic route over Cynth's body and making his blood boil.

"Who's your lady friend, Peach? She up for a party?"

Even in heels, Cynth didn't reach Morton's collarbone. She stepped forward, chin up. "You won't like the party I give you, asshole."

Morton grinned. "Feisty. I like it."

Brent tried, and failed, to tug Cynth back. "What do you need, Jerry? As you can see, the lady and I have plans."

"Now that's too bad. Doug wants to meet. He asked me to pick you up."

He'd been buying increasing amounts of coke from Morton for the past five months, aiming to connect with his supplier so he could ferret out the narcotics cops working with these scumbags. Morton was finally coming through. He ignored the tingling in the back of his neck.

He turned to Cynth. "Babe, I hate to cut the night short, but this is important." He turned back to Morton. "I need to drop her off. Where can I meet you?"

"No need for that. Doug will be upset if he doesn't get to meet the lady."

Brent held Morton's eyes, trying to read them. A pair of car doors creaked open then slammed shut. Two men came around the cars, loose shirts draped over the guns stuffed in their waistbands.

He grabbed Cynth, pulling her back. She took the momentum and spun behind him, dragging his arm up behind his back. She gave a hard shove. He screamed as his arm popped out of its socket. Over the shrieking pain he heard her say, "What the *hell* did you drop me into?"

She shoved again, riding him down, his nose smashing on the concrete. Through the haze he heard Jerry laughing.

"Shorty, the man just bought you a very nice dinner. Helluva way to thank him."

Cynth's weight left his back. Brent panted hard, trying to breathe through the pain.

"I'm nobody's shorty," Cynth snarled.

"I know, Detective McFadden. Fine company you keep, Peach. Very fine."

"No one is taking me anywhere."

"Shorty, I think you mistake our intentions. I'm hurt."

The growl of a motor, a car descending the ramp. Cavalry? More thugs? Innocent bystanders?

A voice, one of Morton's bodyguards. "What now, Jer?"

Morton's wingtips came into Brent's worm's-eye view of the concrete. Whatever Morton planned, Brent was incapable of reacting in any way that would be helpful. He stared at Morton's shoes and concentrated on breathing.

Morton laughed. "Sorry to disappoint, Peach, but I doubt Doug wants you bleeding on his carpet. Shorty, I'll catch you later."

Three car doors slammed. The SUVs drove off. The new car, whoever it was, must have parked one level up.

Cynth spoke, her smokey voice brisk. "I'm calling 911 and then you can tell me what stupidity you're into.

He wheezed, "Don't … call."

"Why the hell not?"

"Undercover … Stay off … system."

"You're a cop? Fine time to tell me, *Peach*."

"Don't … ever … call me … that."

Cynth kicked off her heels. "Lay still and don't tense up. I'm going to fix that shoulder."

"Not going … anywhere."

It was an ugly process, but the blinding pain vanished the moment she'd popped it back in, leaving the almost tolerable ache in his face.

Brent pulled himself into a sitting position. "Care to tell me why you tried to rip my arm off?"

She tipped his chin with one finger, surveying the damage. "You walked me into an empty parking garage and grabbed me when guns showed up. I thought you set me up."

"If it was a setup—and I'm not saying it was—you weren't the target."

"And I wouldn't end up collateral damage?"

"I'd have finessed it."

"That so-called meet was bullshit. Your *friend* knew I was a cop. You would have finessed us into fish food."

She might be right. "So your plan was?"

She smirked. "Shock and awe mixed with crazy works best for small women."

"They teach you that at the academy?"

"Skinny little guy who went to prison when he was eighteen. It's how he survived."

"And you chose to demonstrate your shock and awe on me? Thank you so very much."

"You *should* thank me. Your condition was a complication your *friend* didn't want to deal with."

"Your plan was to incapacitate me so they'd leave me behind?"

"My plan was to get out of the garage alive. You didn't figure into it."

"Well, thank sweet baby Jesus for unintended consequences." He dug into his pocket, handed her his keys. "Would you be so kind? I can't drive in this condition."

She dragged him up by his good arm. "I'll drop you at the hospital. Then I never want to see you again."

Morton took a sudden transfer to Colombia, using up all his accumulated vacation days to get out of town forty-eight hours after the confrontation in the garage. The move put Morton beyond reach while eliminating Brent's one path to his targets.

Suddenly, nobody had any coke, nobody knew where to find coke, and nobody, but nobody, knew anyone named Doug. Which meant he'd been burned.

Five months.

Nothing to show for it.

IA wanted to blame Cynth for blowing things, saying she'd acted precipitously and scared Morton off. After all, he hadn't actually threatened them. They hadn't felt the tension in the garage. Easy for IA to disregard his read on the situation. Even easier for them to forget it had been their idea for him to get close to her.

Next came talk of going after her for assaulting an officer—a stupid suggestion born of a desire to punish someone, anyone. Since she didn't know he was a cop, it would never fly.

In the end they swept the entire mess under the rug. Because he convinced them the someone they punished shouldn't be her, they decided it was him.

He landed at District 5 after his shoulder healed, busted to patrol. That had been their little joke, sticking him with Cynth. Working out of the same station forced an awkward dynamic they were both too stubborn to end. He stayed to be near her. He suspected Cynth had too much pride to let his presence push her out.

When Parker put him on the flute theft case, Cynth gritted her teeth and consigned him to liaising with Moore's victims and endless hours listening to variations on the theme of Moore's duplicity, with the bonus of taking the heat when lost instruments never turned up.

What did they expect when they waited years before reporting Moore to the police? Not entirely fair. More than one person reported Moore. They just weren't important enough to merit the DA's attention until Channel 7's coverage of the "Where's My Flute" rap went viral.

She'd also had him liaising with Aubrey Morse, citing the advantage of their relationship and putting italics on the word every time his connection with Aubrey came up.

He'd never satisfied Cynth's curiosity about Aubrey.

He and Aubrey tangled sheets from time to time. Because he ignored Aubrey's hints for an exchange of quid pro for her quo in the form of inside information, time to time became less and less.

Aubrey never burned a bridge and he enjoyed the ego

boost. Pissing Cynth off was a bonus. At least it got a reaction out of her.

The antagonism between them was regrettable, but that had been her choice. He once thought enforced proximity might induce a thaw. He'd been wrong.

TWO YEARS AGO

Cynth hadn't wanted him on this trip, he knew that. But Moore's use of pawn shops in four states to hide the extent of his activity necessitated travel. To show her displeasure, she'd turned every decision into a battle since they hit the road more than an hour earlier.

They agreed on one thing: either of their personal vehicles would have been preferable to driving hundreds of miles in a battered pool car. Everything else was a point to be won. It had taken thirty minutes for them to settle on driving ninety-minute shifts with the driver choosing the music.

Brent slid his eyes sideways, catching Cynth's profile as she drove the aging Taurus, not wanting her to notice he was looking at her. Her eyes stayed resolutely on the road.

He wasn't sure if she was just being a safe driver, or if she was determined to pretend he wasn't there. Girl rage rock blasting from the speakers lent credence to the second option.

He'd thought leaving at nine gave them plenty of time to do their business in Pennsylvania and head back to Columbus. Cynth insisted on leaving at the crack of dawn, with a breakfast break ninety minutes out.

They had a six-hour drive to Pennsylvania. He'd voted for the interstate, I-71 to I-70, easy peasy. Cynth sneered at him and took the back roads, hugging a series of twisty two-lane highways and blowing through podunk towns, dooming him to heartburn at some rancid mom and pop place.

Eighty minutes after they'd started, a sign and a traffic light in the middle of the highway announced Peebles. Golden arches soared overhead, giving him hope. Cynth turned off the highway and onto the ubiquitous Main Street.

"McDonald's is reliable," he yelled over the music.

She didn't even look at him. She yelled back, "I'll drop you there if that's what you want. I'm not eating that crap."

"For Pete's freaking sake." Brent turned off the music. "Do you have somewhere in mind?"

"I do."

She'd been much more agreeable when they'd first met, her clean scrubbed face with the pale lashes and eyebrows giving her an appealing vulnerability.

"Have you been there before?"

"Actually, yes."

"That's something, at least."

"We're in Adams County, home of Serpent Mound and famous for UFO sightings."

"What's Serpent Mound?"

"World's largest effigy mound. It's nine hundred years old."

"Relevant because?"

"Woo-woo tourists are fussy about their food. The eggs Florentine is good, but if you order it, you'll miss out on the best biscuits and sausage gravy north of the Mason-Dixon Line."

She'd been right about the sausage gravy, though he'd felt compelled to point out that they were so close to the Mason-Dixon Line that it hardly seemed fair to lump it in with Yankee food. She'd snorted and said it wasn't horse-shoes or hand grenades, you either won the war or you lost the war, and the south had lost, no matter how they liked to make heroes out of the men who got the south into a mess it never fully recovered from.

He'd mumbled something about carpet baggers. She said if they hadn't seceded, there would have been no carpet baggers. At that point, he shut up and focused on his food while she stared at her phone, texting and giggling sporadically. Had to be the-red headed neanderthal she'd been seeing.

It had been conversation of a sort.

She handed him the keys as they left the restaurant. "Don't worry, I'll navigate."

"Very kind of you." He was annoyed with how amused she sounded and how stiff he felt. Still, the prospect of having control of both the wheel and the volume knob—on top of a stellar breakfast—eased his mood.

He started the car, putting Coldplay on the stereo (courtesy of the playlist on his phone) and lowering the volume to a level comfortable for talking before easing the Taurus into traffic.

"Which way, boss?"

"You're kidding, right? We're still on Main Street."

He sighed. "You really lost your sense of humor."

"Never had one. Back the way we came, left at the highway. You'll be done with your leg before the road does anything squirrelly."

"Besides putting a traffic light in the middle of the damn highway?"

"Besides that."

He waited until they were well beyond Peebles and said, "We'll be in this car for two days. Are we going to talk about it?"

"There is no 'it' to talk about. Me having no choice about bringing you along on this little field trip doesn't give you the right to impose your bullshit on me. If you want to live to see District 5 again, you will drop it."

Brent gave up. He settled back into his seat and turned the volume up a few notches, preparing himself for a hundred miles alone with his thoughts.

Perversely, he'd enjoyed those two days and her endless sniping. He didn't know what that said about him.

He admired her ability to hold a grudge. She spoke to him when she had to, coolly professional in front of brass. The rest of District 5 knew she despised him though no one knew why.

Their involvement with Moore ended a year ago. He was too much the realist to imagine this was a second chance, too much in love with her to give up hope.

Cynth filled Brent in on the case as she drove down the hill from District 5, turning off Hamilton Avenue at Haight

Street. The street curved around until it paralleled Hamilton, woods on the left, lovely older houses on the right.

Not Victorians like Peter and Lia's place. These were World War II era, wide and homey with big porches and little front yards so full of flowers there was nothing to mow. Houses he would have fantasized about when he was in foster care, if he'd ever seen anything like them.

Cynth jerked her head at the woods. "Parker Woods."

"I remember from last time. Brandt's house is four doors up."

Cynth snuck him a suspicious look. "I don't see Bailey's truck. She must have left. Can't blame her. Brandt is a piece of work."

"You like Brandt for this?"

"Bailey says she was home all night, but when isn't it the spouse?"

"Bailey wouldn't lie."

"No, but she could be wrong." She slowed at the corner, pointed out the walkway leading into the preserve. "If Brandt did it, she probably went through here. I'm going to circle around to the spot where Moore entered."

She turned right on Bruce, picking up Hamilton, then looping up to Glen Parker and a long line of sagging clapboard houses. Folks did their best here. They kept things clean, but were either too old or too poor to keep things up with any style. That or they'd lost the ambition to do so.

"Let's pull over," Brent said. "I'd like to get a feel for the neighborhood."

"Whatever," Cynth said,

He and Cynth strolled to the end of Glen Parker, where a tiny park clung to the curve. Swings, a solitary picnic table, an ancient iron grill. No sign of kids in any of the yards. That was just sad. A street light meant the entrance to the preserve was well lit at night. The house opposite sat on a rise, giving it an excellent view. With luck, they had a camera.

Brent nodded at the lone picnic table. "Let's sit."

"Why?" Cynth asked.

"I want to soak up the ambiance."

Cynth shrugged and sat, giving him an odd look that meant it hadn't occurred to her he intended to be a fully functioning member of the team.

He pointed his chin north along Langland, indicating a tall screen of bushes at the far end of the little park. "That where Moore was staying?"

"Up on the corner. Only house this side of the street."

Her clipped answers irritated him. "However I ended up here, we're stuck together for the foreseeable future. Are we going to talk about the elephant in the room?"

He turned his head as he spoke to catch her expression. She gave nothing away.

"What elephant? There is no elephant."

"You know what elephant."

"There. Is. No. Elephant. Never was."

"Look, I'm happy for you and the caveman—"

"His name is Duff, and he's not a caveman."

"Okay, *Duff* is a Rhodes scholar, and he's going to invent a car that runs on greenhouse gases and save the world. I'm happy for you. I just thought we could clear the air."

"For what purpose? You want to tell me some story that makes you feel better?"

"I—"

"There's nothing you can say to fix it."

"I know I can't fix it. I just thought—"

"You being the best of bad choices doesn't give you the right to impose your bullshit on me. If you want to live to see this case resolved, you will not bring this up again. Ever."

Brent said nothing and stared at the bushes across the street.

He'd never gotten over Cynth, no matter how regularly she expressed her disdain for him. Perverse of him to prefer her contempt to all those cultured Hyde Park women with their high maintenance looks. Looks that washed off, and once gone left the woman underneath unrecognizable.

He recalled climbing out of a strange bed one morning and not being sure the woman pouring coffee in the kitchen was the one he'd slept with the night before until she put a mug in his hand and kissed him.

It had been a kick being with women so far out of his league, or it had been until he realized all he was to them was a bit of rough in a decent suit. A story for their book club. Arm candy at a fundraiser. A good lay.

Worse, if any of them wanted more he would have been sick of them in a week. He was tired of them and their glossy pretensions. He was tired of himself and his own glossy pretensions.

Cynth was always Cynth and she'd never gone for the goop. Her eyelashes were long, but nearly invisible due to their wheat color. She'd never indulged in mascara to show them off. Instead of the smoldering looks of other woman, the pale ruff of lashes made the steely gray pop when she was angry—as she had been since she dropped the binder on his desk.

He'd had no choice but to lie when they met. There was

no changing that. He wondered if she was right, that he only wanted to make himself feel better.

Cynth broke the silence. "Enough ambience. Let's go."

She headed up the street, leaving him to follow. Beyond the screen of bushes lay a tiny clapboard house with an aging paint job and a DIY deck on the back. A skinny dog ramp wound around the deck. Bowser was not big and Bowser had arthritis.

"Moore stayed here? Big comedown for him."

"I doubt anyone else would take him in. Nygaard is a million years old and dying. She barely has enough to keep a roof over her head, and Moore sponged off her. Anyway, I figured he came out the back—"

"Why?"

Cynth shrugged. "Less likely to be seen, but it's not critical."

Moore wouldn't bother. Narcissists always thought they were invisible when it suited them. He followed Cynth back to the park and into the preserve. She stopped where the sidewalk merged with a lateral walkway, pointing at a patch of trampled vegetation.

"Arseneault figures the assailant waited here."

"I see wrecked plants everywhere. Why here?"

Cynth smirked. "The rest is Arseneault's guys tearing up the crime scene looking for clues."

"I take it they didn't find any? No hair, no monogrammed lighter, no footprint with a distinctive tread?"

"They spent hours looking for the murder weapon. Junior found it under the body."

"Score one for the coroner."

"For Junior, anyway. The new assistant coroner is an ass."

Cynth backtracked up the walk, stopping at a stain on the concrete. Someone had cleaned it up, but the discoloration remained.

"The awl?"

Cynth pointed to a small blotch in the center of the void created by Moore's body.

Brent walked to the south side of the stain, shaking his head. "Now that's just weird."

"Ya think?"

He considered the moves. Get close to Moore, stab him in the neck, then … logically, the killer would have taken the awl with him or thrown it in the bushes. "You think he stabbed Moore, pulled out the awl, then ran past Moore and dropped it where Moore conveniently fell?"

"That, or he shoved it under the body to make it easier for us to find."

"Doesn't make sense."

"It gets weirder."

"Do tell."

He followed Cynth down the lateral walkway. She turned off on a dirt path. A hundred feet down the path, she stopped where several felled tree trunks made a lop-sided circle that invited you to sit.

"This is the Lounge."

"I can see generations of students getting high here. An odd choice for a senior citizen hookup, don't you think?"

"Nostalgic. Moore was a student here."

Brent sat on a log, thumping the heel of one foot while he thought. "I'm trying to work out why someone lay in wait fifty feet from a lit street when Moore was headed for this conveniently dark and isolated spot where no one could hear him scream."

"Doesn't make sense to me, either."

"I don't see the trash I expect at a party place."

"Maybe Gen Z doesn't know about it."

"It's not that hard to find." He got up and walked further down the path. It dropped into a steep ravine. Something glinted in bushes below. "Anyone check that out?"

Cynth joined him, peering over the edge. "Knock yourself out."

"You coming?"

"You go ahead. I'll call for help if you break a leg."

"All heart, McFadden."

"Watch your pants."

Brent sighed. He'd put on his second favorite slacks for church. As long as he remained upright they should be safe, but his shoes with their glossy uppers and slick leather soles would need serious work after he got home.

He made his way, edging sideways down the steeper parts, abandoning all hope for his slacks as he pushed through the vegetation at the bottom. All to follow a glint of chrome.

Cynth yelled down. "What is it?"

"It's a wheelchair. What the sweet bleeding Jesus is a wheelchair doing here?"

Cynth, bless her parkour-conditioned heart, bounced down the trail in a fraction of a minute. "Just trash. Somebody dumped it."

"Too shiny to have been here long."

"You think our killer left it?"

"Doesn't fit our narrative, does it?"

"Not one I can think of. But that's this case. Lots of parts don't fit."

"Too far from the road to dump trash here." He scanned

the gully. You might find remnants of a homeless camp in a place like this. Then the wheelchair would make more sense. But he'd seen no detritus, no trash, nothing but pristine woods. "I'm going to poke around."

He hadn't gone four feet when he tripped over the car battery.

LIA

The patrol car was gone. Kita and Chewy sniffed downed crime scene tape while Gypsy lunged at the tiny Lazarus lizards darting across the sidewalk in the afternoon heat. The lizards were a problem. Seventy years after a young boy brought ten of the wall lizards home from an Italian vacation, they were now too numerous for Gypsy to ignore and played hell with discipline.

Bailey said, "Is it okay to go in? Shouldn't they have taken the crime scene tape with them?"

"You'd think. If they expect people to stay out, they need to post an officer here." Lia gathered up the tape and stuffed it into a nearby trash can.

"If I get arrested, you're posting bail. Why are we here?"

Lia headed for the woods. "C'mon. I want to look around."

"Ghoulish, don't you think?"

The woods closed in around them as the walkway rose up the incline. Bushy wildflowers lined the walk. Trunks of downed trees scattered across the slope. Virginia creeper floated above a carpet of last year's leaves like green stars. It was dim and peaceful and nothing she could sell if she painted it, though she was tempted to try.

"Ellen will freak until they find out who sent those texts. I want to help them along."

"In the woods?"

Gypsy strained her leash, attempting to get to what had to be fascinating smells since the lizards didn't care for shade. Lia stopped. Gypsy looked back at her with a mixture of hurt and mulishness.

"Girlfriend, that's not going to work. Look at your brother. He understands the concept of a leash. Heel."

Chewy had to be snickering. Gypsy sulked, then circled into heel position as Lia moved forward.

"Let's try this again." She sighed. "I really ought to stop and put her through some remedial leash work, but that would take too much time. What would Daniel do if Ellen asked him to come home? Would he buy it?"

"He'd eat it up. He'd string it out and play hard to get, but he'd be all in."

"After a year? From a number he didn't recognize?"

"He expected her to beg him to come home. It would never occur to him he was being played."

"I bet the texts were used to arrange a meet. Do you know where he was staying? This is kind of on the way to Ellen's."

"Not a clue. Not knowing made Ellen crazy. But I think this was the destination. Arseneault mentioned the Lounge. You remember, Ellen told all those old stories while we were waiting for court to start."

"I remember now. Any idea where this lounge is?"

Bailey shook her head. "We need to talk to her."

"I just want to do this one thing. I don't want to get

involved. We tell Ellen we're looking around and she'll decide we're going to solve Daniel's murder."

"What are we looking for, and how will we know when we find it?"

"Disturbances in the vegetation will tell us where the crime scene people were."

"Or a big bloodstain?"

"That might be too much to hope for." Gypsy jerked her lead, lunging toward the downed trees. Lia tightened her hold. "No you don't, girlfriend."

Gypsy turned around, backing up as she yanked her head out of her collar. She raced down the slope, stopping to dig at the base of a fallen log. Lia handed Chewy's leash to Bailey and stalked down the slope. Gypsy danced out of reach, circled back to the log, whined.

Bailey called down from the path. "Some jerk massacred an entire bed of touch-me-nots up here."

Lia scanned the base of the fallen log. No dead thing, no baby possums. Nothing there. "I'll be there as soon as I grab the menace." She approached quietly as Gypsy continued to dig, waiting for the right moment, placing a firm hand on her shoulder and pressing her down into a submissive pose. Gypsy looked up, hurt.

"Sorry girlfriend. Leashes are the law of the land." She knelt in the dead leaves and snapped the collar on, giving Gypsy a neck ruffle. Girlfriend gave her an appeasing face lick.

"I love you too, baby girl, even when you're bad."

Chewy huffed when she returned, annoyed Lia hadn't taken him on her field trip. Kita rolled her eyes. Lia dusted leaf litter off her knees.

Bailey said, "You want to tighten her collar?"

"It's as tight as I can make it and still slip two fingers under it. Show me the abused touch-me-nots."

Bailey pointed. "Just up there."

Sure enough, someone had thrashed what had once been a lovely bed of the exploding flowers.

"What are we looking for?" Bailey asked. "I can't imagine the police left anything behind."

"They didn't find the phone."

"How do you figure that?"

"If they had the phone, they could get DNA and finger-prints off it. They'd find a way to compare that with Ellen without letting her know. Telling her about the texts and showing her the number was a stab in the dark, looking for a reaction. They don't have the phone."

"Makes sense."

"So I'm catfishing Daniel on my burner phone. Something goes wrong and I kill him, or maybe I planned to kill him all along. Our suspect pool is smart people, but they aren't crooks. I bet they panicked and tossed the phone. I also bet Arseneault hasn't gotten around to deciding it's worth spending the manpower to search 90 acres. It's still here."

"How do we find it?"

Lia pulled out her phone.

Bailey said, "You're going to call it."

"I doubt the battery is dead yet. If they tossed it, chances are it's near the path and we'll hear it."

"And if someone answers?"

"Good point. Maybe I'll block my number first."

"They won't answer if it's blocked. Pretend it's a wrong number. See if you can get something out of them."

"And how would I do that?"

"You know, someone answers, and you say, 'Joey?' and he says, 'I'm not Joey,' and you say, 'who are you?'"

"You think that will work?"

"Yeah, kinda lame. When he answers, put on your best sexy voice and say—" Bailey's voice transformed to breathy and low. "Joey, honey, I'm so horny I'll explode if you don't get over here right now."

"You sound like you've done this before."

"I put myself through college doing phone sex."

"Wow. You know how to keep a secret."

"The hours and the pay were great but the energy was negative and sad. I had to go on a retreat for six months to cleanse. That was before I learned how to invoke white light to protect myself."

"I don't know what to say."

"You don't need to say anything. If a woman answers, it can still work. More women are bi-curious than you'd think. If they get outraged, you fall all over yourself apologizing."

"You're sneakier than I ever gave you credit for. Maybe you should do this."

"And deny myself the pleasure of watching you try to pull it off?"

"You're a true friend," Lia grumbled. She dialed, counting six rings before the call went to voicemail. A mechanical voice recited the default message. No clues there.

They moved along, the dogs taking the time to sniff and pee every time Lia stopped to call the catfish phone. They reached an intersection where a sidewalk from the Glen Parker entrance connected to the main walk.

Gypsy whined and strained. This time Lia let Gypsy drag them to a dark patch in the concrete. Girlfriend dropped her head, sniffed, and licked. The sickeningly sweet smell of cola hit Lia's gut as she realized what she was looking at.

"Stop that!" She yanked the lead harder than she intended, dragging Gypsy away from the stain. Gypsy stared at her, hurt all over her face.

Lia stooped and gave her a hug. "Murder blood can't be good for you, little girl." *The blood is gone. It's just a stain and I'm being irrational.*

Bailey stood at a distance. "A bloodstain wasn't too much to hope for after all."

Chewy whined and pulled on his leash, wanting to get away from the ugly spot. Little man was picking up bad vibes. "Um, yeah. I wasn't ready for that."

"Can you feel it? The air is thick with rage. I can't get any closer."

"I'm a little nauseous, but I think that's the smell."

Bailey sniffed the air. "Smells like someone spilled a case of coke."

"They use it to clean up blood. Do you often pick up feelings like that?"

"Almost never, but I don't hang around places where people have violent feelings anymore. Came in handy in when I was younger."

"I bet." Lia handed her leashes to Bailey. She took a few deep breaths, then aimed her phone at the concrete. Just a stain, an amorphous puddle like a backward question mark smeared on the top curve. Below that, sprays of blood that had been propelled with some force, like you would get if you loaded a brush and flicked it, like you were cracking a whip. *Or painting a Jackson Pollock knock off.*

Early in her relationship with Peter, she'd expressed

interest in spatter patterns, since it was spatter that tipped Peter that her ex-boyfriend had not committed suicide. He'd obligingly showed her different formations.

"I'm no expert, but I think someone stabbed Daniel in an artery and he bled out."

"You can tell that?"

"Once you lose about two quarts of blood, you die."

"It doesn't look like two quarts."

"Some of it ran off the sidewalk into the dirt. Blood is sticky. It wouldn't spread as far as water."

"They could have shot him."

"A gunshot creates an explosive burst expanding from the exit wound, like mist. This is more like a lot of pressure coming out from the end of a hose. It spurts because of the heartbeat." She traced arcs in the air with her finger. "See, it has a rhythm."

"He wasn't shot? Ellen told Cynth we didn't hear a gunshot. Cynth didn't correct her."

"She wouldn't, would she?"

"I guess not. What else can you see?"

"There are three easily accessible arteries. Carotid in the neck, brachial on the inside of the arm, and femoral on the inner thigh. Carotid is the only one that's usually exposed. It's more vulnerable and easier to hit. No big muscle masses around it. It's not hidden under layers of fat."

"You think someone stabbed him in the neck?"

Lia used her finger to trace the inner border of the stain in the air. "You can see the silhouette of a head and shoulder in the negative space where the blood pooled. It was a right-handed attacker."

"How can you tell?"

"Nearly impossible to reach the carotid from the back,

so Daniel's killer faced him. All the blood pooling on the left side of his body means the wound was on that side."

Bailey looked at her right hand, then at Lia. "Makes sense."

"Whoever it was, Daniel either let them get close to him or they snuck up on him and struck fast. Either way, he didn't have time to fight them off. There's no broken vegetation here."

"You should have your own show. *CSI Northside.*"

"Not in a million years. But this is ground zero." She glanced up the walk to Glen Parker and the trashcan by the entrance. "I bet the techs were all over that trashcan. If the phone was there, they already found it." Still, she shushed the dogs and hit redial on her phone. Nothing.

They backtracked to the main walkway and continued on. Lia stopped at a wood post designating a dirt path as Trail B. This time when she hit redial, she heard something faint coming from the trail.

More confident now, she led her crew forward. Lia stopped near an arrangement of mossy, decaying logs that might have provided suitable seating for late night partying at one time. Today, who knew what crawled over and around them?

She dialed again. A standard ringtone came from the other side of the party place. She walked toward the sound, scanning the ground. That wasn't right. The sound was above her, not below. She spotted a tree with a hollow and beelined for it.

Her phone beeped. Cynth's face popped up on the screen. Lia froze, aware Cynth would not appreciate what she was doing. *Fake her out. She doesn't know where I am or what we're doing.* She accepted the call.

"Cynth—"

"Turn around. Right now."

"I don't—"

"I'm armed. Don't test me."

Lia whipped her head around, looking for Cynth and seeing no one. She dragged the dogs back to the path. The voice in her ear said, "Thank you. I expect to see you at the picnic table by the Glen Parker entrance in three minutes. Then you can tell me what the hell you think you're doing."

Lia opened her mouth to respond when Cynth beeped off.

They found Cynth at the picnic table, staring at her phone, ball cap pulled low with her fat braid protruding from the hole in the back, eyes hidden by sunglasses, wearing rumpled shorts and a T-shirt. She kept her eyes on her phone as they approached.

"Have a seat," she barked. "And act casual. We are having a friendly conversation."

Lia and Bailey sat. The dogs picked up on Cynth's mood and crawled under the table.

Cynth continued to stare at her phone. "Who knows you're here?"

"No one," Lia said. "This is all on me. Bailey just came along for the ride. She didn't know what I planned to do."

"What exactly, was that?"

"Ellen is freaking. She's convinced you think she killed Daniel, because of those text messages. I figured if you didn't have the phone, maybe we could find it—"

Cynth looked up from her phone, over the top of her

sunglasses. The steel in her gray eyes brought Lia's explanation to a stumbling halt. Cynth's next words were so dry they sucked all the saliva out of Lia's mouth. "And how did you plan to do that?"

"She—she wrote down that phone number you showed her. I thought if I called it while we walked through the preserve, we might hear it ring. And it worked. We found it—"

"Did you now?"

It dawned on Lia why Cynth called when she did. She dropped her eyes. "You already found it. You left it there on purpose. You have a game camera on it."

"It took doing to get that camera here so fast. You may have blown our one chance to solve this quickly."

"Sorry. I didn't know."

"You aren't supposed to know. Nobody is supposed to know. If Moore's killer is nervous, they might second guess themselves and come back for the phone. Stupid, because even if we found prints on it, we'd have to have them on file for a match, and the flutists with a hard-on for Moore aren't the type to have a record. But they *are* most likely to come looking for the phone as soon as they could after we got out of there. You see anyone while you were tromping around my crime scene?"

"Not a soul."

"So you were strolling through the preserve, calling that number repeatedly. I sure hope my guy did not come in from the other end of the trail and hear that phone ringing, since the only person on the call log is dead. What do you suppose he did if he heard it? You think he'd pick up that phone? And if he does come back for it, all those unanswered calls will be on the log. He might show up on your doorstep."

"Why do you keep saying 'he'? Most of Daniel's victims were women."

"Force of habit. Men commit ninety percent of homicides. Don't change the subject."

"Maybe the women just get away with it," Bailey cracked.

Lia elbowed Bailey.

"Whatever," Cynth said.

"I screwed up. But maybe you shouldn't have handed that number out."

Cynth muttered obscenities under her breath. "I knew that was a bad call."

"You can't trace the phone?"

"Pay as you go, the choice of criminals everywhere."

"Fingerprints?"

Cynth leaned back, folded her arms. "Does Peter tell you this much about his investigations?"

"I guess I deserve that. Are you stuck here all day?"

Cynth smirked. "Better staring at my phone than knocking on doors for non-existent witnesses and camera footage. I assigned that to Brent."

"You don't think he'll find anything?"

"Doubtful. They roll up the sidewalks before sunset around here."

"I'm really sorry. I thought you were done because the crime tape was down. So you really don't think it was Ellen?"

"Maybe I think it was you, and I stopped you from getting that phone so you couldn't confuse the issue with fresh fingerprints."

Lia's mouth dropped open. "You can't think that."

"No, but any savvy defense attorney will."

Lia bit her lip. Under the table, Chewy head-butted her leg. She reached a hand down and gave him a scratch to keep him quiet. "I'm sorry?"

Cynth continued, "Since it's just us, tell me who you think did it."

"I-I—" Lia stared blankly at Bailey. "We hadn't gotten that far. But it wasn't Ellen. I can guarantee that."

"Convince me."

"Bailey, you explain."

"Daniel named Ellen executor in his will. She doubts he bothered to change it."

"So?"

"Now she'll have to deal with dozens and dozens of former clients who still believe their money is in the Caymans. And there's the court, too."

"Maybe she didn't think about that."

"We talked about it."

"Oh? She talked about killing Daniel?"

"Not that. Just that Daniel was too lazy to redo his papers and it would be just like him to get hit by a bus and leave his mess for her to clean up. And how sick she was of being harassed by his victims like she had anything to do with it."

"So it wasn't Ellen. You went to the sentencing?"

Lia and Bailey nodded.

"Who was the most pissed when Moore got probation? You know the person who did this, I'd bet money on it."

They left Cynth at the table, heading back the way they came. The dogs must have caught her mood because Gypsy was no longer trying to drag her everywhere.

"Stupid, stupid, stupid," Lia said.

"You didn't know," Bailey said.

"I should have."

"You were just trying to help."

"Fat lot of good I did."

"*We* did."

"It was my idea. You're an innocent bystander. At least we know they found the phone. I'm betting Ellen's prints aren't on it. I think they're looking in another direction."

"Ellen will be so relieved."

"You heard Cynth. We can't tell her. This never happened."

Bailey sighed. "We need to tell her something so she'll stop worrying."

"Why would she stop? Drama gives Ellen a sense of purpose." Lia caught the look on Bailey's face. "Sorry. I shouldn't have said that."

"So walk away. Ellen isn't your problem."

"No, she's yours, and I care about you."

"At least she won't need me to protect her from Daniel anymore. I'm so ready to move back home."

BAILEY

Juggling an armload of toiletries, Bailey emerged from the bathroom and found Ellen staring at the explosion of dirty laundry in the open roller bag laying on the coffee table.

Ellen turned, her voice disbelieving. "You're *leaving?*"

The stack of bottles and jars shifted in Bailey's arms. If she didn't set them down, there'd be shampoo all over the rug.

"You don't need me anymore. You'll be fine."

"Don't you get it?" Nati whined and Connie rooed from their bean bags. Kita, muzzle on paws, groaned. Ellen's voice rose. "I'm *next.* I'm not *safe.* I *need* you."

Bailey snapped, flinging her arms up, sending Tom's of Maine toothpaste and Dr. Bronner's lavender soap flying across the room with the rest of her personal hygiene products.

"I need me, too. I need my space. I want my things. Sleeping on your couch kills my back. I want my life back."

Ellen jerked back as if slapped, lip quivering. "I thought you *liked* it here."

Bailey stooped, gathering her things. Ellen stood between Bailey and her suitcase, not helping.

"Get out of my way, Ellen. I need to finish packing."

Ellen didn't move. "Don't leave."

This could turn ugly. Bailey closed her eyes and took a deep breath, something she did when her circuits over-loaded. *Respond. Don't react.* It took several very long seconds to get unstuck and visualize the way forward.

She headed into the kitchen, dumped her stuff on the table and grabbed a plastic grocery bag from under the sink. Toiletries safely in the bag, she returned to the living room, stepping over a dribble of Dr. Bronner's on the rug. Ellen would have to deal with that herself.

"I gave a year of my life to help you get away from Daniel. I stayed in Cincinnati instead of going to Knoxville last winter. I barely got to see John all year."

Ellen's voice was calm now. "I didn't realize I was such a burden."

"You didn't realize giving up sex was a burden?"

"There's no need to be vulgar."

"If you don't feel safe because some anonymous person *might* have a grudge against you, that's not my problem. Kita and I are going."

"Who will walk the girls when I'm at work?"

Bailey shoved past Ellen and dumped the rest of her things into her suitcase. "You had a dog walker before I moved in. I'm sure she'll come back."

Ellen sat on the couch, lip quivering. "What if they arrest me?"

Bailey forced the top of her bag down and yanked the zipper closed with several angry moves. "Goddess, Ellen. They found the phone. They know it's not you."

3

DAY 1, PART 3

SUNDAY, AUGUST 10, 4:20 P.M.

BRENT

BRENT LEANED AGAINST A STEEL AND CONCRETE BOLLARD, one of several protecting the entrance of District 5 from enraged motorists. They hadn't been necessary at the old Frank Lloyd Wright inspired station on Ludlow Avenue.

Cramped as it had been, he missed the lovely old building. But with district personnel tripled, the move was inevitable. The city, in its wisdom, stuck them at a seedy strip mall. He had a theory someone thought their presence would reduce shoplifting.

More like the locals consider us a challenge and year-end statistics will show they upped their game.

Aubrey Morse had Cynth positioned on the sidewalk in front of the building. The orange brick made an ugly backdrop, designed to make Cynth look washed out compared to Aubrey's bold looks. Preferable to the sea of patrol cars in the parking lot, but knowing Ashley, she considered making Cynth look plain on camera a bonus.

He wondered who suggested the location. Parker Woods would have been his choice. Bless Cynth. The nuances of setting would go over her head. And if they didn't, she wouldn't care.

Aubrey's tattooed cameraman hefted the cam to his shoulder and gave a nod, coppery dreadlocks falling over his shoulder. He should have seen it before now. This was the neanderthal in the photo Cynth used for computer wallpaper. In the photo he was in high testosterone mode, with sweat pouring off his scantily clad bod as he jumped over a wall—no doubt a designated obstacle on a parkour route.

Appallingly unlike him to not make the connection sooner.

Aubrey smiled at the camera. "With us is Detective McFadden, lead investigator in the mysterious Northside death of Daniel Moore." She held the mic to Cynth. "What can you tell us about the attack?"

"Daniel Moore was stabbed in Parker Woods Nature Preserve between eleven and one last night. It appears to be a targeted attack. We do not believe the public is at risk."

"That should be a relief to area residents. Why do you believe Daniel was targeted?"

Cynth's face remained serious, though Brent knew she was dying to give Aubrey a snotty look. "We can't release that information at this time."

"Do you have suspects?"

Cue the standard line.

"We are following all leads. If anyone has information about this attack, please contact the Cincinnati Police through the website or by calling …."

After Aubrey wrapped the interview, Cynth wandered off to talk to her boyfriend. Aubrey joined Brent at the bollards.

"Are you on this case, too? Why aren't you lead?"

"Detective McFadden is an excellent investigator and nobody knew Moore better."

"Can I quote you on that?"

Brent smiled at Aubrey, but kept his eyes on Cynth and the caveman. "Nothing I say is quotable. You know that."

Aubrey pouted. "I wish you'd let me put you on camera. You're so photogenic. It would do wonders for your career."

"It would get me busted to crossing guard at the nearest pre-school if it wasn't brass's idea."

Annoyed at Brent's split attention, she followed his eyes. "Detective McFadden must like a challenge."

Cynth tossed her head, laughing at something the caveman said. She caught Brent watching her and dismissed him, turning back to the neanderthal and touching his arm.

"Oh?"

"She's wasting her time with Duff. Women are constantly chasing him. He's always nice to them and they take it the wrong way. They never get anywhere."

Because he has Cynth. He doesn't need anyone else.

"It's enough to question the existence of a benevolent God that He created such a gorgeous man and made him gay."

Brent hid his shock. "Gay men shouldn't have someone pretty to date?"

"You know what I mean."

Cynth couldn't be trying to make him jealous. Had he pestered her so much she enlisted a gay guy to be her beard? *Maybe you're an asshole and it isn't about you. Maybe she doesn't want anyone at District 5 trying it on with her.* She'd be justified. They all talked about her behind her back. He and Peter shut it down more times than he could count, but it still went on when they weren't around.

Aubrey said something. Brent returned his focus to her with eye contact and a smile. "Darlin', gay or not, if he resists your charms he must be dead."

LIA

Starting with Venetian red was a mistake. Lia tapped a foot impatiently on the upended crate she used for a footstool, squinting at the mess on her easel that would eventually be a close-up of tree bark.

Under the drab outer layer, the living bark was lovely, rust and a salmony rose. She wanted to capture that hidden richness. She'd started there, building her bark from the inside out.

She'd taken to her studio to forget the blood-soaked concrete she'd stood over earlier, but the swirls of red paint took her right back to the memories that surfaced while she deciphered the spatter.

Bucky hadn't entered her thoughts in years. Today as she considered that single strike penetrating Daniel's carotid artery—or was it the jugular vein?—it was impossible not to remember what it felt like to thrust a knife into flesh.

She rubbed her thigh, stopping when she realized she was massaging the dimple scar from Bucky's bullet.

I've got to fix that color.

She pawed through her tubes of paint, digging out raw

sienna, Naples yellow, and radiant red—which wasn't red at all but a fleshy pink—squirting globs onto the sheet of glass she used as a palette, then taking an old filbert worn to stubble and scrubbing color into the red until her canvas no longer looked like murder.

She felt a tug on her foot. Gypsy had the sole of her sandal in her teeth.

"Why can't you bark like other dogs?"

Gypsy let loose and grinned up at her. Chewy stood several feet back with a hopeful, expectant expression. Lia took off the sandal and examined it. *Teeth marks.* Gypsy barked. Lia checked the time.

"You're right. I need a break."

She fed the dogs and took them outside to play, tossing balls for Gypsy while Chewy performed his usual perimeter check. She stretched her back—cramped after hours hunched on her stool. The sun had disappeared behind the hills, reminding her to eat.

Not yet.

She returned to her canvas, studying the photo she'd tacked on the side of her easel. The exterior of the bark wasn't brown. Not gray, either. Neither and both, so utterly bland. Cracks revealed those lovely hints of rust and that fleshy rose shade underneath. Bits of pale turquoise and green freckled the not gray, not brown where lichen sought a foothold.

She wanted to capture that, the drab surface and the rich hints of color you discovered if you looked closer. She mixed dabs of cadmium orange and ultramarine blue in a glob of white to make gray, leaving the mixture streaky so she'd get variations. She picked up her large filbert and lay irregular patches over the red.

She'd taken her source photos at Wesleyan as afternoon sun cast hard shadows in the grooves between thick, peeling slabs of ancient bark. She switched to raw umber to lay in those shadows, jagged hairlines and fat crevasses forming a network across the canvas. In a few days she'd glaze those shadows with Prussian blue to pump up the color.

Solving the problem of how to translate her perceptions into paint absorbed her, and as she lost herself in the paint, the tension of the day slipped away.

The hand on her shoulder made her jump. She dropped her brush, leaving a brown streak on her leg as it fell. Peter kissed the top of her head.

She dropped her head back into his shirt, inhaling the scents of pine and smoke and sweat as she looked into his upside-down face.

It was a plain face with deep blue eyes like summer twilight in a Parish print. Peter was like that bark, unremarkable until you looked beyond the surface. He grinned at her and his unremarkable face became extraordinary.

"Is sneaking up on me any way to say hello?"

"It is when you're covered in paint. Commission for dead flowers?"

"It's bark. Can't you tell?"

"Not your usual fare."

"Not my usual day. It suited my mood."

"I came bearing gifts." He set a grocery bag on her work table.

She dug into the bag, smiling as she pulled out a pint of Ben & Jerry's Chocolate Fudge Brownie. "Dinner. You are the best of boyfriends."

"I hear Cynth was mean to you."

She stood, giving him a hello kiss. "And you want to make it better? It's okay, I deserved it. She tell you about it?"

"She sent a text with the broad strokes."

Broad strokes that likely included a lot of profanity. "Cynth was doing her job, and she was right. That's not what's bothering me."

"Oh?"

"I saw the bloodstain and imagined Daniel bleeding out. It reminded me of Bucky."

Peter took her shoulders, looked her in the face. "Not the same. Bucky was trying to kill you. You would have run, but she didn't let you. This was a premeditated attack, lying in wait. Why didn't you call me?"

"I figured we'd talk after you got home. It's okay. I mostly worked it out on the canvas. How did it go?"

Peter shrugged. "Lots of manly posturing. An excuse to run around the woods on the city dime. The zip line was fun. I'm unclear how it related to leadership."

Lia headed into the kitchen with her pint of ice cream, prying the lid off, grabbing a spoon out of the dish drainer, scooping out that first bite, feeling the cold, fudgy stuff slide down her throat. "I repeat, you really are the best of boyfriends. Bailey's the one having a hard day. I should save this for her."

"Oh?"

"She had to cancel a client to babysit Ellen after Cynth showed up with Arseneault. When she decided to move back home because the big bad wolf is dead, Ellen threw a fit. She thinks Daniel's killer is coming for her next. They had a huge fight."

"I hope she didn't cave."

"She's back home. She doesn't want to talk to Ellen."

"Might be the best thing for her."

"At last count, Ellen's number popped up on her phone five times. Bailey has resisted checking her voicemail so far. Do you think Ellen could be right? That Daniel's killer is coming for her?"

"I doubt it's a credible threat. It sounds like she's making Daniel's death all about her. "

"A client punched her." This was old ground, covered before. She didn't know why she felt compelled to bring it up. At least Peter would humor her.

"She report it?"

"She didn't know who they were and didn't want to pursue it."

"Easy enough to identify them from a photo array of people who lost flutes."

"She told Bailey they wore a hoodie and she couldn't see their face."

"More than a year ago. Anything since then?"

"Those protestors outside her house. We saw that on the news."

"I remember." Peter thumbed a spot of ice cream from the corner of Lia's mouth and tapped the nearly imperceptible dent in her chin. It was something he was fond of doing, touching this place no one else knew was there. "Woman Who Thinks Too Much, you're letting Brandt take up residence in your head. You don't even like her."

"I don't dislike her."

"Sure you do. You just feel guilty about disliking her."

The spoon stopped halfway to her mouth, her eyes flicking around as she examined what he'd said. She sighed in defeat. "I ought to be more sympathetic. She's been a good friend to Bailey for years."

"And she continues to find reasons to rope Bailey—and by extension you—into her drama."

"Not entirely her fault. Daniel gave her hell after she tossed him out, including removing his ankle monitor and stalking her."

"I remember that. They ever prove he did it?"

"No, but—"

"You or Bailey ever call the Electronic Monitoring Unit to verify she contacted them about it?"

"Of course not!"

"You see the black eye after that client punched her?"

"He punched her in the stomach."

"Where it wouldn't show."

"You think she made it all up?"

"She roped Bailey in with events no one can verify. That bugs me."

"Can you call the EMU?"

"That wouldn't prove Daniel showed up where she said. She could have sicced EMU on him for fun."

"That's a horrible thought. But even if she made it all up, Daniel dead in the woods isn't nothing."

Peter pulled her into a hug, the chilly carton of ice cream sandwiched between them. "I'd say Daniel dead in the woods puts a cap on things. Give it time to settle."

K LEE

K Lee dumped spaghetti in a colander to drain for a slapdash dinner. Lily would have to live with tuna pasta tonight.

She'll probably toss it and order pizza. At least her wife would be considerate enough to hide the box in the neighbor's trash.

She looked at the clock. *I can just make it.* She'd happily arrive late for the meet and greet if Lily would come, but that was a non-starter. Lily would rather eat cat vomit than have cocktails with the Hopewell crowd. She gave the faux Alfredo sauce a stir and turned off the stove.

In the living room, Lily barked a laugh. "Come quick! You won't believe this."

She wiped her hands on a towel and hurried into the living room, stopping in shock when her eyes met the oversized TV screen.

Aubrey Morse stood in front of a police car. Woods rose behind the yellow crime scene tape blocking the sidewalk. A pair of officers searched the underbrush. The chyron read "Flute Scammer Murdered."

Daniel's dead.

"Early this morning, the body of a man was discovered in Northside's idyllic Parker Woods Nature Preserve. The victim has been identified as Daniel Moore, a former flute shop owner sentenced last week—"

Ensconced in her recliner, Lily toasted the screen with her glass of wine. "You have a better chance getting my money from him dead than living. Think that's why someone killed him? Wish I'd thought of it. How do you think they did it? I hope they strangled him. Better yet, a gallon of gas and a match."

"This is awful." K Lee dropped into the matching recliner, twisting the towel in her hands.

Lily took a generous sip of her wine. "Bastard got what he deserved. I bet mom gives him a piece of her mind when he shows up—no, that's not right. No way they let him into Heaven."

"—Daniel Moore's death dashes the hopes of dozens of musicians desperate to learn the fate of their stolen—"

Lily had a right to schadenfreude. When K Lee discovered Fiona sitting in a pawn shop, her only option had been to buy her flute back. Rescuing Fiona meant canceling a trip out west to see Lily's mother, who died of a stroke weeks later. Lily had yet to forgive her.

How was I supposed to know she'd keel over like that?

The screen cut away to a shot of Aubrey Morse with Detective McFadden in front of a brick wall. "With us is Detective McFadden, lead investigator in the mysterious death." She turned to Detective McFadden. "What can you tell us about the attack?"

K Lee said, "You don't need to be ghoulish about it."

"Why not? Bastard put us through hell. Cost plenty to get your flute back, and we still had to pay to get it overhauled. If I were younger, I would have done it myself."

Knowing Lily, she would have.

LOIS

Lois checked her watch before unlocking the front door of her darkened house. Seventeen minutes after eleven. Tony should be rattling the windows with his snores. If God loved her, he hadn't seen the evening news.

Four hours earlier, Kris and Marcus waved her over, wine glasses in hand. Kris, arching a perfectly shaped eyebrow, placing a confiding hand on her back, leaning in, breathing Chablis in her ear, "You can tell us. It was you, wasn't it?"

Marcus, dapper in a linen suit, tilting his head with a raised eyebrow. "We don't blame you. Losing Xavier's contrabass had to be excruciating. I was still in Kansas, or it might have been me. Nice of you to take care of him for us."

"What are you talking about?"

Marcus and Kris examining her face. Marcus turning to Kris, "She doesn't know."

Kris wrinkling her nose. "Could be an act."

Marcus taking a sip of wine, giving her a shrewd look. "I don't think it's an act."

Kris took pity on her. "Someone murdered Daniel last night. It happened just off campus."

Lois's glass slipped, splashing her dress, spilling on the carpet. Kris caught the glass before it hit the floor. "Marcus, grab a napkin. We need to fix you up. You really hadn't heard?"

Lois, mutely shaking her head.

Marcus, dabbing at her skirt. "Sorry darling. We shouldn't tease you. We thought you knew, being local. It's all anyone is talking about."

Lois said stupidly, "I just arrived." She swiveled her head, noting all the eyes on her. Because she just made a fool of herself, or because they thought she was involved in Daniel's death?

She spent the rest of the evening parsing every sentence, every glance, wondering what her colleagues thought and how much any of them knew. She smiled until her teeth hurt, hiding the sick fear in her gut as speculation spiced every conversation and spite glittered in every eye.

Daniel hadn't listened to her. Now he was dead, and

with Daniel dead, her dreams were dead, too. She just wanted to be alone to grieve. *Please, God, let Tony be asleep.*

She took a deep breath and opened the door, stepping into the dark. Blue TV screen light glowed in the family room at the end of the hall. Murmuring voices meant Tony was watching the late news.

If God loved her, it was tough love.

"Lois?"

Sinuous fur wrapped around her legs. She stooped, scooping Sheba into her arms, rubbing her cheek against the soft pelt, Sheba's purrs vibrating against her chest.

"Lois! You need to see this."

"Coming."

She entered the room cradling Sheba for comfort, or was it protection? Tony sat on the leather sofa, gesturing at the sixty inch flatscreen with his evening nightcap of scotch on the rocks.

Aubrey Morse, life-sized on the enormous screen, talking. "—Police have no suspects in the mysterious murder of Daniel Moore in Parker Woods last night. His death dashes the hopes of dozens of musicians desperate to learn the fate of their stolen—"

"Someone murdered Daniel Moore. Good riddance."

Lois sat at the far end of the sofa. "I know. It was all anyone would talk about this evening."

"Xavier won't recover the contrabass now. Without tenure, you'd be out of a job."

"Ellen stole those flutes, not Daniel."

"Keep telling yourself that. At least this happened before you threw away our money on his latest scam."

It wasn't a scam. The words were on her lips but she didn't say them. The new flute line would be out by now if not for horrible bad luck, and it would have been spectacular. She said nothing.

"Lois? You didn't give him money?"

She stood up, dumping Sheba on the floor. "It's late, and I'm tired."

"Lois?" Accusation in his voice.

She turned away.

"How much, Lois?"

She left the room to the sound of Tony's glass hitting the wall. The glass was heavy and would bounce, not break. But it would be hell getting the scotch out of her brocade throw pillows. Tony would just have to pay to get them cleaned.

4

DAY 2

MONDAY, AUGUST 11

LIA

Terry held up a bakery box as Lia and Bailey approached their usual picnic table. "All hail the prodigal daughter! I brought donuts from Bonomini in honor of the occasion."

"Welcome back, stranger," Jim said.

"We want gory details," Terry said. "That's the price of your donut."

Bailey reached into the bakery box, selecting a plain cake donut. "We have no details."

"How many times was he stabbed?" Terry asked.

Steve jabbed him with an elbow.

"Why would you want to know that?" Lia asked.

"He's still on his Agatha Christie kick." Steve pointed at Lia's leather bracelet. "There's a story where the murderer does leatherwork."

"That was lace-up kits like kids do in summer camp," Terry groused. "Ellen obviously does real leatherwork."

"Summer camp fifty years ago," Steve said. "Still, bad for Ellen. Looks like she's going to jail."

Bailey's fist tightened around her donut. It crumbled into bits, falling on the ground. Kita and Chewy scarfed up the evidence. "Ellen didn't do it."

Terry goofed, "Then tell us, Madam Zoloft, who murdered Daniel Moore? What do the cards say?"

Bailey glared. "The cards say you're an asshole."

"The gods have spoken," Steve said.

"That's Goddess to you," Bailey said. "I forgot what jerks you guys can be."

"You can't abandon us to babysit Ellen and not expect hazing when you return," Terry said. "My donuts should count for something."

Jim said. "*I'm* not a jerk. How's Ellen handling everything?"

Lia stepped in. "About how you'd expect. And no, I don't have inside information." *Not that we can share, anyway.* "Bailey and I went to the crime scene yesterday."

Bailey selected another donut, breaking off a hunk for Kita. "We saw bloodstains on the concrete. Lia read them like tea leaves."

"Do tell." Steve said.

Gypsy, who missed the crumb detail, sat at Lia's feet and whined. Lia broke off a piece of donut that was not slathered in chocolate and gave it to her, tossing a tennis ball after she wolfed it down. "He knew the person who killed him," Lia said.

"That's a given," Terry said.

"I mean someone he didn't expect to attack him."

"What makes you say that?" Jim asked.

"Someone got up close and stabbed him in the neck when he didn't expect it. There wasn't a fight."

"How do you figure?" Steve said.

"Spurts of arterial blood." Lia traced arcs in the air to demonstrate. "And a void in the blood pool for his head. That's the carotid."

"Impressive," Terry said. "How can you be sure there was no fight?"

"The pattern of blood spray was uninterrupted. With a fight, you'd have voids where the attacker was, smears, changes in direction, like that. Someone got close, stabbed him in the neck, then left him to stagger, fall, and bleed out."

"Hit and run?" Steve asked.

"Could be. He knew them well enough to let them get face to face in the dark."

"Someone he expected to meet?" Jim said.

Across the table, Bailey fed the last bit of donut to Kita before selecting another. *Carb-loading because she's upset.*

Bailey said, "Cynth said Ellen was texting Daniel, but there was nothing on her phone. Daniel had to be talking to someone else."

"His next dupe?" Steve said.

A reasonable assumption, if you didn't know someone impersonated Ellen. Lia caught Bailey's eye and shook her head.

Bailey caught the hint. "I bet Daniel was looking for someone to sponge off. There was something else. Captain Arseneault asked Ellen if she knew a place called the Lounge. The way Ellen described it, it had to be that spot where we—"

Lia gave Bailey a hard look. Bailey stumbled to a

mumbling halt. Lia said, "That spot off the trail with all the fallen logs?"

"Um, yeah," Bailey said. "The way Captain Arseneault talked about it, it sounded like that's where Daniel died. But he bled out by the street. Nowhere near."

"Curious," Terry.

"Confusing," Jim said. "Where was he living?"

"Cynth has to know," Terry said.

"Fat chance getting her to talk about it," Steve said.

"He has no income that anyone knows about," Jim said. "Maybe it's not about the flutes."

"Like his latest dupe finally saw through him?" Steve said.

"We need to know who he's been talking to," Terry said. "Bailey, can't your friend help?"

Accessing phone records would be child's play for Bailey's winter beau, but John wasn't communicating these days. Probably because Bailey skipped her trip south last winter.

Bailey stared at the remaining half of her third donut. "He's ... busy."

"You can always ask," Terry said.

Bailey stared at Terry, her eyes bulging more than usual. "You want John to risk arrest to get information Cynth already has access to? You think she's not competent to follow up?"

"Um, when you put it that way. ... Can we talk to Ellen? There may be things she didn't tell Cynth."

In unison, Lia and Bailey glared at Terry, saying, "NO!"

Terry looked hurt. "Why not?"

Bailey looked stressed and miserable. Perhaps she could

give a portion of the truth. Lia said, "Ellen doesn't need to be stirred up right now."

Bailey's phone, lying face up on the table, squawked. On the screen, a text read:

Ellen: 911!!!!!!

Bailey said, "Too late."

BAILEY

Bailey spread a towel over the Kita prints on the passenger seat of her truck, then opened the door for Ellen. Ellen settled herself on the towel, staring out the windshield at her SUV. Last night someone spray-painted "THIEF" in foot-tall letters on the rear window, the windshield, and the hood.

"Thank you for picking me up. I can't drive like that. Can you take me to Hertz after the morgue?"

Bailey had rescheduled two clients so she could drive Ellen out to Blue Ash. Dropping her off might allow her to fit one of them back in. She put the truck in gear and pulled away from the curb.

"Sure. Any idea who did it?"

"It could be anyone. Where I parked, the camera's no help."

"What did the police say?"

"I haven't spoken to them. What can they do?"

"Don't you have to make a report for your insurance?"

"I can't think about that right now. I'm frightened. I told you they were after me."

"You need to tell Cynth."

"I don't have your faith in the police. Let's just get this over with."

"It isn't necessary to put yourself through this."

"I spent half my life taking care of Daniel. He *was* my life. It won't feel real until I see him."

Says the woman who spent the last year wishing him dead at every opportunity. "I've met the Assistant Coroner."

"Do you like him?"

"Her. I do. Amanda's—" Warm, sassy, and fond of bold colors wouldn't impress Ellen. *How to explain her?* "She's strong and competent."

"Hard to imagine a woman putting her hands in dead bodies. I suppose she couldn't make it as a doctor."

Bailey decided she didn't need a pointless argument while she was driving. She used the excuse of morning traffic to avoid conversation and spent the trip reminding herself charity is never wrong.

Goddess knows I have my irrational moments when I need unconditional support. But the steady dose of Ellen's neediness had eroded her resources—never good for someone with bi-polar disorder, no matter how well she managed her medication—and she had little to give.

I'll do this one thing. Then I can disengage.

The new coroner's office looked like someone built it with an erector set: several stories of antiseptic, soulless glass sitting in the middle of an endless asphalt parking lot, dwarfing a handful of recently planted saplings.

Survivors needed comfort, and those who worked here needed relief from the death surrounding them. She would surround it with color and living things, but no one asked her.

Their footsteps echoed through the giant, empty lobby as the sun beat down through a two-story wall of windows. Filling the space with living plants would soften the environment while generating negative ions and dampening the sound, but again, no one asked her.

Bailey expected Amanda with her medusa braids and African print scarves. Instead, they were met by a slender black man straight out of millennial hipster GQ. He greeted them with a crisp, professional voice too deep for a man who topped out at 5' 7".

"I'm Doctor Langston. If you'll follow me, I'll take you to the viewing area."

On rare occasions, Bailey could see a colored haze around people with powerful personalities. This man carried a dirty red aura she associated with resentment. If anyone worked here because they couldn't make it with living patients, it was him.

He led them to a small, empty room with purple drapes covering the back wall. Dr. Langston pressed a button by the door and the drapes retracted, revealing a long window and a curtained cubicle beyond.

Daniel lay on a gurney, his skin almost as white as the sheet covering him up to his chin. *No aura there.*

Ellen placed one hand against the glass as if she could reach through and touch him. "I thought I'd be in the room with him. This feels so … impersonal."

Langston said, "I apologize. Protocol. Do you have any questions?"

"Why is the sheet pulled up so high? Is something wrong with his neck?"

"That's a question you should ask Captain Arseneault when the autopsy is completed."

Ellen snapped, "Why did you ask if I had questions if you won't answer them?"

"Again, I apologize. Would you like some time alone here?"

Ellen huffed. "No, I would not."

"When you're ready, we can fill out the paperwork to release the body."

He's not a body. He's Daniel. Don't you have any compassion?

"I beg your pardon?" Ellen said.

At Ellen's confused look, Langston said, "Captain Arseneault said you were next of kin. We need you to tell us what funeral home to release the body to."

"I have to go through Daniel's papers. I'll get back with you. Bailey, let's go."

Ellen hurried out the door. Bailey followed her down the long hall, looking over her shoulder to see Dr. Langston just outside the door, staring after them and frowning.

Heat rose from the parking lot asphalt, the infant trees giving no relief from the sun. *Need another twenty years for those.*

Back at the truck, Bailey said, "You don't have Daniel's papers."

"What was I supposed to say?"

"I think he expected Daniel's spouse to know his wishes."

"Daniel refused to pay for arrangements. He didn't have any. You think I want to explain that?"

"You have power of attorney, if Daniel never changed it."

"Your point is?"

"You're just going to leave him there?"

"You have a plan that doesn't involve me spending thousands of dollars?"

Bailey's preference would be a Tibetan sky burial, exposed to the elements in a forest where she could feed the coyotes and vultures and become part of the cycle of life. Someone could leave her in the back of Wesleyan Cemetery. Plenty of vultures and coyotes there. Ellen would find that repellant.

"Did you get what you needed?"

"I don't know what I need. I have a headache."

You aren't the only one. Bailey looked at the sun. *About eleven.* They'd hit traffic all the way back, but she'd be able to make her afternoon appointments. "Do you still want me to drop you at Hertz? Are you okay to drive?"

"I'm feeling faint. Can't we get lunch first?"

Bailey pictured herself repeatedly jabbing a sharpened pencil into her eye, and sighed. "I'll make time."

FLORENCE

Snickerdoodle stirred in Florence's lap, lifting his head, chuffing. Someone was coming. When he felt good, he raced to the door and yapped his head off. This was a bad day.

Those bad days came more and more frequently. It would be a near thing, which of them passed first. She hated the idea of leaving him behind, of him with strangers or put down because he was too old and ill for anyone to adopt. She often thought the only reason she held on was to see him safely to the rainbow bridge.

A car door slammed. Gail, back from the store with the week's supply of microwave dinners. Daniel had cooked actual meals for her. That had been nice, even if she rarely ate much. Now she was back to dressing up frozen mac and cheese with sardines.

She stroked Snickerdoodle's head. "Don't feel much like moving, do you? Can't say I blame you."

Gail fumbled the lock, shoving the door open with one shoulder while she carried a half dozen plastic grocery bags in each hand. She was solid-built and boring as her mousy hair. But Gail was reliable, if stuck on her own way of doing things.

Gail elbowed the door shut. "I'll put these away, then I'll take Snickerdoodle out." She dumped the bags on the counter. "Do you want me to pop one of these in the microwave for you? It's no trouble."

"Did you bring the fudge cremes? I'll take a few with a glass of milk."

Gail brought her a plate, setting it down on her night-stand. Two miserly cookies. That was Gail, trying to control her sugar intake.

I'm dying. Worrying about sugar is stupid. When Gail left, she'd get the box and hide it. Gail expected her to do this and skimped to make a point. A stupid pretense, but allowing Gail to bully her a bit meant she wasn't bringing home diabetic cookies.

Gail sat on the sofa, an expectant look on her face. *I suppose I should thank her.* "It's good of you to step in after what happened to Daniel."

"It's what neighbors are for. The police stayed a long time yesterday. What did they say?"

"Only that he died."

"Nothing else?"

"They said a dog walker found him. I wondered if it was you."

"I didn't want to upset you."

"It's all right. How did he look?"

Gail's small eyes glittered for an instant before settling into a subdued expression. "It was awful. Channel 7 says it wasn't a mugger."

"Why would anyone want to kill him?"

Gail pressed her lips into a disapproving line and finally said, "Ellen had me walking the greyhounds after Daniel's arrest."

"Don't talk to me about that woman." Suspiciously, "Did you tell her he was here?"

"Of course not. She wouldn't let me in the house if she thought I was in contact with him. Last thing I needed was for either of them to think I was spying."

"That's silly."

"I know having Daniel here was a blessing for you, but Ellen said some things. It had me worried he was taking advantage of you."

"What of it? Not like I have anyone to leave it to." Florence looked at her shelves of treasures gone shabby with age and neglect. "What little there is."

"All these dust catchers are bad for your lungs. I can clean them, but the dust will just pile up again. Have you thought about clearing out? You'll breathe easier."

"Those are my memories."

"Of course you'd want to keep a few that are special."

Florence felt her face set in mulish lines. "They're all special."

"If you change your mind I can take them to Saint

Vincent de Paul. I can sell them on eBay if you like, though I don't know how much they'd get."

Florence munched a cookie and said nothing.

"So hard for you without Daniel's help. I'm happy to do errands and walk Snickerdoodle, but you need someone to look after your bills."

Florence drank her milk and gave Snickerdoodle a scratch.

Gail continued, "I help my brother-in-law with his bookkeeping. I could take a look for you."

"It's kind of you to offer, but I'm fine."

"Florence, what was he doing out? It makes no sense."

"How would I know? I was asleep." She turned her attention to the remaining cookie.

Gail put her hands on her knees and shoved herself off the sofa. She slapped her thigh twice. "Come, Snickerdoodle. Walkies."

Snickerdoodle looked up at Florence and sighed, then clambered to the floor.

Gail hooked Snickerdoodle up. "I have other dogs to walk, but I can come back this evening if you need me."

"That won't be necessary. I'll let him out in the yard tonight."

They left. Florence grabbed her walker and heaved herself up. Gail hid her fudge cremes on the top shelf, forcing her to risk breaking a hip to get them down. She put the box in the basket of her walker and carried it back to her recliner, stashing it in the bottom of her nightstand.

All she had were memories and indulgences. Daniel understood. He'd been good company and he'd treated her well. Despite everything, she would miss him. She already missed him.

CYNTH

Cynth sat in the Homicide conference room, vibrating with the effort to remain polite. This was *supposed* to be a progress meeting to keep the DA's office looped. The asshat across the table did not want to be looped. He wanted to grab the ball and run with it, with her career on the line.

Charles effing Hobbs's attitude went with his expensive suit and quarterback build. With dark hair and a huge, toothy grin, he could have played young King George in that Bridgerton spinoff. She suspected he had his hair buzzed to play up the resemblance.

The table hid his lower body, but his posture suggested the classic jock pose: relaxed with his legs spread wide as if his balls were too big to be contained. Everything about him said "I'm hot shit king of the world, and I know it."

He glanced at Arseneault and Brent before raising his hands palms up in faux confusion. "You have the bloody knife with the estranged cohab's fingerprints, and you say there was plenty of animosity between them. I don't see the problem."

Cynth drew herself up to her full height, as much as she could in her chair. It left her eight inches shorter than God's gift to justice. "There are holes in the case you could drive a truck through."

"You'll fill those holes before trial."

"And if we don't?"

"I have faith in the department."

Arseneault stepped in. "Charles, let's hear Detective

McFadden out. We don't want to make a mistake at this point."

Cynth both appreciated and resented the assist. It would bother her less if it was Parker. But Parker would have shut pretty boy Hobbs down half an hour ago.

She nodded at Arseneault, keeping her face neutral. "We don't have the autopsy report."

"Is there any question what killed him?" Hobbs asked this like he was genuinely interested and not telling her she was stupid.

"Brandt has an alibi."

"Soft, easily discredited," Hobbs said.

"There are surveillance cameras around the house. She doesn't show up on them."

"Blind spots on the property?"

"No camera on the back yard, but there's a six-foot privacy fence. The camera on the side yard catches anyone coming or going through the gate."

Hobbs reverted to type and raised a cocky eyebrow. "Ever climb a fence?"

Arseneault leaned in. "The woman in question is sixty. Detective McFadden, what does the video footage show?"

"Bailey Hughes enters the house at eight. There's no activity until we woke Hughes the following morning. Hughes states they watched videos until ten-thirty or eleven. She slept on the couch by the front door and is a light sleeper. "

Hobbs asked, "Any other concerns?"

Cynth ticked off her objections. "Everything prior to Friday was wiped from the burner used to lure Moore out. We won't know what it can tell us until we recover the data.

We need bloody clothes. We need to know who put a tracking device in Moore's man purse. "

"Why?"

"If they aren't involved, that person has information about Moore's movements after his ankle monitor was removed." Cynth continued her list. "We can't prove Brandt knew about the meeting. We need to link the texts to Brandt or an associate to show premeditation. The finger-prints on the phone aren't hers. And we absolutely need to explain how Brandt beat her cameras."

"I'm confident you'll resolve all your questions after you search her house and review her electronics."

"Which I'd like to do before we arrest her. We've been on this case less than thirty-six hours. We need to interview other suspects. If we arrest now, we're guilty of tunnel vision."

Charles effing Hobbs stood, shoved his suit jacket back, hands on hips like he was Superman. "Stephen, I don't see any of this posing a problem with a quick resolution, but I'll run it by the DA and get back to you. Take the win, Detective McFadden. "

He grabbed his briefcase and left. The room was silent for a moment. Then Arseneault stood.

Brent said, "I know I'm the third wheel here, but what's the rush?"

That Mr. Cut All Corners asked confirmed how brain-less this was.

Arseneault sighed and sat back down. "This goes back. Our failure to charge anyone with the Geoffrey Lawrence murder soured a lot of donor class people on the DA. He barely scraped by in the last election. Moore came along with a case tailor made to redeem him with those same people."

Middle-class people with expensive instruments and artsy aspirations. Cynth said, "Only it didn't."

"You know better than anyone. Huge case, international exposure, dozens of sympathetic middle class victims, many of them students. If they'd gotten a full confession with the whereabouts of those instruments, he'd be golden right now."

Cynth nodded. "Instead Moore stonewalls and victims drop out of the case. The case shrinks, taking prison off the table. Moore has no reason to confess."

"Exactly," Arseneault said. "Someone takes him out days after sentencing, so even the tiny hope of restitution is gone. Moore's death means no justice for anyone."

Brent said, "I can't imagine how anyone expected him to raise a quarter million to pay them back. The shop was gone, he'd lost his meal ticket, and he never held an actual job in his life other than running his business into the ground."

"You're right, of course," Arseneault said. "But we're talking optics. Moore would have dropped out of the news cycle long before it was clear he'd never pay a dime."

Cynth scoffed. "So the DA wants headlines."

Arseneault said, "More like Hobbs is positioning himself to be the heir apparent and is desperate to gift the DA with those headlines. All speculation, of course."

Brent said, "If this goes wrong, Cynth will be the one who takes the hit, not Captain America. Bad if Brandt is innocent. Worse if she walks because we were premature."

"Point taken. But is there anything to give us a suspect

pool bigger than one? Anything in those victim statements or Moore's communications?"

"Phone calls both ways with one of his victims," Cynth said. "We need to find out what that was about. Brent is chasing down the out-of-towners."

"Trying to, anyway," Brent said. "People all over the country hated him. Random strangers posting on Facebook. Angry emails and texts, but nothing I can point to as an overt threat of violence."

Cynth said, "We're looking at the Tile tracker. Someone had to get near him to plant it, but nobody knew where he was. The only time he showed his face was at court."

"Didn't he skip most of his hearings?" Arseneault asked.

"He had to be there to plead, and again for sentencing. Someone planted the tracker one of those two days. We know who attended his hearings, but we haven't talked to them."

Brent said, "Hopewell's flute camp is in session. Teachers and flute sellers fly in from all over the country. Maybe someone came early. We don't know enough about these other people to rule them in or out."

Arseneault pursed his lips, nodding. "This all needs to be nailed down."

Ya think?

"But it begs the question: was anyone angry enough to kill him over a few thousand dollars?"

"Respectfully, sir," Brent said, "Those women talk about their flutes like they're children or prize poodles. Any number of them would be happy to kill Moore if they had the constitution for it."

Arseneault sighed. "We have Brandt's fingerprints, and he expected to see her. Would he let any of those other women get up close and personal after they said horrible things about him in court?"

"Ellen said horrible things about him in court, too," Cynth said.

"But he believed she was ready to reconcile. Usually it's the intimate partner."

"Sir, it's usually the intimate partner when the victim is a woman. With male victims, it's usually a friend or acquaintance."

Arseneault leaned back, steepled his fingers. "And in those cases, the offender is usually male. Everyone connected to this case is female, except for dealers who wrote off the loss of their flutes. That puts it back on Brandt. Again, who else could get close to him at midnight on a dark sidewalk?"

"That's the sixty-four thousand dollar question," Brent said.

"Write up your search warrant, but hold off executing it until we hear from the DA."

"And if the DA says to arrest?" Cynth asked.

"We're a team. If the DA wants to move forward, we move forward. McFadden, you do your job. Politics are on me."

BRENT

Standing in the hall outside the conference room, Cynth backhanded the wall with her fist. "Write it up but don't move on it," she mocked. "What are we, children?"

If at any point Brent chafed at not leading the Moore

case—which he hadn't, not really, or not much—Arseneault ended that when he made clear Cynth was expected to be a cog in Homicide's machinery.

He tipped his head toward the break room, which housed a vending area far superior to the one at District 5. In Brent's mind it did not make up for being jammed in a cubicle within a field of cubicles. "I need something to drink."

Cynth took the hint and headed down the hall. "You were quiet in there."

"Did you need my help? Looked to me like you were doing fine."

She gave him an odd look. "Thank you for not stepping on me in front of the big guys."

That hurt. "What kind of asshole do you think I am?"

"You wouldn't do it on purpose. I just expected Mr. Testosterone to find your impeccable suit eminently relatable. I'll buy you a caramel fudge toffee cappuccino to make up for it."

The thought of all those chemicals and sugar made his stomach churn. "You're all heart, McFadden. The manly choice is black coffee, burned to tar."

"Get real. You want Evian water."

"Truth." He eyed the coffee machine selections and felt his stomach churn. "Starbucks on Court Street?"

"Starbucks is for prissy assholes."

Brent looked at his watch. "There's a Lebanese place a block from here. We can beat the lunch rush."

"You want to eat?"

"Best gyros downtown. I'm buying."

"Fine. We're taking the stairs. I need to walk off my mad."

Eight floors. At least I'll work up an appetite. Brent held the stairwell door for Cynth. She rolled her eyes as she walked through.

Cynth broke her silence four floors down. "Yesterday, Arseneault gives me this lecture. 'Murder isn't like other crimes' he says. 'The stakes are higher' he says. He tells me, 'You allow the littlest hint of reasonable doubt and the defense will smash the case apart. Every bit of evidence has to be accounted for.'" She scowled. "Then he has the nerve to pull this shit."

"What's the plan while we wait for word from on high?"

"We need to get everything we can on Brandt in case the DA wants to arrest."

"If we had that search warrant, we could do a deep dive into Brandt's electronics."

Cynth exited the stairwell at the lobby and pushed the exterior door open. Summer humidity hit Brent in the face, melting his shirt into a damp mess clinging to his chest.

Unfazed, Cynth continued, "You can press the button on a tile tracker and make the phone it's tied to ring. I'd love to try that when we talk to Brandt."

"Too risky. If it isn't hers we'll alert the person it belongs to, who will then dump the app."

"Will it trigger the phone if it's out of range?"

"Don't know. But if a phone can track the tag miles away, who's to say the tag can't alert the phone? Either way it will leave a record on the account. Safer to get the search warrant and check her phone for the app."

Cynth scowled. "Spoilsport."

"One more thing to research, anyway."

"Feel free to add that to your list of grunt work."

"Waste of time," Brent said. "We'll have our search

warrant before we see Brandt again. What's our next move, Wonder Woman?"

"Lunch. I hear you're buying."

CYNTH

Brent set a tray piled with Middle Eastern food on the table and sat across from Cynth. "I have a request."

Cynth froze, one hand hovering over a basket of pita bread. "Which is?"

"Let's not talk shop. I'd like to enjoy my meal."

She tore off a piece of her pita bread and dug into the baba ganoush. "Whatever. What do you want to talk about?"

"There's movies, books—"

"Why do you like Harry Potter?"

Brent took a bite of his gyro, chewed, swallowed, shrugged. "Why do girls like Cinderella?"

"You got me. Cinderella is a wimp. I was a Mulan girl myself. Why Harry Potter?"

"Magic, adventure, overcoming evil. Flying on a broomstick. Big Truths, with a capital T. What's not to like?"

"The stories are totally illogical."

"Rowling is a brilliant political satirist. If you look at Harry Potter through that lens, they're no more illogical than the current state of the world."

A stock Brent Davis answer, slick and meaningless. "And what do your Hyde Park lady friends think about her politics?"

Brent took another bite of gyro, making her wait for his response. "Which is your not-so-subtle attempt to understand why I have a Harry Potter mug. You really want to know why I like Harry Potter?"

"Yes, I do."

Brent put his gyro down and folded his arms. "Why?"

"Because it's inconsistent with the rest of you."

He gave her a steady look. "All right. If you promise you won't repeat this to anyone?"

"Stick a needle in my eye."

"I was in foster care."

Cynth's gyro fell in her lap, spilling onion and tzatziki sauce on her suit. *Slick, metrosexual Brent in foster care?* She ducked her head, focusing on her sandwich and her pants to cover her confusion. Brent kept talking as she used a wad of napkins to mop up the mess.

"It was an ugly place. The bigger kids were bullies and my foster parents were in it for a paycheck. There was a closet under the stairs. That's where I went when things got hairy."

Which meant everything he'd ever told her about himself was a lie. But he was undercover then. They'd had exactly one personal conversation in the years since the blow up—and that got interrupted by copper thieves. There were secrets in Brent's past. Despite the invitation, she wasn't ready to go there.

"Harry hid in a closet?"

"He lived there. That's where his aunt and uncle put him."

"How did you get started with the books?"

"I became a big brother in Atlanta. One of my kids kept picking up odd stuff when we were at the park, coke cans, lost frisbees, that sort of thing. I asked him why he kept picking up trash and he said he was hoping to find a portkey.

"I didn't know what that was. He explained it and I started reading the books to have something for us to talk about. And I helped him pick up trash. We had a deal. If either of us touched a portkey, we'd come back for the other person. He gave me the mug."

"That's … really nice. What happened to him?"

"Drive-by shooting."

"I'm sorry."

"Yeah, so am I."

Cynth would knock over any can of worms within ten miles. Then she'd trample the worms. She reassembled her sandwich and chewed a healthy bite before speaking. "That was years ago. Why do you still like Harry Potter?"

"Millions of adults read Harry Potter. It's the ultimate battle between good and evil."

"You can get that from the Marvel Universe."

"A phenomenal coming of age story rife with life lessons."

"Name one."

"You can't do it alone."

"I can't do what alone?"

"That's the biggest theme. You can't do it alone. You need friends."

"Pretty basic."

"Not to everyone. My turn. Why did you become a cop?"

"Why did you?"

"Nuh-uh. You first."

When she thought she was dating a P & G executive, she gave him the "cops in the family" bit. She could give Brent the foster kid the truth.

"Boys grabbing my boobs in middle school pissed me off. I discovered I enjoyed punching their lights out."

"I imagine that was before the guys got their growth spurts."

She snorted. "Growth spurts didn't save them."

"I stand corrected."

"My brothers were into Krav Maga. I made them teach me. I spent a lot of time in detention before I learned to wait until we were off school grounds before I hit someone."

"You were defending yourself. Why did you get into trouble?"

"Excessive use of force. Some of those kids had litigious parents. Bratty rich kids hate public humiliation and they lie like Persian rugs."

"Not public school then. They deserved more than embarrassment."

She smirked. "Some of them still cross the street when they see me. My cousin got me in with the skate boarding crowd. I was unimpressive on a board, but they appreciated my ass kicking skills."

"I'm sorry you went through that."

Cynth shrugged. "Everybody goes through something. But seeing the principal hush up everything those entitled asshole kids did—it gave me a taste for justice."

"I bet Moore's butter-wouldn't-melt act got under your skin."

"Give me your typical dirtbag any day. So why did you become a cop?"

"I'm a cop because being a criminal didn't work for me."

"Oh?"

"Wrong side of the tracks and limited supervision. Petty

crime was the most popular social activity. The other kids would get juiced over stealing cars, vandalism, B and E. Shoplifting was considered girlie, but that went on too. None of it made me feel good."

"You had a conscience."

"It was highly inconvenient."

"You were in a gang?"

"Not that organized, but you didn't want them thinking you were a pussy."

"What did you do?"

"I learned how to be on the fringes, how to extract myself from dicey situations without calling attention to myself, how to stay cool with the guys so they wouldn't see me as a problem."

"Good education for undercover work."

Brent rubbed the back of his neck. "I liked playing doper like you liked punching assholes. … Until it went pear-shaped." Brent gathered up his trash, dumping it in his empty gyro basket. "I moved up here because I had to. I snuck out of town in the middle of the night. My captain had a friend here—since retired—and they worked out the deal to bring me in for that undercover assignment."

"Looking for dirty cops. Who knows about this?"

"You and that retired cop."

Brent never mentioned family. He never talked about going home.

"You can't go back."

"Good thing there's nothing to go back for."

"I'm sorry. I didn't mean to get so serious."

Brent shrugged. "It is what it is. What's next, boss?"

"Work on that search warrant. We need more info about Brandt and Moore."

"Where do you propose we find it?"

"We go to the source."

Cynth entered Lia's kitchen and slung her blazer over the back of a chair. Peter and Brent followed with bags of Chinese, leading a parade of salivating dogs. As Peter and Brent unloaded food, Lia put out plates and silverware. Cynth snagged three beers from the fridge, placing two on the table and offering one to Lia.

"Want?"

"No thanks. I have wine."

Cynth twisted the cap off and took a generous swig. "We need to know what's been going on between Ellen and Daniel."

Brent pulled a chair out for Lia, giving Cynth a pointed look. "I apologize for my colleague's breech of manners. She means well."

"It's all right. I expected this."

Cynth seated herself across from Lia, leaning forward on her elbows. "I know we're putting you in an awkward position, but we need to understand the dynamics between Ellen and Daniel. You're the most trustworthy source of information we have."

Lia dumped rice on her plate from one of the white carryout cartons. "Almost everything I know is secondhand. You need to talk to Bailey."

"You're more clear-eyed than she is," Cynth said. "And we can count on you to keep your mouth shut."

Brent cleared his throat, raising his eyebrows when Cynth glared at him. She shoved a beer at him. "If you can't take a chill pill, drink a beer. Lia won't talk to anyone we don't want her to, that's all I'm saying."

Lia kept her eyes down as she spooned mu shu pork onto her plate. "I can tell this has been a fun day in the world of law enforcement."

Cynth grabbed an egg roll, took a bite. "I haven't had contact with Moore or Brandt since I handed the theft case to the DA more than a year ago. We need the lay of the land. We're hoping you can save us time." Pain, in her shin. Cynth narrowed her eyes at Brent, giving him her best mean face. "Stop kicking me."

Brent sighed, looking up at the ceiling—appealing to the Virgin Mary for patience, probably.

Lia poked her chopsticks at her rice. "All breakups get ugly at some point. I'd hate for you to think Ellen killed Daniel because of something stupid she said when she was mad."

"It's up to us to verify anything," Cynth said. "You're just giving us a place to start."

Lia used her chopsticks to make a zigzag pattern in her rice. "I think Ellen was afraid of Daniel."

"What makes you say that?"

"When this started, Bailey wanted Ellen to change her will and power of attorney, and tell Daniel she'd done it."

Cynth was sure she knew, but asked anyway. "Why was that?"

"Bailey was terrified he'd use Ellen's power of attorney to empty her accounts, or push her down the stairs and inherit everything. She thought he'd feel justified."

"A legit fear. Desperate people, desperate things."

"It took a month for Bailey to talk Ellen into it. She got rid of the old papers, but she never told Daniel."

"Which meant Daniel still believed he could inherit."

"I think she was afraid Daniel would make her life hell if he knew. He wouldn't benefit if something happened to her, but she'd be dead, so what would it matter? Bailey was a wreck worrying about her."

"It sounds twisted."

"It got so confusing. Sometimes I thought she didn't know how to stand up to him, and sometimes I thought she had a misguided sense of obligation. Sometimes I thought she was too attached to cut Daniel out of her life. I could never make sense of it."

"Could be all of the above. Your impressions are helpful, but we're mostly interested in events."

Lia said, "You already know it wasn't her, so I guess this is okay."

Cynth caught Brent's eye and said nothing.

"After you served the search warrant on the house, she said she wanted him gone. I said to change the locks and make him move into the shop. She said it wouldn't be right."

Cynth suppressed her unkind thoughts. "She try telling him to leave?"

Lia dragged her chopsticks, replacing the zigzags with a rice road. "You ever get Daniel to tell you what he did with the flutes he misplaced?"

"Point taken. How'd she get him out?"

"Ellen went to see him in jail. She told him then. I guess she felt safe with bullet-proof plexiglass between them."

"Did that work?"

"The next week the Electronic Monitoring Unit called to tell her Daniel was bailing out on his own recognizance to her address. Since it's her house, they needed her approval for monitoring. I bet he thought he could give her address, show up at the front door, and claim she had to let him stay since he bailed out there."

"What a piece of work."

"She freaked out. We said if she had to give her consent, that meant she could deny it. It never occurred to her to say no."

"What happened after that?"

"Bailey convinced the prosecutor something bad would happen if Daniel got near Ellen—"

Cynth could imagine how it went down. Once Bailey turned those wild eyes on the prosecutor and her hands started flapping around like deranged birds, she wouldn't need to articulate a credible threat. If the prosecutor did nothing and something happened, it would ruin everyone involved.

Lia continued, "—Anyway, he arranged the stay away order in case Daniel got out. We figured he'd be stuck in jail until the trial. We didn't know they were going to dump all non-violent offenders on the street a week later."

"You ever find out where he was staying?"

"Not a clue. Then he started harassing her through a lawyer, claiming wrongful eviction and theft of property. You don't want to hear about that."

"Months of stupidity," Peter said. "Lia and Bailey wanted to move Moore's stuff to a storage unit so he'd have no excuse to gain access to the house. Brandt refused to spend the money."

Lia said, "He demanded the dogs, though that was a non-starter."

"How so?"

"GAGC takes their dogs back if you can't care for them.

Easy for Ellen to tell them Daniel had a pending criminal trial, no home, and no income."

"That would do it." Cynth's eyes weren't bleeding, but she suspected her brain was. Against her better judgement, she asked, "Was there anything else?"

"There was that business at Wesleyan."

Cynth caught Peter rolling his eyes. "Tell us about that."

"Ellen runs her dogs behind the cemetery every morning. One day she saw Daniel sitting on the bench by the veterans memorial when she pulled in. She was really upset and drove home. We encouraged her to call the electronic monitor people. They said Daniel had been miles away at a shopping center."

Brandt lied or Moore cheated the monitor. Cynth voted for the lie. "What did you think about that?"

"I don't know. The bench is a good thirty feet from the drive. She might have mistaken someone else for Daniel."

"But?"

"Daniel has edema in his ankles. I can't imagine them clamping the ankle monitor very tight if he complained about circulation issues. He might have been able to slide it off."

"You make an excellent point," Brent said.

"It got weirder. Ellen saw him a week later. Same place, walking a dog. This time, the EMU verified he was there. Turns out Daniel volunteered to walk dogs for the shelter next door—"

Cynth scoffed, "The guy too sick to come to court was walking dogs?"

Lia drew her chopsticks across the rice road in hard strokes, erasing it. "—On advice from his doctor, he said. The walking, anyway. Don't know if the dogs came into that. He made a sad face for the judge. Said he was denied visitation with his own dogs. This was the only bright spot in his otherwise miserable existence, and he couldn't help the shelter schedule. Judge said she couldn't bar Daniel from a public place. Ellen switched up her routine for months before we found out he quit volunteering a week after the judge sided with him."

"So he did it to screw with her," Cynth said. "He'd have reason if she invented the original sighting."

"Sounds ugly," Brent said.

"Ugly and exhausting. I made Peter promise we'd never be so awful to each other."

"It's true," Peter said. "She did."

Lia stopped playing with her rice and looked up. "I don't understand how anyone can be so entitled. It got back to Ellen that Daniel was saying if she wanted to split up she could have just said so, and it would have been handled amicably. That about gave her an aneurism."

"How did she hear that?" Cynth asked. "Who was she in contact with?"

Lia gave Cynth a blank look. "I—I don't know. She never said."

BRENT

Brent arrived at Urban Artifact as Cynth emerged from the decommissioned church with a pair of beers. She jerked her head at a patio strung with colored lights, empty on a slow Monday. With no audience, the love of his life might not revert to her usual antagonistic self. The alcohol couldn't hurt.

He accepted the beer and took a seat. "What's your take on the monitor business?"

"There was that woman who faked a sprain by injecting saline into her ankle—"

"—to make it swell. I remember."

"Bailey knew. Bailey tells Brandt and Moore about it back when they're all friendly. When Moore gets his fancy accessory, he remembers the story. He gets a doctor's note saying he's at risk for blood clots, injects both ankles with saline, and hobbles into the EMU. They loosen the monitor to avoid a wrongful death suit. Swelling goes down in a few hours and he comes and goes as he pleases."

"Sounds like television."

Cynth set her beer down and folded her arms, smirking. "Which of Moore's schemes *didn't* sound like television?"

"Point taken. Interesting that he wasn't home when the alleged event took place. If he removed the monitor, he had to make it look like he was somewhere else."

Cynth picked up on his thoughts. "Because if he left it at home, someone could ask Nygaard if he was there. You think he arranged for someone to go shopping during Brandt's daily dog run? Easy to slip the monitor in their car and retrieve it later. If this person went shopping for him, he'd have the receipt. I doubt EMU bothered to check video footage at the store."

"Still sounds like television, but it could have happened. *If* it actually happened and wasn't just a story Brandt told Bailey for sympathy. Not sure it's relevant."

"You know what I don't get?" Cynth said. "I don't get refusing to spend money on a storage unit when it's the easiest way to deny Moore access to the house. That's stupid. Brandt confuses me."

Brent laughed. "She would."

"What's that supposed to mean?"

It means you spend too much time around guys. "You're the most direct person I know. It's a compliment."

"What does that have to do with Brandt?"

"You ever see a kid threaten to go eat worms? The adults in the room will trip over themselves to stop him. 'Oh Trevor, what's wrong? Will cake make you feel better? Let me buy you ice cream.' Trevor has no plans to get anywhere near any worms."

"Trevor sounds like a piece of work."

"Works for him. She conned Bailey and Lia into fixing everything for her."

"Sounds right," Cynth said. "But that's cunning, not smarts. Cunning doesn't require her to do logistics."

"You don't think she's smart enough to escape her cameras? She has a management position."

"Supervisory, which means she implements other people's plans. Everything we've heard says Lia and Bailey were the strategists when it came to dealing with Daniel."

"Neither of them would plan a murder."

Cynth arched a pale, delicate eyebrow. "You think?"

Brent laid his empty bottle on the table and flicked it to make it spin. It was how he felt. "Brandt doesn't know what she wants. She's an attention seeker. A master manipulator. Intellectually challenged. Pick one. Pick all or none. We need to talk to Bailey."

Cynth put a hand on the spinning bottle, making it stop. "Not yet. There's no way she doesn't tell Brandt."

"Then we circle around. Kill two birds with one stone.

Interview the women who attended Daniel's hearings. We say we're looking for their take on Brandt—"

Cynth grinned. "While we suss them out—"

"—and cure our tunnel vision problem." They were completing each other's sentences. It was downright cute.

Cynth's phone rang. Arseneault's name popped upon the screen.

Brent checked the time. "What does he want at 10:45 in the freaking PM?"

Cynth shook her head, warning him to stay silent. She accepted the call, turning away so he couldn't hear.

She ended the call and let loose a heavy sigh. "Drink up. We have a big day tomorrow."

5

DAY 4
WEDNESDAY, AUGUST 13

BAILEY

BAILEY BROKE OFF A PIECE OF PLAIN CAKE DONUT AND GAVE IT to Kita, who stretched full length across the top of their usual picnic table. Chewy head-butted Bailey's leg, looking for his share. Lia sat beside her, tossing balls down the hill for Gypsy.

Sunshine and dogs. Simple. Uncomplicated. Goddess, she'd missed this like water in the desert.

She was only beginning to realize what a drain the last two years had been. Ellen had needed constant reassurance to own her right to set boundaries and take care of herself. Bailey didn't regret it. But after a year of helping Ellen understand that loving someone didn't give them the right to suck the life out of you, she looked in the mirror and saw the need to apply that lesson to herself.

How ironic.

Baby steps. Monday she drove Ellen to the morgue and

ended up wishing she'd told her to call an Uber. Yesterday Ellen texted in a panic because someone smashed her car window.

She hadn't responded. Ellen didn't need her, not really, now that Daniel was no longer a threat. Maybe, just maybe, if she was strong and didn't jump every time Ellen called, Ellen would start handling things herself instead of begging for help five times a day.

She passed the bag of donuts across the table. "I thought the guys would be here. Take the rest of these before I eat them."

Lia peered into the bag. "Jelly isn't my thing, but Peter will enjoy them."

"Just so I don't have to look at them. Don't let me forget. I have a present for you in the truck."

"A present? You shouldn't have."

"It's nothing special. I found a piece of steel pipe in my basement. It's the right size to prop up the hood of your Volvo. You won't need one of us to hold it up for you next time you check the oil."

"Thank you. That will come in handy."

The engine on Lia's thirty-year-old 240 ran like new. Not so the little things, like hood hinges and pieces of trim. Lia intended to drive it until the engine fell out. Bailey estimated she'd get two years, tops.

Bailey's phone rang.

Lia sent a ball bounding down the slope. "That has to be Ellen. Is she still freaking about the text messages?"

"That's not her ring. I haven't talked to her since we went to the morgue."

"You ghosted her?"

"I drew the Hanged Man this morning."

"And what does that mean?"

"It usually refers to a time-out."

"So, ghosting."

"I'm slow walking communication. If she gets tired of waiting, she might figure things out for herself."

Bailey pulled her phone out of her pocket and put it on the table where Lia could see it. The screen listed a number she didn't recognize.

"Put it on speaker," Lia said. "Just in case it's a handsome Nigerian prince with a lovely accent."

Bailey accepted the call. A robot voice said, "This is a collect call from the Hamilton County Justice Center from —" Dead air, then Ellen's frightened voice. "Ellen … Ellen Brandt." The robot returned. "Press one to accept these charges."

No, no, Goddess, no. Bailey punched one.

Ellen screamed loud enough to make Kita jump off the table. "YOU SAID THEY WOULDN'T ARREST ME."

"Ellen, what happened?" Bailey asked.

"WHY AM I HERE? I DON'T DESERVE TO BE HERE."

Lia, her never-rattled rock, leaned in. "Calm down, Ellen, or the 300 pound fentanyl addict next in line for the phone will bounce your head off the concrete for annoying her."

Ellen whimpered. In a small voice, she said, "I don't understand why I'm here."

Lia was always better at getting Ellen to focus. Bailey shoved the phone closer to her friend.

Lia said, "What did they tell you? They had to tell you something."

"I don't remember all of it. They said I killed him with a

leather awl and they had my fingerprints. How can you kill someone with an awl?"

Bailey recalled Lia's analysis of the bloodstains. *By sticking it in a place that makes blood shoot everywhere.*

Ellen sobbed, "You have to help me."

Bailey said, "What can we do?"

"They took the girls to the shelter. You have to get them out. They won't understand. They'll be traumatized. They'll be euthanized."

Cincinnati Animal CARE was no-kill, and Ellen knew it.

Lia said, "We can do that. Who's your lawyer?"

"I don't know. Some guy the county sent."

Lia mimed poking her eye with an invisible pencil. "Ellen, this is murder. You can't rely on a public defender."

Ellen turned snippy. "Daniel Moore cost me more than a hundred thousand dollars. I'm not losing my house and the rest of my savings just because someone killed him."

Lia mouthed, *Is she crazy?*

Bailey didn't know the answer to that.

Ellen continued, "They can't convict me if I'm not guilty."

Bailey thought she heard Bertha, the 300 pound fentanyl addict, laughing in the background.

"I have to go. Save my dogs and come see me." The line went dead.

So much for my time out.

LIA

Incessant barking echoed off the cinder-block shelter walls. Lia eyed the bowl of complimentary ear plugs wistfully as Bailey handed her power of attorney to the harried woman at the counter.

It had to be hard for Bailey, catching vibes from a hundred traumatized dogs. Dumped and homeless was dumped and homeless, no matter the ground-breaking level of care dogs received here.

The woman tilted her glasses as she scanned the document. "Are you Daniel Moore? I need to see ID."

Bailey sighed, pointing at a line further down the page. "I'm Bailey Hughes, the backup. Daniel is dead."

And the reason we're here in the first place.

"Oh. This is … irregular. I'll have to get my supervisor."

It took a twenty-minute explanation and a call to District 5 before someone went to retrieve the girls. She returned five minutes later.

"They won't leave their enclosure. We need you to come back."

Enclosure. Such a benign word for a cage.

She led Lia and Bailey down the heartbreaking chain-link row, some dogs wagging tails, some huddled in corners, some narrow-eyed with suspicion. A volunteer pushed a cart down the aisle, handing out dog biscuits glued together with peanut butter.

Connie and Nati shivered in the middle of their cage like they were experiencing sub-zero weather. Connie whined when she saw Bailey.

"Poor babies," Bailey crooned. "We're here to rescue you."

Cage unlocked, Connie stumbled into the aisle, panting and leaning against Bailey as she trembled on her toothpick legs. Nati froze, eyes wheeling.

Ellen has to be feeling the same way.

Bailey leashed Connie, handing her to Lia before she entered the cage. When a proffered peanut butter biscuit failed to gain cooperation, Bailey wrapped one arm around Nati's chest and the other behind her haunches and scooped her up, cooing to her as they passed through the gauntlet of dogs now at the front of their cages barking at the top of their lungs.

When they finally exited the building, the girls scanned the parking lot for Ellen, turning those large, liquid eyes on Bailey in hopes of an explanation.

"We got them," Lia said. "What do we do with them?"

Bailey chewed her lip. "They'll be happiest at home."

"You don't get bail on murder cases. If they don't convict her, it will be months before Ellen comes home."

"They can't convict her. She didn't do it."

"They have fingerprints."

"Someone framed her."

"Meanwhile, the girls are alone and you're running back and forth."

"I could leave Kita with them for company."

"You might as well move back in."

Bailey tick-tocked her head, thinking. "Okay."

"You're really moving back in to keep the girls company?"

"When you're right, you're right. At least I'll have a bed to sleep on."

Lia sighed and held out her hand. "Give me Ellen's keys. I'll take the girls home while you go pack."

Connie and Nati refused to get into Lia's Volvo. Bailey ran a hand through her hair in frustration. "I can't lift them in with their legs locked like that. I'll have to drive them in the truck."

Bad idea. "Hand me some biscuits. Maybe we can tempt them."

"I'll do it. You hang onto Nati. If I can get Connie in, Nati will follow." Five minutes of tugging and cajoling got Connie into the back seat. Nati scrambled in, frantic to stay with her fur sister.

Lia spent the drive wondering what she'd find at Ellen's. If they took the dogs, that meant they searched the house. That was the reason she sent Bailey home to pack. She couldn't let Bailey walk in on whatever the team left behind. *Like a door bashed open with a fifty-pound battering ram.*

If Ellen had been home, she would have crated the girls and called Bailey. That meant they arrested her at the bank servicing center and perp-walked her past the dozens of people she supervised.

Not "they." Cynth and Brent. Poor Ellen.

The door was intact, but the living room looked like someone grabbed it and shook it. Cushions, books, drawers; everything was a bit out of place. Bailey would soak up the sense of violation. If only she could erase the vibe before Bailey arrived.

If only I knew how.

The girls fled to the kitchen, attacking the water bowl in a race to see who could splash the most water on the floor before it was dry. Then they stared at Lia as if doing so would telepathically communicate their needs.

I bet prison did a number on their appetite. She found a bag of kibble inside the kitchen island scooped generous amounts into the twin bowls. That would do for now.

She mopped up the water puddles, then looked around.

Two sheets of paper lay atop the kitchen island: the search warrant, and the search warrant return documenting everything Cynth's team took from the house. Peter said it was standard to leave the paperwork on a kitchen counter when no one was home during a search.

Further evidence Ellen wasn't here.

She photographed the documents before examining the inventory of confiscated items. Ellen was minus two computers; her shoes—likely looking for blood, or a soil match; dryer lint—a handy place to get blood evidence if you don't know what someone was wearing; and items of indicia—a fancy term for bills, mail, or other paperwork proving Ellen lived there, tying her to whatever they found.

Items of indicia served another purpose. You can take unlisted items as long as you find them while searching for something on the warrant. But if you're looking for an elephant, you can't open the breadbox. Smaller items on a warrant provide an excuse to look pretty much anywhere.

The list also included cell phone chargers and leather working tools. She reread the list. *No clothes.* They hadn't found anything with blood on it. That was a point in Ellen's favor.

Lia checked the bedroom. Someone rifled through the closet and dumped the hamper on the bed. *I bet they looked in the barbecue grill for the charred remains of bloody clothes.* The thought made her nauseous.

She returned to the kitchen to find the girls wolfing down the last of the kibble. They licked the bowls, then went to the back door, turning that stare on Lia. She let them out and sat on the porch steps.

The girls raced across the yard for exactly thirty seconds, then meandered serenely through the grass. *As if they hadn't spent the night with a hundred pit bulls.* Which wouldn't stop her from sending Cynth a mean text for calling animal control instead of asking her to take the dogs. *I suppose she had no choice. Deviate from protocol and the city gets sued.*

Ellen said Daniel was murdered with one of her leather awls. They already knew someone was impersonating Ellen. Easy peasy to frame her for murder if that person got their hands on her tools. That made more sense than Ellen magically knowing when she'd find Daniel lurking in the woods. Surely Cynth could see that.

Ellen volunteered her cameras. She wouldn't do that if she was guilty. Her fingerprints were in the system. You wouldn't leave your fingerprints on a murder weapon if they were on a federal database. But Ellen wasn't always logical. As she sat with her thoughts, Nati came up and nuzzled her. Time to go back inside. She scanned the yard for Connie.

Connie was gone.

Cynth left the gate open. She raced to the side of the house and found it shut, bolted, and padlocked. *Think, think. Where would one skinny dog go?*

Lia checked the other side of the house. No dog. *She can't jump over a six-foot fence, not at her age.*

Lia returned to the porch. The kitchen door was firmly shut. No dog door because anything big enough for the girls would be big enough for a hopped-up meth head. And if Connie could open doors, Lia would have seen her go past.

I should look inside anyway.

That's just silly.

She sat on the steps. Nati gave her a consolatory lick. *She ought to be freaking out.* She huffed in frustration and placed a hand on Nati's neck. "Where's your sister, girlfriend?"

Nati grinned.

She's laughing at me.

Lia stared at the ten-foot wall of green.

It stared back.

Then she heard the shush of rustling leaves.

She crossed the yard and knelt in the grass, peering through the tightly packed bamboo culms. *Nothing.* She switched on her phone's flashlight utility, playing the beam through the stalks. Connie's eyes reflected green, her invisible black body now showing in sharp relief.

Lia sat back in the grass. Nati licked Lia's ear.

"Think you're smart, don't you?" Nati gave her a bland look.

She stood, swiping grass off her shorts. "You can't be too traumatized if you can play pranks. I'm going inside. Stay, go, I don't care."

Game over, the girls followed her in and settled themselves on their bean bag chairs, posing with heads erect on elongated necks and front paws crossed, languid and elegant as Erté Art Deco models.

As Lia piled clothes back in the hamper, she heard the door open. Bailey entered with Kita, dropping her suitcase and staring at the disarray in Ellen's once pristine living room.

"It could be worse," Lia said. "They didn't break the door down."

"Goddess, it's bad enough. Why didn't they just ask for whatever it was they wanted?"

"They might have. And if Ellen said 'I don't have any bloody clothes because I didn't kill Daniel,' they still have to go through everything."

Bailey sank down next to Nati on her bean bag and stroked the sleek head. "At least they're calm now." She scanned the room. "The energy in here is so disrupted. I need to cleanse the black tourmaline I put here last year. I brought my tingshas and smudge sticks. I hope it's enough."

Lia poked her head in the fridge and came out with a pitcher of tea. She poured glasses for her and Bailey. "I fed the girls and let them out. They should be good for a while."

"What are we going to do?"

"There's not much we *can* do. We can take care of the dogs. We can try to convince Ellen to get a decent attorney."

"There has to be more."

"Cynth told us to back off. I don't want to cause more problems after the way I screwed up her operation."

"We didn't screw anything up. Nobody was there. Ellen's being railroaded. How many times do I need to say it?"

Lia took a long drink of tea, buying time to gather her thoughts. She needed to keep things simple. "You conk out by ten."

"So?"

"She could have slipped out."

"You think she spiked my chamomile tea with Ambien? You think she killed Daniel and was normal as pie the next morning?"

Nothing normal about a death notice, but not a productive point to argue. "You told me she said she'd never be free of Daniel until one of them was dead."

"People say stuff like that all the time."

"All I'm saying, there's a lot we don't know."

WENDY

Wendy found Dianne in Exhibition Hall, straightening the literature table. She waited until a group of giggling high schoolers passed by, then showed Dianne her phone and a video of Aubrey Morse.

"Have you seen this?"

Dianne flashed an impatient look. "What is it?"

"They arrested Ellen Brandt."

She tapped the play arrow. Tiny Aubrey spoke. "I'm standing in front of the home of Ellen Brandt, Daniel Moore's long-time domestic partner. Moore was murdered shortly after midnight Saturday night in Parker Woods Preserve, across the street from this residence." The screen jumped to a shot of the preserve entrance.

"Police arrested Brandt last night after fingerprints on the weapon found at the scene were determined to be hers. Brandt ended their relationship last year when Moore was indicted for the theft of dozens of client flutes from his repair shop."

Dianne shrugged. "Nothing to do with us."

"I can't believe she did it."

"Who else would it be?"

Wendy looked over her shoulder. A high traffic area at the entrance to Exhibition Hall was not the place for this conversation. She grabbed three bags of trash that had been stuffed under the table and shoved one at Dianne. "Let's take these out."

Dianne rolled her eyes. "Whatever." Outside the building, Dianne tossed her bag into the dumpster. "What are you worried about?"

Wendy used the excuse of shoving her bags in the bin to keep her face averted. "We were there."

"Ellen killed him, end of story."

"You went looking for Daniel. Did you see anything?"

"Of course not!"

"You were in an awful hurry to leave after you got back."

"I thought he wasn't coming, and staying was a waste of time. It happened after we left."

Wendy stared at Dianne. Dianne stared back.

Dianne grabbed her arms, gave her a quick shake. "Forget we were there."

"We could get arrested."

"We did nothing. They can't arrest us for doing nothing." She headed back to the building.

Wendy stared after her. *We did nothing.* But that wasn't entirely true.

LIA

The Justice Center consisted of a pair of irregularly shaped, windowless buildings on an enormous concrete plaza. They loomed behind the courthouse like something out of a sci-fi movie, becoming taller and more oppressive the closer they got.

Bailey broke the silence. "Is the depersonalization deliberate, or the result of functionality?"

"Chicken and egg. We're at the juncture of function and intent. There's no telling which came first. Looking at this place ought to be a deterrent."

They arrived ten minutes before visiting hours started. The trash-strewn lobby with its flickering overhead fluorescents and decades of ground-in dirt reminded Lia of too many dystopian movies. The line already snaked down the hall to the entrance, bypassing an out-of-use metal detector.

I guess they don't care if we shoot up a prisoner. Good thing, as her pepper spray was on her keyring and she had no desire to hike three blocks back to the car to stash it.

The waiting women dressed in the same cheap, not-quite-appropriate clothes she'd seen in court, but dirtier—or maybe that was the dingy light. She and Bailey inched forward, finally giving their names to the deputy on duty. The deputy checked them against whatever was on her computer and waved them through.

The elevator opened onto a long, crowded room with packed benches running down the side walls. A half-dozen booths lined the back, with handsets mounted on the partitions and stools bolted to the floor.

Just like the movies.

A depressing environment and a lot of trouble to see Ellen through plexiglass for fifteen minutes. *Probably bullet proof, explaining why they didn't bother to fix the metal detector.*

Ellen finally appeared in one of booths. Everything about her sagged: drooping posture, limp hair, rumpled clothes, dark circles under her eyes. She searched the room, relief in her eyes when she spotted Bailey. Lia followed

Bailey to the booth and stood behind her as she took the stool.

Ellen and Bailey picked up the receivers simultaneously. Bailey said, "How are you?"

Lia did her best to lip-read Ellen's response and caught *terrible* and *I have to get out of here.*

Bailey: "What did the judge say?"

Ellen: *No bail* and more Lia couldn't make out.

Bailey: "The dogs are fine. I'm staying at the house."

Ellen: *Thank You.*

They talked about the dogs. Then Bailey asked what the police had on her. Lia picked out a few phrases: *I was framed, you know that, right?* And *Who would do this to me?* And *I can't talk about it.*

At the end of fifteen minutes, Ellen hung up the receiver and placed her palm on the plexiglass. Bailey matched it, her long, lean, work-hardened hand dwarfing Ellen's small, more delicate one.

Another movie cliché.

Outside on the plaza, Lia asked, "What did she say?"

"Just that the lawyer said not to talk to anyone about the case, and knowing we're taking care of the girls keeps her sane."

Time to give Bailey a gentle nudge. "There's no reason not to tell us what the police said. There's something Ellen doesn't want us to know."

Bailey stopped in the middle of the flow of pedestrians and turned to Lia. "You're so suspicious. She's scared, and she's doing what her lawyer told her to do."

"I'm worried about you. The more you help her, the messier it gets. Now you're involved in a murder investigation."

Bailey stared at her, hard. "What did Peter tell you?"

Lia tried, but she held Bailey's eyes too long for a credible lie. *Not a lie. He hasn't told me anything, not yet.* "You know Peter can't tell me anything."

"Just because he can't doesn't mean he didn't. What did he tell you?"

Someone pushed past Lia, jogging her elbow. *Stupid, stupid, stupid.* They were surrounded by people, and she had no clue who they were. She jerked her head at a short brick wall away from pedestrian traffic.

"Let's go sit." Lia bit her lip until it hurt. "If anyone shared information with me about the investigation—which they haven't—do you expect me to break a confidence when it could get them fired? You need to ask Ellen. She owes you that much."

"How'd she get out? Astral projection? Hard to stab someone if you lack a corporeal body."

"Maybe you were asleep."

"We had this conversation yesterday. She didn't leave."

"It would help me if you explained how you know."

Bailey rolled her eyes. "Fine. We were watching *Meet Joe Black.*"

"Voluntarily? That's three mind-numbing, ridiculously self-important hours."

"Ellen's choice, not mine. I kept nodding off, so Ellen went back to her room to finish it. That was around ten-thirty. Funny thing, as soon as I stopped watching the movie, I woke up."

"I don't doubt it."

"I could hear the television."

"That's not conclusive."

"She never left her room. Kita always woofs when Ellen

goes to the bathroom in the middle of the night. She didn't wake me up until three. You can't tell me she met Daniel at three in the morning."

They didn't know time of death. *I need to fix that.*

"How did she know where to be? Ellen needs support. As my friend, you should want to help." Bailey jumped off the wall and stalked across the plaza. Lia ran to catch her, placing a hand on her arm. Bailey whipped around with an angry glare she'd never directed at Lia before.

Lia pulled her hand away, speaking with all the calm she could muster. "You're my best friend, and I've been watching Ellen's drama drag you down for more than a year. I'm scared this will cost you more than it already has."

Bailey's expression softened. "It's not her fault. She's in jail, she has no one on her side, and she's terrified. I have to help her, and I can't do it alone."

Lia put aside the question of what Ellen needed or how she was feeling. "You're my friend and I love you. If you need my help, you have it."

PETER

The usual suspects greeted Peter at the door when he arrived home with dinner from the mom and pop taqueria down the street from District 5. As he knelt to rub ears and ruffle neck fur, he caught the aroma of freshly baked bread. Lia only baked when she needed to pound something.

She knew.

She hadn't said anything when he texted about dinner. That was a bad sign. Lia was the reverse of most people.

The more upset she was, the longer it took her to say something about it. And when she finally talked, the more reasonable she was.

Satiated, the dogs turned their attention to sniffing at the bags of tacos and guacamole. Peter rescued dinner and stood up, calling, "Honey, I'm home." The Ricky Ricardo line was a joke between them. Today he used it to test the waters.

"I'm in the kitchen."

No stress in her voice. Her anger wasn't directed at him.

He found her at the sink, cleaning paint off her hands with a rag. He set the bags next to two loaves of cooling bread and wiped a smudge of green paint off her cheek with his thumb.

"You're working late."

"I lost most of my day rescuing Ellen's dogs and cleaning up the mess your storm troopers left in her house. Did you know?"

Snarky, but talking. Peter turned away, getting plates from the cabinet. "I heard. Cynth picked her up at work last night."

He nodded at the counter. "I'll trade you a taco for a slice of that bread." All three dogs stood by the counter, drooling. "Better give them some, too."

They settled into the routine of setting the table and serving dinner, the process buying a little time to make the coming conversation more comfortable.

He'd finished his first taco and half a beer when Lia asked, "What can you tell me? Ellen says you have fingerprints."

There was what he could tell her, which was next to nothing. Then there was what he would tell her to keep her out of it, which was everything. He had a sneaking suspicion that was why Cynth gave him chapter and verse on the case.

"Circle of trust?"

"Who's in the circle?"

"Right now, you and me. Not Bailey."

"How am I supposed to manage that?"

"You're a creative woman. You'll find a way."

Lia gave him the stinky fish eye. She took a bite of her taco, taking too long to chew and swallow. Finally, she lifted one shoulder in a shrug. "Okay. I'd rather be an informed person playing dumb than a smart person who doesn't have a clue."

"Atta girl."

"How about Cynth?"

"We're giving her plausible deniability."

"This secret squirrel stuff stinks. Spill."

"Cynth has a lot more than fingerprints. Daniel was staying with a woman named Florence Nygaard on Thompson Heights."

She shook her head. "I don't know where that is."

Peter launched the maps app on his phone, zeroing in on Parker Woods. He tapped the southwest corner. "This is Ellen on Haight." He maneuvered to the north boundary and tapped again. "Langland and Thompson Heights. Nygaard lives on this corner."

Lia's jaw dropped. "He could practically spit on Ellen from there. He must have been stalking her, just like she said."

"We believe Ellen knew where he was."

Lia looked up from his phone. She stared, gaping.

"She had access to his email and social media."

"How does Cynth know this?"

"Cynth took an old computer from the back room when they searched the house. They didn't bother with it when they arrested Moore because nobody uses CRT displays anymore and Ellen said it was hers. Cynth turned it on just to see if it would boot up."

"Is she supposed to do that? Aren't you supposed to clone electronics?"

"She didn't want to bother the tech guys if it was dead. Then it was in for a penny, in for a pound. She shouldn't have done it and she might get slapped for it later. Anyway, it's so old, there's no password to sign on. But the browser saved passwords for online accounts.

"When Cynth opened Facebook, Daniel's account popped up. It opened right up. Same for his email and his bank."

Lia shook her head in disgust. "Ellen was stalking him, not the other way around."

"They could have been stalking each other."

"I feel like an idiot. There were times Ellen said Daniel was doing something—trying to con someone out of money, or spreading lies about her, stuff like that. I kept asking Bailey how Ellen could possibly know. Bailey just said Ellen lived with him for thirty years."

"But she didn't know he was a crook."

"Doesn't add up, does it?"

Peter took the last taco. "She may have kept tabs on him to protect herself, or for any number of reasons. Haven't you ever checked up on an ex?"

"I never cared to. But I never felt threatened by an ex."

"The interesting question is why Daniel never changed

his passwords. You'd think that would be the first thing he did after he got out of jail."

"Daniel was lazy. I bet he told himself she wouldn't dare get into his stuff—"

"Or maybe they were playing games with each other. The important thing, love of my life, is stay out of it. Don't get caught up in figuring out what really happened. The details don't matter. We have her on this."

"Bailey's too fragile right now. I can't abandon her and she won't abandon Ellen. She'll never believe Ellen got out of the house without waking her up."

Peter sighed. "Can you find a way to be Bailey's friend without falling down the rabbit hole with her?"

6

DAY 5

THURSDAY, AUGUST 14

LIA

THE GANG JAMMED INTO THE LONE PICNIC TABLE IN MOUNT Airy Dog Park's small dog enclosure, a space the size of a large back yard with no shade. Kita and Chester lay on top amid an obstacle course of coffee cups, Chester on his back, hopeful for belly rubs.

Gypsy head-butted Lia. She obligingly lobbed the ball laying at her feet. Gypsy chased it past the girls, who meandered in the naked grass, graceful and slightly alien. Chewy flopped in the grass, bored after a much shorter and less interesting perimeter check than usual.

"We're happy to see you," Steve told Bailey, "But does it have to be on this side?"

"It's either here or not at all. Ellen would melt down like Chernobyl if she knew I brought the girls here."

"I don't get why Ellen makes such a fuss about it," Lia said.

"It's the dug up mole tunnels on the other side. Greyhound legs are fragile. One wrong step could snap a bone."

"I saw animal burrows at Wesleyan big enough to swallow a small child."

"She worries about aggressive dogs, too. Their skin tears so easily."

Lia raised her eyebrows. "Aggressive dogs, but not coyotes?"

"We're all irrational about our fur babies."

"How is Ellen doing?" Steve asked.

Bailey snapped. "She's locked up for a murder she didn't commit. How do you think she's doing?" She took a deep breath. "Sorry, Ellen has me taking care of her stuff on top of everything else. I guess I'm a bit on edge."

"Their only evidence is an awl?" Jim asked.

"And fake text messages claiming to be from her," Bailey said.

Lia focused on scooping up the sopping ball Gypsy laid at her feet. She hurled the ball as far as she could, watching it arc across the park as an excuse to keep her face averted.

I know nothing. I know nothing. I know nothing.

"How did someone get one of her tools?" Steve asked. "She throw a party recently?"

Bailey crinkled her forehead, bit her lip. Then her mouth dropped into an "O." "I know how they did it."

"Who did what?" Steve asked.

"Whoever framed Ellen. I know how it was done."

Terry's eyebrows raised. "Do tell."

"Ellen didn't have a party. She went to one. Remember Dog Day?"

Face under control, Lia returned to the conversation. "That feels like forever ago."

"It was Saturday," Bailey said. "Ellen brought tools."

"I remember. She had to punch an extra hole in Chewy's collar."

"What time was that?" Bailey asked.

"Two-ish? Maybe three? Peter and I got home about four."

"Did you see a ceramic cup shaped like the head of a poodle?"

"A poodle cup? I'm surprised I didn't notice it."

"Someone filched it. Ellen kept spare tools in it."

Jim said, "You think the murder weapon was in that cup?"

"I'm sure it was," Bailey said.

"Why would anyone kill over an instrument?" Terry asked.

Bailey's hands did their butterfly dance as she gathered her thoughts. "Flutes are individuals, like people. They don't feel alike, they don't sound alike, they don't respond alike. The right flute is a friend that brings out the best in you."

Steve said, "Like, a dog isn't worth killing over, but *my* dog is worth killing over."

Bailey continued, "What Daniel did was like kidnapping dozens of family pets while telling people he would give them back—"

"And never doing it? That could drive someone crazy." Steve scratched Penny's ears. "If he did that to Penny, I'd kill him."

Lia said, "When did you realize the cup was missing?"

"Ellen noticed it when we were packing up. Neither one of us remembered seeing it after lunch."

Terry looked skeptical. "Someone saw Ellen's tools at her booth and thought, 'Why not kill Daniel tonight?'"

"They could have planned it," Lia said. "Everyone at the sentencing knew Ellen would be there with sharp implements. Anyone stalking her on social media would know."

Jim scratched his beard. "They'd be able to tell if someone else used Ellen's awl, even if the killer used gloves. Her prints would be smudged."

Terry turned to Lia. "We need to see the lab report."

Lia snorted. "Sure, I'll just ask Cynth to email it to me."

Bailey said, "How do we know the prints aren't smudged? We have to do something."

"You're the witness," Lia said. "Call Cynth and tell her what you told us."

"Cynth thinks I'm a nutcase."

"No, she doesn't," Lia lied.

Terry said, "We need to tell Aubrey Morse. Then the idiots at homicide have to listen. I'll do it if you won't."

Steve said, "You just want an excuse to talk to a hot blonde and get on television."

Terry shrugged. "It's a sacrifice I'm willing to make."

"Plan your funeral first," Lia said. "Because that move will bring the wrath of Cynth down on you like napalm." She turned to Bailey. "I'll text Cynth and tell her you have information. Important information."

CYNTH

Bailey always looked a bit wacky. Today she was wacky times five, her pop-eyes wide with intensity as her fingers scrabbled on the arms of Cynth's visitor's chair. If she didn't know better, she'd think Bailey was having a bad drug episode. Whatever her opinion, she needed to be polite.

"I agreed to see you, but I can't talk about cases, especially not with people who are involved."

"Fine," Bailey said. "I'll talk. Ellen said Daniel was killed with an awl and it had her fingerprints on it."

"And your point?"

"Someone framed her. It was Dog Day."

Dogs framed Brandt? Maybe she was mistaken about the drugs. She leaned back in her chair with folded arms, schooling all expression from her face.

"Explain."

"Spring Grove Cemetery hosts Dog Day every summer. Ellen always has a booth for Greyhound Adoption of Greater Cincinnati."

The penny dropped. "Dog Day is the event you mentioned last week."

"Charity booths, a wading pool for the dogs, a 5K, stuff like that. It's the only time they allow dogs inside the cemetery. Sometimes it doesn't go well if dogs misbehave. Ellen sells leatherwork to raise money. I help with the booth."

Cynth had no clue where this was going, but impatience wouldn't help. "And?"

"Someone stole a mug full of tools she used for customizing collars."

The back of Cynth's skull throbbed, threatening to blow up into a major headache.

"You think someone took the tools and used one to kill Daniel?"

"Only if Ellen's fingerprints were smudged. Were they smudged?"

"What part of 'I can't talk cases' did you not get?"

Bailey chewed her lip, defeated.

"I'll tell you this much. The texts started before Saturday. The person who killed Daniel Moore planned it long before Ellen's mug of tools ended up on that table."

Bailey popped up, the intensity back on her face. "That doesn't matter. Everyone knew she would be there."

"Define everyone."

"Ellen invited everyone at the sentencing and said she had gifts for them."

Cynth hated that she could put it together.

"So a handful of Daniel Moore's most rabid victims knew when Ellen would be in a busy spot with sharp implements."

"More. She posted about it on Facebook."

Where hundreds of musicians had been vilifying Moore for two years. Anyone stalking him online could stalk Brandt as well. "And the sharp instruments were accessible?"

"Pretty much."

Cynth shoved a legal pad across the desk, added a pen. "Show me."

Bailey sketched a square on the pad with quick strokes, then drew two horizontal rectangles inside the square. "GAGC had an eight by eight canopy with two tables. The front table was for literature and finished leather goods. The one in the back held supplies and a workspace for customizing the collars. Stamping names or adding holes, things like that." She added a square and some circles on the left side of the rear table. "This is the workspace." She pointed at the circles. "These are the jars she used to hold her tools."

"Which one was stolen?"

Bailey pointed to the circle closest to the edge. "It was a handmade poodle mug."

"She kept her tools in a fancy mug? Where anyone could snatch it?"

Bailey shrugged.

"You're sure that's where it was?"

Bailey picked up her phone. "I have photos."

Why didn't you just say so?

Bailey handed her the phone. Ellen smiled back at her, presiding over an array of fancy collars. Cynth pinched out the screen. Behind Ellen, tools exploded like angry thoughts out of the poodle head. She pinched out the screen more and spotted a brown wood handle identical to the one sitting in evidence.

Cynth kept her face bland, as if she were only going through the motions. "You were at the booth all day?"

"Ellen shooed me away when Lia and Peter came. We spent at least an hour wandering around."

"When did you notice the mug missing?"

"I spent most of the afternoon talking to people. I wasn't paying attention to anything behind me. Ellen noticed it when we packed up."

"What's your best guess when it disappeared?"

Bailey rubbed her throat. "We set up at eight-thirty and the crowd thinned out around two. I doubt it happened after that."

"Who came by the booth?"

"Hopewell isn't far from Spring Grove. I'm sure plenty of people from the school were there. I saw Lois and K Lee. Wendy came, but she didn't lose a flute. She wouldn't have done it. She was with Dianne. Dianne couldn't steal it without Wendy seeing her. I don't think it was her, not unless Wendy was in on it. I can't see that. But the mug was behind us. Anyone could have come down the side of the booth and taken it. It was that crowded."

Cynth stood and walked around her desk to the door, signaling an end to the meeting. "Thank you for bringing this to me. We'll look into it."

Bailey leaned in close, grabbing her hand with an iron grip you wouldn't expect. The whites showed around those deranged eyes. "You have to get her out. She doesn't belong in there."

Cynth hefted the murder book onto her hip and rang Lia's doorbell. The interior erupted with barking dogs. Lia's voice called from the back of the house.

"Coming."

This is a bad idea. She asked herself for the dozenth time what she was doing. The answer remained the same. *We moved too fast. Now there are questions.*

An hour earlier, Cynth called Lia to tell her Bailey was coming unglued. Lia countered with a request to see the murder book so she could figure a way to get Bailey to chill out.

Concern about Bailey's state of mind wouldn't be enough to get her to do something this stupid, but she and Brent were coming up empty. Fresh eyes could help.

Lia opened the door. Cynth waded through swarming dogs and wagging tails. The dogs followed, settling down to watch when they arrived at Lia's studio.

"Do they stare at you like that all day?"

"You're a novelty. I rarely get visitors in the middle of the day."

"It's creepy." Cynth set the huge binder on Lia's work table. "I don't know why I'm doing this."

Lia dragged an extra stool over, patting it in an invitation to sit. "Because you love me?"

"You aren't my type."

"I'm *crushed*."

"I'm pissed. Is Brandt really so brainless she didn't think to tell us someone stole her tools hours before Daniel was killed?"

"She didn't tell you she was framed?"

"Sure she did. She gave us the usual bullshit we hear from dirtbags and left out the part where someone got one of her awls."

"Maybe it hasn't occurred to her yet."

Cynth opened the binder, ran a finger down the tabs, and turned to a section in the middle. "I'm not saying I buy her story."

"It's Bailey's story. She unpacked the tools when they set up. They were gone at the end of the day."

"About that, why did you inflict Bailey on me? You could have told me."

"She's the witness. It's only hearsay coming from me."

"So Ellen put her spare tools in a poodle mug any larcenous dog lover would take because it was cute. The way Bailey described it, it was the next thing to parking your car in a dark alley and leaving keys in the ignition."

"Truth. Thank you for bringing the file."

"Pieces of the autopsy came in from the coroner's office this morning, but the final report hasn't been written yet. I haven't had time to do more than glance at it."

She set the binder on Lia's work table. "I must be out of my mind. I'll be busted to crossing guard if Arseneault finds out. Bailey is outside the cone of silence. You can't let her know you saw this."

"Understood. I'll find a way to redirect Bailey that doesn't involve you."

Cynth turned the binder so Lia could see a photo of an awl with a fat, blood-smeared shaft. The awl had a steel bezel at the base of the shaft and a shellacked wood handle. Judging by the ruler next to the awl, the shaft was four inches long.

"We can't get an exact tool match because Moore's killer jammed this into his carotid, then ripped it around. Either widening the wound to get a nice spray, or Daniel jerked his head and that did it. But we know it was a fat spike and the blood matches. Junior found it underneath the body when he moved it."

"Was Daniel face up or face down?"

"Face up. You're wondering how the awl wound up under the body. Could be a number of things. It's not important."

"It's still weird."

Cynth said nothing, flipping to a photo of the awl after it had been dusted for fingerprints. The largest print—the thumb—overlapped the bezel with smaller prints side by side in a vertical stack down the handle.

"No defensive wounds. Moore let his killer up close and wasn't expecting an attack. We know from the text messages he expected to see Ellen. Think about it. It's midnight in an urban park. Would you let a stranger walk up to you?"

"Daniel knew his killer."

"If it wasn't Ellen, it was someone he felt comfortable encountering in a secluded spot. That leaves out dozens of angry clients he ripped off."

Cynth turned to a diagram of a neck and shoulders that showed the downward angle of penetration from the front and side, with measurements scribbled underneath.

Lia frowned at the drawing. "I thought he was stabbed in the carotid. I can't imagine this would be fatal."

"Slipped behind the clavicle and hit the subclavian artery. You never hear about that one."

"It's almost vertical. An overhand strike, then."

"Only way to pull it off, unless Moore was doing a backbend."

Lia grabbed a screwdriver from a jar of paintbrushes. She returned to the fingerprint photo and arranged her hold to mimic the prints, with her thumb where the bezel would be.

"Like this?"

Cynth gave a nod.

"This is how I would hold it if I was piercing leather." She picked up a loose piece of paper and punched the screwdriver through it.

Cynth shrugged.

Lia stood and dropped her hand down by her side, then swung the awl up in an underhand arc. Gypsy jumped up, snapping at the screwdriver like it was a new toy. Lia held it out of reach and pointed at a cushion. "Go to bed."

Gypsy gave her a hard stare and didn't move.

"Now!"

Gypsy dropped her head and slunk away.

"Girlfriend is stubborn." Lia held the screwdriver up. "This works if I want to jab him in the crotch."

She swung the awl overhead, then twisted her arm so it pointed downward. "Awkward way to stab someone in the neck. Can't get any leverage, especially when you're nine inches shorter than your target."

"Shit."

Lia reversed the screwdriver, holding it in the classic position from the shower scene in *Psycho*, her thumb covering the bottom of the handle. She stabbed downward a few times. "Wouldn't you hold it this way?"

"It's not conclusive."

"Here," Lia said, handing Cynth the screwdriver. She pulled a shallow wood crate from under her work table and stepped up on it. "This makes me about nine inches taller than you. I'm Daniel, and I think you're dying to reconcile with me."

She held her arms open, as if expecting a hug. "Try to stab me."

"I'm ready to do that anyway," Cynth muttered. She held the screwdriver with the shaft pointed skyward and brought her arm up. She rotated her elbow up to point the shaft down for the correct angle of entry. Lia stepped back as she brought it down.

Gypsy growled low in her corner.

"Hush," Lia said. "You know Cynth. She won't hurt me."

Gypsy turned her head away, resting it on her paws.

"Girlfriend, I love that you want to protect me, but today is not the day." Gypsy huffed and continued to stare at the wall. Chewy held his head high and grinned. "See? Chewy isn't worried." Viola strolled out of the room, bored.

"Do you always talk to them?"

"They're wonderful listeners."

Still holding the screwdriver with the underhand grip, Cynth jabbed a few times. "You're right. No leverage."

They resumed their positions and Cynth tried again, this time sweeping her arm out to the side and twisting the screwdriver as she came down. Again, Lia dodged her.

"Time consuming, and telegraphing your moves," Lia said. "The first time you had to raise the screwdriver high enough for me to see it before you could turn it over. The second time, your arm moving sideways registered as the start of a slap."

Cynth narrowed her eyes. Reversing the screwdriver, she stepped in and placed her free hand on Lia's chest. "Oh, Daniel," she cooed, batting her eyelashes. "I've missed you so. I've been a fool."

As she held Lia's eyes, she brought the screwdriver up between them and had the point at Lia's throat before she could move.

"I didn't see your hand until it was by my collarbone, and I couldn't tell you were holding something. If I'd been Daniel, I would have thought you wanted to hug me or pull my head down for a kiss."

Cynth stepped back, giving several powerful jabs with the reversed screwdriver. "Yeah, this is how I'd do it." She snorted with disgust. "This is problematic, but it's not conclusive. They *are* Brandt's prints. Nice clean ones."

"No chance Daniel's killer wore gloves?"

"That's a question for the experts, but doubtful."

"Then this wasn't the awl that killed Daniel."

Cynth knew the answer, but asked anyway. "And the blood?"

"I'm sure Daniel had plenty to spare." Lia flipped back

several pages in the binder. "You plan to repeat our demo with Brent?"

"Might be the best way to get the point—pun intended—across."

"While terrorizing Brent."

"A small side benefit."

Lia skimmed the report, stopping at the diagram of the neck and pointing to a scrawled notation. "According to your photo, the business end of the awl is four inches long. This says the wound track is four and a half inches."

"There's going to be some tissue compression with a forceful strike. That could account for the difference."

"But you'd have to jam the awl up to the hilt, right?"

Cynth nodded. "And?"

Lia returned to the first photo of the awl. "No blood on the bezel. And wouldn't there be a bruise where the bezel pressed into the skin?" She leafed through morgue photos till she came to a close-up of the neck wound, then traced a crescent over the top. "Wouldn't you have a mark of some kind right here?"

"Dammit, I need to talk to Jeffers."

Lia looked back at the diagram, then picked up the screwdriver again. "Something else is wonky."

Cynth felt her temples throb. "Please don't tell me."

"This is a left-handed grip. Your killer was facing Daniel. The wound should be on Daniel's right. It's on his left."

"Crap. This is what happens when you move too fast. You can't tell Brandt. Or Bailey."

"You're going to ignore this?"

"Of course not. But Langston is the kind of prick who will tell me to go play with my taser because he's the expert. I have to figure out how to proceed. More than one person in the food chain will want to dismiss this, and if they can't dismiss it, they may want to shoot the messenger."

Only makes it worse that we warned them.

Cynth continued, "They'll drop the charges with the understanding we are continuing the investigation and may file again later. But it will take time."

"So I act surprised when you cut her loose?"

"That would be best."

"When will you let her out?"

"That's up to the DA. Worst case, he may not let her go."

"But—"

"—I can't snap my fingers and get her released. I promise we will look at other people. We have to now. But this doesn't exonerate Brandt. It just means we don't have a solid case yet. If we go to trial with this, the right defense attorney will create reasonable doubt on this alone."

"Fat chance of that. Ellen refuses to pay for an attorney."

"Then that's her problem." Cynth sighed. "Look, if she doesn't get released, tell her to demand a speedy trial. That's her right. Even Charles effing Hobbs won't want to go to court without the murder weapon nailed down. Whatever happens, keep your mouth shut. And I never showed you *any* of this."

"But—"

Cynth put on her fierce face. "—I will be fired for showing you this file. I have to claim I figured this out on my own. You can't tell anyone about this. Not Bailey, not even Peter."

Lia's eyes widened. "I don't keep anything from Peter."

"You want to put him in a rotten position? I wasn't here. You know exactly what Bailey told you about the stolen tools, nothing more. If you can't keep mum about the rest, tell me now. I promise to bury your body in a pretty spot. I'll say nice things at your funeral when we finally declare you legally dead. Peter will grieve, but you can't fix everything."

LIA

Lia stood in her open door, biting her lip as she watched Cynth pull away. At her feet, Gypsy whimpered. She knelt and ruffled the motley ears. Jealous, Chewy butted her hand. She gave him a hug.

"You are just the perfect little man, little man." She turned to Gypsy. "As for you, what got into you today? You know better."

Gypsy propped her front paws on Lia's thigh, stretching up to lick her face.

"Poor baby. You were just looking out for me. But Cynth is a friend."

How could I be so wrong? She'd hoped to find an angle, something she could turn into a vague hint, a possibility that needed to be considered, a toehold in rationality, anything to pull Bailey out of the morass that was Ellen. Instead, she proved Ellen was framed.

And she couldn't tell her.

I have to say something. She sat on the floor with the dogs in her lap, rubbing her cheek against fur as she thought. It had been three hours since Bailey met with Cynth. She had to be bouncing off the walls.

She pulled out her phone. Bailey answered on the first ring.

"Thank the Goddess. I tried to call earlier, but it went to voicemail."

"Sorry, I was painting. How did it go with Cynth?"

"I—I don't really know. You know how it is with Cynth, she can go all cop and she's impossible to read."

"I think they teach that at the academy. Cop Face 101. Did she at least listen to you?"

"She asked questions and had me draw a diagram of the booth to show her where everything was."

"That's legit. It means she took you seriously."

"You think so?"

"It's Cynth. She doesn't placate people. What did she say?"

"She said she'd look into it. But that could mean anything."

"That's all she can say."

"But Ellen's still in jail."

"It will take time. They have to look at everything again and she doesn't have final say."

"What if they don't let her go?"

"Then you get up on the witness stand and tell your story. You hand the jury reasonable doubt and Ellen comes home. Double jeopardy applies, so they won't be able to charge her again. We need to be patient. Have you talked to Ellen about the stolen tools?"

"She hasn't called yet. I don't know what to tell her."

"Tell her nothing. If she brings it up, act like it's new to you and be helpful."

"That's dishonest."

"No, that's not getting Ellen excited about something that won't happen for a while. It's slowing things down so Cynth can do her job."

CYNTH

Cynth drove up the hill, working through her next steps. *This could blow up in my face. Need my ducks in a row before I go to Arseneault.*

She needed an objective review of the evidence before she torpedoed the case. She wished she knew Langston better. New guy struck her as hostile to criticism and prone to passive aggression. He'd ask her where she got her medical degree and tell her to take a hike. If he shut her down, she'd have to go over his head and that would be a mess.

Can't risk it, not if it turns out to be nothing.

Maybe Jeffers is back.

She trusted Jeffers. If there was nothing to it, it wouldn't go any further. If Jeffers supported Lia's theory—*scratch that. As of now, this is my theory*—she'd have to take it to Arseneault ASAP.

Handing him an open can of worms.

Politics is his job. He said so.

What to do with Brent? She didn't care to examine her motives, but she wanted to keep him out of it until she had it worked out. No matter what, they still needed to nail down everything she'd pointed out to Charles effing Hobbs. Plenty of that to keep him busy.

She drove past District 5, heading up Hamilton Avenue toward Ronald Reagan Highway, the fastest route to the morgue. Decision made, she pulled over and called Brent. He answered on the second ring.

"Hey, boss. Where are you? I stopped by your office, but you were gone."

The best defense is a good offense. "How are you coming with the electronics?"

A long pause, then, "The guy assigned to Moore's phone had a medical emergency, and it fell into a black hole. I reamed Tech a new one. They promised it to us tomorrow. They loaded Brandt's clones onto my laptop an hour ago. Lots of calls and texts between Brandt and Bailey, but we knew that."

"Anything that supports our case?"

"Nothing that makes my spidey sense tingle, but it's early days. She doesn't have the Tile app."

"She could have deleted it."

"I thought of that. I asked the tech guy to dig to see if she ever had it. He said it'll be next week before he can get to it."

"I'm more interested in her communications. Can you read through those texts?"

"You sure this is what you want me doing? You've always been so much faster at analyzing data."

"Suck it up, buttercup. This is an opportunity to upgrade your skills."

"You're so thoughtful, boss."

"I'm done for the day. Since we've been on this since Sunday, I'm taking comp time tomorrow. You might want to do the same."

"Um, yeah, I might do that. With Brandt behind bars, there's no urgency."

As she ended the call, the words popped into her head as if Brent teleported them there: *Comp time, my ass.*

7

DAY 6

FRIDAY, AUGUST 15

CYNTH

THE TEXT CAME AT SEVEN A.M.

> Parker: My office 08:00 7:00 AM

Not good, not on my day off. If Parker wanted her to have more information, she would have called. Saying nothing meant she didn't want Cynth to have time to prepare before the meeting. Whatever it was, was serious and Parker was furious. At her? For what? Best play was to stay noncommittal. She texted back:

> Cynth: I'll be there 7:01 AM

She thought about calling Brent to see what he knew, but whatever the problem, better to be legitimately clueless when Parker brought it up. Stomach churning, she skipped breakfast and opted for a travel mug of black coffee, knowing full well it would burn in her gut.

She arrived at Parker's office ten minutes early. Parker's admin said, "She's with someone. Have a seat."

Usually chatty, Donna turned her face to her computer monitor, shutting Cynth out. Seven minutes later, the door opened and Brent came out. He gave her a cryptic look as he left, heading for the lobby instead of his office.

Cynth waited, vibrating with anxiety. At eight exactly, Donna's phone beeped. After three seconds of conversation, she hung up.

"You can go in now."

Cynth entered. Parker nodded at the visitor's chair. "Have a seat."

Cynth sat, the heat from Brent's recently departed glutes seeping through her pants in an odd intimacy that made her squirm.

"We have a problem."

"Sir?"

"Did you see the news last night?"

"No, sir."

Parker swung her laptop around. A paused video featured a frozen Aubrey Morse in front of familiar trees. *Parker Woods.* Cynth's already queasy stomach sank like lead. Parker punched the play arrow.

Morse's stoplight red lips moved. "Eight days ago, Daniel Moore walked into Parker Woods Preserve to meet estranged domestic partner Ellen Brandt. Instead of the reconciliation he expected, he was stabbed in the neck. He bled out on this spot. Police arrested Brandt after fingerprints on a bloody awl found with the body were identified as hers."

Old news, so what's the crisis?

"Today, a source within the police department spoke on condition of anonymity, saying Brandt claimed the awl had been stolen from her prior to Daniel Moore's murder. Further examination of the awl proves it could not have been used to kill Moore.

"No other evidence connects Brandt to Moore's death. Despite the existence of exculpatory evidence, Ellen Brandt remains in jail, victim of an attempt to frame her."

Cynth watched in stunned silence. When the story was over—a mere thirty seconds that lasted ten years—she looked up, shaking her head. "How the hell did that get out?"

Parker's voice was deadly dry. "That's what the DA wants to know. Who knew about the fingerprints?"

Cynth called on everything she knew about dishonesty tells to lie to Parker, something she never thought she'd do. Eye contact, but not prolonged. A fast, absolute denial, but don't go on about it. Avoid fidgeting, and whatever you do, don't touch your face.

"No one. Jeffers, Arseneault. That's it."

"Arseneault says you know Morse's cameraman."

"Duff is a cousin."

"And you enlisted him to get Morse away from the crime scene. Did you exchange information for that favor?"

She didn't need to fake shock. "No, sir! It wasn't a quid pro quo. I fed him a fake tip so they wouldn't follow us to Moore's residence."

"You lied to your cousin, who I presume you've known all your life?"

"The situation called for it, sir."

"What did you tell him?"

"I said we saw the woman who discovered the body walking a great Dane on Haight, and they might catch her if they hurried. That's it."

"She own a great Dane?"

"I have no idea."

"You do this often?"

"They've never been at one of my crime scenes before. My cases don't warrant media attention."

Parker sighed. "Any idea how this got out?"

There was Brent's long-standing flirtation with Morse. Hold that back and lose trust. Talk and throw Brent under the bus. Maybe she could thread the needle.

"Sir, Davis is friendly with Morse."

"Is he now?"

"But he didn't know about the awl."

"You didn't tell your partner?"

"Arseneault asked me to stay mum. We figured the fewer people who knew, the better." She'd held it back because she was a spiteful bitch, but no need to make herself look bad.

Parker, tapping tented fingertips, giving her that assessing look. "I see."

"Davis wouldn't feed her something like this, anyway."

"And what would he feed her?"

How should I know? "He wouldn't. He knows how to make it sound like he's giving you something when he gives you nothing."

"Like sending a reporter after a non-existent witness?"

"I have no clue what happened. I told Jeffers and Arseneault. Nobody else." *The honest truth. I didn't tell Lia.*

She told me. "I never wrote anything down. Not a text, not a post-it." Lia could have told Peter, and Peter could have told Brent. *Maybe he traded for sexual favors. No, not going there.* If Lia told Bailey, Bailey would call Morse because Brandt was still stuck in jail.

But Lia knows what's at stake.

"The DA will have someone's head for this. Arseneault wants you and Davis off the case until this is resolved, if only to make the DA happy. I told him my people don't get dinged until he proves they did something wrong."

"Thank you, sir."

"Don't thank me yet. If you did this, you won't have a head left for the DA to take."

"I swear to you, I didn't do this."

"There will be a lot of finger pointing. Expect internal affairs to call. If you have any ideas about the source of the leak, float them by me first. Say the wrong thing to the wrong person, and it won't matter that it wasn't you."

BRENT

Brent leaned against one of the ugly yellow bollards protecting the entrance to District 5, wishing he still smoked. A stupid adolescent habit perfectly suited for fuming and one that gave legitimacy to loitering on a strip mall sidewalk.

Cynth barreled out the door, nearly running into him.

"Careful, sweet cheeks. I might think you like me."

"Screw you."

"In front of the teeming masses? What will they think?"

Cynth glared. She wanted to punch him, he knew it. He pushed off the bollard. "Let's take Celeste for a drive."

"Why would I go anywhere with you?"

"You want to hash this out here?"

He strolled to his beloved midnight blue Audi A4, clicking the fob to unlock the doors. Cynth slunk back in the passenger seat, arms folded tightly across her chest.

Brent said, "No feet on the dashboard. You scuff the walnut inlay and I will toss you off Ludlow Viaduct."

Cynth made a scoffing sound and looked out the side window as he headed south on Hamilton Avenue. She said nothing until they entered the Northside business district.

"Where are we going?"

"Wesleyan."

"What the hell for?"

"I hear tell that's where Brainard takes his girlfriends when he's on patrol."

"You wish."

He kept his eyes on the road. "We're going there so all of District 5 won't hear it when you yell at me for no reason."

"Ha ha."

"If we're lucky, we'll run into a drug dealer you can punch out. Don't talk. You'll only get madder and I'm driving. I do not want to run over a pedestrian. It would ruin what's left of my day."

He saw her glower out of the corner of his eye.

"And will Celeste's suspension survive Wesleyan?"

A legitimate concern, not that he'd admit it. "My girl is tough."

Brent pulled into the cemetery, parking behind the ancient brick garage inexplicably located atop the ridge bisecting the cemetery. Cynth jumped out before he could turn off the ignition. She slammed the door, stomping away. He exited the car and leaned against it.

Rage vibrated off her as she spun around. "Did it bother you to trade my career for sexual favors from Ashley? Was that a bonus? Did you consider me at all?"

"Is that what you told Parker?"

"Of course not. What do you think I am?"

"The question is what you think I am. For the record, you occupy my thoughts every time I look in the damn mirror."

"Oh, get over yourself. Nobody sees the bump on your nose except you."

"Now explain to me how I leaked information that I— as the only other member of your team—was not privy to."

Guilt flashed on her face, gone before he was sure he'd seen it. She looked away, mumbling, "There was a path for you to get it."

"Care to explain that?"

"You did it to get even with me for not telling you. You did it to screw me over and get ahead."

"How does leaking to Aubrey accomplish that?"

"Future favors. Good press when you need it. How should I know?"

"You're the one getting all sweaty with her cameraman." Not true according to Ashley, but as long as she wanted him to believe it, he'd oblige her. "Why shouldn't I think it was you?"

She shoved him. "Leave Duff out of this."

He shoved her back.

She brought her fist up in a wide arc, aiming for his face.

Brent grabbed her arm, twisting it behind her back. "You're slipping. You were tougher when we met."

She stomped his instep, pain making him stumble.

He repressed a grunt. "For the record, I let you break my nose."

"Yeah? You let me dislocate your shoulder, too?"

He twisted her arm up a notch. "Do I have to cuff you to get you to listen?"

"Go screw yourself."

"Cuffs it is, then."

Cynth slipped out of his grip and punched him in the eye. She pivoted, preparing to deliver a roundhouse kick. Brent tackled her. He lay along her back, gritting into her ear, "No more Mr. Nice Guy."

Cynth flipped over, rolling him until she straddled his hips.

Her heat pressed into him. Blood flooded his groin, surging into a monster erection.

Cynth jumped up as if burned. "Asshole."

"You were the one grinding your crotch into my junk. Don't give me a lap dance and complain about the result."

"It's all about sex with you."

"Actually, it isn't. Which you ought to know."

Cynth snorted.

"I didn't do it and you didn't do it. Beating each other up plays into the hands of the person who did. We need to figure out who that is."

"If you didn't do it, why did you expect me to yell at you?"

"Since when have you stopped to think before yelling at me?"

Cynth looked steadily at him. Finally, she said, "You're getting one hell of a shiner."

"At least I don't need the hospital this time."

"That's debatable." She held out her hand. Brent took it and she hauled him up.

"When did you plan to tell me about the awl?"

"I had orders."

"Let's not repeat the past."

"What are you talking about?"

"Things blew up back then because we didn't talk. I should have trusted you."

"No." The air went out of her. She looked at him, deflated. "That's stupid. You didn't know who was involved."

"So let's talk."

"Have a seat. I'll grab some ice across the street."

She got in the car, turned on the ignition.

Brent yelled, "Don't bottom out Celeste."

CYNTH

Cynth braked at the Wesleyan gates, waiting for traffic to clear on Colerain.

Why jump on Brent like that? She'd bet her Mustang he wasn't the leak. Now they were both stirred up in ways she didn't want to contemplate. She needed time to think before she did something else stupid.

She stared at her phone, wishing it was 11:00 so she could order pizza. Then she sent a text.

Cynth: Picking up breakfast. I promise to come back. 8:53 AM

Brent: No White Castle. 8:53 AM

Cynth: You get what I give you. 8:54 AM

Brent: You're a hard woman. 8:54 AM

Cynth: Be thankful it's not pickle pizza. 8:54 AM

White Castle was the only place open. He'd have to live with sliders and he knew it. She needed more information. She pulled into the line of cars at White Castle and tapped Lia's face on her contact list, making the call she dreaded.

Lia's voice sounded worried. "Cynth?"

"Are you alone? You aren't at the dog park with a bunch of your friends?"

"I'm in the back. There's no one in shouting distance. What's up?"

"You see the news last night?"

"Who watches the news?"

"Not us, apparently. Who did you tell about the awl?"

Shocked silence on the other end. Then, "No one. You said not to."

"Not Bailey? Not Peter?"

"I didn't want to end up in a shallow grave."

Cynth waited a beat, but Lia didn't continue. "I know you. You said something."

"Of course I said something. I let Bailey tell me about her meet with you. Then I told her to be patient and not tell Ellen because we didn't want to get her hopes up. I told Peter what Bailey said, and that I sent her to you. That's it. Nothing to anyone about you coming over. Peter's under the impression I'm staying out of it and I feel like a jerk. What's wrong?"

"Aubrey Morse knows. She told the entire world. It's on YouTube."

"No! How did she find out?"

"Wouldn't the DA like to know."

"It wasn't me, I swear."

"Okay. That means it wasn't Brent, either."

"Brent? How could you think that?"

"I didn't, not really. He was the handiest target."

"That poor man. What are you going to do?"

Cynth ignored the guilt that had been niggling her since she took Brent's car. "About Brent? Nothing. He's a big boy."

A ping sounded on Lia's end of the call.

"Nuts. I just got a 911 from Bailey. What do I tell her?"

"You know nothing. You haven't talked to me since you sent her to see me. Our little demonstration never happened. Encourage her to stay calm."

"What about Peter? Is he still outside the cone of silence?"

"For now. I have to think."

BRENT

Brent sat on the Donald and Charlotte Addis Memorial Bench, which was conveniently located under a hundred-year-old mulberry tree. The tree had been pruned to look like a weeping cherry, a neat trick taking decades back when someone cared how the cemetery looked.

Cynth had been gone long enough for him to name the Easter bunnies romping on Charlotte's grave. Long enough to count thirty-three miniature American flags decorating veteran graves—ragged leftovers from Memorial Day, soon to be replaced for Veteran's Day. Long enough to count seventeen vultures circling overhead. Long enough for the deflation of his inconvenient erection.

Celeste returned with no obvious dings. Cynth handed him a cup of ice and a steaming white bag before popping Celeste's trunk. "What did Aubrey say? I know you called her."

It burned, what Aubrey had said. "If you pull up the back of my shirt, you'll see tire marks."

Cynth, rooting around in his trunk, snorted. "Bus tires?"

Brent mimicked Ashley's breathy voice. "Brent, *dahling*, what kind of reporter would I be if I gave up sources? I'm happy to call IA and say it wasn't you, but I doubt they'd believe me."

"So the honeymoon is over?"

"There never was a honeymoon. Maybe a Splenda moon."

Cynth stopped rooting around in the trunk of his car long enough to pull her head out. "Don't be a baby." She pulled a dirty T-shirt from his gym bag and thrust it at him. "You can wrap the ice in this."

The shirt reeked, but at least it was his own sweat. "You're the reason I need a damn ice pack. Least you could do is fix it up for me."

"Pushing your luck, Davis."

He sighed, folded the shirt to make several layers, drained melted water from the cup of ice, poured the ice into the shirt, wrapped it in a bundle, and held it against his aching eye.

"I can't unpack my meal one handed."

Cynth rolled her eyes, emptied the bag, and flattened it on the bench. She pulled sliders out of their cardboard sleeves and lay them where he could reach them. Waitress duties completed, she peeled the top off a tub of ketchup, dipped an onion chip, and took a bite.

"It's not Jeff Ruby's, but you'll survive."

"Don't be so nice. The cognitive dissonance is making my brain explode."

"I did punch you."

"Your heart wasn't in it. You were more frustrated than mad."

"Oh?"

"You were flailing at me like a girl."

"That's low, even for you. You talk to Aubrey yesterday?"

"I thought you didn't care."

"I don't, but they'll get our phone records."

"As if I'd leak information from my own phone. No worries there." He took a bite of slider, narrowing his eyes at her while he chewed. "When did you plan to tell me Brandt wasn't our man?"

Cynth looked away. He followed her line of sight. Nothing there but a half-deflated mylar balloon struggling to stay afloat over a headstone that had to be a hundred years old.

"That's just it," she said. "We don't know it's not Brandt, do we? We have one piece of evidence that doesn't fit."

"The murder weapon? A big stinking hole in the case, to my mind, considering it was the only reason we arrested her."

"It's not ideal—"

Brent gave her a look. A waste of effort since she was still staring at the balloon.

"—We still need to investigate Brandt. I saw no reason to change anything."

"That's bullshit and you know it. I'm not your errand boy. Stop treating me like one."

"Isn't that how everyone treats me at District 5? House Data Drudge?"

"Which you allow so you can answer more SWAT call-outs. I get it if you hate me."

Cynth paused, looking at him oddly. She said quietly, "I don't hate you."

"Could have fooled me."

"I'm a woman in a man's job. One guy flirts with me and everyone gets ideas. Then nobody takes me seriously."

"Which you could have told me years ago, so why didn't you?"

She continued as if she hadn't heard. "—I don't care who you are or how I feel, I'm not letting you or anyone tank my career, so you can—."

"So you still have feelings for me."

"Stop twisting my words, asshole. We're here because someone screwed us over."

It was more than she'd said in the years since everything

blew up. He let the moment pass without pressing for more. "How did you find out the awl was planted?"

Cynth consumed half a double cheese slider in one bite, then took her time chewing. *Giving herself time to think about what to tell me.* Finally, she swallowed.

"Do you want plausible deniability, or do you want to know?"

"What I *don't* want is to be blindsided."

"All right, then. I didn't figure it out. Lia did."

He felt his eyebrows raising and said nothing.

"Yesterday, Bailey came in—you were out—and told me someone stole some of Brandt's tools while they were at that Dog Day thing at Spring Grove."

She took a bite of cheeseburger and a slurp of coke.

Brent prodded, "And?"

"You know Bailey."

"I do."

"She wanted Brant out of jail right that minute, and her voice was going up the way it does and her hands were flapping. I needed Lia to cool Bailey's jets. I called her. She asked to see the file."

Brent opened his mouth, but Cynth hurried on before he could say anything.

"Against regulations, but she's sensible and we trust her. I figured if she saw the evidence, she'd understand the case was bigger than the awl and keep Bailey from going off the rails."

"So that bullshit about comp time?"

"I went to the morgue to consult Jeffers."

"We know she didn't leak. Aubrey said it was a police department source. Arseneault?"

"I called him as soon as I left the morgue."

"Plenty of time for someone to tip Aubrey before the late news. Does Peter know?" Brent caught the guilty expression on her face. "Of course he doesn't. I can't believe you put Lia in that position."

"You know Peter."

Brent sighed. "The ethical dilemma would torment him. Nice of you to include me at this late date."

"Do you want me to finish the story?"

Brent waved the last slider in a flourish. "Be my guest."

"Lia spotted the problem with the fingerprints right off. Moore was killed with an overhand strike, but the prints show Brandt was holding the awl in an underhand position. We did a reenactment trying different scenarios and we just couldn't make it work. The awl isn't long enough to make the wound, and the wound is on the wrong side for a left-handed person."

"How did Jeffers miss all that?"

"It was the new guy. Jeffers would have spotted it. She was appalled when I showed her."

"You showed it to her instead of the new guy?"

"You haven't met Langston. He's an asshole. Point is, the awl at the scene is not the murder weapon."

"Duly noted. This shouldn't be our problem. You told them to wait."

"Won't stop them from throwing us to the wolves. Who do you think it was?"

"I favor Heckle and Jeckle."

Cynth sucked up the last of her coke, making a gurgling noise. "I bet everyone in Homicide is pissed Arseneault gave Moore to us."

"True, that."

"Hobbs is an arrogant prick. Maybe someone in the DA's office wants to jam him up."

"You'd never do anything so sneaky. You'd break his face instead."

Cynth's phone sat on the bench between them. It rang and a number with a city prefix popped up on the screen. Frustratingly, she didn't put the call on speaker.

"McFadden." Silence for ten seconds, then, "I can be there in twenty minutes." She ended the call. "Internal Affairs, calling before we can get our stories straight. I expect you'll hear from them next. How do we handle this?"

Brent stuffed the detritus of their meal into the bag, scrunched it into a ball, and lofted it into a nearby trashcan. "We did nothing, so there's nothing to get straight. We work the case from the beginning and we let IA do what IA does."

"What about Lia?"

"Lia who?"

BAILEY

Bailey unlocked the front door. The girls rushed out, pushing past her to get to Ellen, sniffing her all over, whimpering. Ellen sat down in one of her Adirondack porch chairs, gathering them in as they covered her face with frantic licks. "My sweet, sweet girls, I missed you so much. I'll never go away again."

Bailey headed to the kitchen to give Ellen privacy for her reunion. She turned on the coffee pot and opened the fridge, pulling out lettuce, a tomato, a bell pepper, and the chicken breast she'd cooked in anticipation of Ellen's return.

Ellen entered with her furry escort, coming over to the counter to snag bits of diced chicken, which she fed to the girls. "It's so good to be home. You don't need to make lunch."

She said it the way people say, "I can't let you pick up the check," when they really can and expect you to insist on paying.

"I thought you'd be desperate for a decent salad after four days in jail."

"You're not wrong." Ellen held a fold of her shirt up to her nose. "I hope you don't mind if I take a quick shower. I'm even more desperate to get out of these clothes."

Too insecure to let Ellen out of their sight, the girls followed her into the bathroom. Thirty minutes later, Bailey glanced at the clock. She had clients waiting. As she debated whether to stay or leave a note and go, Ellen returned in fresh clothes, hair washed and blown dry, all smiles.

"Sorry I kept you waiting. It just felt so good to shower without wondering what diseases I might catch or who was watching. Those women are so coarse. You know half of them have HIV. You never hear about it anymore, but it's still out there. I bet it's rampant in jail." She plucked a bit of chicken from the bowl of salad sitting on the counter and popped it into her mouth. "This is wonderful."

Bailey was finally learning to be direct. "I'm glad you're home, I really am. But I need to get back to work."

Ellen gave her that trademark stricken look. "You can't. We need to talk."

Bailey sighed mentally. "About what?"

"My case!"

Remain calm. Stick to facts. "They released you, Ellen."

"They can refile at any time. They still have their eyes on me. I can feel it. My lawyer says he's in the business of defending me, not hunting down murderers. You can't abandon me."

Try logic. Channel Lia. She ticked over everything Lia ever told her about prosecutions. *Goddess, give me something, anything, to chill Ellen out.*

"They can't refile unless they find evidence that will stand up in court. And the frame job means they have to work extra hard to prove guilt if they want to arrest you again."

"Don't you care about who hates me enough to send me to prison for the rest of my life?"

Goddess, give me strength. "What do you expect me to do?"

"Everyone who knew about Dog Day is at the conference. Can't you go and ask around? See what people are saying?"

Never do for others what they can do for themselves. It was a lesson she'd been trying to pound into herself for two years. "If it's that important to you, you should do it. You have history with them. You can ask them directly because you have a legit reason for wanting to know. I'm not a musician and they know it. It would look stupid for me to act like I had a reason to be there."

Ellen's eyes narrowed into snake eyes, her voice hard. "I can't believe you want me to go bumbling around where a crazed killer will be in arm's reach and I won't know until it's too late."

"But it's okay for me to do it?"

The salad bowl exploded against the wall, sending the girls yelping away from raining greens and ceramic shards.

"They don't want to kill *you*. Get out," she screamed. "Just get out!"

Bailey shut the front door behind her, cutting off the sound of Ellen sobbing.

K LEE

K Lee groaned inwardly as Lois set her lunch tray across the otherwise empty table and sat. She'd hoped for a few minutes alone between sessions. The last thing she needed was Lois and her Daniel delusions.

Lois swiveled her head, looking to both sides before leaning forward and hissing. With her long neck and over-sized glasses, K Lee couldn't decide if she looked more like a periscope or a snake.

"Did you hear the news?"

K Lee sighed. "What news?"

Lois continued hissing, though no one was near enough to hear. "They let Ellen out of jail. They say she didn't do it."

K Lee opened her mouth to respond, then paused as a pair of giggling students walked by. "That makes no sense. They have her fingerprints."

"It's her awl and her prints, but now they say it doesn't match up with the attack. They claim it was planted. Ellen is getting away with murder. They'll pin it on one of us now."

K Lee returned her attention to her salmon. "If you didn't do it, what are you worried about?"

"It's estimated six percent of people in prison are inno-cent. I looked it up."

"How exactly, was one of us supposed to frame Ellen?"

"If it wasn't Ellen, who was it? You must have an idea."

K Lee bit into a soggy broccoli floret. "Why would I know anything?"

"You're the only one I can talk to. You got your flute back, so I know you didn't do it."

"Considering the damage Daniel did to your career, you have as much motive as anyone."

Lois leaned back, now looking like an affronted turtle. "You can't believe I did it."

"I don't. Even if I cared to speculate, I don't know anyone crazy enough to stab Daniel."

"Ellen killed him before he could prove she stole everything."

"Are you still on about that? He pled guilty."

"No one else would kill him, not as long as they believe he can tell them where their flutes are."

"Maybe he told them and they killed him on principle. I don't get why you still believe Ellen was supposed to deliver the contrabass to Xavier and he didn't know it was missing until you called looking for it."

"He felt so awful about that. He sold me my beautiful Burkart for peanuts to make up for it. I know he took an enormous loss."

And made three times as much off the contrabass. "Then explain his signature on those pawn slips."

"His intern mis-marked repairs as inventory. It was bad luck he couldn't redeem them, and it was only a few flutes—"

That we know of. "So Daniel forgot the flute he sold me and serviced for decades was in the shop, and when he saw a Powell 3100 with 9-karat Arumite tubing, open holes and pointed keys with a 14-karat Haynes gold head joint, he thought it was his?"

Lois had the decency to look uncomfortable.

K Lee pushed. "What about the rest? He never said."

"He never said because he didn't know what happened to them. Because he didn't steal them. Daniel had a plan to fix everything. Ellen killed him before he could make things right."

"Keep believing that."

Just like Lois to assume everything was fine with her just because she'd gotten Fiona back. It had been shocking to discover her only right as Fiona's owner was the right to buy her back for the price Quick Pawn paid for her. She'd been lucky. Customers who bought stolen goods in good faith got to keep them. If Quick Pawn had sold Fiona, she'd have had no legal right to her. Never mind Fiona had been her partner in music for thirty years.

Imagine if parents had no right to their kidnapped children.

Lily still held it over her head that she paid Fiona's ransom and missed an opportunity to see her mom before she died. *No sign she'll ever forgive me, either. Woman always could hold a grudge.*

THIRTY-TWO YEARS AGO

They'd met decades ago, when she was bi and Lily had yet to embrace her attraction to women. When they were both seeing Derrick the Dick. When Lily used her key, expecting to surprise the man she loved and caught him in bed with K Lee.

Lily was gorgeous when she was angry, so K Lee didn't mind the screaming. Then Lily wound down. She blinked, looking around the trashy grad school slum of an apartment, finding an open door and no Derrick.

"That asshole," she'd said. "Did you know?"

K Lee shrugged. "We weren't exclusive. Looks like he didn't explain that part to you."

"I'll kill him."

"Think he's worth all that energy?"

"No point yelling if he can't hear it." Lily narrowed her eyes at the painting studio taking up half the living room. Then she smiled. "How long before he has the balls to come back, do you think?"

"Not until we leave. He's watching the door from the bar across the street."

"You know this how?"

"I just know."

Lily had ethics. An artist herself, she left the canvases alone because it was wrong, wrong, wrong to touch another artist's work. Instead, she squeezed his acrylic paints into cups and diluted them with water until they were the consistency of blood. His brushes weren't big enough, so she ripped Derrick's favorite bath towel into rags and used them to slop obscene invective all over his walls and bed.

As Lily spewed rage all over the apartment, K Lee fell in love. No cell phones back then, so no photos to record Lily's creation. Crying shame, that. It was possibly her best work.

Ninety very energetic minutes later, a happy, satisfied Lily dropped the last of the paint-soaked rags onto the accumulated pile on the rug.

"That was better than sex," she said. "How come you didn't join in?"

K Lee shrugged. Truth was, she wasn't mad at Derrick because she always knew he was a dick and didn't care what he did. "More fun watching you turn this place into a crime scene. That was amazing."

"It'll be hell repainting the walls. Think he'll get his deposit back?"

"Doubtful. Want to get a beer?"

Betrayal and rage. Daniel's murderer felt both. Had to, to stab someone like that. Lily had that kind of passion thirty years ago. That glorious passion had faded into silence and passive aggression. K Lee missed it.

How could Lois believe Daniel was the victim after everything that had happened? She should be angriest of all.

LIA

Banging on the kitchen door caused Lia's brush to stutter, leaving an ugly splotch on her canvas.

Dammit. Have to fix that.

The dogs thundered to the kitchen, howling as their claws scrabbled against the door. The sunroom Lia used as a studio jutted out from the corner of the house, allowing her to see Bailey on the porch, sans Kita. Her usually sleek Cleopatra do frizzed wildly in all directions.

Just what I need. A new episode of As Ellen Turns.

She parked Bailey at the kitchen table and brewed her a

cup of chamomile and lavender tea, wishing she had some valium to drop in it.

Chewy, always the comforter, head-butted Bailey until she took him up on her lap, working her long fingers into fur that badly needed a trim Chewy didn't want. Gypsy gnawed on Lia's sandal for attention. Lia armed herself with a handful of dog biscuits and sat down, prepared to listen until Bailey ran down.

"—so she screams at me and throws the salad against the wall, glass everywhere. I walked out. I swore I'd never talk to her again." Bailey took a sip of her tea. "Every time I try to disengage, something happens."

"What is it now?"

Bailey handed Lia her phone. "Read the texts."

Ellen: Sorry to bother you. I think someone doxxed me while I was in jail. I don't know what to do. Forwarding so you can see. 2:27 PM

Ellen: God will punish you if the law won't 2:27 PM

Ellen: You deserve all the fires of Hell. 2:28 PM

Ellen: You profited from the pain of others and protected a man who stole from children. You committed murder to hide your guilt. Truth will out. 2:28 PM

Ellen: Time to confess, killer 2:28 PM

Ellen: Blood is on your hands 2:29 PM

Ellen: You should have died instead of Daniel. 2:29 PM

Ellen: You deserve to have your naked body tossed in the street for dogs to eat. 2:29 PM

"Does she have the numbers these came from?"

"I don't know. I haven't talked to her. But anyone can use an app that lets you text from a fake number." Bailey stared into her cup. "I'm sorry to dump this on you."

Gypsy amped up her work on Lia's sandal, making growly noises as if the sandal were prey. Lia snuck a biscuit under the table to distract her. "What are friends for?"

"Apparently they're for skulking around looking for murderers."

"You got her out of jail," Lia said. "That's enough."

"I know you had something to do with it. All I did was say Ellen had an awl stolen hours before Daniel was killed. It's not anything I can prove. Why isn't it enough they let her go? Their case against her won't stand now."

"There's a lot I don't understand about some people. I still don't understand how Daniel could steal from his clients."

Bailey's mouth quirked up in a half-smile. "That's because you're not an entitled asshole who believes any money you get is your patriarchal God delivering the abundance that is your divine right, no matter how you get it. Prosperity Gospel bullshit. The divine never sanctions hurting people, no matter what 'God's special purpose' is for you."

"Plenty of New Age types see freeloading as a form of manifestation."

"True, that. Whatever you believe, you can twist it up and cherry pick to justify anything. Maybe it just boils down to Daniel being an entitled asshole."

"We would have saved ourselves a lot of angst if we'd come to that conclusion two years ago." Chewy poked his head over the edge of the table, sniffing at the pile of biscuits. Lia nudged one over to him and he gobbled it down.

Bailey scratched his head. "Why can't people be as easy to please as dogs?"

"You mean after we provide for their every need?"

"You have a point." Bailey traced a callused finger along the rim of her cup. "What am I supposed to do about these stupid texts? Am I supposed to hover over her for the rest of her life? You know the worst of it? I feel guilty."

For the umpteenth time, Lia wished she could share everything she knew about Ellen. It might make Bailey feel less obligated. *Or it might blow up our friendship.* "I know you owe her for loaning you the money to start your business, but when does that end? You paid her back years ago and you've done more to help her than anyone else she knows. More than ten friends."

"I keep thinking about how I'd feel. I'd be terrified if it was me getting random hate texts."

Gypsy gnawed on Lia's other sandal. She fed her another biscuit. "Would you abuse the only person willing to help you?"

"I think she's too embarrassed to ask anyone else."

"You mean she's willing to dump on you, but heaven forbid her book club finds out? You ever wonder what she tells the other people in her life?"

Bailey cuddled Chewy, eyes down on him. "Maybe she

has some evolving to do. But she has legit reasons to be scared."

"Where's this going, Bailey?"

A long pause, then, "I think we should help her."

"If she needs help, she should hire a private detective. I'm sure she can afford it."

"I don't know if she even has a job after they arrested her in front of her team."

"Why does it have to be your problem?"

Bailey took Lia's hand with a desperate iron grip. "Please, I need you to be there for me. Don't make me choose between you."

Lia looked into Bailey's pleading, overlarge eyes. "What do you want to do?"

"The flute people know us. It's dumb for us to act like we want to buy flutes, but Jim has granddaughters. We could take him to the conference and he can pretend he wants to buy a flute for one of them."

"And we'll spot some random flautist walking around in a blood-spattered shirt?"

"You're right. It's a stupid idea. I knew it was stupid when Ellen suggested it. Let's talk about it at the park tomorrow morning. Maybe the guys will have an idea."

"Maybe they will." *At least I can put off dealing with this until then.*

PETER

Peter found Lia bent over her easel, hair pulled into a messy bun secured with a paintbrush. He stood behind her, watching as she scrubbed a dingy brown color into another dingy brown color. The overall effect was dark and edgy. His love was in a foul mood.

"More bark? How will you feed the kids?"

"David thinks I'm onto something."

"He can sell bark?"

"Not like this. He has a plan."

Lia set her brush down and opened her laptop, bringing up an email with a photo of an office. A huge, squiggly painting hung behind a commanding executive desk. It took a minute to decipher the image as a section of one of Lia's bark paintings, blown up to six feet square. At that scale, it was unrecognizable as a piece of tree.

"David playing with Photoshop?"

"He says it will appeal to his corporate clients and open up a new market for me."

Peter poked his tongue in his cheek. "Knows how to make lemons from lemonade, doesn't he?"

Lia poked her fist gently into his gut. "Philistine. He's thrilled to have something in manly colors to offer corporate clients. He's tired of hand-tinted hunt etchings."

"Reducing bad hunt etchings is a noble cause."

"He says wives will be delighted to bring their men into the 21st century. He wants to do giclée prints and make me rich. I could decorate boardrooms all over the country."

Peter looked around the sunroom. "Can you fit a six-foot canvas in here?"

"I still have the old space. Just need to move things around a bit."

"Plenty of room in the attic if we knock down a few walls. You know, you could upload this stuff to Zazzle and print your own camo socks, make your millions that way."

"Now I have to hurt you."

He leaned over her shoulder, examining the small canvas. "A bit dark for you, isn't it?"

"David says there's a subliminal suggestion of rage that will resonate with the corporate kill-or-be-killed mentality. I don't see it."

"Maybe you have to squint and hold your mouth right. I heard Ellen was released. This should be a happy day."

"Ellen wants Bailey to exonerate her."

"Wasn't Bailey the one who set the cat among the pigeons and got her out of jail?"

"Apparently that's not enough."

Explaining the foul mood. "The woman needs to learn gratitude and let Cynth and Brent handle it. Bailey isn't equipped for this."

"Bailey knows that, but she feels obligated. Then there's the vandalism. Now there are threatening texts."

"Ellen report any of it?"

"I don't think she trusts any of you after she wound up in jail."

"She didn't much trust us before she wound up in jail."

Something was off. Lia should be pumping him for information. He threw out a lure. "It's a huge leap from saying someone took Ellen's tools to putting a hole in the case big enough to get Ellen released."

Lia stared at her canvas, making a swipe with her brush. "I guess."

He dragged a stool next to Lia and sat so he could look her in the eye. "What aren't you telling me?"

Lia blinked, her face otherwise immobile. "What do you mean?"

"I'm wondering why you don't want to talk about a case that involves your best friend."

She opened her mouth, then stopped, looking everywhere that wasn't him. *Working through options.* Finally, she slumped with an audible sigh.

"You know how we have the circle of trust?"

"Uh-huh."

"What happens when the circle of trust runs into the cone of silence?"

"Huh." It was his favorite response when he wanted more from someone. He shouldn't need to use it on Lia.

She placed a hand on his knee, imploring. "It's not mine to tell."

He picked up her hand, thumped their clasped hands against his thigh a few times. "Will this thing you aren't saying allow a criminal to go free?"

"No. I don't want to say more because explaining could create a problem. Can you trust me?"

She looked at him with eyes like damp moss, biting her lip. If it wasn't about protecting Ellen, it had to be on the other side of the case. That meant Cynth or Brent. Brent was unlikely to tap Lia for anything, not without telling him. Had to be Cynth. In light of the IA investigation that no doubt started five minutes after the Channel 7 broadcast, ignorance was bliss.

He pulled her into his arms. "Always. I'm sorry someone put you in this position." And when this blew over, he'd rip Cynth a new one wide enough to drive her truck through. "About Bailey ..."

Lia mumbled into his shirt, "What about Bailey?"

"I know you love her."

"But? I hear a 'but'."

"You have no control over Ellen or what Bailey chooses to do about her. You can't fix people. It's one of the first things I learned about cop work."

"No, but I can hurt for them."

He pulled her tighter, resting his chin on top of her head. The paintbrush she used to secure her bun poked him in the clavicle.

"What do you plan to do?"

"As little as possible. Listen, mostly."

"That's my girl."

"How are Cynth and Brent doing? They can't be happy about the Channel 7 story."

"Sam said they were in with Parker first thing. Nobody at District 5 has seen them since."

"You haven't heard from Brent?"

"Not a word." *And that was troubling.* "Let's take the kids to Putz's for ice cream. I'll tell you dumb stories about idiots who steal catalytic convertors."

She turned in his arms, relief in her eyes. "You are the best of boyfriends. Give me five minutes to clean my brushes."

WENDY

Wendy sat on the floor, staring at the game board on the coffee table. Should she build or explore? Ron was grabbing territories, while Dianne amassed armies to block him. She needed to ally with one of them, but who?

Ron slouched on the sofa, his bushy afro obscuring his face as he stared down at his phone. Dianne braided another pencil-thin lock of hair, something she did when she felt fidgety.

I'm taking too long.

Ron took a long toke, holding his breath as he turned the phone so Wendy and Ellen could see the bold headline.

Charges Dropped in Moore Murder

Ron croaked, trying to hold in as much smoke as he could. "They released Ellen Brandt."

Wendy placed a card for building a defensive wall. "What do you think it means?"

Dianne drew a card, scowling at her hand. "It means that bitch will get away with murder after she made sure I never find my flute."

"They must have had a reason," Wendy said. "What does it say?"

Ron scrolled, squinting at the tiny print as he exhaled a long stream of skunky-smelling smoke. "Blah, blah, blah. A lot of nothing, except saying they can charge her later. Something's messed up about their case." He held the phone out again, this time displaying a photo of Ellen leaving the Justice Center in the company of a tall redhead. "She looks ragged for someone who only spent a couple days in jail. Who's the scarecrow?"

Wendy took the phone, examining the photo. "Like you'd come out of jail ready for a fashion shoot. That's Bailey. She worked for Daniel ages ago. She gave a statement in court."

Dianne snorted. "About how Daniel was always lying and she quit instead of telling us?"

Wendy waved away the joint. "That's harsh. What good

would it have done? Daniel would have said she was a crazy homeless person who wandered in off the street and answered his phone. Everyone would have pretended they believed it and still taken their flutes to him."

Dianne played an attack card on Wendy's new defensive wall, rolled the dice. "Boom! Down it goes. Everyone said Daniel was the best."

"You had to blow up my wall, didn't you? The point is, if they let her go, she probably didn't do it. So who did?"

Ron turned his attention to the game board. "I bet it's Lois. All that moral high ground. Bet she cracked."

"And get blood on her fluffy scarf? I doubt it," Wendy said.

"Good thing I stopped you from telling that cop we were there," Dianne said.

"But we didn't do anything."

Dianne nodded at the phone. "You think they care? They arrested Ellen and it looks like she didn't do anything, either."

Ron played a parlay card, seeking alliance with Dianne. "Stop giving Wendy a hard time. *She* didn't leave the phone behind."

Dianne took a drag on the joint and passed it back to Ron. "They'll have fun trying to trace it."

"You wipe off your fingerprints? If you did, I didn't see it."

"I've never been arrested. They don't have my prints."

Ron stared at Dianne. "You made us dump the wheel-chair. Why were you in such a hurry?"

THREE WEEKS AGO

It had been fun, a game. Just a game to cheer Dianne up. It started weeks earlier with Ron complaining for the umpteen-zillionth time that Dianne's flute rap was ruining his life.

"Lamest no-rhythm, white-girl lyrics ever. People think I wrote it."

"You offered to perform."

"Because you can't rap worth shit. That thing will follow me for the rest of my life." Ron pointed the joint at Dianne. "My career is over."

"Stop being such a drama queen. You're a drummer. No one cares how you rap. If it bothers you, get a stage name and move to Chicago. Shave your head. Grow a soul patch. Nobody has to know it was you. If you get famous enough for anyone to dig up the stupid video, you can squash them because you'll be rich. I'm the one who lost a fifteen thousand dollar flute. That video was supposed to humiliate Daniel into confessing."

"Should have worked," Ron said.

"The prosecutor said he's getting probation. He'll never talk."

"Maybe we give him a reason."

Dianne sneered. "How do you plan to do that, genius?"

Ron burned through the remainder of the joint before he answered. "We go Gitmo on him. We need props. Can't do it here. Has to be someplace no one will hear him scream."

Dianne glared at Ron, looking as fierce as she had that night.

Ron wasn't intimidated. "What happened when you went looking for Daniel?"

"You really want to know, asshole? I stabbed him. Are you happy now? Is your life better now you know?" She looked from Ron to Wendy, back at Ron. "Why would I stab Daniel before he told me where my flute was?"

Wendy kept her head down. *Maybe because he told you and he deserved it.* "We didn't say you stabbed him."

"We need to go back," Ron said.

"Why do we need to do that? I reject your alliance, asshole."

"Maybe you don't care about the phone, but if the wheel-chair is gone, the police have it. If they figure out where it came from, they're coming for me. Because you were in such a big freaking hurry to get out of there." He stood up. "I'm tired of this stupid game."

8

DAY 7

SATURDAY, AUGUST 16

LIA

BAILEY ARRIVED AT THE DOG PARK WITH DONUTS, PRESUMABLY to soften the guys up. As she passed the box around, she kept flashing Lia looks, as if she expected Lia to take the lead. Lia kept her eyes on her Bavarian cream. If Bailey wanted to pursue this, she needed to do it herself. *Besides, I promised Peter.*

Finally Bailey said, "I've got a problem. Ellen expects me to find Daniel's killer, and I don't know how to do that."

Steve spoke around a mouthful of cruller. "Real crooks don't do frame jobs. This isn't television."

Terry licked glaze off his index finger and jabbed it in the air. "Excellent point. Our murderer is inspired by fiction. Agatha Christie is the mother of every murder plot ever invented. We must look there."

Jim said, "She didn't invent *Murders in the Rue Morgue*."

"Bah! I consign any plot requiring an orangutan to the seventh circle of fiction hell."

"A week ago you said a dozen flutists stabbed him with the same knife."

"In pursuit of justice denied. It's an apt corollary."

Steve said, "Shame it didn't fit the facts."

Jim said, "Christie's plots are too contrived."

Terry dug his heels in. "Philistine! They are perfect storms of human nature and circumstance."

Steve said, "You think that's what we have here?"

As they often did, the guys were arguing over nothing. Jim brought the conversation back around. "We know the circumstance, but we're lacking in the human nature department."

"What do you mean?" Bailey asked.

"Everything you know about Daniel came from him or Ellen. That's a problem."

"I see what you mean," Bailey said. "We need a different perspective. Ellen wants us to skulk around the flute conference."

"Why would any of them talk to us?" Steve said. "We need an insider."

Everyone looked at Lia.

Lia feigned ignorance. "What?"

"Aren't you friendly with the Hopewell Admin?" Steve asked.

"Hannah? I haven't talked to her since I finished the Hopewell frieze."

"But she likes you, right?"

"Oh, no."

"You helped her out the night Professor Lawrence died," Bailey pointed out.

"What's the harm?" Steve said. "She knows everything that goes on there. You chat her up. Maybe she tells you stuff, maybe she doesn't."

Bailey's eyes begged for help. "I'd do it, but she doesn't know me."

Peter would want her to say no. But Peter wasn't here, and it wasn't him turning his back on his friends. "Upscale baked goods are required. Who's funding a trip to Happy Chicks?"

The student manning the reception desk blinked huge fake eyelashes at Lia. Those eyelashes sat under a pair of manicured caterpillars that fashion claimed were eyebrows. The eyelashes and eyebrows battled for dominance while pale, puffy lips sulked underneath.

Young, trendy, and not Hannah. "Is Hannah Kleemeyer in?"

The caterpillar eyebrows scrunched together, the head tilting as if assessing Lia's mental competence. She jabbed a pen over her shoulder. "In her office."

The pen pointed at an open door, through which Hannah could be seen working on a computer.

No wonder she thinks I'm stupid.

Before Lia could knock on the jamb, three lap dogs leapt out of their baskets and raced to her, tails wagging.

Hannah looked up from her computer and smiled, looking more relaxed than when Lia last saw her.

"They remember you. They don't cavort for everyone."

Lia set her bag of goodies on Hannah's desk and knelt to pet the dogs crowding around her. "I brought tribute. May I give them treats?"

"Absolutely. To what do I owe the honor?"

Lia fished in her pocket and produced tiny duck treats to the capering delight of the dogs. "Do you have time for a break? I was hoping we could have a private chat."

"For you, always. Let's take the boys out to the patio."

Hannah led Lia to the staff picnic table. Hannah untied the string on the pastry box, cooing over giant lemon-raspberry cupcakes while Lia poured lattes from a thermos.

Hanna sighed over her cup. "This is just what the doctor ordered. Thank you."

"My pleasure. It looks like you've moved up in the world."

Hannah, her expression arch, smiled. "They invented a position for me and gave me an office. I'm now in charge of special projects."

"Well deserved."

Hannah tipped her head modestly. "People always compliment the trumpet vines you painted in the auditorium. I can't tell you how many society wives have asked what kind of flowers they are because they want some. I can only imagine the reaction at the greenhouses on Gray Road when they go in asking for an invasive weed."

"You're so bad."

"I get my pleasures where I can. We're years away from breaking ground on the—" she hooked finger quotes "—Geoffrey Lawrence Memorial Concert Hall, but Dr. Wingler has me researching architects and specs. There will be a budget for art. I hope you'll submit a proposal when the time comes."

"More murals?"

"We're planning a circle drive out front. I saw the solstice sculpture you created for the Solomons. Something along those lines would be spectacular. Enough of my business. What brought you here today?"

"Daniel Moore."

Hannah scowled. "People keep talking about finding the offshore account where he stashed the money. They're idiots."

Nothing new, but Lia wanted Hannah's take. "Where do you think the money went?"

"Oh, it's gone."

"You sound certain."

"Would you sign on for eighty-four percent APR if you weren't desperate? You go to pawn shops because you need money right now. I heard he pawned flutes to get other flutes out of hock so he could turn around and pawn them again. This was robbing Peter to pay Paul, taken to stupid lengths." She gave Lia a speculative look. "Surely you've thought of all this?"

"You're one of the smartest people I know. I wanted your opinion."

"Flatterer. In his way, Daniel was worse than Geoff. Everyone knew Geoff was a shit. Underneath all Daniel's helpfulness and old school Christianity was a sociopath who liked to torment people."

"Torment them how?"

Hannah took a bite of cupcake, chewed. "This is mostly hearsay and conjecture, so please don't repeat anything I say. The non-verifiable parts, anyway."

I hate secret squirrel stuff. "Understood."

"Daniel dropped out of the graduate program at Bloomington a month before his thesis recital. Rumor is he stormed out after an argument with his advisor and never went back."

"That's stupid. Suck it up, get your degree, and move on."

"So speaks a rational woman. He stopped performing and learned to build and repair flutes."

"Why do you think he stopped performing?"

"Some of the people he went to school with went on to have international careers. I think he couldn't compete and he couldn't stand it."

"Where does torture come into it?"

"Again, this is conjecture."

"Understood."

"You're an artist. You understand the pressure to excel. But people don't get to judge what you make until you choose to reveal it. Performers have to do their very best at a particular place and time with no do-overs. Sometimes one performance can make or break your career."

"I imagine the anxiety is enormous."

"Take what you imagine and multiply it by ten. So you have Daniel. Daniel fails to fulfill his ambition to play for adoring audiences all over the world. He adopts plan B. In this new role he discovers he has a kind of power and influence."

"How so?"

"Daniel's genius lay in matching a performer's ability and style to the perfect flute. People loved him for it. "

"I'm not seeing the problem yet."

"A lot of the kids tell me stuff they won't tell their teachers. Some of them went to K Lee. She discounted what they said and made them feel foolish."

"I bet she regrets that after he pawned Fiona."

"You think? He really did know his stuff. He could tweak flutes to get more out of them than they were designed for and he would often give free mini lessons to students to help them maximize their performance. But he had time management issues."

"Because he was too busy impressing people with his brilliance to fix their flutes?"

Hannah took a sip of her latte. "Exactly. After someone was his client for a while, he'd slack off on their repairs, miss due dates, take three times as long as he should to turn their flute around.

"When that started, everybody followed the same playbook. They continued to send him instruments because they wanted the Daniel touch. But they also want their flute when they need it. They try different things: impressing on him the importance of meeting the date, allowing for him to take twice as long as he said he needed, inventing concerts or auditions weeks in advance of the actual event."

There was something compelling about the way Hannah covered old ground. "Sounds exhausting."

"As time went on, his excuses and delays would get worse and worse." Hannah picked up a Bichon frisé named Dasher and looked in his adoring eyes. "You wouldn't put up with that, would you, precious boy? You'd go somewhere else, I know you would."

She settled Dasher in her lap and continued, "So you have young hot shots and mid-career flautists who have spent the price of a car on a flute because together they sing like angels weeping. But they have a concert or an audition coming up and regular angel tears are not enough. Those angels better weep golden tears. You entrust your baby to Daniel and you give him a thousand dollars or more in advance for an overhaul, because he's the guy who can perform this miracle.

"The due date passes and there's a problem. There

continue to be problems. Your concert is getting closer and you're practicing on the beater you played light sabers with in high school marching band. Now you're getting sick in your gut because it's not enough to know the music. You need to practice on the right instrument."

"Why is that?"

"The responsiveness of the keys will be different and that puts your timing off as well as the amount of pressure you use. You have to hold your mouth differently because the lip plates are not the same. A hundred little things that make the difference between a stellar performance and mediocre one.

"Daniel keeps making promises, but you're losing sleep. You beat yourself up because you knew he had issues with due dates, but you had to have that magic touch. If you're local, you could go to the shop and get your flute, but by now it's beyond thirty days so Visa won't go to bat for you to get your money back, and nobody else can turn it around in time."

This is what she needed, the emotional nuance. "How often did something like this happen?"

"Too often. Usually they got their flute hours before the event, with Daniel telling stories about his heroic efforts, never mind he caused the problem to begin with."

"How awful."

"Those poor musicians had to smile and be grateful when they were such a wreck by that point it didn't matter that they had their magic golden angel tear flute back, they were going to blow the performance."

"You think he did it on purpose?"

"Maybe not consciously, but I can't help thinking he envied performing musicians. I think at some point he started enjoying the power he had over them, and how they had to thank him for making their lives a living hell."

Lia could see it. "That's sick."

"Any decent human being would change how they did things after the first time they screwed someone like that, don't you think?"

"You could end up with PTSD from that."

"There was a high school student, a very talented girl with a promising future. She was a scholarship kid. Her grandmother scraped to buy her a gorgeous pro flute and got her into our summer program.

"She had an audition to go on a European tour and play for the Pope. You know how it is when you're young and you have a shot at the brass ring. It's the only thing in the world that matters. If you don't get whatever it is, your life is over.

"A month before her audition, one of her keys screwed up. A minor repair Daniel could have turned around in a day. He kept making excuses and she had to practice with this miserable Bundy. She got her flute back two hours before her audition. She flubbed it."

"That poor girl."

"She ran out of the auditorium. Friends found her in the ladies' room an hour later with blood pouring from both wrists. They administered first aid, but it was too late. Daniel had the nerve to go to the funeral."

Lia stared at the rest of her cupcake, appetite gone. "That's horrible."

"When the whispers got around, people started taking their flutes elsewhere and his business took a hit. But he had clients all over the country. I'm sure he traumatized others."

"Just curious, who got to play for the pope?"

"That's the sad thing about it. Her best friend got the spot. The grandmother gave her the flute. Then Daniel stole it."

Lia thought back to court. "Small, long hair with a lot of tiny braids and the personality of an enraged dock worker? Dianne something?"

"Lovato. That's her."

"No wonder she's so angry. What are people saying about Daniel's murder?"

"People have been giving each other the hairy eyeball all week. Lois Buchanan is wafting around and tearing her hair out like she's auditioning for *Hamlet*."

"She say anything specific about the murder?"

"Not around me. I'm sure she knows I don't want to hear about the tragedy that was Daniel. I suspect she's continuing her fairy tale that Ellen destroyed Daniel. Ellen's arrest is proof in her mind that Daniel was never at fault."

"She didn't blame Daniel? But she sat with us in court."

"Optics. After the contra-bass poofed, Lois was on thin ice at Xavier. She wants to make it to retirement."

"She wasn't tenured?"

"You can fire tenured professors for fraud and criminal activity. Rumor is her director made noises that she was in on it. I doubt he believed it. I think he mostly did it to push her, in case she had any influence with Daniel. A secondary benefit was shutting her up."

"I don't understand why some people refuse to accept the obvious."

"She's the only one still on Team Daniel. Everyone else has had two years to accept that he wasn't who they thought. I think his refusal to tell the police what happened to the flutes was a reality check for everyone who thought he was a decent guy who made bad decisions and got in over his head."

The tricky thing with gossip is you have to give to get. Lia had a few carefully curated tidbits to share. It was time to use them. "Bailey and I met up with Ellen right after Dianne did her act for Channel 7."

"How did Daniel react?"

"He said Dianne was nuts and refused to go out and talk to her. Aubrey Morse was on the porch with her cameraman banging on the door. Ellen took the dogs and left, leaving the door wide open. I'm not sure who she wanted to torture more with that move, Aubrey or Daniel."

"I saw the clip on Channel 7. It was quite a performance."

"Wasn't it though?"

"Dianne is a force to be reckoned with. She really stirred things up here. Online, too. She's the one who started things on Facebook. K Lee had already found Fiona in that pawn shop, but it wasn't a story until Dianne dug up all those folks across the country who lost flutes. They didn't know about each other. They all thought their problems with Daniel were isolated."

"Are any of the out-of-town folks here for the conference?"

"I couldn't say. Does this really matter?"

Lia sighed. "Bailey insists Ellen didn't do it."

"Didn't the police release her?"

"They reserve the right to refile charges. Ellen is desperate for someone to find Daniel's killer before they arrest her again."

"Don't you think the lady doth protest too much? Sounds very O.J. to me."

The door to the patio opened. The young lady with the caterpillar eyebrows escorted Cynth and Brent through the door and pointed at Hannah. Cynth spotted Lia and narrowed her eyes.

Oops.

Lia stood, gathering the remains of their feast. It was an excuse to look away from those steely eyes. "Looks like you've got things to do."

As she passed by, Cynth said, "We'll talk later."

CYNTH

Cynth examined the faint blue splotch on Brent's cheekbone as they waited for Kleemeyer to round up the women. He'd been right. Ice or no ice, it would have purpled by now if her heart had been in it.

She grinned when he caught her looking at it. "Don't worry. The ladies won't notice it under the fluorescents."

"You're enjoying this entirely too much."

"You want to borrow some concealer?"

"Careful, I'll think you care."

"Just keep your mind on the ladies. Shouldn't be too hard for you to do."

"I suppose you think that hurts. What do you think Lia was up to?"

"Snooping. I'll get it out of her later."

The conference room door opened. Hannah Kleemeyer, with their four new suspects. Cynth hadn't seen the women who attended Moore's court hearings in more than a year, so she took a minute to attach names to faces.

Of the two senior citizens, the bony refugee from the 90s with oversized glasses and blonde wedge—that was Lois Buchanan, the Xavier teacher with the missing contrabass— whatever a contrabass was. K Lee Demyanovich—the Hopewell teacher who named her flute—had to be the sturdy, practical woman with the silver boy cut.

Dianne Lovato was easy to pick out with her signature tiny braids in her long, dark hair. That left a heavyset girl with pale skin and shampoo-ad blonde hair held back by a too-cute flute barrette, currently biting her lip. *Wendy Harrison-Green.*

Each wore some combination of curiosity and anxiety on her face. *Now that Brandt is out, none of them want to look uncooperative.*

Brent said, "Thank you for agreeing to talk to us. You were regulars at court. We believe you might have helpful recollections."

"Are you sure it wasn't Ellen?" Buchanan asked, one hand fussing nervously at the fluffy print scarf around her neck.

"Nothing is certain at this point," Cynth said.

Demyanovich's face went righteous. "It had to be Ellen."

"Why do you say that?" Brent asked.

"Well, I—"

Lovato interrupted, defiant. "Why isn't Bailey here? She followed the case just as much as we did. She could be Ellen's accomplice."

Buchanan gave her a stern look over the top of her glasses. "We want to be *helpful*, Dianne." She turned to Brent. "I think what K Lee meant was, Daniel and Ellen's relationship had been volatile for a very long time."

"And you know this how?" Demyanovich asked with a

dangerous sweetness. "And no, that wasn't what I meant. It had to be Ellen because it wasn't any of us, and no one else came to the hearings. If they didn't care enough to come to the hearings, they wouldn't risk prison to kill Daniel."

"Why wouldn't it be you?" Brent asked.

"I got Fiona back."

"But you still went to the hearings." Brent said.

"Thousands of musicians followed the case and were desperate for updates. Somebody had to let them know what was going on."

"Daniel was my friend for decades," Buchanan said. "I would never hurt him."

Lovato gave Buchanan a disbelieving look. "He screwed your career. Doesn't that matter to you?"

"You're the one who lost an heirloom flute," Buchanan said.

Lovato popped out of her seat, glaring. "Wendy and I were home that night. We were nowhere near the woods." She turned to Cynth. "You can ask Ron. He's our roommate."

Until now, Harrison-Green had her head down, hiding behind all that hair. She gave Lovato a pleading look. "Dianne, this isn't helping."

Buchanan said with exaggerated dignity, "*I* was home with my *husband*."

Lovato and Buchanan looked at Demyanovich.

"Don't look at me. Lily and I went to Columbus for Picnic with the Pops. I have the ticket stubs."

"And got back when?" Dianne demanded. "What time did Daniel die? You still could have done it."

Harrison-Green chewed her lip, looking too uncomfortable for a bystander. *Something going on there.*

Brent stood and patted the air in that universal signal to calm down or lower the volume or freaking shut the eff up. "Ladies, please. We aren't suggesting any of you are responsible for Daniel Moore's death."

"I bet you're thinking it," Dianne muttered.

Brent caught Cynth's eye, raised an eyebrow in a are-you-going-to-do-this-or-not look. She reached into her pocket for the small plastic square and pressed twice.

A calliope tune interrupted the bickering. Lovato and Buchanan looked around, confused. Demyanovich froze, eyes wide and terrified.

"It wasn't me," she stammered over the music. "I swear it wasn't me."

"We'll talk about that," Brent said.

The noise stopped.

"What just happened?" Buchanan asked.

Cynth stood, signaling the end of the meeting. "We need to talk to Ms. Demyanovich. We'll catch up with the rest of you later. Our apologies for the inconvenience."

Lovato's eyes swiveled between Cynth, Brent, Demyanovich, and Buchanan.

Buchanan rose, craning her long neck to look over her shoulder at the miserable woman shrinking in her chair. "Why do you need to talk to K Lee? She was in Columbus."

Holding the door, Cynth said, "I'll walk you out."

"Detective Davis," Buchanan said primly, "Will you call me when you're free? I have some questions about the case."

Before he could answer, Cynth said again, a bit more firmly, "*We'll* be in touch later this afternoon."

She dumped the women in the hall, watching long enough to ensure they wouldn't listen outside the door.

Brent—master of "work smart, not hard"—had

suggested gathering the women to activate the tracker from Moore's bag. Annoyingly—because she hadn't thought of it first—it had worked.

She returned to the conference room. Brent sat across from Demyanovich, tipped back in his chair with his arms folded. Demyanovich stared down at the table. She looked up when Cynth shut the door, fear in her eyes.

"I don't understand why you kept me."

Nice try, buttercup.

Cynth removed the white plastic square from her pocket, setting it on the table with the silver circle logo facing up.

"What's that?" Demyanovich asked unconvincingly.

Cynth tapped the silver circle twice. The calliope noise returned, emanating from the purse Demyanovich clutched in her lap.

"That," Cynth said, "Is a problem."

Demyanovich's eyes fell back to the table. "I've never seen that before."

"We found that tracker in Daniel Moore's bag and it just alerted your phone. Feel free to turn it off so we don't have to talk over it."

Demyanovich stayed silent.

Cynth continued, "We now have probable cause to get your fingerprints. I wonder if they'll match the prints we pulled off it."

The music died.

"Would you like to try again?" Brent asked, gentle solicitousness masking the snark.

"It—it must have been an accident."

She glanced up from the table, eyes darting between Cynth and Brent. Cynth gave her a skeptical look.

"I was standing behind him in the line for the metal detector. It must have fallen off my keychain."

Brent shook his head sadly. "K Lee, K Lee, K Lee."

"I don't know what you want me to say."

Cynth folded her arms. "You lost your tracker and never hunted it up on your app?"

Brent said, "If we turn on your app, will we find a map with all the places that tracker has been for the past month?"

"You don't have a warrant."

Cynth shrugged. "Fine. You and I sit here for three hours while Detective Davis writes it up and finds a judge. Then we confiscate your phone. Not sure how soon Tech will copy it, they get so backed up. You might want to buy a new phone while they do that. Then we get call history, texts, browser, emails, social media, private chats."

Demyanovich flinched.

Wonder what that's about. Probably lots of talk about all the ways she and her thousand flute friends wanted Moore to die.

"If I show you my phone, will you let me keep it?"

Cynth caught Brent's eye. He twisted his mouth in an expression that meant "I don't know. Your call."

Thanks a lot. "Tell your story, the truth this time, and show us the app. We'll take it from there."

Demyanovich pressed her lips together. "I didn't do anything, not really."

Brent, in his gentle, coaxing voice, "What didn't you really do?"

"You understand, Daniel pawned Fiona and jerked me around for six months until I found her in that shop. Then I had to buy her back. Daniel *claimed* it was an accident—not that he ever apologized. He kept saying he'd fix it." She snorted. "It was a new song and dance every week about money coming in any day. Then he stopped taking my calls. People online started talking about Daniel keeping their flutes, so I realized it wasn't just me. I took him to small claims court and called Aubrey Morse."

Her face screwed up in anger. "That asshole. When he saw the camera in the courtroom, he turned around and walked back out."

They knew this, but letting Demyanovich tell the story her way would ease her into what they needed to know.

"You arrested him, but you let him go and he kept making excuses to miss his court dates. Health issues. Hah!" Her face turned pleading. "I had to pay eight thousand dollars to bring Fiona home while he spent two years mocking all of us. I just wanted a little of my own back."

"So, how did you get it?" Cynth asked.

"No one knew where he was. He finally showed up to change his plea. I decided to tag him, just to know where he'd been hiding. It was harmless, really. He'd continue to think he was pulling one over on all of us and I could get to him whenever I wanted."

"And did you?"

"I thought about doxxing him, but just knowing was enough. It was my little secret."

"You knew where he was for a month? If we pull your phone's GPS records, how many times will it show you went there?"

Demyanovich couldn't hide her guilty expression. "I don't know. A few times. He was staying with an old woman. I thought about telling her not to trust Daniel, but I doubted she'd believe me. If she did and she threw him out, she'd be alone. I could tell she wasn't well. She needed someone around."

Demyanovich fiddled with her phone, handing it to Cynth with the app open to the tracker history. "I found out where he lived, but that's all. I guess he only took that bag to court. You can see where he went to the sentencing."

This wasn't getting them anywhere. Cynth looked at Brent, made that face that let him know she was out of ideas.

Brent said, "How long have you known Daniel?"

Demyanovich sat back, shoulders slumping in relief at the change of subject. "I started teaching at Hopewell his last year there."

"A long time then. What was he like back then?"

"Attractive and knew it. Smart, a fair amount of native talent, but not enough discipline. You could tell it pissed him off when someone he considered less talented beat him in an audition."

Cynth sat back, happy to observe Demyanovich while Brent drew her out.

"And how did he react when someone beat him?"

"How do you mean?"

"Dirty tricks? Revenge? Or did he hole up in a practice room?"

"I don't know about dirty tricks. He didn't work harder. His problem was he preferred talking theory to practicing. He always had sycophants."

This didn't appear to be going anywhere, but more background was never a bad thing.

"Did his theories include why judges had it in for him?"

"I wouldn't be surprised. I'm sure those theories never

mentioned spending too much time taking female students out to the woods. "

"Sounds like you didn't like him much."

"I liked him fine until he sold Fiona. I just knew his limitations. He found his lane with the shop and he fell into a natural mentoring role with younger clients. I always thought Daniel was helpful as a way to be admired, but the students benefitted from it. Some people thought he was the best in the country."

"Not you?"

"I'll give him best in the tri-state, maybe better. He was good enough for me to send students to him. I helped him build that business. It's his own fault he ruined it."

"When was the last time you had contact with Daniel?"

"That would be the day before I filed suit against him in small claims court, unless you call seeing him in court contact. But you should talk to Lois. She always had a soft spot for him."

Brent ushered Demyanovich to the door. She stopped and turned. "There's something you should know."

"Oh?"

"One night I drove by Daniel's place and I passed an SUV that looked just like Ellen's."

"Did you see the driver?"

Demyanovich shook her head. "It was too dark."

"Do you remember the date?" Brent asked.

"I couldn't say. Maybe a week after I slipped the Tile into his bag? You're wasting time with us. Why aren't you looking closer at Ellen?"

Cynth was tired of everyone treating them like they were stupid. "Tell us how she left her house without showing up on her cameras, and I'll take another look."

Damn my stupid temper. With IA investigating them for leaking, this wasn't the time to spill case details to witnesses. She pulled out the notebook she kept in her inside blazer pocket and scribbled, keeping her head down. Better her chicken scratch than the expression on Brent's face.

Brent returned from ushering Demyanovich out. He sat across from her, saying nothing as she pretended to review the notes she couldn't read. She counted to ten before he cleared his throat and said, "What did you make of Ms. Demyanovich?"

Ignoring my stupid lapse in judgement? Fine by me. She set her pen aside. "Eager to redirect our attention to Buchanan and Brandt after we nailed her on the tracker. You think she told the truth? That she got her jollies just knowing where he was, and that was it?"

"Better to let her think we bought it. We'll get her GPS history, but I think she's too smart to lie about anything we can verify and too sensible for direct action. I'm more interested in her Ellen sighting."

Cynth shook her head. "That's a non-starter. Too many SUVs around, and she was careful to say she didn't actually see Brandt. Brandt's phone records don't show her going anywhere near Thompson Heights."

"A smart person would leave their phone home. I bet her SUV has GPS."

Cynth's phone buzzed. Duff's photo popped up on the screen. *Take it or let it go to voice mail? Either he doesn't know I scammed him or he does. Might as well get it over with.*

She put on a cheerful voice. A mistake because Duff

would know she was hiding something, but she couldn't help herself. "Hey, big guy. What's the word?"

"Word is no Danes—great, harlequin or otherwise—have been seen on Haight since 1996."

"Is that a fact?"

"No, but I knew you were up to something."

He sounded amused, not mad. "I hope I didn't get you into trouble with Aubrey."

"Nah. I spotted a honking big imaginary dog turning onto Donaldson. By the time we caught up, it disappeared. Musta gone into a house. Aubrey had a new shiny to chase thirty seconds later."

"You are the best."

"Blood's thicker, cuz. Next time, let me in on the joke. By the way, what *was* the joke?"

"Nothing huge. We just needed to get past you. We didn't want a news van outside while we did the death notification."

"Understandable."

"So we're good?"

"We're always good. I have a quick question for you."

"Shoot."

"You know a skinny black guy with a seventy-dollar buzz cut and a chinstrap beard? Tats not nearly as fine as mine?"

Asshat Langston, "What about him?"

"Nothin'. And you didn't hear that from me."

"Hear what?"

"Exactly. In fact, this conversation never happened. David wants to know if you're up for omelets tomorrow."

"Tomorrow is tight. Next Sunday? Run first?"

"As long as we jump a few walls. Food always tastes better after a hard sweat."

She ended the call.

Brent said, "What about who?"

He would pick up on that one piece of the conversation. *Tell him? Don't tell him?*

"I'd tell you, but then I'd have to kill you."

He examined her face. "That bad?"

"We can't do anything with it."

"Then what good is it? What the hell are we talking about, anyway?"

She put on her best guileless face. "Who's on first?"

"I don't know's on third. Spill, McFadden. You know you want to."

Cynth busied herself, closing her notebook and stashing it back in her pocket. "The leak? It's my fault."

"How the hell did you work that out?"

"I went around the new assistant coroner and he got pissed."

Brent's eyebrows raised. "He leaked his own autopsy mistakes to Aubrey? That's hard core. I guess I can stop sticking pins in my Heckle and Jeckle dolls."

"Don't you do that as a daily practice, anyway?"

"Right after I brush my teeth. But now I will leave the family jewels in peace. How do we handle this?"

"We don't. I can't know. You can't know. I give them Langston, and IA demands my source. I refuse to say, I lose my job. I give up Duff, he loses his job." *And my family disowns me.*

"And we wouldn't want your *boyfriend* to end up homeless. I don't know about you, but I want IA off our backs."

"There has to be something we can do. A week ago, I

thought Homicide would be an excellent gig, even if I had to put up with Heckle and Jeckle."

"Would be if Arseneault had some cojones. Who knows? Maybe he does, when it's his own people. He doesn't know us."

"Parker stood up for us," Cynth said.

"That she did. I'm going to channel Peter's zen mode and say we must wait for the deer to enter the clearing."

"What's that supposed to mean?"

"As the man frequently says to me, 'Let events unfold, grasshopper.'"

"You being the grasshopper? That's so cute."

"Never mind that. If Langston's that big an asshole, he'll trip himself up sooner than later. Meanwhile, we can stop worrying about who the leak is."

"Or," Cynth said, drawing the word out. "We give the deer a kick in the ass."

"Like what? How would you do that?"

"We point IA at the coroner's office without looking like that's what we're doing."

"You're as subtle as a flash bang, so you expect me to do the invisible nudging. The first person they'll go after is Jeffers. You want that?"

Cynth sighed. She could forgive herself for being a rat if Heckle and Jeckle were in the line of fire. There weren't enough Hail Marys between now and eternity to absolve her of siccing IA on Jeffers.

"No, I don't."

"We wait. More will be revealed."

BRENT

Brent counted three boys in the river of chirpy young girls exiting Lois Buchanan's classroom. *Nice odds, if you can get them.*

The girls gave Brent sidelong glances and coy smiles as they brushed by. *Crying shame they didn't look at me that way when I was their age. I might have stayed out of trouble.* Cynth looked bored, which meant she noticed the attention he was getting and was not amused.

The last blonde lemming passed by. They found Buchanan bent over her desk, a sharply cut wedge of blonde highlights—no doubt intended to hide encroaching gray—floating over a gauzy scarf fluffed to artistic effect.

She was a more polished version of a type of teacher he'd disliked when he was in school: rigid, never a sense of humor, always favoring prissy suck ups; a brittle woman whose attempts to look youthful gave her a strained look. Women like that never realized they'd be more attractive if they embraced the crow's feet and the gray hair and meant it when they smiled.

She looked up, a single finger resetting her glasses at the top of her nose as she gave them a tight, pro-forma smile. "Detectives, I thought you were going to call first."

Brent went with conciliatory. "I hope it's no trouble. Ms. Kleemeyer said you had a gap in your schedule."

She took a deep breath and held it, as if she intended to sigh but thought better of it. "No, no trouble at all." She waved at a table in the back of the room. "We can sit there."

Cynth took a chair and shoved it back several inches, out of Buchanan's line of sight. It was a sneaky move to focus Buchanan's attention on him while allowing her to observe without being seen. It would also force Buchanan to turn around and look at her when Cynth spoke.

Her impatience with a certain type of woman was the reason she'd asked him to take lead in this interview. He was impatient, too. He just hid it better.

"I'm going to get some water," Buchanan said. "Can I bring you some?"

"We're fine, ma'am," Brent said.

Buchanan went to the carafe on her desk, turning her back and taking longer than necessary to pour herself a glass. A delaying tactic, giving her time to wonder what they wanted and how much to say. When she reseated herself, she took a sip to demonstrate the legitimacy of her thirst.

Brent gave her a minute to settle before he spoke. "You have questions for us, and we'll get to them. We'd like your help to clear up a few things first."

"I'm not sure what I can say that will help you."

Cynth forgot he was lead and dove in. "Let's start with your relationship with Daniel Moore."

She flinched. "We didn't *have* a relationship. I'm *married*."

"Forgive me, ma'am," Brent said. "We didn't mean to imply anything untoward. But you knew him for a long time. When did you first meet him?" He snuck a glance at Cynth, caught her stifling an eye roll.

"Oh, I see. I've known him forever, I guess. We were in the same class as students."

"How did you get along?"

"I didn't run with his crowd. After he opened his shop, I found him knowledgeable, a true professional. It's a shame about his COPD. That's when the shop got into trouble. He never recovered, not his health, not the business. All that talent." She sighed. "What a waste."

He caught Cynth's eye. She twitched her eyebrows up in a kind of facial shrug. This was the first mention of COPD, though Moore claimed a litany of other ills.

"You sound sympathetic."

"Any Christian would be. It could happen to anyone."

"When was the last time you spoke to Daniel?"

A hesitation, then, "After the sentencing. Poor man, to be humiliated like that."

Something about that hesitation bothered him. He held her gaze and said, "Not since a week ago Wednesday, then?"

She dropped her eyes and took a sip of water, stalling.

"Ms. Buchanan, it's vitally important we have an accurate picture of events if we want to catch Daniel's killer."

She bit her lip, chewing off her lipstick. "We had dinner Friday."

Cynth's eyebrows zoomed down over those formidable steel-gray eyes. "You had dinner with the man who stole a university flute it cost eleven thousand dollars to replace?"

Buchanan turned back to Brent, identifying him as good cop. "I had to file the criminal complaint for the university. I had no choice about that, but everyone had it wrong. He didn't steal the flutes."

"He pled guilty, Ms. Buchanan," Brent said, oozing a soporific dose of magnolia in his voice. "We have his signature on dozens of pawn slips. Help me understand." He didn't dare look at Cynth. There was an excellent chance he'd catch her sticking a finger down her throat.

"Daniel pawned those flutes by accident, and he owned up to it, even though his intern mis-marked them and put them in inventory."

An intern with no digital footprint bumming her way across Europe. For two years.

Buchanan continued, "He doesn't—didn't—know what happened to the others. That's why he delayed the trial. He was trying to find them, to make things right. He couldn't put it off anymore, so he made the plea bargain to stay out of prison."

She believes this. Time to probe, but gently.

"He never told us that."

"You wouldn't have believed him."

"What wouldn't we believe?"

"Ellen stole them. She has them stashed somewhere."

Absurd on too many levels, but necessary to engage with Buchanan on her terms. "Why would Ellen steal from him? Everyone says she held the purse strings."

Buchanan toyed with the edge of her scarf, a substitute for clutching pearls she wasn't wearing. "Daniel was about to take his business to the next level and she couldn't stand it."

"Ellen wanted him to fail?"

"I hate to speak ill of others."

"Ms. Buchanan, it's inevitable when you investigate crimes. Anything you tell us will help. We will discard anything that's irrelevant."

"Daniel ran with the—I'd guess you call it a loose crowd. Ellen wasn't a Hopewell student, but she showed up to party on the weekends. They all hung out in the woods."

"She hooked up with him then?"

"I really shouldn't say anything. I didn't know her until later."

Brent said, "What shouldn't you really say?"

Buchanan pursed her lips. Then she said, "This is only rumor, you understand, and it's decades ago."

"Everything helps," Cynth said.

Buchanan blinked and turned, obviously surprised to find Cynth there. "Ellen was a trust fund baby. Can't have been much of a trust fund since she works, but I'm sure it was impressive to starving musicians. The rumor is they all counted on her to bring the drugs."

"She bribed her way into his crowd?"

"I'd say so, yes. Daniel had a lot of girlfriends, but he dropped them for her. I overheard two of them talking about how she bought him. Now that it's common knowledge she supported the shop, I wonder if it was more than just spite."

"But she stopped giving him money for his business."

"I don't pretend to know what goes on in Ellen's mind."

Brent knew his cue. "But?"

"She needed him to need her, didn't she?"

Cynth jumped in again. "Friday's dinner, where was it?"

"We met at Ruth's and stayed until a little before ten. I've known the owner since they opened. He'll remember us."

Maybe he'll remember who paid.

Brent said, "You go anywhere after that?"

"We said goodbye in the parking lot and I went home."

"Tell us about dinner."

"We talked about business, about repairing his finances now his ordeal was over."

"What is your interest in this?"

"That's why I wanted to talk to you. I was his partner."

"In the shop?"

"Not the shop. The shop was a money pit. Daniel was a genius with flute engineering. He designed a quality student flute we could sell at an irresistible price point. We were getting ready to go into production when this nonsense about flute theft hit."

Brent didn't dare look at Cynth. "That's unfortunate."

"The Kazé flute would have made us rich. That's why I know it was Ellen who stole the flutes. She wanted to keep him under her thumb."

"Didn't the state revoke his right to do business?"

"There was a workaround. I offered to put the company in my name, with him as my employee."

"Seems like a comedown for a man who ran his own shop for decades. He okay with that?"

"He needed my name to build back trust. He understood that."

Not exactly an answer.

"Detective Davis, the judge barred Daniel from his own home after you arrested him. There are a lot of things Ellen never returned. We were wondering if you took his papers when you searched the house, and if you still have them."

"You don't have a copy of your business contract?"

"Not that." She looked embarrassed. "We were still working out the details. He contracted with a company in South Korea to manufacture the flute, but catastrophic floods shut the factory down for more than a year. Maybe you saw the news stories? When I saw him Friday, Daniel said the prototype would be ready in ninety days. That's my granddaughter's college fund. I need to follow through."

Buchanan's earnest eyes stayed focused on Brent. Beyond her, Cynth's eye roll engaged her entire face in a "can you believe this shit?" expression.

"What's the problem?"

"I don't have the contract or contact information. He meant to give them to me, but his life was so chaotic after the arrest. I don't know if they'll honor the contract if I can't produce it."

Brent was tempted to ask if she'd ever seen the contract, but in that direction lay madness.

"We don't have anything like that, Ms. Buchanan," Cynth said. "This is out of our wheelhouse. Your best bet is to get a lawyer."

Buchanan bit her lip. "I was hoping to avoid that."

"Did he have a will?" Cynth asked. "Who is his executor? You should talk to them."

"Oh, that's a problem."

"In what way?"

"I don't think he ever changed it, so that would be Ellen."

"And?"

"I have no paperwork supporting my partnership with Daniel. If you didn't find a new will at Florence's house, there isn't one. Ellen will be his primary beneficiary. She'll own the whole thing, won't she?"

Back in the car, Cynth asked, "Do you believe she didn't run with his crowd back in school?"

Brent considered Buchanan and her careful grooming. "Maybe she was mousy and beneath his notice. Maybe she was intrigued, but too repressed to walk on the wild side. Whatever happened back then, she paid attention to him. She's in love with him now."

"You're not wrong, but what makes you say that?"

"Would you give me your life savings to fund a Glock that doubles as a taser?" Brent asked.

"No, but I'll list it on Kickstarter for you if you give me fifty percent."

"You're a hard woman. You run across any money transfers to South Korea while you were digging into his financials last year?"

"You remember. Cashier's check for forty-five thousand. Came in a few months before we got the case. We couldn't trace it, and he wasn't talking. Went out immediately to the IRS. Bet that was hers."

Brent shook his head. "What was supposed to happen in ninety days when the prototype didn't show up?"

"Shipwreck, fire, the next pandemic. Wouldn't matter as long as he could kick the can down the road."

"Somebody else said he wanted to manufacture his own flute line. He may have started with good intentions."

Cynth snorted. "Good intentions to enrich himself. Did you read his notebook of sermon quotes and his thoughts about them? Everything comes from God. Other people are the vehicle through which God provides."

"Nothing wrong with that."

"His interpretation was creepy, like if it was there for the taking, God meant it for him."

"So God provided Lois's money to save him when Uncle Sam came calling. That appeared to be his rationale every time he pawned a flute. What is it about women that makes them believe stupid lies?" Brent asked.

Cynth took her eyes off the road and stared at him. "You're kidding, right?"

"My lies weren't stupid. And I never asked you to empty your IRA."

"Whatever."

Nobody held a grudge like Cynth. He admired that about her and he never blamed her for being pissed. When everything fell apart, he figured she'd be over it once she kicked him around enough, since his lies had been part of the job. Instead, he'd had to settle for a working relationship that amounted to keeping a polite distance while suffering constant low-level hostility.

"If you hate me so much, why did you ask Arseneault to bring me on board?"

"Because he offered me Heckle and Jeckle. I find you barely more tolerable."

Low blow, comparing him to the Neanderthal twins.

"That's something, at least. Where to next?"

9

DAY 8

SUNDAY, AUGUST 17

CYNTH

THE REEK OF BURNT COFFEE PENETRATED THE LOBBY OF District 5, a real feat since the pot was back by her office. The foul smell would last for hours. Yelling at the officer on the desk would be satisfying—until he asked Cynth if she was on her period and she had to deck him.

A burnt crust coated the pot's bottom after sitting overnight. She brewed new in a clean pot, pouring the entire pot into a thermal carafe to take to her office and leaving the burnt pot in the sink for the boys on graveyard shift to find when they returned.

They want coffee, they can make their own. Not that any of her fellow detectives were around. They had better things to do at six a.m. on a Sunday morning. *Like sleep.*

Yesterday had been mostly a bust. Once they finished with Buchanan, they'd prowled the conference for people who knew Moore, assisted by the annotated attendance list Hannah Kleemeyer provided.

People cheerfully told them how much they hated Moore. No one was sorry he'd died except in that abstract way people are sorry because they ought to be, when you know they don't mean it. The appetite for details about his death bordered on ghoulish.

When they talked to Lia, they understood why.

We investigate Moore for months and nobody tells us he drove someone to suicide. That was the way of it. People rarely trusted cops enough to share the important stuff.

The sum total of the day: Demyanovich was a stalker; Buchanan had been scammed for forty-five grand still didn't know it; and Moore had been a secret sadist. Plenty of motive to go around. Nothing concrete to move the case forward.

Arseneault expected an update in twenty-four hours, while IA lurked, ready to pounce. Which meant a restless night and her grinding in the office when she ought to be on a pre-brunch run with Duff.

She booted up her computer. After days of waiting, the recovered files from the burner phone popped up in her inbox. She poured herself a cup of coffee and settled in.

The data showed up as a series of spreadsheets for texts, contacts, and call history. No camera meant no pictures or videos. Shame, photos would be the fastest way to learn about the owner.

She opened the contact list and began scrolling. Whoever owned the phone did not believe in last names. Everyone was identified by a first name or a nickname, except Moore Flutes. No epiphany there. Everyone with a grudge against Moore did business with the shop at some point.

She switched to the call history, toggled the sheet so the most recent call was first and checked it against the contact list. Moore Flutes. She checked the date.

Four years ago.

Why no calls for so long? *Owner upgraded to a nice smart phone and tossed this in a drawer because you never know when you'll need an anonymous phone to entice a creep to his death.*

Daily calls to Moore Flutes, going back weeks. Desperate appeals for the return of a flute?

She began working through the other calls, checking them against the reverse directory. The next three had no obvious significance. She hit pay dirt with the fourth.

Someone had weeded Florence Nygaard's flower beds. As Cynth speculated about changes in Nygaard's circumstances, Brent whined, "I can't believe you woke me up at seven."

"I gave you an extra half-hour."

"Only because it would be indecent to roust Nygaard before eight. I take that back. Eight is indecent. Why are we here?"

"Pull up your big boy panties and stop complaining."

"Confess, McFadden. The only reason I'm along is to charm the little old lady."

"Now that Aubrey is persona non grata, I thought you should meet more women."

"Harsh."

A Sunday sermon penetrated the siding as they stepped

onto the porch. Cynth rang the bell, launching Snickerdoodle into a yapping fit. The TV went silent.

"Who is it?" Nygaard called, her voice quavery.

"Mrs. Nygaard, it's Detective McFadden. I'm here with Detective Davis. We need to ask you some questions about Daniel."

"Come on in. The key's under the mat."

Nygaard looked even more fragile than she had a week earlier. Snickerdoodle guarded her lap, aiming those blind eyes at the intruders, grumbling. Someone had given him a bath and a trim.

Disorder still reigned on Nygaard's side table. Otherwise, the house was clean and less depressing than the week before. The army of figurines glowed. Cynth didn't want to think how many hours it had taken to rid them of grime and cobwebs. *I hope Nygaard's helper gave her a respirator while they raised all that dust.*

"Have a seat. Sorry I couldn't come to the door. This is not one of my better days."

"Ma'am, I'm Detective Davis," Brent said. "We appreciate you talking to us, but if you're ill, we can come back later."

"If you wait until I feel better, you'll be talking to me in heaven."

Cynth asked, "Is there someone here with you?"

"I have a girl who comes in the afternoon. Not good company like Daniel, but she's much neater. What do you want to ask me?"

"Your number is in the call history of a phone associated with the case. We're hoping you'll recognize it."

She handed Nygaard a card with the burner number written in bold marker for her ailing eyes. Nygaard stared at the little rectangle. Her hand shook violently and the card dropped to the floor. Tears spilled down her cheeks.

"Do you know it?" Cynth asked gently.

"It—it's not possible."

Brent caught her eye, shook his head imperceptibly. Cynth said nothing.

Nygaard lifted her head to the array of Natalie photos holding pride of place on the mantel. "That's Natalie's number."

Cynth paused—a moment of silence out of respect for the dead—then asked, "What happened to her phone after she passed?"

"The room Daniel stayed in, that was Natalie's. It should still be there."

"Captain Arseneault and I didn't see a phone when we went through Daniel's things. Where else might it be?"

"I left everything pretty much as it was in her room. I meant to do something about it after Daniel moved in, but I never had the heart."

"No one but Daniel has been in there?"

"I was getting to that. Two of her friends came over a few days after the funeral. I gave them her music things because she would want them to be used."

"Do you remember their names?" Cynth asked. "We need to talk to them."

Disapproval replaced grief on Nygaard's face. "You can't think they had anything to do with this."

Brent soothed, "We don't think anything. We just need to track down the person who last had the phone for our file. We wouldn't be bothering you if our captain hadn't insisted on it."

Liar, liar. Nobody sold stupid and necessary lies better

than Brent. Necessary, because upsetting Nygaard could give her a heart attack. Stupid, because who would believe they were tidying paperwork when they hadn't caught Moore's killer?

Nygaard pointed to a photo of Natalie next to a small girl with a dozen skinny braids peeking through her long, dark hair. "That's Dianne. She was Natalie's best friend. She brought another girl with her. Big girl, blonde hair. I forget her name."

Dianne Lovato, who Cynth hadn't recognized when she'd first seen that photo; who'd starred in the YouTube protest video; who they kicked loose yesterday.

Nygaard extended a trembling hand to a drawer in her side table and pulled it out a few inches. "My address book is in here, if you can find it. I don't have much use for it anymore."

Brent rummaged through the drawer and withdrew a miniature binder. "Dianne have a last name?" He asked, flipping through the book.

They had Lovato's contact info, but following Nygaard's lead would encourage the flow of words.

"Dianne Lovato."

"Have you seen Dianne recently?"

"Not for years. Covid messed with everything. People stopped visiting. Guess they didn't want to kill me."

Outside the house, Cynth asked, "Think she'll call Lovato?"

"Hard for her to do when I buried her address book in the wrong drawer."

"We had Lovato in that conference room and sent her away. I should have made the connection then."

Brent shrugged. "We were pursuing other matters."

"Lovato kicked off the investigation and kept it in the news. I can't believe Moore slept in that room with her staring at him. Why didn't he turn the photo around?"

"Not odd at all, if you don't have a conscience."

BRENT

They found Dianne Lovato sorting literature at a booth in Hopewell's exhibition hall. Brent called her name. She turned, jerking when she realized they were inches behind her. She ran a nervous hand through her hair, fingering one of her many braids.

"I thought you were done with me yesterday."

Brent grimaced, then sighed. "I wish. Do you have a few minutes?"

"I have rehearsal."

"Rehearsal?" Cynth said. "Isn't the conference over this afternoon?"

"This is for something else. What's this about?"

Girlfriend recovers fast.

"We talked with Florence Nygaard. She says she gave you some of Natalie's things after she died."

"So?"

"Do you remember what you did with them?"

Lovato gave them an overdone "WTF-does-that-have-to-do-with-anything" look. Then she shrugged, as if it didn't matter.

"It was mostly music stuff. Why would you care about that?"

"We're looking for Natalie's phone," Brent said.

"Her phone?" Lovato's confused act wouldn't win the Oscar any time soon. "I don't have it. I never did."

"You don't remember who you gave it to?" Cynth asked.

"We took the stuff we didn't want to Saint Vincent de Paul. If we ever had it, it probably went there. Look, I'm late. Gotta go."

She turned, tiny braids flying as she whipped around, moving through the crowd as if she wanted to run but knew it was bad optics.

Brent nodded after her. "She knows who has the phone."

"You think?"

"What we need are fingerprints."

Cynth gave him an ironic, wide-eyed look. "You can follow her. She'll toss out a gum wrapper, eventually."

"Aren't you a laugh riot. We should have hit her up for fingerprints for exclusionary purposes."

"Too late. Public knowledge the prints on the awl are Ellen's."

Wendy Harrison-Green entered the hall, scanning the crowd. She spotted them and hurried over. "I just saw Dianne. She says you're looking for Natalie's old phone."

Brent raised his eyebrows. "You know something?"

"We offered to go through Natalie's things with Mrs. Nygaard. Make it easier for her. Like ripping off a band-aid, you know?"

He didn't know. But he knew others who had been over-whelmed by the process.

Harrison-Green continued, "Anyway, she said she

wanted to keep Natalie's room like it was. But she gave us her music stuff and some other things."

"And the phone?"

"Mrs. Nygaard, she hasn't been well for a long time. Natalie helped her with meals and stuff. After Natalie died, Mrs. Nygaard had a helper who came in for a few hours every day. Mrs. Nygaard said she didn't want the phone. Can't blame her, it was a piece of junk. I never told Natalie that. She couldn't help it if she couldn't afford better. The helper asked me if she could have it, and I gave it to her."

"When was this?" Brent asked.

"I don't know. Sometime after the funeral."

"You know her name?"

"I wish I could remember, but I can't. Does this help?"

Brent flashed her a smile. "Sure does. Thank you for coming forward."

Harrison-Green turned to leave. Took two steps.

Now I lower the boom. "Ms. Harrison-Green?"

Harrison-Green paused. Her head turned back toward them while her feet pointed hopefully toward the door.

"We'll need you to make an official statement. When can you come in to District 5?"

The soft mouth dropped into an "O" as her eyes darted, thinking. She turned the rest of her body around to face them, head drooping. "Umm … that's on Hamilton Avenue, right?"

"Just up the hill," Brent coaxed. "By Family Dollar. Can you come by after class today?"

"No, um … I'm working. Can I come tomorrow?"

Brent looked at his watch. "How about now? I'm sure we can square it with Ms. Kleemeyer. If we give you a ride to

District 5, we can have you back in thirty minutes. Twenty if Detective McFadden drives. "

He winked.

Brent took the rear, observing Harrison-Green as Cynth led the way to the interview room. Shoulders tense, head swiveling in search of an escape route, face paler than even her natural color; everything about the girl screamed, "I'm doomed."

There's more to get from her.

Cynth did her best with chatty stuff—she'd improved in that area—to get Harrison-Green to relax so they could read her baseline responses. It wasn't working.

They stopped at a vending machine. Cynth asked, "Can I get you something to drink?"

Voice barely audible, Harrison-Green said, "No thank you."

They needed fingerprints. *Push a little and she'll accept to be polite.*

Cynth said, "You sure? We have soda and iced tea. I can get you coffee, but I don't recommend it."

Good. Make her focus on the choice instead of whether she wants anything. Condescending to mentally coach Cynth, but he couldn't help himself.

Cynth raised her eyebrows, waited.

Harrison-Green chewed her lip. Surveyed the offerings. "Tea, I guess."

Cynth ushered her into the interview room, while Brent took a minute to duck into the closet with the hidden video camera controls. Better to have it on before

Harrison-Green entered the room, but you couldn't have everything.

A change in policy replaced big conference room tables with small side tables, eliminating the shield that hid eighty percent of body language from investigators. Harrison-Green had no protections.

She sat, ankles crossed and tucked under her chair. Her hair fell in a curtain, hiding her lowered face as she ran a thumb up and down the side of the unopened can of tea in her lap. *If she can't see us, we won't see her.*

Brent took a seat opposite Harrison-Green and said in his kindest, luring-kittens-out-of-trees voice, "No need to be nervous. We just want you to repeat what you told us for the record."

Harrison-Green's head popped up. "Don't I need to write it down?"

"We're recording now. We'll transcribe your statement for your review."

Cynth jumped in, rattling off the Miranda warning. Harrison-Green's mouth dropped into that same "O" they'd seen earlier. Good. Their tough cop, nice cop rhythm had Harrison-Green off kilter.

He walked her through everything she'd said at Hopewell.

She said, "That's it I guess."

Cynth spoke. "We're hoping you can clarify a few details?"

Harrison-Green jolted. "Details?"

Gently, McFadden. Ease her into it.

"Florence Nygaard may not be as sharp as she used to be."

Harrison-Green dropped her eyes to the can she never

opened and shrugged. "I haven't seen her since she gave us Natalie's things."

"She doesn't remember the helper. Anything you can tell us about her will help."

We haven't had time to talk to Nygaard, but she's too rattled to realize that.

"I don't remember her name. I said so before.

"Do you remember what she looked like?"

"Umm ..."

Didn't expect that, did you?

"She was just normal looking." She uncrossed her ankles, hooked her feet around the chair legs.

"Let's start with her build. Tall as you? Short as Dianne?"

"Kinda in the middle, I guess."

"Your age, middle-aged, or older?"

Eyes darting now. Harrison-Green's heart rate had to be spiking. Brent leaned in. "If you're having trouble remembering, we can put you with a sketch artist. Our guy is amazing at pulling out details."

She shook her head, fear etched on her face.

"There was no helper, was there?" Brent said.

"Someone was there, I swear! I gave her the phone."

Cynth said, "Florence's insurance has no record of an aide until a month after Natalie's funeral."

Another bluff. Good one, McFadden.

"I got the dates wrong. Or it was a neighbor." Harrison-Green set the can aside and planted her feet. "I can't tell you any more."

"Wendy," Brent said, moving into his un-spook-the-horse voice, "You aren't in any trouble right now. But if you leave this room after making a false statement—what's the penalty, Detective McFadden?"

"180 days in jail and a $1,000 fine."

Full deer-in-headlights now.

"The phone had nothing to do with it! I swear!"

"All right. Let's start over."

Harrison-Green's head dropped again, her voice tiny behind the screen of her hair. "We didn't hurt him. Nothing happened."

"Okay," Brent said, "you didn't hurt him and nothing happened. Tell us what you did do."

Harrison-Green swallowed hard. She popped the tab on her tea and drank. When she finished stalling, Harrison-Green said, "Dianne and Natalie were best friends for years."

"We thought it was something like that," Cynth said.

Good, encourage her. Cynth was doing fine. He was ridiculous for worrying about it.

"Natalie was amazing. A real prodigy. Mrs. Nygaard was on disability, but she somehow scraped together the money to buy Natalie a handmade Burkhart. It was an awesome flute. She let me play it once."

Harrison-Green took a sip of tea, staring at nothing.

"She was upset. We let her go, to work it out in private. If we'd known how bad off she was, we would have stopped it. "

Another sip.

"I don't understand," Cynth said, all empathy. "What would you have stopped?"

Harrison-Green looked confused. "Didn't Mrs. Nygaard tell you? Daniel kept her flute for weeks longer than he should have and didn't return it until the morning of her audition for an international tour. She was a wreck going in, and she flubbed it. She killed herself."

This was the student Lia told them about.

"We thought she was going off for a good cry. We thought giving her space was the right thing to do. She cut her wrists in the bathroom."

A tear rolled down the pale cheek. "When we went to help Mrs. Nygaard, she said she couldn't bear to sell Natalie's flute and it should go to someone who loved her and would appreciate it. She said Natalie would want Dianne to have it."

More than a fancy flute. The last bit of a dead friend.

"When Daniel disappeared it, Dianne felt like she'd let Natalie down again. By then, we all knew going to Daniel was risky, but he knew the flute and she was afraid to trust it with someone new.

"Dianne was desperate to find Natalie's flute. She said she'd never feel right until she got it back."

"The phone?" Cynth prompted.

Abrupt, but the tone was right.

"I kept it. For an emergency, you know? Anyway, we were talking about how you never made Daniel confess. We started goofing on how to do it."

"And your plan was?"

"It didn't matter. Nothing happened."

"You and Dianne? Anyone else?"

Harrison-Green's eyes brimmed. "I don't want to get anyone in trouble."

Brent jumped in. "Wendy, did you commit a crime?"

"We pretended to be Ellen. That's a crime, isn't it?"

Cynth said, "If the DA wants to be a hard-ass about it, telling us everything now is your best defense."

WENDY - 8 DAYS AGO

They would have broken their necks that night if the moon wasn't full. They wouldn't have been able to see their hands in front of their faces, much less the trail.

It shouldn't have mattered, but Dianne—always Dianne telling them what to do—Dianne wouldn't let them use a flashlight, not even the measly light on her phone. Even with the full moon, it had been a near thing.

It would have been so easy to drive the stupid wheelchair to Hopewell and push it a few hundred feet along the walk, but Dianne said they couldn't risk being seen and Ron's car in the parking lot could get them caught.

They'd parked at the far side of the preserve, loading the wheelchair with the car battery and jumper cables, wrestling and sweating the stupid thing over the trail, down and up gullies, over tree roots and rocks. Between the elevation and the switchbacks, they must have traveled a mile. That and the heat had Wendy sweating like a pig before they made it to the Lounge.

"Window dressing," Ron had said when he proposed his ganja inspired plan. "We go Gitmo on him."

"How do you plan to do that?" Wendy asked.

"We zip tie him to a wheelchair and threaten him with live jumper cables. If I touch the clamps together, they'll spark and scare the piss out of him. That doesn't work, we roll him to the edge of the ravine and threaten to let go. He'll tell us anything."

It was Dianne's idea to impersonate Ellen. But Wendy was the one paying attention to Ellen's stories while they waited in court for Daniel to not show up. She'd provided the details necessary to sell the con—something Dianne hadn't appreciated, not enough.

They giggled over Daniel's texts and how easily they reeled him in. It had been a game. Just a game to cheer Dianne up.

The final text came as they sat on fallen trees in the Lounge. A simple "OMW," then nothing. They sat in tense silence, sweating under their balaclavas and slapping at mosquitos.

Finally Dianne stood up. "He should have been here twenty minutes ago. I'm going to see if he's around."

"We'll come with you," Ron said.

"You stay in case he comes the other way."

Five minutes later she was back, balaclava stuffed in her pocket. "He's not coming. Asshole."

She pulled the ancient tracfone out of her pocket and shoved it into the hollow of the tree where they'd kept it since they sent the first text.

There was something Dianne wasn't saying, but she had that look on her face, the one where you knew she'd blow up if you said anything. So Wendy hadn't.

CYNTH

Harrison-Green spent a long minute chewing her lip before speaking. "We were just goofing. Ron—Ron Coleman—he shares a house with me and Dianne—he said we should do some theater on Daniel, scare the crap out of him and find out where all the flutes went. We'd wear masks so he couldn't identify us."

Theater. Freaking theater.

Harrison-Green's face screwed up, angry and red. "He deserved to be scared after what he did to everyone, after the judge gave him probation and never made him say what happened to all the instruments. Daniel was never going to pay restitution. Dianne didn't want money, anyway. She wanted her flute."

"Okay," Cynth said. "What was the plan?"

"We had to get him somewhere nobody would see us. I had Natalie's phone. It felt like poetic justice to use it. I didn't think anyone could trace it."

"We read the texts."

"We figured it was legit that Ellen might change her number. They make you do that sometimes when you switch providers. Ellen and K Lee used to talk about the old days when we were stuck waiting in court."

"That's how you learned about the Lounge?"

Harrison-Green nodded. "Nobody parties in the woods anymore. I guess we don't need to. I knew I could make it sound like Ellen. We sent the texts to get him in the woods, and we had props."

"What kind of props?"

"We had a wheelchair. We were going to zip-tie him in it. We had a car battery and jumper cables."

Dammit, why did Brent have to be right?

Brent said, "How exactly was this little play supposed to go?"

Harrison-Green took a long swallow.

Stalling? Hiding embarrassment?

"Ron—um, Ron planned to hook up the jumper cables and make them spark like they do when you touch the clamps together. If that didn't work, we were going to push him to the edge of the gully and make like we were going to dump him down that steep part where it drops off." She broke off there.

"And?" Brent drew the word out, not letting Harrison-Green off the hook.

"It was just theater, honest. We sent a few texts, and he said he would come. Then he texted and said he was coming. We waited ages. Dianne told Ron and me to stay while she went to see if she could spot him. She came right back and said he must be onto us because he wasn't there. She said we needed to go home and forget we were there."

"Why hide the phone in the tree?" Cynth asked.

"That was stupid, wasn't it?"

Cynth shrugged and said nothing.

"It's an old phone, but we didn't want to chance that it had GPS. We kept it in the tree so if you traced it, it wouldn't come back to us. But it did anyway."

Harrison-Green's face turned mulish again. "Dianne didn't kill him. She didn't have any blood on her, and she wasn't messed up from a fight. She looked just like she did when she left."

"Okay," Cynth said.

"There's a bigger reason she didn't do it. She never would have killed him before she found out what he did with Natalie's flute. She wants it back."

Cynth shot Brent a glance. *Something more here.* They stayed silent.

Harrison-Green's eyes blinked rapidly, anxiety written on her face. "Do you think someone killed him while we were there?"

"What do you think?" Brent asked.

"But we never heard it. Wouldn't we have heard it?

Dianne swears she saw nothing. I guess she didn't go far enough down the path."

The walkway where Moore died was well-lit from street lights on Glen Parker. If Dianne came that way, she saw him.

"Who did you tell about your plans?" Cynth asked.

"No one, I swear!"

Cynth gave Harrison-Green her meanest stare down and said nothing.

Harrison-Green looked at Brent for help. He said nothing. She looked back at Cynth, desperation in her eyes. "Nobody knew! Honest!"

Cynth put on her mean look again. "We'll take you back now, and we'll have a statement for you to review tomorrow. If you tell Dianne or Ron what we discussed, I will charge you with obstruction."

Harrison-Green's lip trembled.

Brent said, "You can talk to them after we do, not before. Can you do that?"

"I can spend the night at Mom's and not answer the phone."

Brent rubbed her shoulder. "Atta girl."

"I'll have to move out. They'll murder me after this."

BRENT

Brent returned from driving Harrison-Green back to school, shaking his head as he dropped into Cynth's visitor's chair. "Did you have to give her the basilisk stare? That poor girl is a wreck."

Cynth snorted. "That poor girl was prepared to torture an old man."

"The same old man you wanted to torture on many occasions. We should've tried a car battery."

"Nothing else worked. Do you believe her?"

"Yeah, I do. Moore told someone."

"Another effing thing to chase down." Cynth looked at the clock. "Barely eleven. Lunch before we run down Lovato and her boyfriend? You try the barbecue place yet?"

The restaurant across the parking lot had gone through several incarnations in recent years: barbecue, Lebanese, fish. This month it was back to barbecue.

"Fine. It will give us a chance to strategize." Brent reached for the stack of menus Cynth kept on her desk. The phone rang. He picked up the receiver instead, handing it to her. She narrowed her eyes at him and punched the speaker button. "McFadden."

The desk sergeant's tinny voice came through the phone. "There's a Gail Cook here who wants to talk to someone about Daniel Moore."

She muted the phone. "You know a Gail Cook?"

Brent rubbed his chin. "Connected to Moore? I've seen the name recently. She wasn't part of the original case."

Cynth snapped her fingers. "She's the dog walker. There goes lunch."

Gail Cook was sturdy, with lank hair of that no-particular-color common with middle-aged women. Underneath a nervous obsequiousness, Brent sensed pugnacious tendencies. *This woman is a secret bully.*

She sat in the interview room, twisting her hands in her lap. *Waiting for us to pry out of her whatever she came to say.* Cynth vibrated with impatience. The love of his life was so much better with dirtbags she could go head on with.

Start with the easy stuff. He cleared his throat. "How do you know Daniel Moore?"

"I never met him. Florence told me who he was. I do a bit of everything for people in the neighborhood. Have done since the place I worked went bankrupt during covid. I did errands and housework for Florence after Natalie died. When Daniel moved in, she didn't need me anymore."

Resented him, did you?

"You know I found him? I didn't know it was Daniel. The dogs were way ahead on their flexi-leads, and it was dark under the trees. I saw them standing in all that blood and sniffing him and I dragged them away."

"Understandable," Brent said. Sometimes you see a body and you know it's dead. Maybe it was like that for Cook, but he doubted it. He wanted to ask how she could be so calloused, to not bother to check if Moore was still alive.

Cook continued, "I only realized it was Daniel when the officer asked me if I knew him. That's when I went to look. I suppose I should have told that police officer—"

Told him what?

"—but I expected someone would call me. I waited a week."

So whatever this is, is on us?

Cook dropped her head. "I don't want to get anyone in trouble."

Brent felt himself moving into I-want-to-poke-my-eye-out-with-a-broken-pencil territory. Skittish women found his Georgia accent soothing. He poured magnolia into his voice. "It's all right. Whatever you tell us, we have to verify with evidence."

"I saw Daniel the night before. Must have been right before it happened." Her head popped up. "I didn't know she was going to murder him!"

Cynth jerked her chin, signaling him to keep going. He plied Cook with more magnolia. "Deep breaths. Go back to the beginning. What were you doing out that night?"

"I'm house sitting on Glenn Parker. Cleo and Patra are old. If they don't go out late, they won't make it through the night. "

Cleo-Patra. Cute. "What time was this?"

"I'm not sure. Sometime after eleven-thirty. They like to walk in the woods. It's safe there, never any trouble in the preserve."

"You were in the woods?"

"We never got there. I saw Daniel walking down Langland. A woman got out of her car and they were arguing on the corner. I went the other way."

Cynth jumped in. "What were they arguing about?"

"I don't know. The dogs had already done their business, so I took them home."

"You couldn't hear them?"

Cynth's directness got Cook's back up. "They weren't loud."

"How did you know they were arguing?"

Cook huffed, "Because she was waving her arms like a maniac."

Brent shot Cynth a look and slid in. "What can you tell us about her?"

Cook's temperature came down a notch. She shook her head. "Nothing, really. It wasn't anyone I recognized."

"Was she tall or short?"

"I don't remember."

Brent heard frustration in her voice. He leaned in and put a gentle hand on her arm. They couldn't afford to alienate their one witness. "It's all right. Close your eyes and picture her standing next to Daniel."

Cook closed her eyes, opened them. "I guess she was about as tall as Daniel."

"Close your eyes again. What shoes was she wearing? Flats or heels?"

"I'm sorry. I'm not very good at this. She was skinny, and she wore a dress, something nice, like you wear to church. I guess she wore heels. It was that kind of dress."

"How about her hair?"

"A wedge. Big glasses and a scarf around her neck."

Lunch was two six-month-old power bars on the drive to Hopewell. It would have been three, but he'd given the last one to Cynth.

Gail Cook's revelations meant pivoting the investigation. Dianne Lovato and her accomplice would have to wait while they chased Lois Buchanan down. He promised himself they wouldn't get lost in the shuffle, if only for Harrison-Green's mental health.

He didn't approve of vigilantism, but he understood their frustration with a legal system that often failed to provide justice. Daniel told someone about the meet, and that person hijacked their play. Being young and stupid shouldn't wreck their lives, not if their involvement was what Harrison-Green said.

Cynth wanted to go at Lovato and Coleman with both barrels. Couldn't blame her with the game Lovato tried to pull on them. If he convinced Cynth to take a diplomatic approach, they might preserve Harrison-Green's friendship with them. It would come down to what Lovato saw and how forthcoming she was. But that would be after they dealt with Buchanan.

They arrived at Hopewell shortly before noon. Hannah Kleemeyer directed them to the same staff area they'd seen during their first visit.

Buchanan sat alone at the secluded picnic table. "Detectives, is there more I can help you with?" She glanced at a small, diamond-encrusted watch. "I have a few minutes before our closing luncheon."

Brent sat across from her. "This shouldn't take long. We're still trying to nail down Daniel's movements that last day."

Buchanan looked away. "I wouldn't know anything about that. Can't Florence help you?"

He leaned in, pitching his voice low and confiding as if they were alone. "We've got a problem. Someone saw a woman talking to Daniel at the entrance to Parker Woods minutes before he died."

Her head jerked as if she'd been slapped, wide eyes magnified by those glasses. She looked like a startled alien.

Gently, he said, "Our witness identified you. Would you like to start over?"

A lie. They hadn't shown photos to Cook, not wanting to influence her memory in case they needed to set her up with a sketch artist.

Buchanan chewed her lip, getting lipstick on her teeth. It would horrify her next time she looked in a mirror.

"I didn't know she would do this."

"Who, Lois? What did she do?"

"Ellen, of course. Who else?"

He exchanged a quick look with Cynth. This wasn't what they expected.

"Ms. Buchanan, the awl was planted. We have no evidence Ellen was there."

"Of course she was there. She's the reason Daniel was in the woods in the middle of the night."

"How do you know this?"

"He told me."

"What exactly did Daniel tell you?"

"He said she'd been texting him and she wanted him back."

Cynth said, "The texts weren't from her. She didn't know about them."

"Oh, she knew about them," Buchanan snapped.

"How is that, Ms. Buchanan?" Brent asked.

"We talked about it."

"Come again?"

"I confronted her."

Time to regroup. "Let's go back to the beginning. How did you know about the texts?"

"Daniel showed them to me. He thought it was funny. He said he wanted to see what she had to say. I could see her reeling him in, just as he was getting back on his feet. You know how it is when two people are together so long. They can't let go, even when the relationship is toxic."

"Ms. Buchanan, why did that matter to you?"

"She's the reason he landed in that mess, and it was starting all over again. I had a significant investment at risk."

Investment, my foot. You were trying to buy him the way you say Ellen did.

"How did you leave it with him?"

"I told him he knew best. It's pointless to argue with Daniel when he's in a certain frame of mind."

Then why did you show up the next night? But it wasn't time to ask that. "Then what happened?"

"I went home."

Brent read irritation behind Cynth's placid expression. It reminded him to take it slow. "When did you decide to talk to Ellen?"

"I planned to keep my mouth shut and let it work out. But she'd invited me to Dog Day. And it just burst out."

"You thought she stole from Daniel. Why did you go?"

"I wish I hadn't. I wanted to be civil going forward, since Daniel and I were partners."

"Lois, think carefully about what Ellen said. How did the texts come up?"

Buchanan looked away. "It was all very heated. You know how arguments are. Remembering who said what is impossible."

Maybe with context, she'd remember more. "Were you at the booth?"

"I stopped by. She gave me one of her tacky key fobs."

"Did anyone see you?"

"There were people all around. Bailey was there. I thanked Ellen and went to the refreshment area."

"And then what happened?"

"Ellen took a break and saw me throw the key fob in the trash. She got right in my face about it."

"What did you do?"

"I walked away, but she followed me. I said I wanted

nothing from her. That she was a hypocrite, claiming she wanted Daniel out of her life when she was begging him to come back."

"How did she react to that?"

"She said I had a lot of nerve to suggest she wanted Daniel back. I told her I read her texts. I said she was pathetic, and Daniel was playing her."

"Think back. Did either of you say anything about the meeting?"

Buchanan chewed her lipstick. "I may have said something like, 'If he shows up tonight, it will be to watch you humiliate yourself.'"

"What did she say?"

"She told me to look in the mirror. The nerve!"

Brent probed, but got nothing more. He had to count it as a win. Histrionic personalities—which he suspected Buchanan was—often remembered nothing after going into a rage.

"How did you wind up at Parker Woods?"

"I didn't mean to go. I couldn't get over what a liar she was. I went for a drive to clear my head and the car sort of drove itself there."

Bunny boiler. Brent nodded, all empathy.

"I guess I had to find out for myself."

"Was he surprised to see you?"

"I—I don't know. He said not to worry. He needed to see her face to face, so she'd know he meant it when he told her it was over."

A mature statement that in no way should have provoked the crazed arm-waving Cook reported.

"What happened after that?"

"I left."

Cynth jumped in. "You left? Just like that?"

Buchanan sat up straight, all primness. "Staying would have been undignified."

Cynth pushed. "Ms. Buchanan, why didn't you come forward?"

Eyes magnified by those overlarge glasses grew even wider now. "You arrested Ellen right away. You didn't need me."

"And we un-arrested her," Cynth said.

"Do you think I want to be involved? I won't be able to show my face in church if I'm dragged into this."

Brent put on his most reassuring face. "You've been very helpful. We'll do our best to keep you out of it."

As he stood, Cynth gave him her basilisk glare, a sign she wasn't finished. Tough. She assigned him to conduct this interview. She'd have to live with it. He turned to leave, confident Cynth would follow.

CYNTH

Cynth dropped into the driver's seat and slammed the door. She wasn't ready to leave, but this was the only place she could yell at Brent in private. She turned on him, unleashing everything pounding in her brain since they'd left Buchanan.

"What the hell was that? We have her at the scene. We needed to push. And if you tell me to calm down, I will punch your other eye."

Brent's lip twitched. She folded her arms and stared out the windshield so she wouldn't have to look at him struggling not to laugh.

He waited several seconds—probably to stifle the laugh he was holding in—then said, "There's more than one way to catch a fish, boss lady."

She wasn't ready to give in. "We should have hammered her and ended this."

"She was cooperative because she thinks we believe her. Miranda her, go hard at her, we lose that edge. She's still willing to talk to us. We can circle back later."

"So you didn't buy it."

"Our lady doth protest much, but we aren't in a position to say she's lying about Ellen. Not yet."

"So we hammer Ellen."

Brent gave her a patient look that pissed her off all over again. "Brandt will never admit to knowing about the meet. We need a witness. Shame they didn't have that blowout in front of Bailey."

"Someone saw it. A volunteer from one of the refreshment booths?"

"I hate needles in haystacks, especially anonymous needles."

"The dogs have to register."

"We interviewing dogs now?"

She grumbled, "Don't be cute."

"We have to assume Lois spewed the particulars at Ellen. You know—" His voice went up an octave. "'Stop playing innocent. I know all about your midnight rendezvous at the Lounge tonight, you bitch.'"

Brent's falsetto made her laugh, as Cynth was sure he intended. She retrieved a canister of emergency nuts from the glove box, offering it to him.

He waved it off and continued, "So we have Dianne and

Wendy and Ron plotting terroristic theater, and Lois attempting to head off the lovers' reunion—"

Cynth spoke around a mouthful of almonds. "So she says."

"So she says. She admits to being angry and on autopilot most of the day. She could have been mad enough to kill Daniel."

Cynth folded her arms, giving him a bland look. "And the awl?"

"People in that state do stupid things on impulse. She could have grabbed the poodle mug for spite, and it was still in the car. You know how often assholes tell us they don't know how the knife got in their hand. It could have been like that."

"Daniel wasn't killed with the awl. She had a handy alternate weapon to kill him with?"

"It's not clear in the photograph how many awls were in that mug. Could have been another one. She kills Daniel, realizes she's sunk, has a brainstorm, plants the second awl, and disposes of the first."

"The smashed vegetation where Moore's killer lay in wait?"

"No proof Moore's killer trampled that patch. Could have happened earlier."

Cynth sneered. With her mad blown out, it was just for form. "Crime of opportunity? Heat of the moment? She just happened to have a sharp implement in her pocket?"

Brent shrugged. "Playing devil's advocate. If we don't, the defense will. She has the argument with Moore, dashes back to her car, spots the poodle mug shoved in the cubby above her gear shift, grabs the first thing that comes to hand in a rage, and chases Moore down."

"A sixty-year-old woman in pumps accomplishes this in less time than it takes for Moore to walk a hundred feet? Gets in front of Moore and stabs him with no defensive wounds after they just had an argument? Want to buy a bridge?"

"You should have more faith in your sex."

"We need blood evidence."

"Our viable suspects provide each other with reasonable doubt, whether they know it or not. We have to resolve this."

Cynth looked at the dashboard clock. "We still need to track down Lovato and Coleman."

"Maybe try a little deep breathing first? Giving those kids the full SWAT treatment might be problematic."

"Asshole. I'll call Spring Grove first thing in the morning. If we're lucky, they haven't tossed the registration forms."

Brent grumbled, "If you call chasing down hundreds of casual passersby lucky. This is pointless. We need fresh eyes on the known players."

"You want to go to Arseneault?"

"Considering our current situation with the brass, I'd rather have a solid theory before we do that. We nail down Lovato and Coleman. After that, we go back to the well."

Cynth raised her eyebrows and gave Brent that bland look.

He backpedaled. "That's if you agree, boss. If we don't come up with something tonight, I'll chase down every one of the registered Dog Day attendees and toss in the volunteers."

10

DAY 9

MONDAY, AUGUST 18

LIA

THE SUN BROKE OVER THE TREES AS LIA ARRIVED AT THE DOG park, casting long shadows across dewy grass. *No one here. Good.* Chewy bolted through the corral, off on his usual patrol of the fence line. Gypsy stood just inside the gate, grinning.

She set her coffee and the tote bag containing her iPad on the garbage bin and launched a tennis ball, taking a moment to watch her girl chase it down. She'd be back in seconds, with the ball soaked in saliva and an expectant look in her wild, bi-colored eyes.

She headed for the picnic table furthest from the gate, tossing the sopping ball as she went. It would be a solid hour before anyone showed up. *That ought to be enough time.*

Last night Cynth and Brent came over with barbecue, beers, and a request to pick their brains. Brent hooked his laptop to the ridiculously huge TV in Peter's man cave and

293

opened the virtual murder board he'd created with mind mapping software.

They'd talked out the case for hours, looking for angles and holes and adding notes until her head swam. Cynth allowed her to load the file on her iPad, a gift that came with the expected threat of death and dismemberment if she broke cone of silence.

She was here at daybreak, hoping quiet and a night's sleep would lead to an epiphany. Her sandal tugged. Gypsy grinned at her, tongue lolling, wagging her entire body as she stood with the sopping tennis ball between her front paws. Lia flung the ball as far as she could, aiming for the slope so it would roll downhill and make Gypsy hunt for it. Beyond the fence, the parking lot was still empty.

She settled in with her coffee and iPad, coming up for air whenever Gypsy showed up with her ball.

Daniel's killer lay at the intersection of people who knew about Wendy's texts to Daniel and those who attended Dog Day or otherwise had access to Ellen's tools. While hundreds took part in the event, only Wendy, Dianne, Ron, Lois, Ellen, and Daniel knew about the texts.

None of their suspects benefitted from Daniel's death, and that was a problem. That suggested the attack was an impulse. Planting a fake murder weapon said premeditation.

What if one of the six told someone?

Not the students. They would have thrown that person under the bus as soon as Brent and Cynth came knocking. Daniel might have told Florence, but her infirmity put her out of it. It would be stupid for Lois to protect anyone, since she argued with Daniel minutes before he died. Ellen would have told Bailey about the texts if she'd told anyone—if she even knew.

Brent added K Lee to the list. No evidence she knew about the texts, and they couldn't place her at Parker Woods. But the stalking—you don't do that unless you're obsessed. Still, they agreed there wasn't enough there. K Lee's name went to the bottom.

Dianne blamed Daniel for her friend's death, a much better motive than the loss of an instrument. She'd finally admitted to seeing Daniel's body. She hadn't told her friends, figuring one of them would crack and tell someone. *That had to piss Wendy and Ron off royally.*

A search of the house did not yield the poodle mug or any potential murder weapon. Ron and Dianne were too cooperative about giving up their clothes and balaclavas to be hopeful for Daniel's blood or DNA.

Peter said the scene didn't fit. Why attack Daniel near a lit street when he was on his way to a secluded spot? Lia suggested Dianne didn't want her friends involved.

Peter countered, "Then Dianne needed to send her friends to the Lounge and say she wanted to keep an eye out for Daniel and would text when he showed up. Instead, she waited until he was late to hunt him up. Either they all did it or none of them did. And if they all did it, why do it in view of the street?"

He had a point.

Cynth insisted Ellen remain at the top of the list, regardless of her security cameras and Bailey's alibi. "Just because we don't know how she did it doesn't mean she didn't." Which meant the space labeled "Opportunity" contained a huge question mark. Under motive, anger over years of financial exploitation was contraindicated by Bailey's assertion that Ellen did not want to be stuck with Daniel's financial mess and the inevitable lawsuits from victims.

It bothered her that Ellen hadn't told Bailey about the bogus texts. *Maybe Lois lied. Maybe she never confronted Ellen.* But Ellen had a habit of leaving out the most important fact in any story. *Like not telling Cynth her tools had been stolen while screaming about being framed.*

It made her head hurt to think about it.

That left one obvious suspect. Lois argued with Daniel half a block away, minutes before the attack. And she'd been angry.

Why kill him? *Because she found out he used her money to pay back taxes instead of sending it to a non-existent factory? Because he was going back to Ellen?* Easy to fly into a rage if you thought your future was falling apart. Daniel was the sort to placate you with a hug. *Putting Lois in the perfect position to strike.*

Brent had put her and Bailey on the list. He said they were part of the gestalt. Under Bailey, Cynth added "Ellen accomplice?"

"You can't believe that," Lia snapped.

"No," Peter soothed. "But some lawyer will tell a jury Bailey covered for Ellen if they don't account for it."

"And me? What's my part in all this?"

"You were around," Brent said. "Adjacent, but not culpable. You add much needed context. Thankfully, you have an unimpeachable witness that you were nowhere near the food booths when Lois allegedly had her confrontation with Ellen."

"So I'm up there, but my unimpeachable witness isn't? No one knows who was in earshot when Lois and Ellen got into it. Knowing Ellen, it got loud. Anyone could have heard. Anyone could have stolen that mug."

Cynth huffed. "Sure, add everyone at the freaking cemetery. Toss in Santa Claus and the Tooth Fairy while you're at it."

Brent closed the file. "We're going in circles. More beers, or ice cream at Graeter's?"

A shadow fell across Lia's iPad. She tried to swipe the file off screen and succeeded only in replacing Bailey's profile with Ellen's.

"Hiding from us, I see," Terry said, leaning over the table to look closer. Lia tried to pull the iPad away. Terry put a hand out, blocking her. "What's with Ellen?"

Steve joined them, saying, "Didn't anyone teach you boundaries? Oh, wait, I forgot who I was talking to."

Kita climbed up on the table and sniffed the iPad before laying down with her head on her paws. *Bailey's coming.* Lia pulled the iPad away, holding the screen against her chest.

"What's this about Ellen?" Bailey said, sitting next to Lia.

Lia stuffed the iPad into her tote bag.

"So much for privacy," Lia grumbled.

"Ellen is in my book club," Terry said. "How do you know her?"

Bailey gave him an are-you-serious look. "Flutes? Murder? Where have you been for the past two years?"

"This is the Ellen driving you crazy all this time?"

I knew she had a book club. "What are you reading? *Under the Tuscan Sun? Eat, Pray, Love?* I thought you were working through all the Star Wars paperbacks."

"That's his other club," Steve said. "No women in it."

Terry shot Steve a repressive glare. "*This* club engages solely in detectival pursuits. We've been reading Agatha Christie all year."

Steve jerked a thumb at Terry. "He tells me middle-aged women are a blood-thirsty bunch."

Lia frowned at Steve. "Is that why you two have been cracking with all the Poirot references? Why didn't *you* recognize her?"

"They meet when I'm at work. I read the books, but Terry's the only one who hears my opinion. She's your suspect?"

"One of them."

"Ellen never said she was involved in a criminal investigation," Terry said. "You'd think she'd offer her unique perspective on verisimilitude, in view of our genre."

Bailey glowered. "She couldn't get out of the house without waking me. How many times do I have to say it?"

Terry punched a finger in the air. "Aha! A locked room mystery in reverse!"

Steve said, "Is there a Christie plot for that?"

"She's done many locked room mysteries. *The Mysterious Affair at Styles comes to mind.* Did Ellen have an opportunity to slip something in your wine? Did you sleep heavier than usual?"

Bailey shut her eyes, enunciating carefully, "There. Are. Cameras."

"A mere detail. We can discard Dr. Fell's famous locked room lecture in *The Three Coffins* as it focuses on absurd mechanics like stabbing one's self with an icicle or blowing your own brains out with a gun attached to a helium balloon. Any chance our victim committed suicide?"

"Narcissists don't kill themselves," Lia said.

"At any rate, all of Fell's methods rely on finding a dead body inside the locked room. Here we are looking for how a killer escaped her house without detection."

"Keep going, Captain Obvious," Steve said.

"Jane Kalmes is more useful in this regard. She postulates one of four things must occur in any locked room mystery. One caveat: she does not mention that the murderer could have committed the act from outside the room by some means—"

Bailey's voice bordered on shrill. "You think Ellen murdered Daniel from her bedroom? With what? A killer drone?"

"An intriguing theory," Terry said. "Has Ellen ever flown a drone?"

Lia expected to see smoke coming out of Bailey's ears.

"Getting back to Ms. Kalmes, the first option is the death occurred outside the accepted time frame."

"Nope," Lia said. "Two witnesses saw Daniel shortly before midnight and another saw his body twenty minutes later."

Terry nodded appreciatively. "I see our lady has the inside track."

"And there's a coroner's report," Bailey gritted out.

"Don't interrupt. Second, a deception made it *appear* the murder happened while the room was locked, typically by the murderer locking the door from the outside after committing the murder, then slipping the key inside the room as the body is discovered. A classic, elegant solution, irrelevant to these circumstances."

Bailey's eyes shot daggers at Terry. He continued to pontificate and failed to notice.

"Three, the murderer was inside the room the entire time and did not leave until the body was discovered. This would mean Ellen slipped out instead of going to bed and slipped back in as Bailey answered the door in the morning."

Bailey's face was now bright red. "So, where was she for eight hours?"

"One problem at a time. This is unwieldy, and Ellen couldn't count on anyone providing a distraction that would allow her to reenter unseen."

Steve snorted. "Ya think?"

"That leaves number four. As Sherlock Holmes said, 'When you eliminate the impossible, whatever remains, however improbable, must be the truth.'"

"And what remains, Sherlock?" Steve said.

"There's another way to get out."

Bailey's voice was now sharp enough to cut cheese. "Ellen tunneled through the floor? Maybe she was a trapeze artist in a past life and climbed up on the roof—but oops, can't do that, the windows are swollen shut."

Terry asked, "And you know this how?"

"Who the hell are you? The Spanish Inquisition?" Bailey jerked up off the bench and stormed toward the gate. Kita lifted her head, sighed, and followed.

"That was uncalled for," Steve said.

"It's a legitimate question," Terry insisted.

Lia stood, gathering her things. "You're such an ass. If the prosecutor has his way, he'll have Bailey on the stand, doing to her exactly what you did here. How do you think she'll handle court? He'll tear her apart."

"Yeah, asshole," Steve said.

"I'm just pursuing a logical inquiry."

Lia discovered Gypsy cowering under the table. She knelt down and ruffled her ears. "It's okay girlfriend, fireworks are over." Once she lured Gypsy out, she said, "This is a waste of time. It's someone no one's thought of, someone who wanted Daniel gone for reasons we haven't considered."

"Daniel's secret illegitimate love child?" Terry offered. "Any of the students have questionable antecedents?"

"That's as good a theory as any." Lia scooped up Gypsy's ball, tossing it in Bailey's direction. Chewy, her independent little man, was already halfway to the gate.

Lia found Bailey in the picnic shelter outside the fence, sitting in lotus pose atop a table. Kita lay beside her. She had one hand in Kita's fur, eyes shut. *Probably trying to meditate.* The tendons standing out on her neck said she wasn't succeeding.

"Hey, girlfriend."

Bailey's eyes flew open, landing on Lia. She patted the tabletop, inviting Lia to join her. Lia climbed up, Chewy scrambling after her. Gypsy, equilibrium restored, wagged her tail in expectation of ball flinging.

Bailey picked up Lia's chucker and obliged. "I wish I could be like Gypsy, happy as long as I have a ball."

"It's not all biscuits and chew toys. Viola still bullies her."

"I never think about dogs being assholes. I guess they're more human than we give them credit for."

"Terry didn't mean anything."

"He thinks I'm stupid."

"He's not thinking anything. He's just chasing ideas. You know how he gets. He'd grill any of us the same way."

Chewy climbed into Lia's lap, head-butting her hand until she petted him. Gypsy returned, propping her front paws on the bench seat, soggy ball in her mouth. Bailey tapped the bench with the chucker. Gypsy dropped her ball. Bailey scooped it up before it could roll off the bench and sent it flying.

"Their lives are still so much simpler."

"If you reincarnated as a dog, you couldn't spend your next life on Alpha Centauri with John."

"If he ever talks to me again. He hasn't forgiven me for choosing Ellen over him last winter."

"I'm sorry about that. Have you talked to Ellen?"

"Not since she threw that salad at me. She keeps texting. They're lurking on my phone. It's like knowing there's a dozen snakes in your underwear drawer."

"I suppose reading them would only make you feel worse."

"Everything is about her. Nothing I do is enough. There's not a thing she could say that would make me feel better. I'm glad I helped her, but I'm done. I don't care who killed Daniel."

Lia: Can you send me the Christie list from book club? 11:17 AM

Lia wasn't sure why she'd sent the text to Steve, except she hadn't pictured Ellen as a mystery buff. *Maybe I'll get a clue what goes on in that brain of hers.*

Steve: Sure. Why do you want it?
11:19 AM

Lia: Curious, I guess. Don't tell Terry, he'll make something of it. 11:20 AM

Steve: It's a lot of reading. 11:20 AM

Lia: I'll check out the plots on Wikipedia. 11:21 AM

Steve: BBC's Poirot is close to original. You'd love the visuals. You could binge them in a day. 11:23 AM

Lia: Sounds like a plan 11:23 AM

Steve: Whole year or just what we've read? 11:24 AM

Lia: Whole year. Can you mark which ones you've read? 11:25 AM

Steve: Don't ask much, do you? I'll get back to you. 11:26 AM

Lia carried a giant bowl of popcorn up to Peter's man cave and his giant TV screen. Peter and Brent had tickets for tonight's Reds game, giving her twelve hours for her private Christie marathon. Chewy scrambled after her. Gypsy sat at the bottom of the stairs and whined.

"The evil princess is spending the day at Alma's, girlfriend. It's safe to come up."

Gypsy thumped her tail a few times but stayed where she was, unconvinced. Lia put the popcorn out of reach and went back down, scooping up her forty-pound chicken. She climbed the stairs, grunting under Gypsy's squirming weight.

Gypsy licked her face.

"You have to stop being such a wimp. You're bigger than her now, even if she's meaner."

Peter built his man cave for screen viewing. He'd positioned the screen opposite the foot of his extra-wide couch, making it perfect for cuddling during a movie.

Lia stretched out, Chewy on her lap, popcorn on the coffee table, and her back propped up to the perfect viewing angle with an oversized cushion. Gypsy settled on the floor beside her, refusing to climb on the sofa. *Must smell like She-Who-Must-Not-Be-Named.*

The Poirot adaptations showed well on Peter's TV, the lush Art Deco creations appealing to her artist's soul even if she'd hate living in such a fussy environment.

She enjoyed the acting, though the plots were ridiculously contrived: Rube Goldberg conspiracies; identical twins; disguises that shouldn't fool anyone; murderers setting themselves up as intended victims; fake identities; evil serendipities. More plausible than Doctor Fell's icicle, but too much work for any sane murderer.

Dianne and Wendy went to a lot of trouble to lure Daniel into Parker Woods, and it hadn't worked. *Only because someone else stepped in with the exquisite timing necessary to pull off a Christie plot.*

She plodded on and had to admit Terry was right: If you looked past the showy machinations, character ruled. The murders were often born decades before they occurred, arising out of pitch perfect psychology. She suspected the same was true for Daniel's murderer, but beyond that little nugget and a lazy day of escapism, she'd achieved nothing.

She was about to give up when Viola's claws scrabbled on the steps with Peter's size twelve shoes clomping behind. She paused the video, freezing the opening credits as a cartoon Poirot looked over his shoulder and winked.

Gypsy tried to crawl under the sofa. Her butt hung out, tail curled under her body. By the time Peter entered, Viola lay crouched on the floor, giving Gypsy's protruding haunches the evil eye.

Peter shook his head. "That's pathetic."

"What do you expect? Your girl traumatizes her."

Lia dumped Chewy off her lap and dragged a protesting Gypsy out from her refuge. Lia cuddled her, sh-sh-shushing in her ear. Gypsy squirmed around until she had her eyes on Viola.

"Law of the jungle, dog mom." Peter sat and chucked Gypsy under her chin. "Viola thinks it's funny you're scared of her. You need to butch up."

"Like that's going to help."

"You going to carry her around when she hits sixty pounds?"

"Can we change the subject?"

"Sure." He grabbed a handful of popcorn and tossed a kernel at Viola, who snagged it. Viola and Chewy expertly snatched the kernels Peter launched into the air. Despite Gypsy's mastery of tennis balls, she looked sad and confused as the projectiles bounced off her muzzle. They landed on the floor, where Viola gobbled them up.

"Stop tormenting her," Lia said.

"She has to learn," Peter said.

"Then I'll teach her while Viola isn't around to intimidate her."

Peter shrugged and held out a kernel for Gypsy. She sniffed warily, as if it might jump up and smack her in the face, then flicked it into her mouth with her tongue.

"Thank you," Lia said. "How was the game?"

"We won, which puts us third in our division. Still a long shot for the playoffs. What are we watching?"

"Turns out Ellen is in Terry's book club."

"You just now figured this out?"

"Don't get me started. They've been reading Agatha Christie all year. I'm watching adaptations."

Peter raised an eyebrow. "Life imitates art?"

"Not according to what I've seen. The series is excellent, if you ignore the contrivances."

"English murder mysteries are too polite. Either the murderer shrugs and gives up when they're found out, or they commit suicide and save the courts the expense of a trial."

"I've noticed that. I have one left. Are you up for it?"

Lia unfroze the screen, which transitioned to a handsome, charismatic doctor visiting his artist mistress in advance of a weekend house party. As everyone gathered at the family estate, complex relationships unfolded.

"All these undercurrents," Lia said, grabbing a handful of popcorn.

"Are all artists so amoral?" Peter asked. "There's something twisted about the mistress being the only person who's genuinely nice to the wife. Everyone else patronizes her, and her husband treats her like dirt."

"Who's your choice for victim?"

"My money is on the doctor. Everyone in the house wants to kill him."

Lia shook her head. "They like him too much. I vote for the former fiancée."

"Setting the doctor up as the prime suspect? Interesting choice."

Poirot arrived for lunch to find the wife standing over the doctor's body with a gun in her hand.

"Why do they always do that?" Peter said.

Lia hit pause. "Why do innocent people pick up murder weapons, or why do writers make their characters do stupid things?"

"It never happens in real life. It made sense exactly one time out of the hundred I've seen it on TV."

"Oh? What was the reason for that?"

"He heard a noise and thought the killer was coming back. He picked up the gun to defend himself."

"Now that we know the wife didn't do it, can I start the movie again without you interrupting?"

"Can I throw popcorn at the screen when they do more stupid stuff?"

"It's your television, dearest."

Halfway through the program, a ballistics report proved the gun in custody was not the murder weapon.

Lia sat up, dumping Chewy and Gypsy off her lap.

"Huh," Peter said. "Maybe life does imitate art."

"Damn it. I should have been taking notes."

"Not to worry. We'll find out who done it at the end. It's in the rules."

Lia focused her attention, but nothing made sense.

Until the end.

The mousy wife—the one everyone thought was too

unintelligent to keep up with her brilliant husband and her brilliant relations—got away with murder by framing herself. The gun in her hand meant the police had no reason to search for the gun she'd dumped in a bush. It also gave her a pass when the ballistics report came in.

Lia said, "This is insane."

"You think Ellen did it? Based on this?"

"The first hijackers got the idea from Rod Serling."

Peter stood and stretched. "Really? I thought his claim to fame was writing the screenplay for *Planet of the Apes*."

"Don't change the subject. I don't know if Ellen did it, but it makes sense. Daniel believed he was meeting Ellen and expected her to fawn on him. He'd let her get close. The awl and Bailey are the only things keeping her out of jail."

"We still don't know how she got out of the house and off the property. None of the other programs you watched provided a solution?"

"I should be so lucky. I need to talk to Bailey."

Peter placed a hand on her arm. "We should talk to Cynth first."

"You want to unleash Cynth on Bailey so she can accuse her of holding back? Bailey's already on edge. Cynth will send her over. Let me talk to her first."

Lia checked the clock. *Eleven-thirty. Bailey will be in bed.* Just as well. Considering how Bailey reacted to Terry that morning, she'd need to think through how to approach her.

"I'll catch her in the morning."

BAILEY

Bailey slouched in her truck several houses down from Ellen's, praying the neighbors walking their dogs in the failing light wouldn't notice her as she waited for Ellen's dog walker to finish with the girls. She rubbed Ellen's key between her fingers like a worry stone.

Goddess, hurry up!

She needed to get into the back yard before full dark, and she needed time to poke around, time to think, before Ellen got home from work. She'd be gone already if the dog walker hadn't been late.

Damn Terry for making me doubt myself. She hadn't been able to stop thinking about the night Daniel died since she left the dog park that morning. Seeking guidance, she'd drawn The Moon: a card of illusions, of things not being what they seem, of fear-based perceptions.

Extracting yourself from decades of toxicity wasn't easy, and Ellen had needed to find her way. That's what she'd told herself. Two years. Dropping everything for Ellen's emergencies. Being her sounding board and her place to vent. Putting her own life on hold.

Did she repay me by setting me up to be her alibi?

It was an insane idea, and it wouldn't go away.

Did I shut out the truth about that night?

She should talk to Cynth—or at least Peter—but what if she was off on one of her spastic mental trips and had everything wrong? Everyone acted like they'd forgotten how she went off the deep end after Catherine died. She'd been gaslit and drugged out of her mind, but she should have realized she was losing her grip. She hadn't fully trusted herself since.

How could she subject Ellen to more suspicion after she'd been through so much?

What if I'm nuts?

What if I'm not?

The night Daniel died, she'd been ready to crash thirty minutes into *Meet Joe Black,* the second worst movie she'd ever seen (nothing could steal the title from *Zardoz*). Casting Brad Pitt in an exploration of the afterlife, then turning it into an unwatchable bore—it had to be a crime against humanity.

She'd said as much.

Ellen had sniffed, "I picked this for you. It ought to be right up your alley." She left to finish it in her bedroom while Bailey pulled out the pillow and comforter stashed behind the sofa. She settled in, one hand dangling off the side of the sofa, resting on Kita's neck where she lay on the floor.

Ellen had the volume up high enough to hear bits of it through the walls. Ironically, once out of sight, the noise kept her up. If Ellen left the house while the movie was on, Bailey would have known.

What if the noise was meant to cover something?

The windows were swollen shut.

What if they weren't?

Then there was the second gate that opened directly onto the property behind Ellen's, a relic of the time when sisters owned the adjacent properties. After Ellen bought the house, she had Bailey plant bamboo along the fence line, to block noise from the traffic on Hamilton Avenue. The gate hadn't crossed her mind in twenty years. Surely Ellen forgot it as well.

What if she hasn't?

The bed of bamboo was over four feet deep. There wasn't enough room for Ellen to squeeze through.

What if there is?

What if, what if, what if? She was making herself crazy. The only solution was to get inside, examine the windows, and take a hard look at the wall of bamboo. If she had time, she'd search for the poodle mug—though it would be insane to keep it.

Ellen can't be that stupid.

She might be that arrogant.

This is crazy.

It's not housebreaking if you have keys.

Down the block, a stocky figure with a pair of greyhounds moved through the increasing darkness and turned onto Ellen's walkway.

Finally.

It took five minutes for the woman to settle the girls and leave. Three more minutes for the street to clear.

Bailey opened the truck door, willing the hinges not to squeal, closing it softly.

Goddess, open my eyes that I may see, and make me invisible while you're at it.

11

DAY 10, PART 1

TUESDAY, AUGUST 19, 8:00 AM

LIA

BAILEY WASN'T AT THE DOG PARK. LIA SENT A TEXT, THEN tossed balls for Gypsy. Fifteen minutes later, there was no return text and no Bailey. Fifteen minutes was long enough for Bailey to drive from her house, long enough to get out of the shower.

She called. It went to voicemail. She grilled her friends. No joy. She waited another fifteen minutes, then dragged Gypsy and Chewy out of the park and drove to Bailey's. The truck was gone.

She tried Bailey one more time.

No response.

She checked the time.

Eight-fifteen.

Bailey was impulsive when stressed. She'd been upset the day before, the pressure building since Bailey asked her to meet at Wesleyan Cemetery two years earlier. If her mind had been racing all night, who knew what state she was in?

Wesleyan?

Surely not.

She's working. An early appointment.

Then why hasn't she returned my texts? Why won't she answer the phone?

She went to Wesleyan. she's off the rails.

BAILEY

Bailey pulled into Wesleyan Cemetery with her head throbbing, knuckles white as she gripped the steering wheel. The coffee she'd drunk on the way layered jitters onto the night she'd spent pacing when she wasn't thrashing in her bed.

Confronting Ellen in this mood was dangerous. She didn't care. Not caring was a problem, and she didn't care about that, either.

Kita trembled and whined, sensing her agitation. In her brain, she screamed "shut up-shut up-shut up!" but she had enough discipline left not to yell at her dog.

She stopped the truck in the middle of the crumbling asphalt lane, shutting her eyes, forcing herself to breathe, counting, counting, slowing her heart.

She opened her eyes to see Kita's nose inches from her face, concerned brown eyes watching her and not under-standing. Kita licked her face, doing what she could to comfort. Bailey wrapped her arms around Kita and drew on the animal warmth.

I should turn around. Nothing good happened when she felt like this, like she couldn't live inside her own skin.

I can't go to work like this. I'll lose half my clients.

If she was going to act like a crazy woman, she might as well go off on the responsible party. In the back of Wesleyan, no one would hear. As for Ellen, Ellen deserved every bit of whatever she got.

This isn't the way. What you put out comes back, times three. That is the Law. She had to find her compassionate heart.

Call Lia. The thought was a whisper. Trees said true guidance comes as a quiet thought, easily brushed aside— especially under the onslaught of emotions bumping her heart rate up, pushing, pushing, pushing her to *do something.*

Lia would understand, but Lia didn't deserve the weight of her emotions.

Call John. But he ghosted her when she chose to stick by Ellen instead of making her winter pilgrimage to Knoxville. She couldn't ask him to let her lean on him when she had yet to mend fences.

Kita snuffled her face. Bailey swiped a hand across her cheek and discovered tears.

Two freaking years. After all I've done, Ellen uses me this way. Two freaking years.

Goddess. Bailey lowered her face, rubbing a cheek against Kita's soft, floppy ear.

Her phone chirped. A text from Lia.

Not now.

She put her phone back in her pocket.

Call Lia, Peter, someone.

Once they arrest Ellen, she'll be out of reach. I have to know.

My brain is exploding.

Anger is met with anger. Anger is not the way.

She resumed her breathing, counting until her heart slowed again, visualizing waves of compassion emanating from her heart, penetrating Ellen's heart, eliciting honesty.

She parked the truck by the old caretaker's house and let Kita out. The half-mile walk to the back would give her time to think.

MONDAY NIGHT

Bailey unlocked the door to find the girls standing sentinel, giant ears alert, eyes wide and curious. She stroked the silky heads as she listened for the beeping of a triggered alarm.

Silence.

Despite Ellen's professed fears, she'd canceled installation of the security system.

Of course she did.

Lights on or off? Lights on meant a neighbor might notice someone was in the house. But they were used to her coming and going and she doubted Ellen told anyone about their blow up. If she bumbled around with the light from her phone, anyone who saw it would know she was an intruder. Lights on, then.

The girls followed her through the house. She detoured into the kitchen, grabbing a handful of treats before heading down the hall.

She ducked into the bathroom. With the movie playing, would she have heard Ellen climb out the bathroom window? Possibly not, but Kita would have lifted her head and woofed, the way she did every time Ellen took a middle of the night bathroom break.

Better look anyway.

The tiny window was four feet above the floor as opposed to the thirty-one inch sills elsewhere in the house. Easy enough to climb onto the toilet to reach it. Small as Ellen was, she might squeeze through. The bottom pane rose easily enough, though it made a grinding noise she should've heard. A thin layer of grime lay in the tracks undisturbed.

Bailey knelt on the toilet and stuck her head out, examining the hollyhocks growing underneath. No way to get out without trashing them, and the ground was a good eight feet below. And while Ellen *might* have been able to jump down without breaking a hip, getting back in would've been impossible.

One of the girls butted her ass. Then they stared at her, wide-eyed and innocent as lambs. Impossible to say which one assaulted her. Bailey gave them both a treat and proceeded to Ellen's bedroom.

Three windows sporting curtains and roman shades, one on the side, two facing the back yard. Ellen asked Bailey's help to open them late spring, when it was finally warm enough to open up the house. That had been three months ago.

Had she been planning it back then?

Like the rest of the house, the sills and frames were pristine. Ellen had gone on a stress-induced cleaning binge after Cynth and Captain Arseneault told them about Daniel. If Ellen was upset, she baked. If she didn't bake, she cleaned. Bailey hadn't thought anything about it.

Nothing to see while Ellen destroyed evidence.

If that's what she was doing.

Cynth and Brent and their squad of goons had been

through here more than a week earlier. If there was anything to find, surely they already found it.

I have to prove Terry wrong.

The windows had been raised the previous fall. What had made them non-functional? Ellen blamed a wet winter and the age of the house. She went on about wanting to replace them years ago, but Daniel needed the money for his shop and his trade shows and his slick mailers. The complaint passed through Bailey's head, barely registering because everyone knew Ellen had family money she refused to spend.

She tested the windows, raising the shades to expose the lower panes, unlatching them, then pulling up on the handle on the sash. When that didn't work, she braced both hands against the top rail and shoved, putting her full weight into it. All three resisted her efforts as stubbornly as they had months earlier.

It's like they're glued shut.

Maybe they are.

Wood glue between the jambs and stiles would do it. With the newer adhesives, it wouldn't be hard to find something that set in thirty minutes.

If Ellen glued them shut, you'd have to break the window apart to prove it. But Ellen would need one functional window. How to make it appear like it was stuck long enough to fool her?

She stepped back, stroking the girls' heads, thinking. The eight-foot drop was a problem, and the plantings along the house. She visualized the yard, the plants ... and the air conditioning unit. It wasn't directly under the corner window, but there was an overlap.

Ellen could lower herself onto it. Cynth and Brent

wouldn't consider a sixty-year-old woman capable, but while Bailey hadn't known a thing about Ellen's book club, she'd been well aware of her twice weekly yoga classes.

To make the window appear swollen shut, there couldn't be any movement at all. Something had to hold it down.

When Bailey bought her house, she'd drilled holes in the top corners of the sashes of her downstairs windows with corresponding holes four inches higher in the upper sashes. By sliding a ten-penny nail in, she could lock her windows open wide enough for a breeze while being too narrow for anyone to climb in.

Maybe Ellen did something like that. It needed to be something you wouldn't notice. Maybe Ellen going on about how it was Daniel's fault she didn't have new windows was meant to distract her while she tried to bang the windows open.

Screwing the bottom sash shut would work. Angling screws into the jamb would be most effective, but she would have seen that.

Screw the sashes together where they overlapped? Countersink the screws, cover with wood filler and paint over them for a clean result. Which would later require painstaking work to chip out the filler, remove the screws, and patch it up.

Which Ellen had plenty of time to do.

Bailey ran her fingers across the wood, reading the surface like braille. She felt a tiny dip in the right corner. A corresponding dimple on the left.

Dimples that meant Terry was right. She'd been a dupe.

She sat on the bed, staring at the window. How had it gone? Ellen asking for help because the windows wouldn't budge, rattling on about Daniel. After Bailey gave a couple of hefty tugs on the third window, she'd been ready to get a mallet and chisel to knock it loose. Ellen said not to bother, she'd just call the window people about replacements.

Only she never had.

Instead, Ellen removed the screws, filled the holes, freshened the paint. And after she slipped out to kill Daniel, she waited until Bailey wasn't around and glued the window shut like the others.

A few minutes, that's all it would take. Plenty of time while she and Lia hunted for the phone. Two days for the glue to cure before the search warrant.

I'm an idiot.

Years coddling a woman who couldn't extricate herself from a toxic relationship without help.

So she led me to believe.

Stressing herself out, wrecking her relationship with John.

Stupid, stupid, stupid.

Bailey looked at her phone, checked the time. She needed to finish this and get gone. She hugged the girls, projecting a calm she didn't feel.

"Poor babies. I'm about to destroy the life you know and you have no clue."

They followed her into the back yard, curious at this deviation from their usual schedule, happy for an extra trip outside.

The air conditioning unit sat on a concrete slab, rising about three feet off the ground. That left four feet for Ellen to negotiate. Difficult, but doable.

Peter once discovered footprints in Lia's basement by shining a light at a low angle across the floor. She did this now with the light from her phone. The beam exposed a variety of smudges, none of which looked like sneaker tread. Not an exonerating pristine layer of accumulated grime, but nothing to hang Ellen with either.

Probably a pair of mating raccoons.

The real issue was proving Ellen got to the gate. Bamboo was forgiving and resilient. It would recover from being disturbed.

But maybe not the soil.

The ground was soft. Had Cynth and Brent looked for footprints? No reason for them to think of it.

No telling where Ellen entered the bamboo thicket, but she had to make it to the gate. Bailey moved opposite the place where she knew the gate to be and crouched low. Nati nuzzled her cheek. Connie slid her head under Bailey's arm.

Bailey took a moment to inhale the scent of dog and enjoy the feel of fur against her cheek. "Sweet girls, I'm so, so sorry."

She shined her light across the ground, looking for disturbances in the dirt bed. Hard to distinguish with the bamboo casting long shadows, but it was there, an arc in the dirt, a double curve, the outside of a sneaker print. She moved to the right and found three similar shapes.

She did it. She really did it. I've been a fool.

She could trace the footprints back to the beginning of the thicket, but this was enough. More important to see what else she could find inside. Wood glue? The poodle mug? A journal detailing Ellen's evil plan? Something that explained how she knew Daniel would be in the woods that night?

She looked at the time on her phone.

Ten more minutes, then I'm gone.

The girls nosed delicately through the grass, ignoring the vultures riding the thermals overhead. Ellen looked up, scooting over on her bench as Bailey approached.

Smiling as if all was right in her world.

Bailey joined her, saying nothing, trapping her hands between her knees to keep them from flying away.

Ellen's smile hesitated. "You're quiet today."

Here goes nothing. "I'm trying to understand something."

Perplexed frown of the innocent. "What's going on? Can I help?"

Bailey turned. She had to see Ellen's face. "Why did you do it?"

Ellen shook her head a fraction of an inch and tilted up one side of her mouth, a sign of appeasement, of confusion. "Do what?"

Bailey drew a deep breath and said as carefully as she could, "I'm not talking about killing Daniel. I know why you did that. I'm talking about setting me up as a stooge, making me part of it."

Wide eyes. "What are you talking about? You know I was framed. You were there."

Bailey spoke with a calm she didn't feel. "Where did you hide your clothes? They had to be bloody, and you were on foot. You couldn't have gone far."

"Have you been taking your meds? I'm worried about you."

Bailey's voice turned shrill. "Is that why you chose me? So you could blame anything I said on my diagnosis if you needed to?"

"You're so stressed—"

"Of course I'm stressed! I'm stressed because you made me an accessory to murder!"

Kita whined. Connie and Nati popped their heads up, ready to run.

Ellen pushed off the bench, backing away. "You don't know what you're saying."

"I found the mug."

"What?"

"I searched your place last night. I found the mug and the tools. You used one of them to kill Daniel."

"What are you talking about?"

Bailey jumped up, screaming, "The mug! The stupid poodle mug! Did you slip it in your tote bag when I was off with Lia? Was it that easy? You killed Daniel and framed yourself."

"You're nuts. I haven't seen that mug since Dog Day."

"That's the point, isn't it? Your crazy friend doesn't know what she's talking about. Your precious poodle mug isn't behind that five-year-old bag of chia seed anymore. I moved it so you can't dispose of it before the police search your house again. Did you think I wouldn't remember that old gate behind the bamboo?"

Ellen stood, her face ugly and red and twisted. "I. Was. Framed. I'm still being framed."

"Just stop it! Stop lying to me! I'm done."

Ellen, panicked, moved towards Bailey. "What do you mean done?"

Bailey stepped back, throwing up her hands. "Done! Done is done!"

Bailey turned away, staring at the strip of woods. She strode towards the trees, slapping her thigh , calling, "Come, Kita." Kita fell in beside her, mournful bloodhound eyes making Bailey's heart crumble. She'd make it to the woods and fall apart where no one but Kita would see her. Then she'd call Lia.

Ellen yelled, "We have to talk."

Bailey looked back. Ellen was following her.

"Leave me alone!" Bailey sped up, her long legs eating the ground faster than Ellen could follow, Kita moving faster than she had in years to keep up.

Damn Ellen. Decades of friendship, and Ellen continued to lie to her face.

She reached the trees and pushed through the undergrowth, stopping when she reached the edge of the bluff overlooking Mill Creek. Heart pounding, she leaned against a young tree, taking greedy breaths as she looked over the edge. Water moved sluggishly in the concrete bed forty feet below. *Goddess help me.* Kita leaned against her leg, seeking connection.

The shove came hard in the center of her back. Bailey lost her grip on the sapling. She tumbled forward, her arms and feet flailing at nothing.

LIA

Lia spotted Bailey's truck as soon as she turned off Colerain Avenue.

Stupid for her to think she could wait until morning to talk to Bailey. Stupid, stupid, stupid for Bailey to meet with Ellen without talking it through first.

At least she parked out front. That meant she walked

back and had given herself time: to cool down, to process, to respond instead of react.

The Volvo crested the ridge. Gypsy howled, scratching the door to get out. She propped her paws against the open window, contemplating a jump.

Lia kept one hand on the wheel and grabbed her collar. "Chill, girlfriend. We'll get there soon enough."

Ellen's SUV sat in its usual spot in the back corner, a flock of vultures circling over the woods beyond. She headed that way while Gypsy continued to howl. Chewy curled into a ball to shut out the noise.

Ellen turned on her bench as Lia pulled up, no doubt responding to Gypsy's racket. Lia opened her door. Gypsy jumped over the back seat, digging her toenails into Lia's thigh as she boosted herself out. She raced to the back of the cemetery, her leash dragging behind her.

Chewy gave her a grumpy old man look, snorting as he followed Lia out of the car. Lia heaved an exasperated sigh as Gypsy disappeared into the strip of the woods. At least she wouldn't go far. The drop-off in back was not girlfriend's cup of tea.

Ellen said, "This is a lovely surprise. Is Bailey coming, too?"

"You haven't seen her? Her truck is out front."

"That's strange. Maybe she popped into the store across the street."

The store was a quarter mile from where Bailey parked.

"I need to catch Gypsy. No telling what she's up to."

"Don't go in the woods. I spotted a pair of coyotes earlier. Wait for Gypsy to come back."

"Coyotes?"

"They come down Mill Creek from Mount Airy Forest."

Which explains why you let your girls out in the back meadow.

A dozen vultures wheeled overhead. Vultures could mean dead things. *The coyotes are partying with a carcass and Gypsy ran right into them.*

"I'm not standing around while coyotes eat my dog."

Lia picked Chewy up and dumped him in the front seat. She drove across the field, praying she didn't puncture a tire, her mind racing as she considered options. For the first time, she wished she had a newer car, with an alarm you activated with a key fob.

That would scare predators away.

She felt her vest pocket for a slim metal cylinder, hoping the pepper spray she hadn't used in years was still good. There was the steel pipe Bailey gave her to prop up her hood. Pipe or ball chucker? With only one ball, the chucker would soon be useless. *Pipe, then.*

She ruffled Chewy's ears and told him to stay, opening the door and pulling the pipe out from under the seat.

Gypsy barked somewhere in the trees, her tone urgent instead of fearful or angry. *Not coyote dinner, not yet.* A dog bayed in the distance. She followed the sound into the trees, pushing through the brush with her pipe raised, pepper spray in her other hand. Gypsy's bark lured her toward the steepest part of the overlook.

"Gypsy! Come!"

Gypsy paused, then barked frantically. *Maybe her leash caught on a tree and she's trapped.* Lia pushed through the brush, scanning for coyotes.

Gypsy stood by a patch of wintercreeper at the edge of the cliff, bouncing on stiff legs. Lia's heart jumped into her throat as she pocketed her pepper spray and dropped the pipe. She grabbed the leash, tugging as she knelt. Gypsy wouldn't budge.

"Stubborn girl, what's down there? You spot the coyotes? We need to get out of here."

Gypsy shot her a mutinous look and continued barking. Lia moved forward, peering over the edge. Something purple hung in a skinny tree growing out of the cliff.

Movement by the creek, circling and baying.

Kita?

Her eyes jumped back to the purple thing, penetrating the foliage. *A T-shirt?* Carroty hair and tanned limbs took form underneath the screen of leaves.

"Bailey! Bailey!"

No response.

She pulled her phone out, thumbed it awake.

Rustling behind her. *Coyotes.* She turned. Grabbed her pepper spray.

Ellen emerged from a thicket, concern written on her face.

Lia sighed, relieved. "Thank God you're here. Bailey fell. I don't think she's conscious. I'm calling 911."

"I'll call. You keep your eyes on her."

Lia turned back, leaning over the edge, searching for movement, trying to figure out how Bailey landed in the tree and whether it was strong enough to hold her.

Pain exploded in her head

BAILEY

Barking. Pain. Confusion. Someone calling her name. Something hard, pressing into her face, her hip. An arm and leg dangled, the weight pulling her body sideways.

Bailey opened her eyes. One eye saw nothing. The other, leaves and sky. She turned her head, unable to make sense of anything.

She looked down. Twenty feet below, Kita circled, baying at her like she was a treed raccoon.

Which is exactly what I am.

Panic snapped her fully conscious. *I could fall any second.* She slid her hands over the trunk, groping for a handhold, shifting her weight until she felt more secure.

Ellen pushed me.

She'd landed in a tree growing out the side of the cliff, straddling the cantilevered trunk, her hip wedged painfully in the crook where a branch grew out of the trunk. You couldn't call it a bough, it was too slender.

The tree was too slender. *Too slender to bear my weight?* The trunk shifted. Had it bent under her weight, or was it pulling up at the roots? She couldn't see to tell.

Someone calling for me. Ellen? To see if I'm alive? Someone else? Who? She looked down again. No humans. Kita continued to baroo and circle. She turned the other way, carefully, looking up. *Too many leaves. Can't see. Should I yell?*

The tree shifted again.

Above her, someone screamed.

LIA

Ellen screaming, Gypsy snarling. Lia fought through the haze of pain, pushing up on her hands. Chewy leapt out of the car window, barking.

The pipe lay on the ground. Ellen reached for it while Gypsy harried her, leash dragging in the grass. Ellen snatched her hand back. Tried again for the pipe.

She'll smash Gypsy's head. Have to stop her. Too dizzy to stand.

Gypsy dodged, whipping the end of her leash in front of Lia. Lia lunged, looping the padded handle around her hand, pulling it tight as Gypsy ducked between Ellen's legs. The leash popped up. Ellen tripped, sprawling in the grass.

The ground shifted. Lia's legs slid over the edge of the cliff, feet dangling in air. She tightened her grip on the lead as Ellen tried to kick it away. Annoyed at the pull on her neck, Gypsy planted her paws and ducked her head.

"No!" Lia shrieked

Gypsy's collar flew off. With the leash freed, Lia slid through crumbling dirt. She grabbed at a skinny stump inches out of reach, her hand landing in the wintercreeper. It tore out of the ground as she dropped over the edge.

The leash yanked tight, pain shrieking through the shoulder forced to carry the weight of her body. She gasped and flailed, dropping the vine. Gypsy and Chewy popped their heads over the edge and whined.

A car started. Ellen was running.

Lia hung, her extended hand two impossible feet below the top of the cliff. Gypsy's collar had caught on something. The stump? How long would it hold? Pain—in her shoulder, in her neck—made it hard to think. *Have to relieve the pres-*

sure. Need a handhold, a foothold, anything. She groped with her free hand, finding only dirt.

If she was Cynth, she could pull herself up by the leash and walk up the cliff.

I'm not Cynth.

I'm going to die.

ELLEN

Pain. In her leg, in her arms, from dozens of puncture wounds. Blood everywhere.

Damn Bailey for making me do this. Damn dogs. Have to think. Have to figure everything out.

She'd seen no one at Wesleyan except Lia and Bailey, and they were dead. No one could prove she'd been there.

Get the girls home. Get to the hospital. Strays attacked me in Parker Woods.

I can make this work.

Find the mug and destroy it. There would be nothing to incriminate her.

I love that mug. Bury it in the garden?

She drove one-handed, taking a circuitous route up Kirby, to Frederick, to Hamilton, south on Haight. Anyone tracking her movements wouldn't look for cameras there.

Cameras. Should she dump her cameras? Toss them in a dumpster? Say she took them to Saint Vincent de Paul? If anyone asked, she'd say she didn't need them once Daniel died. *No.* They'd show her leaving with the girls and coming back bloody. That fit with her story, and getting rid of them would look bad.

Blood on the seat covers. If she'd been in Parker Woods, there would be no blood in the car.

Dump the seat covers.

Scratch that. Driving to the hospital would explain the blood. But she'd have to walk from the parking garage. Hurting as bad as she did, she didn't trust herself to drive in the traffic around Good Sam.

Drop the dogs off, get back in the car, call 911 and say she hurt too much to drive. That would work.

If I'm lucky, it will be days before they find Lia and Bailey.

BAILEY

Dirt rained down as Lia slid off the cliff, jerking to a stop in mid-air like a hanged man dropping through a trapdoor. She dangled from one arm, held up by something Bailey couldn't see.

Lia kicked her legs and waved her free arm as if attempting to regain her balance on a floor that wasn't there. She stopped, her still body twisting. Whatever she was hanging from, it wouldn't last.

Bailey moved, aligning herself with a gap in the leaves that gave her a clear view of the cliff face.

There, on the left—

LIA

Bailey's voice drifted up like a gift from heaven. "There's a big root sticking out six inches above your left foot. You can stand on it."

"My face is an inch from the cliff. I can't see!"

"Reach your foot out. I'll direct you."

Lia shut out the barking of the dogs and felt along the cliff face with her toes.

"Two more inches. Feel it?"

Lia's foot brushed something protruding from the cliff. She traced the contours. Hard and about three inches thick. The root protruded from the cliff face, then looped back in. It should support her. *It had better. I've got nothing else.*

"I need something to hold while I pull myself up."

"There's a rock over your head."

Lia planted her left foot on the root and lifted her free arm, searching for the rock. Not much of a handhold, but enough. She edged over to get both feet on the root. The pain in her shoulder dropped by 90 percent. She considered letting go of the leash, letting her injured arm down.

Can't. If I slip, it's the only thing holding me up. "Now what?"

"It's not far. Can you climb up?"

Now on secure footing, she was able to look around. "All I see is dirt. You see anything? I don't want to die."

"Can you reach your phone? Mine fell."

My phone. She'd had it in her hand when Ellen hit her. "I dropped it."

"In the creek?"

"Up top, near the edge."

"Just a few feet. Voice command might work."

"I've never done that."

"Luddite. Loud and clear, say, 'Hey Bixby. Activate speakerphone. Call Peter.' Tell Gypsy to hush first."

"That's it?"

"I'd do it, but it's too far from here."

This can't work. She followed directions, expecting nothing. A faint mechanical voice said, "Calling Peter Dourson."

I'll be damned.

Bailey called up again. "Now Pray."

One ring. Two. Three. The voice she loved drifted over the edge.

"Love of my life, I was just thinking about you."

She took a breath and yelled, "Bailey and I are hanging from the cliff behind Wesleyan Cemetery! Send help! Look for the vultures!"

Silence, then, "Dammit, Lia."

BAILEY

Lia's dogs finally stopped barking. Kita still barooed as she circled underneath. *I know you're worried, but please stop. You're making it hard to think.*

The tree shifted under her, dropping an inch? A fraction of an inch? The trunk acted like a lever, amplifying the force of her weight. Every minute that passed made it more likely to rip out at the roots.

Not good.

In the distance, a siren. She called up to Lia, "Is that us?"

Lia shouted the question up to her phone. Bailey couldn't hear Peter's response. A moment later Lia said,

"Peter says yes. Station 20 is just up on Blue Rock. Can you hang on for five minutes?"

The tree lurched, this time dropping several inches. Five minutes was stretching it.

"Tell him about Ellen. If we die, I don't want her getting away with this."

She'd be safest where the roots grew into the cliff. *Have to shinny down. Ten feet, maybe less.*

If she could extricate the leg wedged into the crotch of the tree, she could do this. She used her free leg to feel along the trunk for a foothold.

Then what?

Several branches appeared strong enough to carry her weight, but she'd have to worm the rest of the way down. Unless she slid. She said a quick prayer for her crotch.

Above, Lia yelled, "How are you doing?"

"Shaky. Climbing down."

"Peter says don't move."

Her right leg screamed as she levered it up over the branch. She gasped, and that sent pain shooting through her ribs. She edged back along the trunk, feeling for the next branch, praying her injured leg would hold her weight, taking shallow breaths to control the agony in her side.

"Peter doesn't see this tree coming out by the roots."

Her foot struck something. She transferred weight onto it, then eased backwards.

"Be careful."

"Shut up. I'm trying not to die here."

Sirens, louder. Bailey shut them out, narrowing her world to the unsteady trunk. Weight on her screaming right leg, she hugged the trunk, shifting her left leg off its perch, scooting down a little, risking a glance below, feeling for the next branch, moving slowly to not jolt the tree, not jolt her ribs.

Channel your inner sloth.

The trunk thickened as she inched down, feeling less precarious. She reached the bottom limb.

Six feet to go.

To go further, she'd have to straddle the trunk while hanging onto the lowest branch. Then she'd have to hug the tree for the last few feet. She'd be twenty feet above the very shallow concrete creek, with her arms wrapped around the trunk and no foothold.

Have to risk it, unless they plan to pull me out with a helicopter.

Bailey's ears rang in sudden, siren-free silence. Even Kita was quiet. Men, shouting. Men at the top, somehow pulling Lia up. A skinny rope snaking down. A man, a big, beautiful, burly man in a harness rappelling down and down and down, the rest of her life closer with every foot.

He hung in the air, enfolding her in his arms. "You're okay now. We got you. I'm going to strap you in a rescue basket and we'll pull you up. I'll be right behind you to make sure you're okay. You'll be up in two shakes of a lamb's tail. Can you do this?"

Bailey gave a watery laugh. "Can I shut my eyes?"

"Honey, you do whatever you want."

12

DAY 10, PART 2

TUESDAY, AUGUST 19, 10:23 AM

LIA

WHITE PAPER CRACKLED UNDER LIA AS SHE LEANED BACK ON the cantilevered exam table. It was a theme: white paper, white gown, white cabinets, blank white curtains isolating her and Peter from everything else.

The illusion of privacy was laughable. She heard everything in the corridor. That meant they could hear her, too. At least eavesdropping provided a useful distraction during the interminable wait for her MRI.

Better than thinking about almost dying.

"I hate these stupid gowns."

Peter, sitting in the chair beside her, squeezed her hand. "It shouldn't be much longer. How's your shoulder?"

"Still hurts."

Bailey had been wheeled off elsewhere. Peter said Jim was with her.

Good. She has someone she knows. "You called him. You are the very best boyfriend."

"Sorry I wasn't here when you checked in."

"Someone needed to take care of the dogs."

Beyond the curtain, a wheelchair squeaked down the corridor. A nurse said, "Those are terrible bites. We'll get photos so you can press charges if you identify the dogs later. Are you sure you don't know who they belonged to?"

The squeaking stopped. Steel curtain rings rattled in the next cubicle. A tremulous voice said, "I never saw them before. The pit bull was brown. I don't suppose that's much help. The other one was a ratty little mutt."

Ratty little mutt, my ass. Why hadn't she noticed Ellen in the waiting room? Doh. They wheeled her in on a gurney. All she'd seen was the ceiling. She met Peter's eyes and jerked her head at the voices, mouthing, "Ellen."

The nurse said, "Don't you worry, we'll get a policeman in here to take your report."

"That's too much bother. I'll never see those dogs again."

A rustling sound as the nurse helped Ellen settle herself on the examination table.

Peter squeezed her hand and whispered, "Back in a minute."

Whatever call he intended to make, he did not want to be overheard. That meant leaving her with one thin curtain shielding her from the woman who tried to kill her.

What if she saw them bring me in?

She wouldn't do anything in front of staff.

They'll leave her alone, eventually.

What if Peter doesn't come back?

She scanned the room for potential weapons. Nothing.

Something sharp in a drawer? A tiny scalpel blade would be useless if Ellen attacked from her injured side.

I can still kick with the best of them.

CYNTH

Cynth found Bailey propped up in bed with a cast on her leg, waiting for the all clear to go home.

"What's the damage?"

"I had the stuffing knocked out of me."

"Is that a medical diagnosis?"

"Two broken ribs, a cracked fibula, a bruised hip bone, and a partridge in a pear tree. Did you catch Ellen?"

Up to the gills on pain meds. Cynth took a seat. "I guess you didn't hear. Lia's dogs went after her. She strolled into the emergency room with a story about being attacked by strays in Parker Woods. Cal nodded his head and took her statement while they were patching her up. When they were done, he slapped cuffs on her."

Bailey gave a loopy smile. "Cal's naïve act is a mighty weapon. Where is she now?"

"Brent has her on ice at District Five."

"Don't tell the goddess, but I hope she looks like Frankenstein."

Serious pain meds. "A lot of punctures. I bet it hurts like hell. How are you feeling? Up to making a statement?"

"The hydrocodone is making me fuzzy, but I'd rather get it done now. I have a confession to make. After Daniel tried to bail out to Ellen's house, I contacted the prosecutor and told him something awful would happen if Daniel wound up back in the house."

"Yes, I know."

"Everyone assumed Daniel would hurt her."

"That's not what you meant?"

"Daniel is—was—a master of passive aggression and gaslighting. Ellen has always been volatile. While she was gaslighting herself about Daniel, it wasn't an issue."

"And then it was?"

"Ellen would try to talk to him. First about the charges, later about moving out. He never gave her a straight answer. He'd blow her off or patronize her. She'd get mad and come over to vent. Then she'd go home and Daniel would pretend the conversation never happened. Lather, rinse, repeat. I was terrified he'd push her too far."

"How often did this happen?"

"After you served the first search warrant, it was every weekend. I knew he'd push his way back into the house, and when something awful finally happened, it would look like her fault."

"You're talking about reactive abuse. You were trying to protect her."

"I knew she could lash out. I never thought she was capable of premeditated murder."

Bailey was surprisingly focused for being doped up. That would make this interview much easier. Cynth asked, "What happened this morning?"

She had to exercise formidable control when Bailey reported her housebreaking stunt. That Bailey broke the case open and inadvertently handed them slam dunk felony assault charges against Ellen made it easier to be charitable.

When Bailey finally ran down, Cynth said, "So you found the poodle mug, but you moved it?"

"I covered my hand with a poop bag so I wouldn't leave fingerprints."

An unused one, I hope. Cynth thought she'd stifled the eye roll. Bailey's defensive response said otherwise.

"I couldn't leave it where it was. Ellen would have gotten rid of it before you got a search warrant."

Not if you'd called me instead of confronting her.

"You think I should've called you instead of talking to Ellen."

Maybe she's psychic after all. Scratch that. If she was psychic, she wouldn't have needed to confront Ellen.

"Where did you put the mug?"

"You have to make a promise first."

"This isn't *Let's Make a Deal.*"

"Ellen's greyhounds were traumatized after you took them to the shelter. Don't put them through that again."

"You're in no condition to take them."

"Call Brenda at GAGC. They get the girls if Ellen can't care for them. Ellen's not getting out, is she?"

"Not on a murder charge. We have to follow procedure with the dogs, but maybe the adoption folks can meet them at CARE when they arrive."

They're still there. Cynth could feel the greyhounds behind her, muzzles pressed against Brandt's living room window, huge alien eyes wondering why they wouldn't come in and —Play? Feed them? Let them rampage through the neigh-borhood?

Scratch that. They want their murderous mommy.

She leaned back, an impatient leg jiggling Brandt's over-sized Adirondack porch chair as she resisted the urge to turn around. Beside her, Brent kept his eyes on the woods across the street. His lack of annoyance at the delay irked her more than it should.

She wanted inside the house, but a loose dog on I-74 had already caused a three-car pileup. That put Rampaging Rover above their silly search warrant on the dog warden's list. Waiting chafed. The girls were more likely to throw a party for intruders than bite them.

She needed to relax. A sixty-minute break meant an extra sixty minutes Brandt cooled her heels in a stuffy interview room at District 5. Brandt's head should be ready to explode by the time they got to her. That was a fine thing.

They were in for a long night.

Brent broke the silence. "This is over once we get Brandt's confession. Except for the paperwork."

"And IA."

"I have faith in the laws of karma."

"Yeah, right."

He shrugged. "Karma may need an anonymous tip, but I'll give it another week. When this is done, do we return to unrelieved hostility?"

"God, can't we get through this first?"

"Can we aim for civility? I never intended to drag you into my gang business. I never wanted that. I—"

Cynth turned to him, fierce. "Stop it. Just stop it."

"But—"

"It was my fault. I screwed up your operation, and I almost got us killed. It's all on me, so you can quit with the hair shirt."

"What are you talking about?"

"I ran a background check on you, okay? You had a credible cover, but there were anomalies. When I dug deeper it fell apart."

Brent sat up in Brandt's other Adirondack chair and stared. Quietly, he asked, "What did you do?"

"I was stupid. I told someone you weren't who you said you were, that I planned to rip you a new one at dinner."

Brent continued to stare and say nothing. Behind them, claws scratched the window pane, reminding them two very nice dogs were tragically in danger of starving to death or suffocating or dying from lack of attention. *Not looking. Nope, not gonna do it.*

Confessing hurt, but it didn't count unless you got it all out. "I thought I could trust her to keep her mouth shut. Turns out she thought it was a scream her straight-laced cop cousin didn't realize her hot executive boyfriend was really a dirtbag con."

She shrugged a still-resentful shoulder. Gemma spotted Brent first and had been throughly pissed when he went for Cynth. Gemma was big on spite. "I guess it was too good to keep to herself. Somebody she told must have shared it with the wrong person."

"Did you break her nose, too?"

"Wanted to," Cynth said. "Didn't want the repercussions." Which, since Gemma was family, would have been huge. "Made her piss her pants instead. She stays out of my way now."

"Well, that's something. I never knew what tipped them off or how they found me."

"They knew the restaurant, not the garage. I figure they slipped a tracker on your car. Easy enough to remove it while we ate. I shouldn't have freaked, but you acted like you were with them."

"You couldn't just ask? You had to break my nose and dislocate my shoulder?"

Cynth drew on righteous indignation. "What did you expect? I was ambushed by a bunch of gangsters in a deserted parking garage, and my *civilian* boyfriend is like, 'no worries, these are my *friends*.'"

"They *loved* watching you beat the crap out of me. For the record, you only got the drop on me because I was focused on Jerry and his armed thugs."

"I had no clue there was an operation going on."

"As was proper, since they were working with cops. Cops we never identified."

"Ouch. I bet they left us behind because your good friend Jerry didn't want blood on his upholstery."

"For which I am thankful, since I was in too much pain to defend either of us. My guy in IA laughed his ass off when I explained my girlfriend thought I was one of the bad guys and did her civic duty."

"I reset your shoulder."

"That you did. That little fiasco killed my future in drug enforcement."

"I wasn't aware. Sorry about that."

"I transferred in as a detective. They busted me to patrol and stuck me here."

Not what she expected. "I thought you requested it."

"I wasn't in a position to refuse. I suspect they hoped you'd finish me off."

"Oh."

"Not like it's been a party getting slapped down by you on a daily basis."

Cynth mumbled, "The whole situation was the biggest humiliation of my life."

"So you chose open antagonism?"

"It seemed easier."

"Sweet bleeding Jesus. You're a piece of work. It's nice to know you don't hate me."

"Not all the time, anyway." Several houses down, a white county van slowed, looking for on-street parking. Behind her, the greyhounds made their weird roo-roo-roo noises.

About freaking time.

BAILEY

Bailey sat on Lia's bed, her ribs aching and her head swimming with drugs and fatigue, the cast on her leg dooming her to weeks of inactivity. Kita pressed up against her, those mournful bloodhound eyes glued to her.

Poor baby is just as traumatized as I am. "I don't want to be a bother."

Lia edged the top drawer out of her dresser, tugging one side, then the other, with her good arm. "You're staying here until you can take care of yourself."

"But this is your bed."

"Peter bought an excellent bed when he moved in. It's time it got some use." She pulled a nightgown out of the drawer and shoved it shut with her hip. She sat on the bed, laying the folded nightgown in Bailey's lap. "This should fit. Once you're settled, I'll see about dinner."

"You're concussed and your shoulder is trashed. Why doesn't Peter fix dinner?"

"He's meeting Terry and Steve at Wesleyan to bring our cars back. Let's get those clothes off."

Between the two of them, Bailey eased into the night-gown and only bumped her broken ribs twice. Once appropriately attired, they shifted her so she sat propped up against the headboard with her leg elevated. The process was ludicrously awkward, compounded by Kita occupying the center of the bed and not inclined to move until Lia produced treats.

Lia kicked her shoes off and scooted up beside her. Chewy and Gypsy piled on the bed, sniffing the alien cast.

Warm and cozy and safe and surrounded by dogs, Bailey's defenses collapsed. Eyes wet, she blinked hard, clearing her throat. "Why didn't I see it?"

Lia stroked her hair. "It's easier to see when someone is an out-and-out cad. She needed you, and the need was genuine. Being needed is a powerful thing. I wish you'd waited until we had a chance to talk. We could have gone together."

"I had to look her in the face, just me and her, and ask her why she used me that way. I knew I wouldn't get the chance once I told Cynth what I found." Bailey leaned against Lia's shoulder. "I drew a card. The Tower. I knew I was walking into a disaster, and I didn't care. That was stupid."

"What did Ellen say?"

"She said I was nuts. I've decided confrontation and closure are highly overrated."

"When I was in therapy, Asia said confrontation with someone who isn't acting in good faith is asking them to lie to you. In their mind, you have your evidence. If you come to them about it, you want to be wrong and you're asking them to make it happen. She said you have to trust your gut, and if it feels bad, it is bad. You might not have all the facts, but maybe you don't need them."

"Did she share any other wise words on the subject?"

"She said if someone is screwing you around, you can't expect them to suddenly come clean about it."

"Yeah, that only happens on *Father Brown*. Where were you at nine this morning?"

"I was looking for you."

Bailey sighed. "I wish you'd found me."

"Me, too."

"Do you think something is wrong with her?"

"What do you mean?"

"Daniel was a sick puppy, scamming and lying to everyone the way he did. I'm wondering if Ellen isn't a version of the same thing."

"I think if you stay in a relationship with a toxic person, you can wind up playing by their rules. Maybe because those are the rules your toxic partner understands, or maybe you just get infected. But does it matter? In the end, isn't how she treated you what's important?"

"It would be an explanation."

"You're bi-polar, and you don't hurt people."

"I hurt you."

"You were being fed a scary amount of drugs. You were sorry, and you never did it again. That's different. People can make mistakes. When they put everything on you and gaslight you instead of validating your experience, that's not a mistake. That's someone jerking you around."

"Two years. I let her lean on me for two years, and it meant nothing to her."

"You are a loving and compassionate person. She might

not have had the strength to boot Daniel without your support. And that's to your credit."

"I'm wondering if I ever really knew her. She tried to kill me, Lia. She tried to kill *you*."

Lia squeezed Bailey's hand. "You were a rock back on the cliff. You saved my life."

"Landing in a tree knocked the crazy out of me. As therapy, I don't recommend it."

Lia wrapped her good arm around Bailey, gathering her in. The storm broke. She sobbed, big ugly sobs that eventually trailed off into hiccups. The dogs crowded into their laps, making Bailey laugh.

"Goddess, my nose is running. Hand me my t-shirt." The shirt was grimy, sweat-stained, and embedded with bits of tree bark. Bailey used it to wipe her face and blow her nose.

Lia said, "You must be exhausted."

"I'm never moving from this spot. You should be resting, too."

"You're right. I'm done. Let's let Peter take care of us." Lia dug out her phone, then stared at it. "Texting one-handed will be hell. Good thing you taught me something new today. Hey Bixby, activate speakerphone. Call Peter Dourson."

Bailey felt her appetite returning. "Can we have Indian? I could use some saag paneer."

Peter's voice sounded from the speaker. "How's the one-armed woman and her gimpy friend?"

"Too tired to move and in need of sustenance. Can you stop by Dusmesh?"

"Absolutely, after we drop the cars off. I have a present for Bailey."

"Present?" Bailey said. "Aw, Peter, you shouldn't have."

"Steve and Terry hiked down to the creek and found your phone. That's some case you have on it. Still intact after a forty-foot drop."

"That's great. Thank you."

"Don't thank me. Thank Steve and Terry. They got a call from John. He's frantic to talk to you."

Hope broke through her druggy lethargy.

"John? My John? How did he know to call them?"

"He didn't. He rang your phone. That's how they found it. He'd been calling for hours."

Thank the goddess. "What did he say?"

"Terry spoke to him. I'll get dinner for all of us and you can ask him then."

Lia ended the call. "That's odd, Trees calling while you were in the hospital."

Bailey spoke through tears. "Not odd at all. He always knows when I really need him."

BRENT

Several hours ago, Cal—a softie for seniors—stashed Brandt in an interview room with soft, cushy chairs normally reserved for witnesses and victims and others unlikely to break the furniture apart and rip the cushions to shreds.

Brent and Cynth stood inside a repurposed closet, observing Brandt on a monitor. Brandt sat with her head resting against the high back of a recliner, eyes closed, a bit of drool on her chin. Her hair fell over her face, tangled like a bird's nest. Her body swam in sweats someone dug up from somewhere when they took her clothes. She looked frail and twenty years older.

"Our lady killer is a hot mess. Think she realizes we're watching her?"

Cynth turned away from the monitor, handing Brent a cardboard box. She picked up a stack of file folders that looked ominous but contained junk. "If she's even awake. She'll hate us seeing her like this."

"All to the good if a bad hair day keeps her off balance."

Cynth paused at the door. "You take lead."

"When will you get over your little old lady phobia?"

"Screw that. She thinks she can manipulate you and she won't talk to me. So you might as well lead."

Brent sighed.

Cynth snorted. "Being you is *such* a burden."

They were both dragging. The mini snark-fest had been his gift to Cynth, a warmup to put a little color in her cheeks and get her on her game. And if she knew he provoked her on purpose, she'd break his nose again.

Brandt sat up as they entered. "Finally! If I'd realized it would take this long for someone to talk to me, I would have asked for a lawyer."

"We can still get you one," Brent said. He placed the box on a central coffee table next to Cynth's stack of bogus files and sat in one of the squishy chairs.

"Let's get this over with. I have to get back to my girls. They've been alone for hours."

"About that," Cynth said. "Animal Control removed the dogs so we could search your house."

Rage twisted on Brandt's face. *Maybe breakable furniture was the wrong call.*

"You had no right to take the girls!"

Cynth said, "We alerted GAGC. They may have them."

With the dogs in Moore's name, she might never see her girls again.

Brandt's face paled. Typically, she went on offense. "I was the victim of an attack! What is this?"

Cynth had done a decent job drawing fire. Time for him to present as the sympathetic option. "A pitbull and a mutt in Parker Woods?"

"That's what I told the officer. Then he arrested me and I still don't understand why."

Confusion, exasperation, and an appeal to chivalry. Too predictable. "We'll straighten this out once we go through the Miranda warning." He shrugged. "Procedure."

She signed the paperwork with an angry scrawl. Brent walked her through the statement she gave Cal, allowing her to build her confidence in a rhythm Peter called playing the trout.

Time to change the narrative. He put a little oomph into his drawl. "Ms. Brandt, if you were getting torn up by stray dogs in Parker Woods this morning, how did Bailey Hughes wind up hanging in a tree over Mill Creek with broken ribs and a fractured leg?"

Brandt's mouth fell open. Her eyes dropped, searching the floor as if looking for a convenient trapdoor. Finally she said, "What did Bailey tell you?"

"We're more interested in your side of things. Tell us about this morning."

Ellen paused, then said in a quiet voice, "You're aware of Bailey's history? She's mentally ill."

"Is she?"

"She's bi-polar. If she stops taking her medication, she

gets crazy ideas. I'm sorry I lied, but I didn't want to get her in trouble. She's a good person. "

Full of Christian charity, aren't you? "Just tell us what happened."

"I was at Wesleyan with the girls and Bailey showed up. We had an argument the last time I saw her. That was the day I was released from jail.

"I thought she wanted to apologize. Instead, she went crazy on me. She accused me of killing Daniel. She said she'd been rooting around in my house while I was at work and found my poodle mug. The person who framed me is at it again."

So far it jibes.

"She stormed off. I followed, begging her to listen to me. I guess I grabbed her arm. She jerked away and lost her balance. That's when she fell."

"You left her there?"

Brandt's voice had become increasingly urgent. Now she was frantic. "No! I mean, I did, but I had to go back to my car to get my phone so I could call 911."

"We never got that call."

"Lia drove up, drove right across the field. I tried to tell her, but her dogs jumped out of the car and attacked me."

Brent kept his voice even and pleasant. "Why would they do that?"

"I don't know, I don't know," she moaned. "I had to escape. Lia found Bailey. I knew she'd take care of her and I was bleeding everywhere. I had to get to the hospital."

"Where you told the doctor strays attacked you."

"I didn't expect the hospital to call the police. Bailey's my best friend. Whatever got into her head, I knew she'd regret it as soon as she calmed down."

Freaking amazing. I almost believe her. "That all sounds good, Ms. Brandt, except the part you left out, where you whacked Lia with a pipe and she fell off the cliff."

Ellen screeched, her voice a strident, high-pitched whine that cut like a table saw. "She was *fine* when I left. It had to be someone else."

"Someone else lurking in the woods that you didn't see?" Brent asked.

"Maybe it was coyotes," Cynth suggested with uncharacteristic sugar in her voice.

Brandt clamped her mouth shut, crossing her arms tightly across her chest.

Brent couldn't blame Cynth—sarcasm was hard to resist when the lies were so transparently stupid—but it was the wrong move and shut Brandt down. He continued in that same level voice, "The pipe is at the lab. I wonder whose prints we'll find on it."

He pulled a clear plastic evidence bag from the box and set it on the table. The muzzle of a pink ceramic poodle pressed against the plastic. He set several bags next to it, containing tools and wood filler and adhesive. "Which is where these will go when we finish here."

"That's my mug! Where did you find it?"

"Where do you think we found it?"

"I have no idea. Bailey wouldn't tell me. I think she must have put it there. … She must be the one who framed me!"

Cynth huffed, obviously tired of playing games. "Stop it. Bailey didn't frame you. You pushed Bailey and attacked Lia. These are facts. What we want to know is why you killed Daniel."

Brandt's face froze in a mix of fear and outrage. Her chest heaved. She breathed audibly, about to blow.

Just have to wait her out.

Somehow, she brought herself under control. "I didn't want Daniel dead."

Brent kept his voice conversational. "What did you want?"

"I wanted him to grow up."

"Excuse me?"

"I wanted him to apologize. I wanted him to beg me to let him come home."

"But he wasn't begging, was he? He was sponging off an old woman, and he had a patsy to finance his next business venture."

Eyes wide, Brandt said, "It was Lois, wasn't it?"

Brent put bite into his voice. "Don't play dumb. Daniel was walking away from everything, starting over in another state under someone else's name, so the court couldn't touch him. He'd be gone. He'd never be sorry for anything."

"I don't know what you're talking about."

"Ms. Buchanan told you all about it at Dog Day, same time she told you about the text messages."

Brandt shook her head. "That never happened. She came by the booth, I gave her a key fob and she left."

"You didn't talk to her later?"

"I haven't seen her since then. I didn't know about the text messages, but it sounds like she did and she didn't want you to think she was the only one. What a snake!"

"You're saying she lied."

"Yes, she lied! I never left the house that night!"

"Now see, that's where we have a problem."

"I don't understand."

"Bailey remembered the gate behind your bamboo."

Brandt's eyes jerked up.

Yes, Ellen, you are well and truly sunk. "We discovered footprints behind the bamboo and fibers snagged on the fence. I'm sure they're from your clothes. Sorry about the bamboo. We cut it down to take casts of your footprints."

Brandt lunged for the table. Cynth whisked the mug away as Ellen's outflung arm scattered the stack of file folders and the papers they held. She ducked her head into her hands and wept.

Cynth ignored the mess, ignored the crying. "You glued your windows shut months ago to fake an alibi. Is that when you decided to kill Daniel?"

Ellen said nothing.

"What did you do with the murder weapon? Is it in one of these bags?"

Brandt, head still down, spoke through her hands. "I want a lawyer."

13

DAY 11

WEDNESDAY, AUGUST 20

BRENT

THEY'D EXPECTED A NIGHT AT THE JUSTICE CENTER TO soften Brandt up. The cool look in Brandt's eyes when the sheriff's deputy unlocked the interview room said they'd underestimated her.

Brandt sat at the conference table, chin up, hands folded over a sheet of paper, looking steadily at them without saying a word. She'd found an orange jumpsuit, a mirror, and self-righteous indignation. Pitbull Perry—a stocky man with a shaved head frequently seen chomping a cigar on the backs of bus benches—sat next to her. The stink of tobacco smoke on his suit said the cigars were more than an affectation.

Brent exchanged a glance with Cynth as they sat down. They'd run into Pitbull before. Cynth called him "low-rent representation for lowlifes." He didn't look low-rent today.

He looked like there was a twenty-two ounce ribeye with his name on it at Morton's.

Pitbull grinned, displaying a gold eyetooth.

Make that a thirty-six ounce ribeye.

Pitbull half-stood and leaned across the table, nodding, shaking hands, taking control of the narrative. "Detective Davis, Detective McFadden." He cleared his throat, assuring he had everyone's attention. "Let's get this going. Ms. Brandt will make a statement, after which we will take no questions. Ms. Brandt?"

Brandt straightened her shoulders before picking up her paper. "The events at Wesleyan Cemetery were a tragic accident that resulted from being accused of murder by my most trusted friend. I deeply regret that Bailey Hughes and Lia Anderson came to harm.

"I last saw my poodle mug at Spring Grove Cemetery on Dog Day. I do not know how it came to be in my home. Bailey said she found it in a cabinet on a high shelf I can't reach and never use.

"I have not used the gate behind my house for over twenty years. I go behind the bamboo because Nati is skittish and gets stuck back there. When she won't come out, I have to retrieve her.

"I was not aware of any supposed text messages between me and Daniel Moore before you advised me of them after Daniel's death. Lois Buchanan never spoke to me about them or about any plans she had with Daniel."

She laid her statement down and folded her hands again.

"Is that it?" Cynth said.

Pitbull said, "Your evidence is purely circumstantial. None of it is sufficient to charge Ms. Brandt with Daniel

Moore's murder. As for the assault charges, Ms. Brandt requests immediate arraignment and bail."

"Not assault," Cynth said. "Attempted murder. No bail."

Pitbull stood, aligning his lapels and shooting his cuffs. The smug expression on his face said that ribeye was waiting. "That's for the judge to decide. Detectives, we're done here."

Cynth slumped in Brent's visitor's chair. She flicked a pen laying on his blotter, sending it skittering over the edge and into his wastepaper basket in an apt metaphor for the Moore case.

"Pitbull was wearing his second best suit," Brent observed.

"Murder's a long step up from the DUIs he pulls in with those bus bench ads. Brandt sounded way too credible."

Brent retrieved his pen. "Didn't she though? The gate opened too easily to have been shut for twenty years. Doesn't matter. What matters is she provided a plausible explanation for the footprints. It's that beyond a reasonable doubt thing. "

"She didn't explain the windows."

"Because there is no explanation. As of now, we have a circumstantial case that will be a heavy lift in court. We need a murder weapon. You think Pitbull coached her?"

Cynth snorted. "You think she came up with that all on her own?"

"She was pretty damn creative yesterday."

Cynth's phone rang. She answered, her face clouding over as she spoke, those eyes going gunmetal gray. She ended the call, gripping her phone as if she wanted to strangle it.

"What's wrong?"

"That was Jeffers. We'd be better off if I'd let Brandt smash that mug."

"Why? What happened?"

"Zero fingerprints."

Brent raised his eyebrows. "None? That's a problem."

"You think? You don't wipe fingerprints off something you own that's in your house. It lends credibility to her whole 'I'm being framed story.'"

"No joke."

"It gets worse. Junior found saliva on the side of the mug."

"Not on the lip?"

"Nope. He ran a Rapid DNA test. It isn't Ellen's. Why would someone lick the outside of a mug?"

Brent took a moment to consider, then said, "Didn't your mother ever spit on a napkin to clean your face?"

"What does my mother have to do with it?"

"If it was planted—and I'm not saying it was—whoever hid the mug in Ellen's cabinet cleaned it because they couldn't be sure which fingerprints were theirs and which were Ellen's. At the last minute, they saw something they missed. Maybe they accidentally touched it again."

"They spit on a napkin to rub off whatever it was?"

"It's an explanation."

"It's a dumb one. DNA is better than fingerprints."

"So we take Einstein off our suspect list."

Cynth summarized. "We can prove Ellen had a way out of the house. We can't put her at the scene, and her knowledge of the texts is down to 'she said, she said.'"

"Not even that, since Buchanan is fuzzy about what she said." Brent sighed, recalling the pile of Dog Day registrations. "We need a witness to that argument."

"I'll take the volunteers."

Brent withdrew a file folder from the stack on his desk and handed it to her. "Here's the list. You might as well take Peter's desk."

CYNTH

Cynth hung up the phone. She sneered at Peter's leering Elvis skull bust, wanting to give the bobble head a healthy flick. She resisted, since that risked setting off a rubbish recording of "Jail House Rock." Peter regularly removed the batteries, but someone kept replacing them. Probably the joker who snuck Elvis onto Peter's desk in the first place.

This is getting us nowhere. She swiveled her chair so she could see Brent. After two hours on the phone, his hair stuck out in all directions. He'd hate that. Unlike her drab blonde, his pride and joy was the rich gold of antique coins, and he kept it impeccably groomed.

"I got nothing. You?"

Brent crumpled a sheet of paper and tossed it at the basket sitting on the file cabinet for that purpose. He missed. "A big, fat goose egg unless you count a pair of corgis going at it. The jackass who recounted that story said he didn't notice boy parts on either dog, but they were low to the ground, so how could he tell? I still have—" He scanned his list. "—three hundred and fifty-some names left. You talk to everyone manning the refreshment booths?"

"What do you think? Several of them remember seeing Brandt, but they were too busy to notice who she talked to."

"Buchanan had a week to come up with that story. It was a great way to shift suspicion."

Cynth shook her head. "She wouldn't invent a story unless she knew the texts were fake. We never released that."

"We'd just told her they were fake. Maybe she's a fast thinker."

"Too many damn plot twists."

"This is highly inefficient. We need to view the situation through a different lens."

"How so?"

"Everyone on our list swears they wanted Daniel alive." Brent ticked the points off on his fingers. "His victims wanted to find their instruments or get restitution. Buchanan sank her retirement into his new flute and she was desperate to make that happen. Brandt says she wanted him back."

"She also wanted him to suffer," Cynth said.

"You can't suffer when you're dead. Think about the tit for tat between them, even with a no contact order. The woman couldn't let go."

"But that leaves us nowhere."

"We need to prove nobody could plant that mug. Conversely, if Brandt is innocent—"

Cynth gave him a murderous look.

He held up his hands, palms out. "—Not saying she is, but *if* she is, someone had to enter her house to plant it.

Brandt's window was glued shut by that time. No one could get in that way. It will be on her cameras."

Cynth continued her glower.

"Treat it as an academic exercise."

Cynth snorted. "If we're looking for an intruder, Bailey's schedule was irregular. I don't think anyone would risk breaking in while she was staying there. We can start when Brandt got out of jail and stop when Bailey came back."

"We need to consider that Bailey framed her." When Cynth scowled, he added, "Not that she would."

"Now you're arguing the other side. So Bailey hid the mug, left her fingerprints on the bag of chia seeds, moved the mug, then confronted Ellen, knowing she didn't do it."

"I'm just saying we have to account for it, since that will be Brandt's defense."

"Bailey had the run of the house," Cynth said. "Brandt can just say Bailey planted it while she was in jail. Bailey had to haul bags of clothes and stuff in and out. We can't prove the mug wasn't smuggled in then."

"Making Bailey the perfect patsy." He ran a hand through his hair, mussing it further.

"The narrative makes no sense. Why didn't she 'find' the mug rooting around Brandt's cabinets while she was staying there? Burgling in the middle of the night makes her sus."

Brent gave her a steady look with his impossibly blue eyes. "When has anyone accused Bailey of being logical?"

"Bailey didn't leave the house, not unless she climbed over Brandt's sleeping body. And if she's framing Brandt for someone else, who is she doing it for? Lia? You going after Lia now?"

"Despite your excellent analysis, Bailey is a banquet for the defense, especially if they trot out her history."

"Dammit, the only way to protect Bailey is to prove someone planted that mug."

"Tanking our case against Brandt. It's a lose-lose proposition. Either way, we need to know what we're dealing with."

Cynth huffed a sigh, thinking of the hours ahead. "We need to amend the search warrant to get back into Brandt's account. Fix your hair before we see the judge."

14

DAY 12

THURSDAY, AUGUST 21

GAIL

GAIL EXPECTED A MOVIE SCENE: DINGY ROOM, FLICKERING fluorescents, and a bare table with loops for shackles. That was silly. A sketch artist needed light to work, and she was here to assist the investigation. But logic wasn't sufficient to quell her apprehension as she followed Detective Davis down the hall in District 5.

She couldn't think of a valid reason to refuse when he called. Not fast enough, anyway. As he opened the door to the interview room, she tried one more time. "You arrested Ellen again. Why do you need me?"

Even knowing her movie version of an interview room was ridiculous, the pastel green walls and soft upholstered chairs surprised her. *Just like someone's living room. Maybe this won't be so bad.*

Detective Davis waved her to the softest and cushiest of the chairs and gave her a sympathetic smile. "Pre-trial discovery. Ellen's lawyer will learn about the woman you saw. They'll claim she killed Daniel. That's reasonable doubt and Ellen walks. We have to identify her and get her statement on the record."

"Oh. Now I'm sorry I said anything."

"Don't be. Better we locate your mystery woman now. Imagine if the defense sprung her on us during trial? We find her first, she helps us put Ellen away. Can I get you something to drink? Coke? Water? Coffee? Tea?"

"Umm, water will be fine."

Detective Davis brought her water in a glass and set it on the little table next to her chair before he sat in the chair opposite hers. "Our artist is running late. I'm sorry for the inconvenience."

"How long will this take? I have dogs to walk." Her mouth suddenly dry, she took a sip of water. She couldn't face Ellen in court. If they found this woman, maybe they wouldn't need her testimony.

The door to the interview room opened and Detective McFadden entered, carrying a file folder. She held out a hand for shaking. "Ms. Cook, I'm Detective McFadden. Thank you for coming in."

"Um, happy to help. How long will it take?" She took another sip of water to hide her nervousness. "I'm due at Florence's in an hour. I can't be late." Florence wasn't fussy about time, but anything to get this over with.

"We apologize for the inconvenience," Detective McFadden said. "This is really important. I'll get someone over there to cover for you. No worries, you can have the fee."

Before Gail could protest, Detective McFadden walked to the far side of the room, making a call Gail couldn't hear.

She pocketed her phone and returned, smiling as she sat in the chair next to Gail.

"All taken care of."

If it was meant to be reassuring, it wasn't.

Detective Davis said, "Let's get the Miranda warning out of the way, don't you think, Detective McFadden?"

"Be my guest."

"I don't understand," Gail said. "We didn't do this last time."

"An error on our part," he said. "It's just procedure."

Nerves threatened to become panic. She stuffed it down, too focused on the queasy feeling in her gut to pay attention to the words. Didn't matter. Everyone who'd ever watched a cop show could recite Miranda by heart.

He picked up a clipboard off the table beside his chair and leaned over to hand it to her. "We just need you to sign this."

It was the warning, with a place for her signature. She signed, trying to act like it was no big deal, and handed it back.

As he reviewed her signature, he said, "How long have you been walking Ellen Brandt's dogs?"

"Excuse me?" Where had he heard that? His voice sounded friendly, so maybe it was just conversation.

"In your earlier statement, you didn't mention knowing Ellen. We're curious why."

"Oh. Um, I wasn't walking her dogs when Daniel died."

"You hadn't met her before?" Detective McFadden asked.

"Well, sure, but her friend moved in. I hadn't walked them in ages." She needed to get this off her. "Nobody asked me about Ellen. I didn't think about it. Does it matter?"

"Probably not." Detective Davis said. "Just another of

those things we need to clarify. Ellen's lawyer might make something of your prior relationship."

Detective McFadden cleared her throat. "After we searched Ellen Brandt's house, someone went in and hid a piece of evidence."

"Um, they did?"

"Detective Davis and I spent yesterday reviewing Ellen's security footage. Only one person besides Ellen entered during the relevant period."

"Are you talking about me? I walk her dogs. I don't know anything about evidence."

Detective McFadden narrowed her eyes, like focusing a laser. "Ellen's fingerprints should be on it, but they're not."

"Ellen's a very clean person—"

"No fingerprints, but we found saliva."

Gail picked up the glass and drank, desperate for a reason to avoid those laser eyes.

Detective McFadden said, "We have DNA. When we test the saliva on that glass, we'll find a match, won't we?"

TWELVE DAYS AGO

Ellen—the cause of her problems—sat smug and pretty at her booth, surrounded by people cooing over her junk. The lovely mug sat on the corner of the table, nobody watching it. Easy enough to slip into her tote while Ellen and her friend were busy.

A small revenge. No one would know.

It should have ended there.

Glen Parker was mostly safe, but this was Northside. It

made sense to have protection when she was out late at night.

The awl was the right size to fit in her pocket, something she could hold while walking dogs, better than holding keys between your fingers like she'd been taught as a young girl.

She hadn't meant to follow Daniel into the woods. But when that woman left, her feet pulled her forward as if someone else inhabited her body, her chest ready to explode with the need to say something.

The smug bastard smiled at her when she caught up, crouching down to pet Cleo and Patra in the long shadows cast by the street light.

"How are the old ladies?" he asked. They rolled on their backs for belly rubs like they never did for her.

"They're fine." She bit off the words, reminding herself to be nice. "You must be relieved with your case resolved."

Daniel glanced up, saying nothing.

"You can move on now."

Daniel returned his attention to the dogs. "I don't plan to go anywhere."

"I know what you're doing." The words burst out without her realizing she'd meant to say them.

He had the nerve to look confused. "What are you talking about?"

"Taking advantage of Florence like that. You don't even have the decency to care for her properly. You're just waiting for her to die so you can steal everything."

"Whatever you think, I'm making her last days pleasant. At least she enjoys my company. She calls you Nurse Ratched. Did you know that?"

Daniel began to rise out of his crouch. It was in that moment, her alien Doctor Strangelove hand coming out of her pocket, that hand still holding the awl, the awl somehow sliding into the base of Daniel's neck.

Daniel, stumbling back, blood spurting, Cleo and Patra shrieking. Her heart pounding as she dragged them away, pulling them into her arms, racing down the dark path to Haight to get as far away as she could, barely able to see the walk but not daring to use the light on her phone in case someone should see her. Slipping on the final steep descent and almost falling. Clinging to the sign at the end of the trailhead with her chest burning.

She walked up Haight to Hamilton and back to the other end of Glen Parker, ditching the awl in a storm drain along the way.

Cleo and Patra were too old for such a long walk, so she'd had to carry them. Back at the house, discovering blood in their fur, on her shirt, inside the pocket where she'd stuffed the awl, that awful awl she'd had no business carrying.

She'd washed the dogs twice to make sure no blood remained on their white fur. Then she'd spent a sleepless night waiting for the police to come.

But they hadn't.

She'd stared at the ceiling, wondering what would happen next. She only stabbed Daniel once. That wasn't enough to kill anyone, was it? He was a block from home and had a phone to call someone, call 911. He'd be at the hospital.

She looked at the clock. 5:20 a.m.

If he was at the hospital, the police would be here by now.

What if he's still there?

What if he's dead?

Did that woman see me?

She'd seen no blood on her shoes, no blood on their paws, but what if Cleo and Patra left fur behind? What if their fur was on his clothes? They could test doggy DNA, couldn't they?

She had to have a reason for the dogs to be there. She had to go back and take the dogs. If the dogs were with her and she discovered the body, that would explain it, wouldn't it?

Dog walkers would be out early. *I have to get there before anyone else.*

The awl. Stupid, stupid, stupid. If Daniel died—even if he didn't—the police would search for it. Storm drains were the first place they looked in crime dramas, or maybe second after trash cans.

In a book she'd read, the wife gave the police the wrong gun, so they never went looking for the murder weapon. *Lots of options in the poodle mug.*

She pulled on a neoprene glove, rooting through the tools for a second awl. To avoid smudging Ellen's fingerprints, she held it by the shaft as she placed it in a baggie. She'd take the dogs back to Parker Woods. If Daniel was dead, she'd leave the awl and it would serve Ellen right for booting Daniel out.

I'm worrying about nothing.

She kept telling herself that as she dragged Cleo and Patra down the street and into the woods. She repeated it like a mantra as she shined her phone light on the walk.

Daniel lay on the concrete, his head and shoulders wreathed in a pool of blood. Despite her fears, she hadn't been ready for that, hadn't counted on Cleo and Patra wading into the sticky mess.

She dragged Cleo and Patra back to the street and used a

carabiner to attach their leashes to a signpost, checking the houses to assure herself no one was up. She pulled on a new glove before she removed the awl from her fanny pack, holding it as she considered the best place to put it.

If it's under him, they can't miss it.

She crouched down, lifting the edge of his shirt. She stopped.

Wait. It needs blood.

She dipped a gloved finger in the deepest part of the blood puddle, smearing it on the business end of the awl.

Has to appear like he fell on it.

She lifted the shirt again, shifting Daniel's body just enough to slip the awl under him, lowering his body and arranging the shirt the way it was when she found him.

She peeled the glove off, pulling it inside out, checking her hands for blood, not finding any but grabbing an emergency wet wipe from her fanny pack, anyway. After cleaning her hands, she stuffed it in the inside out glove.

What to do with the glove? *Not the trash can.* She shoved the whole mess in a pocket. They'd find it if they searched her, but they'd need a reason, wouldn't they?

Patra barked, annoyed at being tied up. *Too loud. She'll wake someone.* She rushed to the dogs, shushing them, unhooking their leashes. As she stooped to reassure them, Cleo snuffled at the pocket containing her bloody secret.

A light flicked on across the street. Mrs. McCarthy was awake, and Mrs. McCarthy knew her. Everyone in the neighborhood did. She had to call 911, had to call them now.

She'd messed up with the awl, had hoped to correct that by hiding the poodle mug in Ellen's house. But she'd messed up again. Stupid, stupid, stupid, because she knew about DNA. Cleaning the smudge off the mug had been a reflex. A stupid, thoughtless reflex.

She'd been silent too long. She looked up to find both detectives watching her with flat, no-nonsense eyes.

"There is no artist, is there?"

LIA

It was obvious Florence rarely moved from her aging recliner, anchored by infirmity and surrounded by the detritus of her medical routines. Inertia made everything about her sag: limp hair, her face, a faded, shapeless house-dress. A dust mop of a dog snuggled in her lap, staring at Lia through eyes like moonstones. *Poor baby must be blind.* An arthritic hand rested on the dog, the fourth finger sporting an ancient wedding set.

Florence's eyes shone bright with intelligence. They narrowed on Lia's sling. "Are you sure you can do this? I don't want you to hurt yourself."

Lia stooped and gave the dog a scratch. "I've become an expert at doing things one handed. You won't be a problem, will you, little guy?"

"Gail never mentioned you," Florence said. "Is she all right? I don't understand why she didn't call."

"She's stuck in a meeting." *True enough.* "I work at home, so I'm happy to fill in. What do you need?"

"Can you make a pot of coffee? I have a taste for it right

now. I'd do it, but it's so hard for me to get around. Make a cup for yourself and we can chat. It will give Snickerdoodle a minute to get used to you."

Florence directed from the living room while Lia made coffee. When she returned with two steaming mugs, Florence pulled out the drawer on her end table and pointed a shaky finger at a box of Mallomars.

"Have a cookie. Don't tell Gail. She doesn't like me eating sugary stuff. I don't know why she bothers, always fussing when I'm going to die, anyway. I'd rather enjoy my remaining time."

Lia considered what it would be like, trying to eke out an extra month or year when you couldn't do any of the things you loved. She wasn't a fan of marshmallow, but she took a cookie to be sociable, munching as she wandered around the room.

"I don't blame you."

Shelves and curio cabinets lined the room, packed with figurines and fossils and tchotchkes. The mantel above a decommissioned fireplace overflowed with family photos. A handful of mostly mediocre paintings hung on the walls. As crowded as a museum basement, the room was surprisingly dust free.

"Your things are lovely."

"All my memories. Gail has been after me to declutter. She knows all about selling things on the internet. I told her it was too much bother, but she said we could at least hold a garage sale."

Florence's face turned stubborn. "Memories are all I have left. I can't bear to let any of them go."

"Objects possess a kind of life, don't you think?"

"Oh, I do. These are like old friends. There's a story

attached to every one. Now that my family is gone, they're a comfort to me.

"I told Gail she can declutter after I die. She was kind enough to clean everything for me after Daniel died, they were so dusty. I suspect she wants me to get rid of it all so she won't have to do it again."

A painting hung above the mantel, directly in Florence's line of sight. Tiny barns and farmhouses scattered across a colorful patchwork of fields and mountains and trees, painted in a fourth grader's wonky concept of two-point perspective.

Lia said, "Tell me about this one. It's obvious you love it."

Florence smiled. "My grandad was a traveling salesman during the Great Depression. He bought it at a drugstore in upstate New York for three dollars. Grandma thought it was a waste of money. She was always carping about the three-dollar painting he bought when no one had any money. By the time I was born, it was an old joke with them. I suppose it's not very good, but I like the colors and it reminds me of them."

"I like it too. There's something cheerful about it. Art is about how it makes you feel, don't you think?"

"I agree," Florence said. "Gail likes it, too. She always says she'll be happy to take it if I decide to get rid of it."

"Do you mind me looking at your things? They're so interesting."

"Please, be my guest. You're a good conversationalist, like Daniel." She sighed. "I miss talking to him."

State fair kewpie dolls sat next to Hummel and Meissan; lumpy ceramic ashtrays formed by tiny hands abutted cut glass that might be Waterford. It was a collection assembled over a lifetime with no thought to value, only to the pleasure it gave.

Lia approved, enjoying the memories Florence shared along with her Mallomars. When Florence started to droop, Lia said, "I'm tiring you. I'll walk Snickerdoodle, then I'll leave. Is there anything else you need?"

"So nice of you to ask. This has been the best time I've had since Daniel passed. I hope you'll come back."

"Tomorrow, if you like."

"I need to pay you."

"No worries. I'm doing this as a favor to Gail. You can give her the usual fee."

"She didn't tell you? I don't pay her."

"Not even for walking Snickerdoodle?"

"Other people pay her, but she won't accept money from me. She says it's her Christian duty and I need to save my pennies. That's silly. I suspect she needs her pennies more than I need mine."

Lia called Cynth on the way home. Cynth, as usual, sounded impatient.

"How did it go? I thought I'd hear from you hours ago."

"We spent the afternoon talking. It's sad, her being alone and wanting to live out her life in her own home. What happened with Gail?"

"It will be a matter of record by tomorrow, so I can tell you. We got a confession."

"Ellen confessed? That's great."

"No. Gail Cook confessed."

"I don't understand. What about everything Bailey found?"

"Haven't figured out the window yet, but Cook planted the mug."

"Why would Ellen attack us if she wasn't guilty? Never mind. This is the same woman who threw her welcome home salad against the wall. How did you get Gail to confess?"

"When I told her we had DNA, she got that 'I'm screwed' look on her face and crumbled. Said it was an accident—which is a joke. Broke down crying and asked for a lawyer. It's all over but the plea bargain. We still don't know why she did it. Can't be for the pittance Nygaard paid her."

"I'm sure it wasn't."

"Enlighten me."

"Florence didn't pay her. Said Gail insisted she keep her money. Gail is a neighborhood odd jobber, right?"

"Errands, pet sitting, housework, like that. Lost her job during covid."

"Does she flip garage sale stuff on eBay?"

"Could be. You think she was after Florence's junk?"

"A lot of it isn't junk. Gail had her eye on a painting that I'm pretty sure is an early Grandma Moses. No signature, but the back story is dead on."

"Which means what?"

"Potentially more than a million at auction. That's the star, but plenty of her other pieces are worth thousands. If Gail frequents eBay, she'd know. Florence doesn't have a clue."

CYNTH

With Cook spilling her guts, they knew where to find the evidence. Cook had washed her clothes, but there was always something on the shoes. *Idiots always forget about their shoes.*

Cynth finished her call with Lia and closed the lid on the evidence box, filling in the form printed on the side and sealing it with evidence tape. She glanced around Cook's living room, reassuring herself that nothing was left behind. "That's it for here. Now we get to shine a light down that sewer grate and hope the awl is still there."

Brent shot her a hopeful look. "You volunteering to fish it out?"

"You're the grunt. What do you think?"

"I think these are my third-best slacks." He peered out the front window. "We've got company."

She joined him at the window. A news van sat across the street. A sleek brunette paced the sidewalk, while a tech guy dealt with equipment. *Not Morse.* The signage on the van read Channel 11. That had to be Carol Logan.

"New girlfriend? Aubrey will be pissed."

"She's not my girlfriend. Fine by me if Aubrey gets scooped."

I bet.

Cynth tapped her fingers on the evidence box, unsure what to do. She called Arseneault, who said to limit her statement to Cook's confession, her arrest, and anything else relevant that was part of the blotter. Before he hung up, he told her the right coverage could clean up their PR problem. *No pressure there.*

Cynth put her phone away. "He says make a statement.

Sure you don't want to do it? Wouldn't want to disappoint your new girlfriend."

"You're the boss. I'm just a lowly grunt, suitable only for fishing murder weapons out of sewage."

As they exited the house, she heard him mutter, "I don't *have* a damn girlfriend."

15

DAY 15

SUNDAY, AUGUST 24

PETER

AFTER FIVE DAYS OF CAREFUL NUDGING, BAILEY WAS OUT OF the house. Peter liked Bailey, but Lia had enough trouble managing with one functional arm without exhausting herself tending to Bailey, while Bailey mooned over John on Zoom and fretted about her business.

It was an unsatisfactory arrangement whose only benefit was giving Lia an opportunity to exorcise totally unmerited guilt feelings.

Simple enough to recruit Jim and Terry to take care of her clients. Harder to get Bailey to accept the offer of help until he suggested she supervise in real time over video chat to make sure they didn't trash someone's prize dahlias.

He waited a day before remarking that she could remotely supervise from anywhere. Bailey leapt to the obvious conclusion on her own. "Anywhere" became "Knoxville," and an early pilgrimage south.

Once he ponied up return airfare, Terry was happy to chauffeur Bailey in her truck. Yesterday, Bailey tested the video chat, running things from Lia's bed while Jim and Terry packed her truck.

It was all systems go, with the truck out front and the gang gathered in the back yard to say goodbye. Steve brought donuts and Alma had the huge coffee urn she used at church functions going next door.

Peter breathed a sigh of relief as he stood on the back porch, surveying the crowd of people and dogs. They'd soon be gone, and he'd have his girl back.

He waded through milling dogs and helped himself to a bear claw. Jim scooted over, allowing him to sit with Lia, who was attempting to open a shipping box by picking at the packing tape with her functional hand while she used her elbow to brace the box against her useless arm in its sling.

She turned to him. "Here, you do it."

Peter set down the bear claw and used his pocketknife to slice through the tape. He removed the ubiquitous gift bag and loosened the drawstrings, holding it out to her. She withdrew an arrangement of straps and buckles holding together two pieces of padded fabric, a sort of X shape above a Y.

"Oh!" she said. "It's a harness."

Bailey, enthroned on an Adirondack chair with her cast propped up on an upended planter, said, "It's for Gypsy."

Lia held it out for Gypsy to sniff. "What do you think, girlfriend?"

Gypsy barked, backing away as if the alien object was a hostile entity.

"She's not impressed. What's the occasion?"

"It's so Gypsy can't slip her lead," Jim said.

Lia nodded. "This should do it."

Steve said, "Next time you fall off a cliff, she'll support you long enough for you to grab onto something."

"Or I could drag her over with me. We might need to rethink this."

Peter leaned over and fed Gypsy a bit of his bear claw. "Gypsy's strong, aren't you, girl? You want to be like Lassie and rescue your mom when she falls off a cliff."

Gypsy licked her chops and gave Peter her stubborn look, demanding more pastry.

Steve said, "What's the news with Ellen?"

Lia said, "She's being held without bail. No clue why she attacked us, since she didn't kill Daniel."

Jim said, "What happens to her dogs? Will they be separated?"

Bailey said, "GAGC gave them to the Sheltons. They're long time volunteers. They fostered the girls when they first arrived. Brenda—she's the president—said a woman called her, saying Daniel wanted her to have them. She had a total meltdown when Brenda informed her the girls had been rehomed."

"She give a name?" Terry asked.

"Brenda didn't say, but I bet it was Lois."

"Ellen will plead insanity and get off," Terry said.

"Won't fly," Peter said. "She lied at the hospital. You only lie when you know what you did was wrong. That's consciousness of guilt. Consciousness of guilt means no diminished capacity. A competent lawyer will plead attempted murder down to assault, but she'll have to confess. She'll get time."

Bailey chewed her lip. "Ellen sent me a letter."

"She's allowed to do that?" Steve asked.

"I bet her lawyer doesn't know," Jim said. "What did she say?"

"She's horrified and wonders if I remember everything, since I must be concussed. She ran after me because I was upset and she was worried about me. She believed I was going to jump, so she grabbed me. I jerked away, and that's how I fell."

"When was this?" Lia asked.

"Jim brought the mail over yesterday while you were out. I didn't tell you because I needed time to think."

"What else did she say?"

"She said she was trying to call 911 when you showed up. The dogs attacked her, and she picked up your pipe to scare them off. If she hit you, it was by accident while she was protecting herself. She needs my help to explain it to the judge, because it's all a big mistake."

Lia dropped her donut. "It's *our* fault we wound up dangling off the side of a cliff?"

"She's a piece of work, isn't she?" Steve said.

Lia dusted off her donut and gave it to Chewy. "Didn't you tell me she shoved you in the middle of your back?"

"That's what it felt like, but it happened so fast."

"It's bull. Ellen told me she hadn't seen you. When Gypsy ran into the woods, Ellen said the coyotes were out, and she tried to stop me from going after her. I had the pipe out to chase off Ellen's imaginary coyotes. She wasn't calling 911, and she sure didn't call them after she hit me with that pipe."

"You didn't see her hit you," Bailey said.

"No, I saw the dogs going at her after I came to, which explains why they went after her in the first place."

Bailey's hands fluttered, distressed. "Now I don't know what to think."

Peter reminded himself to be patient. "She's gaslighting you. If she gets you on her side and explains away her fingerprints, she discredits Lia and the case goes away."

Bailey said, "I provoked her. I accused her of murdering Daniel."

Peter said, "You also walked away. She chased you down."

Terry said, "She has no business making you question your memory."

Lia said, "Bailey, look at me. What did you do to justify being pushed off a cliff?"

"I'm so confused."

"That's what she wants. We're sending a photo of that letter to the prosecutor, and we're calling the jail to make sure she can't write you again."

"Can we do that?"

"You have a right to protect yourself."

Jim said, "What was all that business with the window? Ellen could leave by her back door any time Bailey wasn't around."

Terry said, "Maybe the estrangement was a sham, and they were meeting up in the woods."

"Why would they do that?" Steve said.

Terry shrugged. "Protect her assets from litigious flautists?"

Peter said. "They never married. Her assets were never at risk, not unless she was part of it."

Jim said, "I bet she was."

"How do you figure that?" Peter asked.

"This started with Ellen refusing to give Daniel money, right?"

"You can't blame her for that," Lia said.

Jim held up a hand for silence. "Daniel says, 'give me money.' Ellen says no. So Daniel says, 'If you won't give me money, let me pawn your granny's silver. I'll pay it back. My ship is coming in next week.'"

"Why next week?" Steve asked.

"It's always next week with those types. So Ellen says 'you can't have my heirlooms.'"

Steve asked, "Does Ellen have heirlooms? Did her granny have silver?"

"Stop interrupting. It could be anything. The important part is, she says, 'If the money's coming in next week, why don't you pawn one of the repairs lying around the shop? They're worth more and you can get off my back.'"

"Ellen doesn't talk like that," Bailey said.

"I may have the words wrong, but I bet that's what happened."

"Telling someone to rob a bank doesn't make them an accomplice," Peter said. "You need her signature on a pawn slip or video of her at the pawn shop with Daniel."

"I'm sure she didn't participate," Bailey said. "I could be mistaken about the window."

Lia said, "You found the glue. You found dimples in the wood where she drilled it." She met Peter's eyes. He kept his lips firmly pressed together. "Peter can't say anything, but I bet they took the windows apart and confirmed they'd been glued.

"You can't be blamed for picking up a vibe when she really was up to something, even if we never find out what that was. I made the same mistake. I saw that video and decided Ellen murdered Daniel."

Bailey said, "Thank the Goddess you did. I would have died in that tree."

Steve shrugged. "Right theory, wrong perpetrator. Terry saw Gail on the news. Turns out she's in his book club, too."

Terry grumbled, "We would have solved Daniel's murder in five minutes if the two of you hadn't kept everything to yourselves."

Jim glowered. "How do you figure that? No one knew she was Ellen's dog walker. We still don't understand why she did it."

Lia turned to Peter. "I bet Cynth and Brent are relieved this is over so they can go back to their usual cold war."

The fewer people sniffing around Cook and Nygaard and that million dollar painting, the better. He was happy to assist his love with a bit of misdirection.

He rubbed his chin. "It's odd. She hasn't sniped at him in days."

"Do tell," Terry said, wiggling his eyebrows.

"I caught her winking at him yesterday."

All eyes were on him. *Good.*

"Sam said he saw her following Brent in her car. The station is scandalized."

"Surely it was a work-related excursion," Terry said.

"Case is closed, though they might be re-interviewing witnesses. You see either of them, Lia?"

Bless her, Lia was biting her lip to keep from laughing since she knew he made it all up. She shook her head, her expression now schooled into seriousness. "You think Cynth finally caved?"

"If so, the world is not right on its axis." A lie. As long as he had Lia, his world was in perfect order. He'd do whatever was necessary to keep it that way.

As for Bailey, she'd spent too long down the Ellen rabbit hole. This was the third time he'd heard Lia countering her doubts with facts. Today's intervention was helping, but she'd need more deprogramming. Even so, he was confident their friends would help her find her footing again.

LOIS

Lois stood on Florence's front porch, holding onto one slim truth while fluffing the tissue in the gift bag she carried: Daniel had been in contact with the factory since his release from jail. *The papers have to be here.*

Finesse was called for. Daniel never told Florence about the criminal case because her health was too fragile and he didn't want to upset her. Who could say what else he'd kept from her?

Behind the door, a dog barked, high pitched and protective. No more stalling. She rang the bell.

Inside, a quavery voice said, "Come in, but don't let Snickerdoodle out."

Lois cracked the door. Close to the floor, a dingy white blob of fur stared at her with eyes like cloudy mirrors. He humphed and snorted and trotted away.

The voice, again, "Come on in. Snickerdoodle won't hurt you."

She opened the door wider. Florence Nygaard sat in an overstuffed recliner, her body an undifferentiated lump under a floral, tent-like dress. She wore socks with her slippers, which were dingy white blobs resembling nothing so much as Snickerdoodle's littermates.

A miniature set of steps and an end table loaded with medication sat by the recliner. A walker sat on the other side. Shelves stuffed with tacky ceramics took up all available space. Inferior paintings climbed the walls. Photos jumbled the mantel.

"Sorry I didn't greet you at the door. I don't get about so easy anymore. You're Daniel's friend? Lois?"

Lois held out the pretty bag. "Daniel said you like these."

Florence took the bag, pawed through the tissue, and smiled. "Godiva! My doctor won't let me eat sugar, but what he doesn't know, he can't scold me about." She chose a hazelnut truffle from the gold box and waved a hand at the couch. "Please, sit down."

Lois wandered to the mantel instead, using the excuse of admiring family photos to buy time while she decided how to ask for what she needed. Snickerdoodle followed, sniffing at her feet and gazing up at her with those uncanny eyes.

Most of the photos were of a young girl, growing from infancy to adolescence, with a formal portrait holding pride of place. In it, the girl had blossomed into a true beauty with spiraling blonde hair. She held a flute so shiny it had to be new, the light reflecting off it so hard it should have hurt to look at.

In the next photo, a familiar face mugged with the blond girl. Dianne was much younger in this photo, making it four or five years old. The beautiful blonde girl should be in college now.

She opened her mouth to comment, then glanced

around the room. No recent photos of a mature young woman. There had to be a reason.

Florence broke the silence. "My granddaughter. Natalie was so beautiful."

"Exquisite," Lois agreed. *Was? What happened to her?*

"That was the day I bought her flute. She said it was the best day of her life. It took years to scrape the money together, all while flute prices were going up and up. She sounded like an angel when she played it. It was supposed to last her a lifetime. She died a year later."

"I'm so sorry for your loss. … The girl with her, is that Dianne Lovato?"

"They were best friends in high school. I gave her Natalie's flute. A handmade Burkart with a gold lip plate. Fifteen thousand dollars, and me on disability—"

Handmade Burkart with a gold lip plate. Just like the one Daniel sold her for a song three years ago. Lois's gut clenched.

"—I couldn't stand to sell it after Natalie died. I thought Natalie would want Dianne to have it."

"And how does Dianne like it?"

"That flute is cursed. It disappeared. Dianne said Daniel stole it from her. I don't see how. He was a decent man, a Christian. He'd never do anything like that. How do you know her?"

"I don't, really. I saw her at the Hopewell flute conference. She stands out."

"Then she's still playing. I was afraid she gave up after she lost Natalie's flute."

"She didn't strike me as a quitter."

Lois turned away from the photo of the two grinning girls and the prize flute, not wanting to think about the story Dianne told in court only weeks earlier, the rap song that had gone viral in every flute outpost on social media, or the list of missing flutes and serial numbers she'd avoided looking at since it started circulating two years ago.

Daniel wouldn't do anything so awful. He'd been ill. It had all been Ellen. But there couldn't be two identical handmade flutes passing through Daniel's hands at the same time.

She seated herself on the sofa, sinking into cushions that were thick and too soft, the way they were on cheap furniture. Snickerdoodle plopped his butt down in front of her, making her wonder if she was supposed to pet him.

"How are you getting along without Daniel?"

Florence's face turned sad. "It's lonely without him. Snickerdoodle misses him as much as I do."

Snickerdoodle heard his name and climbed the little steps to jump on Florence's lap. He snuffled the gold box. Florence set it aside where he couldn't reach it and stroked his fur.

"Bad for me, much worse for you, baby doll."

"Do you have anyone to help you now?"

"There was a girl after Daniel died, but she's gone. They said she killed him. Can you believe that? The police sent me this nice artist after they arrested Gail. She shops for me and walks Snickerdoodle. She's lovely, though it's not like having Daniel here all the time. He was such a comfort."

"Did Daniel talk to you about his plans?"

"What do you mean?"

"I may be imposing, but Daniel and I were in business together. I'd like to continue our project, but the papers are missing."

Florence shook her head. "That makes no sense. He met with my lawyer about applying for disability. You can own a business and be on disability, but the amount of money they allow you to make isn't worth the risk of losing your benefits."

Disability? What happened to my money? "How did he plan to get by?"

"It was so awful what Ellen did, ruining his business and stealing his house and savings. He said he was too old to start over—"

The judge would've had a hell of a time making Daniel pay hundreds of thousands in restitution if he was disabled. Maybe that was the point. *But the Kazé flute would have solved everything.*

"—and he just didn't have the heart. I told him he could stay here and keep me and Snickerdoodle company as long as he liked."

"Do you still have his papers?"

"What sort of papers?"

"Contracts? A will?"

Florence shook her head. "He didn't have much. He had a used laptop he bought on Craigslist after he moved in with me, but the police took that."

If she had a name, a phone number, she could resurrect the project from there. Lois took a last stab. "I understand everyone keeps numbers on their phone, but perhaps he had an address book?"

"The police took his Filofax. What kind of project were you planning to do?"

"Daniel designed a student flute. We paid for a prototype. It should arrive any day now."

"I don't know anything about that. Can't you call the factory?"

She'd tried emailing the company. They denied having any business with Daniel.

Damn Daniel. He said he changed his will and his power of attorney to protect her since they were in business together, but he kept forgetting to give her copies.

Detective McFadden had refused to share the contents of Daniel's computer. She relented enough to say she'd found a deposit corresponding with the date and amount Lois had given them, but there was no corresponding transfer to a factory. No overseas transfers at all.

Maybe the money is still in his account.

He'd wanted a cashier's check. She hadn't thought she'd need a paper trail, but without one, she had no basis to reclaim her money. The state wouldn't worry about where it came from, they'd just apply it against the court mandated restitution for Ellen's thefts.

"I'll try that. Did he have a safe deposit box?"

"I'm not aware of one. The police gave me a list of things they took." Florence waved a hand at the kitchen. "It's in the junk drawer, left of the sink. Will that help?"

"It might. I'll have a look."

"I still have his things. Nobody can tell me who's supposed to get them. I suppose it would be Ellen, if she wasn't in jail. You can ask her."

Fat chance Ellen will tell me anything.

"Gail moved Daniel's things to the garage. You're welcome to go through them, if you promise to put everything back."

After three sweaty hours in the overheated garage, she'd come up with Daniel's disability application, an email from the lawyer, and a cardboard tube containing a set of mechanical drawings for the new flute. No patent papers, no folder of communications with a factory, no contracts.

Like they never existed.

She looked at the tube of drawings. She'd paid for them. That made them hers, though the court might not see it that way. She closed the last box and replaced it on its stack, taking the tube and exiting, pulling down the garage door. She stashed the tube before stepping back in the house to say goodbye.

"I thought you'd left. You were out there a long time. Did you find what you needed?" Florence asked.

She shook her head, smiling sadly. "No luck. I'll try Ellen next."

"I'm sorry about that. You'll come back, won't you?"

"Absolutely," Lois lied.

K LEE

K Lee woke to the smell of freshly brewed Peruvian coffee emanating from her favorite mug on the nightstand. Beside it sat a plate of assorted pastries: tiny fruit tarts, tiramisu, and a lovely, dense chocolate brownie with walnuts. Lily sat at the foot of the bed with a mug of her own, that gorgeous face wearing a tentative, hopeful expression she hadn't seen in too long.

K Lee pushed up to lean against the headboard. "What did I do to deserve this?"

Lily quirked one corner of her mouth up. "You put up with me."

K Lee took a sip of coffee, wondering where Lily was going with this. "It's not a hardship."

Lily bit her lip and looked away.

K Lee said, "There's something else, isn't there?"

Lily spoke to the wall. "I need to confess."

"Can't be too bad if all it rates is a run to Servatii's."

Lily shook her head, finally looking back. "I'm not a good person."

K Lee set her mug down. She drew her knees up and leaned forward on them. "What's this about, Lils?"

Lily shrugged. "I've been angry about Mom for too long. I was being a martyr. We could have managed."

"I said so at the time. Why didn't you trust me?"

"It was selfish. Sacrificing the trip was a way to make rescuing Fiona about me. I was unable to admit it because that makes it my fault I didn't have that last visit. It was a shit move and I'm sorry."

"That's it? I forgive you."

Lily bit her lip again, tilting her head the way she did, looking at K Lee sideways.

"What else, Lils?"

"I'm not a good person."

"You said that."

"I blamed Ellen."

"Not Daniel?"

"Him too, but no one knew where he was."

"What did you do, Lils?"

"I hit Ellen."

K Lee's eyebrows shot up, keeping pace with her elevating blood pressure. She reminded herself she'd wanted to smack Ellen herself on several occasions. She drew on three decades of teaching to stay calm.

"Any particular reason?"

"I hated the way she made herself the victim. If she didn't know what Daniel was doing, it was because she didn't want to."

A conversation they'd had many times since Fiona wound up in that pawn shop.

"When was this?"

"Ages ago."

"I'm surprised you weren't arrested."

"It was dark, and I wore a hoody. I don't think she recognized me."

"Thank God for small favors then."

"There's more."

"More, as in criminal more?"

"Misdemeanor, probably."

"Oh?"

"Petty stuff. I bought a burner phone and sent her nasty texts. I defaced her car."

"Jesus, Lils."

"I keep wondering if I pushed her over the edge and that's why she attacked those women. They might have died."

"Oh, Lils."

K Lee moved to the end of the bed and opened her arms. Lily curled against her like a child. Her voice was so soft K Lee could barely hear her.

"I didn't know anything bad would happen."

"What Ellen did is not on you."

"I hate thinking I contributed to her state of mind."

"I stalked Daniel. I'm no better."

"You didn't do anything, though."

"Only because Ellen's dog walker got to him first."

Lily sniffed, rubbed her hand under her nose. "We're a pair."

K Lee rocked her gently, thinking of that long ago evening when Lily barged into Derrick's apartment. "Remember how we met?"

Lily sniffled, then smiled. "How could I forget?"

"I love all of you. I even love the bad parts. I especially love the bad parts."

16

DAY 16

MONDAY, AUGUST 25

AMANDA

Clipped footsteps interrupted Amanda Jefferson's communion with her current dead body. Carter stood just inside the lab, file folder in hand, eyes narrowed with animosity.

She set her forceps down and nodded at the folder. "Is that for me?"

"For the record, this is entirely unnecessary. I would have caught it."

"Reviewing your reports wasn't my idea. If you have a problem, take it up with Doctor Arya."

"Your *friend* should have brought it to me."

"She wasn't sure you'd listen. If being asked to accept mentoring twists you up this badly, I can't blame her." She held up gloved hands sticky with body fluids. "Set it on the counter. I'll get to it when I'm done."

He slapped the file down on the counter. "Whatever. You won't find any *mistakes* in this."

He spun on his heel.

"Good to know," Amanda muttered.

Two hours passed before Amanda completed the autopsy and closed the Y incision. She had her own reports to write, but it was her habit to get unpleasant tasks out of the way. She grabbed her salad from the fridge, then changed her mind and settled on a diet coke. Wouldn't do to dribble salad dressing on dickwad's precious report.

She returned to her desk and opened the file. A routine fentanyl overdose, the decedent exhibiting all the usual signs of long-term drug use and supported by toxicology, along with history provided by the decedent's family.

As autopsies went, this one was boilerplate. No mysteries here. She imagined Carter resented being handed such a no-brainer. *That's what you get when you fail to realize you can't make a right-handed strike with your left hand and you don't compare the wound depth to the weapon length.*

She initialed the report, flipping it over as she slid it in her out basket. Light hit the back of the folder, highlighting indentations in the cardstock. Carter had written something on a piece of paper laying on the folder, his aggressive scrawl making grooves in the heavy manila.

All that suppressed anger.

None of her business, but Carter's assholery entitled her to invade his privacy.

She angled the light to create a bit of shadow in the indentations. A phone number, with an extension. She jotted it down on a post-it note, picked up the receiver on her desk phone.

As the number rang, Carter stuck his head in her door.

"Have you looked at it yet?"

She placed a hand over the receiver as if there was a person on the other end. "I just finished with my body. It's going to be a while."

The call connected. In Amanda's ear, a cheerful recorded voice said, "You've reached Channel 7. Your news, your way, every day!"

At the door, Carter snipped, "I wrote down the time I gave you the file. I don't want anyone thinking it's my fault if it's late."

She waved him out. "Fine, fine."

On the phone, the recorded voice had looped back and was now saying, "If you know your party's extension, please enter it now. If you need the operator …"

Heart pounding, she tapped the four-digit number.

Carter stuck his head back in. "I don't know why I—"

"Can't you see I'm on the phone? Shut the door!"

Carter slammed it.

Voicemail kicked in after four rings. "You got Aubrey! Tell me something juicy."

The receiver clattered as she fumbled it back in the cradle. IA was all over Cynth and Brent, when Carter was the leak. She took a deep breath and called reception.

"Angie, has Carter gone to lunch yet?"

"He steamed out of here a minute ago. Guy needs to meditate."

"Thanks, you're a doll." She tapped the switch hook and dialed her boss's extension.

"Zarine? Do you have a minute? There's something I need to show you."

Dianne

Dianne knocked on the doorjamb to Ms. Kleemeyer's office with no clue why Hannah the Hun had summoned her. A trio of dogs jumped out of their baskets and raced to meet her, tails wagging.

Word was a murdered professor willed his entire estate to Hopewell, provided Hannah took care of them for the rest of their natural lives. All Hannah the Hun got from the deal was free rent and job security.

At least the dogs were cute.

Ms. Kleemeyer looked up from her computer and smiled.

"I got your text," Dianne said. "What did you want to see me about?"

Ms. Kleemeyer nodded at a long box sitting on the corner of her desk. "This came for you today, in care of the school. Were you expecting a package?"

Dianne shook her head as she approached. The box was 24" x 10" x 10", standard for shipping flutes.

Somebody's idea of a sick joke.

"I have no clue what this is." She looked at the return address. Plainfield Road, Rising Sun, Indiana. No name. "I don't know anyone in Rising Sun. I don't see any postage. How did this get here?"

"A courier brought it. I was nosy and googled the address. It doesn't exist."

Weirder and weirder. "Can I borrow a pair of scissors?"

She sat in the cushy visitor's chair and used one blade of the scissors to slice through the tape while the dogs wagged and sniffed at her feet, hopeful for treats. She pulled back the box flaps. A folded sheet of printer paper lay on top of packing peanuts. She opened it.

I had no idea. I'm sorry.

No signature.

Hope, something she hadn't expected to feel, bloomed. She dug her hands into the peanuts until her fingers collided with a smooth leather box. Heart pounding, she drew it out. Styrofoam peanuts showered onto the dogs, who snapped at them like they were tiny living things.

"Sorry, sorry."

Ms. Kleemeyer called the dogs. "Dasher! Rory! Buddy! Bed!"

"Sorry."

"Don't worry about them. What do you have there?"

Dianne ran her hands over the familiar leather case. Someone had cared for it. *Please, oh please.* She pressed the latches with her thumbs until they clicked, easing the lid open in case the contents had shifted in transit.

Bright silver, and a slash of gold on the head joint. Burkhart stamped on the tenon.

She looked up, mouth trembling.

Ms. Kleemeyer asked, "Is it?"

Tears poured down her face, onto her lips. She lifted the body of the flute, slid the foot joint on, then the head joint. She blew a single wet note, then ran through her scales. The action was as responsive as she remembered, the sound as pure. She closed her eyes.

Thank you, thank you, thank you.

I've got to tell Wendy.

She opened her eyes again. Hannah the Hun was smiling.

"It is, Ms. Kleemeyer, it is."

BRENT

Brent found Cynth sitting on Donald and Charlotte's memorial bench with the promised lunch. Since it was from NYPD Pizza, there was a risk of pickles.

Surely she didn't.

She opened the lid. Italian sausage and mushroom, thank the sweet baby Jesus.

She detached a slice and held it out for him, hot strings of mozzarella dangling.

He eyed it dubiously. "You bring napkins?"

"Wuss."

"Heathen." Since he was wearing his fourth—or was it fifth?—best slacks, he took the slice and bit in. The medley of flavors and textures flooded his mouth.

He inhaled the slice, then said, "What's the occasion?"

"I got a call from Amanda. Dr. Carter Langston is no longer employed by the coroner's office. We can expect word from on high that the IA investigation has been closed. I thought we should celebrate."

"How did that miracle come about?"

"Amanda noticed an impression of Aubrey Morse's number on a file folder Langston gave her. Dr. Arya was displeased."

"Go Amanda. Think IA will apologize?"

"Fat chance. At least Parker had our backs."

"Still considering Homicide?"

"Too political. I'd rather catch dirtbags than play games. Eat your pizza. It's getting cold."

"Yes, ma'am." He nodded and gave her a serious look as he took another slice.

She must have seen something in his eyes because she said, "This isn't a date."

He took a bite. "Did I say it was? So what is it?"

"How the hell should I know?" She chewed, swallowed. "We're colleagues being civil."

He raised an eyebrow and put a little mockery in his voice. "Is that what this is?"

"That's *all* this is. Being civil."

"You're awfully hostile for someone who confessed to almost getting me killed."

"It's not like I did it on purpose."

"I am fully confident that if you wanted me dead, I would be six feet under. I'm just wondering when the civil part kicks in."

"This is it. This is me being civil."

"Darlin'—"

She scowled.

"Never change."

ELLEN

Voicemail, again. *She might be in the bathroom.* Ellen wanted to wait a few minutes and call again, but the heavily tattooed woman leaning over her shoulder knew she wasn't talking to anyone. She hung up the phone and moved away.

Bailey should have visited by now.

Maybe she didn't get my letter.

I shouldn't be here, not after Gail confessed.

Attempted murder. That's what Detective McFadden said.

All because Bailey had to snoop in her house. Then Lia stuck her nose in before she could figure out what to do.

It was a stupid accident. She had to talk to Bailey. If she could explain, this would go away. Bailey owed it to her to help since it was her fault she was stuck here.

After all, I didn't kill Daniel.

SIXTEEN DAYS AGO

It wasn't supposed to end like that. Daniel was supposed to say he was sorry. Sorry for taking her for granted, sorry for draining her investments instead of managing his shop properly.

He was supposed to beg to come home.

But Daniel didn't beg. She signed on to his accounts to find out how he was surviving. Then she had to see his pathetic existence first hand. She found herself drawn there late at night, while she tried to understand how Daniel could accept living that way.

And it had been pathetic, the sad, tiny house with the aging siding. She'd conned her way in one day while Daniel ran errands, claiming to be looking for a lost dog.

Florence had been so sympathetic, sitting in her broken-down recliner with that stinking mutt on her lap, offering her stale, discount fudge cremes.

Installing the cameras and making Bailey believe the

windows were stuck had been necessary. If anyone spotted her on Thompson Heights, she needed to prove it hadn't been her. Otherwise, the judge would lift the juris monitor, and Daniel would show up at her house like he had a right to be there. He'd ignore her if she asked him to leave. Nothing would change.

Then Lois threw it in her face. They were starting over in Indiana and taking the girls. She said he was showing up at her silly rendezvous to tell her so.

A meeting she knew nothing about.

Daniel is stringing Lois along. There is no rendezvous.

She went just to prove it. She'd wait for him to arrive—which he wouldn't. Follow him to see what happened if he did.

She'd known that horrible movie would put Bailey to sleep. Then she hid behind a patch of weeds opposite Trail B.

Only nobody came.

12:15 and still nobody came. Either Lois lied or Daniel made it all up to manipulate her.

She stood slowly, to work the cramps out from sitting so long. Then she heard it. A surprised grunt. Running feet and a pair of dogs yelping.

She froze.

The sound faded in the distance.

It's only kids.

What a waste of time.

When she reached the fork, she glanced up towards Glen Parker. A lump lay on the walk, visible in the light from the street.

A lump that hadn't been there thirty minutes ago.

A lump that resolved into a human shape as she neared.

Daniel.

He lay on his back, blood pumping sluggishly out of his neck, puddling on the concrete.

He gaped up at her, wheezy gasps escaping his mouth as it worked. A hand lifted six inches off the ground, wavering toward her.

It was over. Everything was over and she felt nothing at all.

"After everything you did, you want me to save you?"

The flow of blood slowed to a trickle. Daniel's hand fell. His mouth quit its efforts and hung open. His eyes dulled. The desperation left his face as it went slack.

"You asshole," she said. "All you had to do was apologize."

Daniel died, and she would never know what he planned to say to her.

All this time, it was Gail. Surely she was here. *They must be keeping us apart. Has to be some way to get to her, ask her why she did it, why she ruined my life.*

She had to talk to Bailey. But waiting for the phone meant an hour in line with brute women who smelled.

I should write her another letter.

Damn you, Daniel. Why couldn't you just apologize?

EPILOGUE
TUESDAY, SEPTEMBER 16

FLORENCE

Florence stroked the furry head on her lap and sighed.

"I was just waiting for you, Snickerdoodle. If you'd been a little faster, so much pain would have been avoided."

The blind, milky eyes did not turn to her voice. They would never turn to her again. She continued to stroke the limp body, knowing it would soon cool and stiffen.

"Well, it's over, and I'll be right behind you. Can't say I'll miss these old bones."

Pretending Daniel was a saint had become habit, one she continued after he died. Better everyone thought she was a fool, than to start them wondering why she invited him into her home.

Daniel caring for her made sense, since he was the reason she needed help. He'd been decent company. It made living with him easier, while creating a kind of cognitive dissonance. He was two people: the kind-hearted man who gave her ice cream and cookies and made her laugh; and the monster responsible for Natalie's death and so much more.

There'd been nothing she could do after her darling girl died. Then Daniel sought her out at Natalie's grave on the anniversary of her death, spinning a ridiculous story about Ellen and needing help. She decided then she would find her own justice.

It had been satisfying to make him clean up Snickerdoodle's accidents and cater to her. But that wasn't enough. He deserved to spend the rest of his life in prison.

She was dying. What would it matter if she went a month or a year early? With proper planning, Daniel would be convicted of murder and serve the sentence he deserved.

But you messed that up, didn't you, puppy? Snickerdoodle had been on his last legs and there was no one she trusted to give him a loving home. If he wasn't euthanized for being old and infirm, he'd wind up with strangers or live out his days in a concrete and chain-link shelter cage. She couldn't bear for any of those things to happen, so she waited.

You weren't supposed to live this long.

She plunged a shaky hand between the arm of her recliner and the seat cushion, removing the cache of Daniel's pentobarbital she'd accumulated months earlier.

More than a year acting oblivious while she laid a trail investigators were certain to follow: she'd mix Daniel's pentobarbital in her food, placing the empty capsules in his trashcan. A search of her papers would uncover the will leaving everything to Daniel for his care of her. A review of her finances would show he'd been abusing his power of attorney and pilfering her accounts. She'd email Ellen— BCC'd to her own lawyer—to give Daniel motive and trigger an investigation:

Ellen,
I'm sorry I doubted you. Daniel was so kind after Natalie
died, and I thought I could help him get back on his
feet. He's stealing from me, after I was kind enough to
take him in. All he had to do was wait, since I put him in
my will. No more! I'm giving him notice tonight.
Tomorrow I am changing my will.

It would have worked.

It had been a good plan, ending her constant pain while
ensuring Daniel experienced accountability for the first
time in his life. Life in prison wouldn't get anyone's flutes
back, but a year of Daniel's bull convinced her he'd never
reveal what he did with the flutes, and he'd never, ever pay
restitution.

She'd felt sorry they arrested Gail. Then that nice Lia
came back with photos of knick-knacks like the ones Gail
encouraged her to throw out. Knick-knacks worth thousands of dollars. Paintings that meant the landscape Gail
admired could be worth a million.

So Gail was as bad as Daniel, maybe worse. She didn't
feel bad for Gail anymore.

Lia talked to her about her options and what she wanted.
She introduced her to Hannah Kleemeyer and that nice
Renee Solomon, who knew all about charities. They'd set up
a charitable trust that would transform all her memories
into scholarships in Natalie's name.

She'd signed the papers. Everything belonged to the
trust now. Renee urged her to attend the auction as guest of
honor. This was better, to go surrounded by her memories.

Tomorrow Hannah would find her when she came to
catalogue the house. She would take care of things, because

she was that kind of person. And Florence would take her place with Natalie at Spring Grove.

She counted the capsules, pushing them around on her TV tray with a trembling finger. Fifteen was more than enough. She would drift off in a pleasant, pain-free haze with Snickerdoodle on her lap, wearing her best dress to meet Natalie again.

DIANNE'S FLUTE RAP

All I want is to be a musician, play my flute and make it sound
pretty.

But my pads won't seat and the springs are loose.

The action is floppy. I sound like a goose.

They say the flute doc is the one for you. He'll fix you up and make
it sound like new.

You got my flute, flute.

Where is my flute, flute.

You stole my flute, flute.

Give me my flute, flute.

I want my flute, flute.

Three weeks come and three weeks go.

Doc says sorry, I broke my toes.

His supplier closed down. He can't get pads.

The shop flooded and he can't get in.

I see a pattern here. I know he's lyin.'

My audition's in two days. Inside I'm dyin.'

You got my flute, flute.

Where is my flute, flute.

You stole my flute, flute.

Give me my flute, flute.

I want my flute, flute.

I say, give it back and I'll go away.

He says your money's not refundable and anyway

your flute's in a safe, and I lost the combination.

You got my flute, flute.

Where is my flute, flute.

You stole my flute, flute.

Give me my flute, flute.

I want my flute, flute.

AUTHOR'S NOTES

Covid broke up my IRL dog park gang, which was ironic since the dog park was one of the few places people could go in Cincinnati during lockdown. Still, it happened, and the day came when Gypsy and I arrived at the park and found only strangers.

My girl (who crossed the Rainbow Bridge in 2024 after a year-long battle with cancer that included the loss of a leg) had always been socially insecure. That day, she sat by the gate and would not move. I started my daily routine of crossing the park ten times to log a mile, thinking she would eventually join me. It never happened. She would not budge, not even to chase tennis balls—her very favoritest thing in the whole, wide world.

I brought her back three more times with identical results, then gave up. That's when I started taking her to Wesleyan Cemetery. I'd driven past it for thirty years but never gone in despite its historic significance. Twenty-eight escaped slaves crossed the Ohio River. Posing as a funeral procession, they walked five miles through Cincinnati in broad daylight to Wesleyan.

The cemetery has a deliciously creepy reputation. The prior owner went to prison for financial crimes, and was rumored to have resold graves, a story that went around after walkers found bones in the grass.

Wesleyan is as described in this book, complete with coyotes and vultures, though this year they are not as numerous as in the past. I exaggerated the steepness of the bluff overlooking Mill Creek (but only slightly).

As in this book, the county shelter is next door, now run by Cincinnati Animal CARE, who took over the contract in 2021. I started volunteering for them after Gypsy passed and cannot say enough about the amazing work they do.

In the book *Dog is Love*, Clive D. L Wynne talks about issues with shelters. Now that there are more and more no-kill shelters, carers are discovering that dogs decline when kept in the shelter environment for extended periods. The more they decline, the less adoptable they become. CAC addresses this problem with strategies based on research into shelter populations, much of which was discussed in Wynne's book.

Cincinnati Animal CARE (CAC) is a pilot shelter for HASS—Human Animal Support Services. The HASS mission is to revolutionize the animal welfare industry, embracing a community-centered sheltering model.

It's an amazing enterprise. Between the two Northside facilities, they shelter as many as 300 dogs and 100 cats. They serve another 200+ dogs in foster homes. In 2024, more than 5,000 dogs and cats were adopted through CAC. More than 1,000 were reunited with owners.

An army of hundreds of volunteers walk the dogs (logging more than 50,000 miles last year), manage play groups, provide enrichment, take dogs out for day trips, and assist with cleaning cages and feeding, totaling more than 29,000 hours in 2024.

Every dog is assessed for behavior and color coded to ensure only volunteers trained for specific behaviors interact with those dogs. Records are kept of their interactions. There is a behavioral team that works to correct problems and an alumni group with resources to address issues that crop up after a pet is adopted. That's just the stuff I know about.

I expect one outcome of the volunteer army is training good pet parents. I've had dogs for more than thirty years, but I am learning new things through CAC. It's a level of care I never expected to see in a county shelter.

Cincinnati's District 5 is no more. After years of wrangling over where to house it after it was moved out of the old Ludlow station, it was torn in half, with the parts absorbed by Districts 3 and 4. Both stations are miles from Northside. As is my prerogative, I am keeping District 5 and the strip mall station alive.

The real Connie and Nati were placed by Greyhound Adoption of Greater Cincinnati, an excellent organization supporting these wonderful dogs for 23 years.

Cynth's favorite author is also mine. Taylor Stevens is the phenomenal writer of the bestselling Victoria Michael Munroe series. She is a friend and her writing advice has done much to elevate my prose. While Taylor is thrilled to get a shout out, she implored me to make sure you know that Cynth saying VMM can learn a new language in five minutes is Cynth's hyperbole and not accurate. I said sure, I'd let you know it takes VMM at least thirty. (Just kidding! VMM's facility with language is one of her superpowers, but should never be construed as instantaneous.)

Peter's smoking gun reference in Day 9 comes from *Castle,* Season 3, Episode 1, "A Deadly Affair." Lia has her epiphany while watching *Poirot,* Season 9, Episode 4.

Also in Day 9, Terry references Jane Kalmes. Jane is a mystery author with a YouTube channel dissecting the mechanics of mystery stories, using examples from television series like *Murder She Wrote* , *Monk,* and *Remington Steele.* It's great fun for anyone who enjoys finding out how the sausage is made.

The tiny lizards Gypsy finds so fascinating are known locally as Lazarus lizards. Lazarus was at one time the premier department store in the region. Many decades ago, a ten-year-old member of the family who founded the stores brought several European wall lizards home from an Italian vacation in his balled-up socks.

They are an invasive species that has overrun parts of the Cincinnati. They popped up in Northside a few years ago. IRL Gypsy never encountered them. They drive my new boy, Padfoot, crazy.

ACKNOWLEDGMENTS

A big shout out to my beta team. Marilyn, Florence, Jerri, Jenna, Sue, Susan, Nancy, Desiree, and Marianne, you are the best.

Thanks to Florence, Dianne, Ellen, Kris, Gail, Lois, Zarine, Charles, and Wendy for loaning me their names. I hope you enjoy the characters I crafted.

Thanks to Adam Richardson of Writer's Detective for technical advice regarding police procedures.

Thanks to Greyhound Adoption of Greater Cincinnati and Cincinnati Animal CARE for technical advice, and for allowing me to feature them and the work they do in this story.

Lastly (but absolutely not least!) I want to thank everyone who has taken the time to write to me about the books. Writing is a lonely profession, and it often feels like shouting into the void. Knowing there are real people who care about Lia and Peter and their two and four-legged friends keeps me going. So thank you.

CAST OF CHARACTERS (AND THEIR DOGS)

GROUPED BY SPHERE OF ACTIVITY

MOORE FLUTES & HOPEWELL MUSIC ACADEMY

Daniel Moore - Owner of Moore Flutes

Dianne Lovato - Flute student

Dr. Wingler - Hopewell director

Ellen Brandt - Daniel's life partner

Florence Nygaard - Daniel's friend

Gail Cook - Neighborhood dog walker

Hannah Kleemeyer - Hopewell special projects coordinator

K Lee Demyanovich - Hopewell flute teacher

Lily - K Lee's wife

Lois Buchanan - Xavier University flute teacher,
Conference guest lecturer

Natalie Nygaard - Deceased student

Ron Coleman - Drum student, shares a house with Wendy
and Dianne

Tony Buchanan - Lois's husband

Wendy Harrison-Green - Flute student, shares a house with
Ron and Dianne

MOUNT AIRY DOG PARK GANG

Bailey Hughes (Kita) Woo woo queen & Lia's BFF
Jim McDonald (Fleece & Chester) Retired engineer
Lia Anderson, (Gypsy Foo la Beenz and Chewy)
Steve Reams (Penny) - Casino security, Terry's roommate
Terry Dunn (Jackson and Napa) - Retired government
negotiator, Steve's roommate

LIA & PETER MISCELLANEOUS

Alma - Lia & Peter's elderly neighbor who dog sits Viola
David - a decorator who brings Lia clients
Renee Solomon (Dakini) - Lia's art patron, also a Hopewell
donor
John Morgan, AKA Trees - IT specialist, hacker, mystic, and
Bailey's long-distance beau

CINCINNATI POLICE DEPARTMENT - DISTRICT 5

Captain Ann Parker - District 5 commander
Captain Bill Roller - Retired former District 5 commander
Detective Brent Davis
Detective Cynth McFadden
Detective Peter Dourson (Viola)
Detective Sam Robertson
Donna - Captain Parker's admin
Officer Cal Hinkle
Officer Paul Brainard

CINCINNATI POLICE DEPARTMENT - HOMICIDE

Captain Stephen Arseneault - commander

Charles Hobbs - prosecutor

Detective Hodgkins, AKA Heckle

Detective Jarvis, AKA Jeckle

Pitbull Perry - 3rd rate defense attorney

NEWS MEDIA

Aubrey Morse - Channel 7 news personality

Carol Logan - Channel 11 news personality

Robert MacDuff - AKA Duff, Aubrey's cameraman and David's significant other

ALPHABETICAL LIST OF CHARACTERS

EXCLUDING THOSE OF LITTLE IMPORTANCE

Alma - Lia and Peter's elderly neighbor, who watches Peter's dog, Viola

Amanda Jefferson/Jeffers - Assistant coroner

Aubrey Morse - Channel 7 reporter

Bailey Hughes - Gardener and Tarot reader, Lia's BFF (bloodhound Kita)

Brent Davis - District 5 detective

Cal Hinkle - District 5 patrol officer

Captain Ann Parker - Current District 5 Commander

Captain Roller - Former District 5 Commander, retired

Captain Stephen Arseneault - Homicide Department Commander

Carol Logan_ - Channel 11 Reporter

Carter Langston III - newly hired Assistant Coroner

Charles Hobbs - Hamilton County criminal prosecutor

Cynth McFadden - District 5 detective

Daniel Moore_ - Owner of Moore Flutes, (Greyhounds Connie and Nati)

David - Decorator who sells Lia's paintings, cohabs with Duff

Dianne Lovato - Hopewell student, shares a house with Wendy and Ron

Dr. Wingler - Hopewell director

Duff/Robert MacDuff/Bob - Channel 7 cameraman, cohab of David

Ellen Brandt - Cohab of Daniel Moore, bank service center manager, friend of Bailey (greyhounds Connie and Nati)

Florence Nygaard - Senior citizen who took Daniel in, grandmother of Natalie (shih tzu Snickerdoodle)

Gail Cook - Dog walker

Geoffrey Lawrence - murdered Hopewell professor

Hannah Kleemeyer - Hopewell Admin (Chihuahua-mix Rory, Bichon Frisé Dasher, poodle Buddy)

Hodgkins/Heckle - Former District 5 detective now in Homicide

Jarvis/Jeckle - Former District 5 detective now in Homicide

Jerry Morton - Target of Brent's undercover assignment

Jim McDonald - Widower, retired engineer (border collie Fleece, Norwich terrier mix Chester)

John Morgan/Trees - Bailey's beau, a disabled, computer tech/hacker and mystic who lives in Knoxville

Junior - Morgue tech

K Lee Demyanovich - Teaches at Hopewell

Lia Anderson - Artist, Bailey's BFF, Cohabs with Detective Peter Dourson (schnauzer Chewy, Catahoula Gypsy, golden retriever Honey, who is deceased)

Lily - K Lee's wife

Lois Buchanan - Xavier University faculty, Teaches at Hopewell summer session (cat Sheba)

Natalie Nygaard - deceased granddaughter of Florence Nygaard

Peter Dourson - District 5 Detective, Cohabs with Lia Anderson (medium-sized lab mix Viola, who spends most days with Alma, a neighbor)

Pitbull Perry - 3rd rate defense attorney

Renee Solomon - Arts maven, a patron of Lia (Collie Dakini, an agility champ)

Ron Coleman - Hopewell student, shares a house with Wendy and Dianne

Sam Robertson - District 5 detective

Steve Reams - Works at a casino, roommate of Terry (small hound mix Penny)

Terry Dunn - Much divorced, retired government labor negotiator, shares a house with Steve (hound-mix Jackson and golden retriever-mix Napa)

Wendy Harrison-Green - Hopewell student, shares a house with Dianne and Ron

Zarine Arya - Hamilton County Coroner

LIA ANDERSON DOG PARK MYSTERIES

A Shot in the Bark

Detective Peter Dourson investigates the suicide of Lia's deadbeat boyfriend.

Drool Baby

Peter's search for the truth brings Lia into the cross hairs of a killer.

Maximum Security

Lia's loyalties are tested when Peter arrests the wrong woman for murder.

Sneak Thief

Lia's kindness to an orphaned beagle draws the attention of an obsessed stalker.

Muddy Mouth

A Fourth of July parade, 89 feral cats, and a missing author. It's nothing Lia and her schnauzer can't handle.

Fur Boys

The drama never ends when Lia stumbles on a dead diva.

Swamp Monster

Rumors from the past dog Peter's efforts to discover the truth about a thirty year-old vanishing act

The Girls

Lia's BFF would never cover for a killer. Why does the evidence say she's lying?

ABOUT THE AUTHOR

Carol Ann "C. A." Newsome is an author and painter who lives in Cincinnati. She spends many mornings at the Mount Airy Dog Park with a Tasmanian devil named Padfoot, digging up her next mystery.

Carol loves to hear from readers.
Contact her at
gypsy@canewsome.com

Would you like to stay in touch?
Sign up for Carol's newsletter at
CANewsome.com

facebook.com/AShotInTheBark

www.ingramcontent.com/pod-product-compliance
Lightning Source LLC
Chambersburg PA
CBHW070232200726

48293CB00005B/1580